Knickers in a Twist

The Trailer Park Princess Cozy Mystery
Book 4

Kim Hunt Harris

Kim Hunt Harris Books, LLC
Lubbock, TX

Kim Hunt Harris Books, LLC
3410 98th St., Ste. 4-157
Lubbock, TX 74923
www.kimhuntharris.com

Publisher's Note: This is a work of fiction. Names, characters, places, and incidents are a product of the author's imagination. Locales and public names are sometimes used for atmospheric purposes. Any resemblance to actual people, living or dead, or to businesses, companies, events, institutions, or locales is completely coincidental.

Book Layout ©2013 BookDesignTemplates.com

Ordering Information:
Quantity sales. Special discounts are available on quantity purchases by corporations, associations, and others. For details, contact the "Special Sales Department" at the address above.

Knickers in a Twist/ Kim Hunt Harris.--1st ed.
ISBN- 978-0-9977734-6-0

Dedication

This book is dedicated to the Trailertopians – you've become my own personal cheerleading squad that keeps me encouraged, but also helps me spot errors. I can't imagine anything more valuable to a writer. You guys amaze me.

Acknowledgements

My most sincere gratitude goes to Matt Sherley for answering my numerous questions about crime scene investigations and police procedure. Any errors in those areas are entirely my own.

My thanks also to Dr. William Lawson, who helped me early on in determining just what the deal was going to be with this book. Dr. Lawson wrote a paper called *Soil Sampling on Sword Beach*, which became the inspiration for Donald Baucum's WWII service. Do yourself a favor: Google that paper and read it. I am going out on a limb to guarantee it will be the most fascinating paper you'll ever read about soil sampling. ☺

Thanks also to Kelly Hunt for helping me get the scenes with Tri-Patrice's job right, for being my sounding board when I get stuck, and for the idea about the difference between how Europeans and Americans write the date.

And as always, my eternal gratitude to Darryl Harris, husband-slash-author-assistant extraordinaire. It all finally started coming together when you got on the team, and I'm loving every second of it.

Note from the Author

This is a work of fiction, but as with most fiction, some of the things in it are true. Here's a quick overview:

Injection wells used in the hydro-fracking of oil are associated with earthquakes: *True. However, these quakes are relatively small, and no major damage has been caused by them such as the damage described in this book.*

People in West Texas don't know what Earl Grey tea is. *False. Sorry.*

Allied forces conducted soil sampling on French beaches before the D-Day Invasion: *True, except in the real mission, no American troops were involved.*

Women pilots flew in the WASP (Women Airforce Service Pilots) program to ferry planes to men in combat, and they trained in Sweetwater, Texas: *True, and you really should visit the WASP Museum there. It's awesome. http://www.waspmuseum.org/index.html*

These women were righteous and amazing: *Also true.*

Everything sounds better in a British accent: *True, obviously.*

If you enjoy *Knickers in a Twist*, I would love it if you could take a few minutes to leave a review on Amazon, iBooks, Kobo, Barnes and Noble, or GoodReads.

Table of Contents

CHAPTER ONE

Somewhat Married

"Okay, now I want you to lift up tall... breathe in... aaaand...lift up tall *tall tall*."

I lifted up tall in my triangle pose. Or rather, as tall as I could, given that I am only of medium height and that I was also trying to keep one hand wrapped around my ankle. I shifted my feet on my yoga mat and tried to find my center of balance. Where was that crazy thing?

I glanced over at Viv, her lean legs in bright pink and yellow tie-dyed leggings, her bare feet planted solidly on her own mat beside me.

I couldn't decide what was worse: the fact that I, a young, healthy woman in the prime of her life, was bad at yoga, or the fact that my best friend, Viv, who was somewhere in her eighth decade of life, was so good at it.

Sweat poured out of every cell of my body, and I felt like my face was about to catch fire.

"Mmmm...this pose is a fantastic stress reliever," the instructor purred.

"Fantastic," I grunted under my breath. My feet were sweaty and felt like they were going to shoot out from under me, sending me into involuntary splits. I struggled to keep them on the mat.

"Just relax and focus on your breath. In... and out. In... and out."

I prayed for it to be over.

"Okay, now, one more breath. That's it. Relax into it."

For the life of me, I could not understand how anyone could relax into this. I felt like my ribs were breaking. Was I supposed to feel like my ribs were breaking? This couldn't be right.

I ducked my head and looked at the other people in the class. No one else seemed to be on the verge of cardiac arrest. I must be doing it wrong.

I checked Viv again. She had never looked more serene.

"Okay, now we're going to go down to our mat, on our shins."

I silently said a prayer of gratitude and dropped to my knees on the mat.

"We're going to go gently down to our mats," the instructor said with a pointed look at me. "On our shins and then down to our forearms."

I cringed, but did as I was told and tried not to imagine how wide my posterior must look to the row behind me. Note to self: always claim the back row in yoga – and everything else, if possible.

"Now, I want you to just relax your heart into your forearms—"

What? Relax my heart into my forearms? How did that...what?

"And breathe into your kidneys."

I started to draw in a breath but stopped. Breathe into my kidneys?

I thought about that for a moment, then noticed that the rest of the class was moving on to a different position. I hadn't even figured out how to breathe into my kidneys yet! Wait!

Everyone else seemed to be lifting in that triangle thing, with their palms and feet on the floor, their booties in the air. I floundered around and finally got my hips up, rocking precariously back and forth before I caught my balance, spread my feet a little further apart, and then tried my best to maintain the pose. The backs of my thighs screamed.

"If you want, you can bring your legs in a little bit closer to your body, and drop the backs of your feet closer to the ground for a deeper stretch."

I was on the balls of my feet, and I felt like the stretch was quite deep enough, thank you. The blood was rushing to my head. My lungs felt buried under every other organ in my body.

My head hung between my shoulders. I tilted it just a bit. Viv's bony feet were flat on the ground. She turned her head and smiled sweetly at me.

I gave her a flat smile in return. "I will not forget this," I promised her.

After the class ended and I could summon the strength to stand, I rolled up my yoga mat and slung it over my shoulder. I could feel that my face was red as a clown nose and dripping sweat. Sweat rolled down my neck and the small of my back. I had been thoroughly disabused of my assumption that yoga was going to be relaxing and easy, kind of like stretching before you get out of bed.

Viv, on the other hand, looked positively dewy as she pulled her jacket on over her form-fitting yoga outfit.

"This is going to get easier, right?" I mumbled as we followed the other students to the parking lot.

"Oh, sure," Viv said with a wave of her hand. "In a couple of weeks you'll really get the hang of it and love it." She stretched her bony arms over her head and did a tree pose.

"Mmmhmmm," I said, because I was fairly sure that, even with my recent weight loss, my body would never be as limber and flexible as Viv's. It seemed patently unfair that she had that willowy, lithe body at 80-something years old while I was stuck with my basic fireplug structure. But it was what it was, and I didn't have enough energy left to do anything but accept it.

"I wonder why Tri-Patrice didn't make it."

Tri-Patrice was my childhood friend Trisha, who had decided to change her name to Patrice when she became a high-falutin' anchor on the local NBC affiliate, KBST. I'd tried to make the change, but my mouth always said, "Tri-" before it remembered she was Patrice now. So, I gave up and went with it. To me, she was either Trisha or Tri-Patrice, and we'd both come to accept it. Much as I'd accepted my fireplug body.

I opened the passenger door on the Monster Carlo and tossed my yoga mat and gym bag inside. As soon as the bag hit the seat, my phone beeped.

"Sorry," I said. I took the phone out of the bag. "She just sent me a text. She probably got stuck at work."

Trisha did the six and ten o'clock news, which was a pretty demanding job. To some people, it looked like she worked for an hour and a half every day, but I knew she put in some intense time at the station.

"Sorry, can't make it (obv). I think they found Peter. Not good."

I flipped the phone around and showed Viv.

She peered at it, then said, "Crikey."

"Crikey?"

"It's a word. I wonder what's not good."

Peter Browning was a hotshot reporter on KBST. He was pretty high profile, even for a big fish in a small pond like Lubbock. He had a reputation for hard-hitting investigative interviews, like the one a few months prior about the collapse of an elementary school following an earthquake that might have been caused by fracking for oil in the area. Or something like that—to be honest, I hadn't paid much attention. I knew there was a little girl who'd been crippled; Browning had gone after the guy who designed the building; and, not long after that the guy had been found dead. Browning was soon showing up in interviews with major networks as some kind of expert on damages caused by fracking-related earthquakes.

Then a few days ago, he'd disappeared. Half the town had been out looking for him. His wife, a pretty young thing with an eight-months-pregnant belly, was on the news several times a day, pleading tearfully for information.

I think they found Peter. Not good.

"It could be anything," I said. "Maybe they found him in Las Vegas, drunk out of his mind and blowing all his money on show girls."

"I saw a story about a woman whose car had gone off a bridge, and she was trapped in the bottom of a ravine for three days before anyone found her. It could be something like that."

"Exactly. Or maybe he got mixed up with the mob and he decided to go incognito—dyed his hair, grew a mustache, changed his name."

"Clearly, we need more information. Let's go up to the station to see what Patrice knows."

I wasn't surprised. Viv lived at Belle Court Retirement Home, and on Tuesday nights she usually found a reason to be gone because of Taco Tuesday. "You can't imagine what they consider a taco there," she said once, and shuddered. "I'd rather eat my own hair."

"I need to check with Tony first. He has Stump tonight."

"You have shared custody of your dog now?"

"No," I said, rolling my eyes at her and pulling on my own jacket now that the early-November chill was starting to hit my sweat. Viv knew about Stump's separation anxiety and why I could never leave her alone at our place in Trailertopia. "Frank is out of town and I didn't want to miss this class—which you promised would be fun –" I slapped her lightly on the arm with the back of my hand. "So, I took her over to Tony's."

"Well, he might as well get used to her if you're all eventually going to be one big happy. Listen, there's no sense in taking two cars. Let's take yours."

"Sure, but only if you'll drive."

"Oh, okay," Viv said, pretending (badly) to be a little put out by the idea. Viv was seriously envious of my 1974 Monte Carlo. Apparently forty-years-ago Viv had wanted a Monte Carlo like Sue Ellen Ewing drove on Dallas and had been deprived of that experience. She was the one who had talked me into buying the ancient metal monstrosity in the first place, and I expected any day now she was going to offer to buy it from me. She just had to come to grips with the idea that the Cadillac she bought around the same time I bought the Monster Carlo was a lemon, at over twenty times the price I'd paid for her dream car. She appeared to still be in the denial phase of her grieving process.

Viv pulled onto Clovis Highway and headed for the loop so we could make the trek to the complete other side of town quickly. I called Tony. "If it's okay with you, Viv and I are going to head over to Channel 11 to talk to Trisha. Apparently, something has turned up on that guy Peter Browning."

"That might be what's on the news right now. They cut into America's Got Pizazz. Right now they're broadcasting from some place out in the middle of nowhere."

"Really? Like, a crime scene?"

Viv looked at me, bug-eyed.

"Eyes on the road when you're driving my car," I told her.

"They haven't said anything about a crime," Tony said. "Just that the body of an adult male was found and the police department would have a press conference at nine."

"Whoa." I pulled the phone away and told Viv, "They found a male body somewhere outside of town and the PD is having a press conference at nine."

Viv floored it.

"You can't tell where they're broadcasting from?"

"No, it looks like any road you'd see outside of town. Dirt road along a stripped cotton field. You're not going to try to find it, are you?"

"No," I said with a laugh. I glanced over at Viv, who most definitely looked like she wanted to find it. "Maybe. Do you want me to come back?"

I was trying really hard to be considerate of the fact that I was a somewhat-married woman now and needed to take Tony's opinion into consideration from time to time.

He was silent for a moment. "No, Stump is fine and I doubt you can get into much trouble with all the news cameras and police around."

I laughed and said to Viv, "Tony thinks we can't get into much trouble with the news cameras and police around."

"Has he met us?"

I turned back to the phone. "I think you've just thrown down the gauntlet to Viv."

Tony sighed. "Well, if you get arrested for interfering with a crime scene or creating a public nuisance or something, just let me know. Stump and I will come bail you out."

"There's a reason I love you two," I said happily. "We'll probably be no more than an hour."

I ended the call and slid the phone into my gym bag.

"Oh, gag," Viv said. "Look at you grinning like a fool."

"You're just jealous because I'm a happily somewhat-married and you're not." I called Tony's and my relationship somewhat-married because, although we were legally married, we'd only recently resumed our relationship after a ten-year hiatus. We hadn't yet made the leap to living together full time because cohabitation was a bit more than either of us was prepared to deal with at the moment.

Viv rolled her eyes. "Believe me, I am not jealous of any married person, somewhat or otherwise. I've been there, done that, got a five-pack of t-shirts. And it just so happens that there is a new gentleman in my life."

"Oooh, Viv," I said. "Who?"

"I'm not even going to tell you."

I waited fifteen seconds.

"His name is Nigel and he is British. All those silly old widows up there are sniffing after him. I call them all The Gaggle. Like a bunch of geese."

I knew she couldn't hold out long. "Nigel the Brit, huh? That sounds like a nice change."

Two of Viv's late husbands had been stinking rich, having made their respective fortunes in oil and Dairy Queen franchises. One of them was nicknamed "Hoss." They'd made it possible for her to live in the lap of the Belle Court Retirement Home luxury, but neither those two, nor the first three ex-husbands who had not been wealthy, were anything but red-blooded American.

"He is charming, handsome, and sophisticated. And British."

"You mentioned that."

"I mean, he could be a lord or something."

"You don't say."

"You should hear him speak. Last week at poetry night he read "Meeting at Night," by Robert Browning. It was like being inside a scene from Downton Abbey." She sighed.

I nodded. Yep. Every last one of those widows up there were sniffing after him.

Viv took the tall flyover about half a mile from Channel 11, and I looked out over the east side of town. Something a couple of miles east of the station caught my eye.

Red flashing lights. A lot of them.

"Viv, I think that might be what Tony was talking about. Don't look!" I said when she shifted her gaze—and the car—in the direction I was looking. "Just get off the flyover and head west."

We headed out of town in the general direction of the lights, and immediately got turned around on the surface roads. We drove down dark dirt roads for a while, until I finally spotted the lights again.

Pulling up behind a long line of cars parked at the side of the road, Viv killed the motor and hopped out. Nothing got her jazzed up more than a possible crime scene. I slid out of the bench seat beside her, since my side of the car was hovering over high grass in a bar ditch. I figured all the rattlesnakes were probably hibernating by now, but why take that chance?

Viv and I joined the crowd behind the yellow caution tape.

"What's going on?" Viv asked a guy standing beside her.

He shrugged. "I really don't know. I was just driving by and saw all the lights." Although he wore jeans and an Eagle Construction t-shirt, something about him said "military" – close- cropped hair, hard body, poker posture.

"They found a body," a woman with a smoker's voice said.

"Dead body," someone else said, as if that level of specificity was called for.

"Murder?" I asked.

"Yeah," "Of course," and "Haven't said," were the immediate replies. I figured the last one was the truth. People tended to immediately jump to the conclusion of murder when a body was found, but it could just as easily have been an accident, suicide, or even natural causes.

A small stand of mesquite trees about fifty yards down the road seemed to be where most of the activity was concentrated. The entire squadron of first responders was there—police, ambulances, fire trucks—and they had the vehicles parked and personnel standing in a way that made it difficult to see anything.

After Viv and I had been there about ten minutes and learned nothing useful from the crowd, except for a rumor that the deceased probably was Peter Browning (but nobody knew for sure,) a group of EMTs emerged from the trees carrying a body bag on a stretcher. They brought it to the back of the ambulance, which faced the other direction, and in the ensuing silence we heard the sound of the doors being shut.

The crowd remained silent and stepped out of the way so the police cars and ambulance could pass. In the stillness, the whir and pop of the news cameras and soft crunch of the tires on the dirt road was magnified. With headlights on, but flashing lights dark, they drove slowly through the somber crowd and toward town.

As they left, several of the reporters were setting up shots to report back to their respective stations.

"Vultures," the military guy said.

I started to point out that he, like the reporters, had been attracted to the sight of flashing red lights and yellow police tape, but unlike him, it was their job to be there. I didn't point that out because, frankly, he looked a bit scary.

So instead I nodded and said, "Tell me about it." Like a complete hypocrite.

His jaw clenched and he shook his head. "I don't know how they sleep at night. Love nothing better than to see someone's misery."

"No doubt," Viv said. "People treat them like they're bloody celebrities or something just because they're on TV. Hey, look! There's Misty Monahan!" She pointed to the young reporter that Tri-Patrice had hired last year. "Let's go talk to her. Maybe she'll interview us!"

"Why would she interview us? We don't know anything."

Viv shrugged. "That never matters. All we have to do is be colorful, and we'll be a viral sensation before our heads hit the pillow tonight. I'll say something like, 'Guuuurrrrl! My friend and me were driving down the loop and she was like, 'Look at those lights!' and I was like, 'Whuuuut?' and she was like, 'Let's go check it out,' and I was all, 'I gotta go home and drink my prune juice, on account of my insides get locked down if I don't drink at least two glasses of prune juice a day, I mean it's like an abandoned factory in there, no output at all if you get my meanin'...'"

I put a hand up to stop her. It was unseemly to be giggling immediately after a body bag had just passed us, and, besides, if I ever went viral, I didn't want it to be as Viv's prune juice-carrying sidekick. "What would Nigel think of that performance? Is he attracted to that kind of thing?"

"Oh, you're right," she said, which surprised me. Viv must have it really bad if she considered altering her behavior in any way for the guy. "Let's see if we can get the scoop, though."

The cameraman was setting up the shot, and Misty fluffed her hair and rolled her lips together, doing this thing with her hand that made me think she must be very keyed up. She held her hand at her side, about breast level, and shook it. Then she raised the other hand and shook her wrists out together, kind of the way a gymnast might do before tackling the uneven parallel bars. She blew through her lips, puffing them out over and over, and paced back in front in the small bit of dirt road she and the cameraman had staked out.

Except the cameraman wasn't a man, I realized as I got closer to them. A short, compactly-built girl with short, spiky hair was fiddling with the camera.

She hoisted it to her shoulder, put it to her eye, then pulled it away and looked at Misty. "Are you going to be able to do this?"

Misty took a deep breath. "No choice. Come on. Let's just get it done."

The camera girl squared up and nodded slightly.

"Patrice and Tom, we are on the scene of a somber discovery in east Lubbock, where Lubbock police have recovered the body of—of –" She stopped, swallowed almost imperceptibly, then went on—" of an unidentified male. Now, two teenagers were riding around this area on dirt bikes this afternoon and discovered the body. As you just saw from that video, an ambulance just drove away –" She stopped and blinked a few times, looking blank, then she pulled it together. "Unfortunately, we don't have any other information at this time, but police will hold a news conference tonight at nine pm. Patrice and Tom, back to you."

She continued to stare into the camera for five more seconds, her face somber and her eyes wan. The camera light flashed off.

Then Misty Monahan burst into tears.

Viv and I looked at each other and decided simultaneously to give Misty a pass. Viv was at least as awkward as I was in dealing with emotional people, if not more so.

"Let's go back to the station and talk to Trisha," I suggested. "We probably have time to chat with her for a little while before we head over to the press conference."

"You don't need to get home to the hubby?" Viv asked.

I didn't care for her tone. "You don't have to get back to Belle Court and make sure none of those floozies are taking off with Nigel the Brit?"

"I wonder what was going on with Misty Monahan," Viv said, by way of changing the subject.

I shrugged. "Dead body is a bit upsetting. And Peter Browning was a co-worker, maybe even a friend, if it really was him."

"Did her reaction seem weird to you?"

"Ummm, no. For the general public, a co-worker turning up dead would warrant a few tears."

"Yes, but she was working so hard to hide it."

"She was trying to be professional."

Viv shook her head. "Maybe. But I have an inkling it was something more than that."

"What's an inkling? Do they hurt?"

Ignoring me, she said, "Let's go back to the station and see if we can get some inside information from Patrice."

Things were crazy at the station, so nobody paid Viv and me any mind as we wound our way through the bustle. Besides, we'd been up there enough times that everyone knew we were there to see Tri-Patrice, and they left us alone.

I expected to find her in the big middle of things like she always was, but she was in her office with her feet propped on a stool made from a couple of stacked boxes.

"Look at you taking it easy," Viv said as we barged in.

"Doctor's orders," Trisha said. She leaned back in her chair, her hands folded over her stomach.

"You look pale," I said. "I didn't realize you were sick."

"I'm not." She smiled this big smile and said, "I'm pregnant."

"Oooh!" Viv clapped her hands. "A baby! That's jolly good news! Brilliant!"

"Seriously? That's fantastic!" I jumped up and maneuvered the box stool to lean over her and give her a one-armed hug.

She remained seated and one-arm hugged me back. "Thanks. We're very excited."

She didn't look very excited, though. I put together the entire picture then. The stool, her absence from the bustle of the newsroom. "Are you doing okay?"

"I feel pretty good, actually. But the doctors are concerned about my blood pressure. I'm only ten weeks along, and I wouldn't have told anyone except I've been ordered to light duty."

"I wondered why that other guy was doing the ten o'clock broadcast," Viv said.

"Yeah," I said faintly. I didn't want Trisha to know I was a complete lightweight and rarely stayed up until ten. When I did, it wasn't to watch the news.

"I'm down to six o'clock only, and when I'm not on the air I'm in here with my feet propped up."

Someone came in and said something in news-ese to Trisha, who answered in the same unintelligible language. He left.

"Anyway. Did you go out to the scene?"

"We did," Viv said. "They didn't say much. Just a male body."

Trisha frowned. "They're still notifying next of kin."

A look passed between us. "It's him, though?" I asked.

"I can't say. But...yeah."

"We won't say anything," Viv said.

"I know. I just..." She shook her head and turned a pen over and over in her hand. She tapped it on her desk and set it aside, then picked it up again. "Poor Bitsy. I feel so awful for her. She's pregnant too, you know."

Of course we knew. Browning had been missing for the past three days, and Bitsy Browning was all over the news, her tearful face pleading for information, for help. Her little basketball belly was a media darling in its own right.

I assumed Trisha got her news directly from someone in the police department. She had a reputation for being professional and circumspect when it was appropriate.

"Did you get any other information? What happened to him?"

She shook her head. "No, my source just gave me the heads up because he knew Peter worked here."

"We saw Misty Monahan out at the scene. She was a bloody mess."

Trisha jerked. "What?!"

"She means she was upset," I clarified. "Viv, careful how you wield your newfound Britishness."

"I simply meant that she looked horrible," Viv said with an eye roll. "You Yanks misinterpret everything."

"Well, it is horrible," Trisha said. "I'm proud of her for being able to make it through the report."

The door opened and a different guy said something to Trisha, equally as mysterious as the last guy. Trisha gave a few orders and the guy left.

"Everyone is tiptoeing around me like I'm a live grenade," she said.

"I would take advantage of it if I were you. Maybe use it as an opportunity to tell people what you've always wanted to say and were too polite to," Viv said.

Trisha laughed. "That could be fun, but no. I want a career to come back to. And no matter what anyone says about respect and accommodation for professional women, this at-risk pregnancy business is not helping my career one bit. Not that I care, at this point, but I know I will eventually."

The door opened again, and another guy stuck his head in. "You ready?"

"Just about," Trisha said. She nodded in our direction. "You remember Salem."

Oh, jeez. It was Scott, Trisha's husband.

I saw him stiffen just as I did. He turned slowly to face me.

"Salem," he said with a reserved nod.

"Hello, Scott," I answered, equally reserved. Scott and I had a history that neither of us wanted to revisit, even for a second. "This is Viv," I said as soon as I could, to deflect attention.

Viv jumped up and shook his hand. "Congratulations on the pregnancy. Jolly good show!"

"Ummm...thanks." He turned back to Trisha. "You need to go."

Trisha smiled and stood with a groan. "I'm fine. I've had my feet up the entire time." She put her feet down and stood slowly. "I am guarded like the Hope diamond these days," she said with a warm smile at Scott. "Normally I'd be home on the sofa by now being waited on hand and foot, but I needed to stay for a while tonight, considering everything going on."

"We'll get out of your hair." I popped out of my chair, relieved when Scott backed out of the doorway and let me pass.

As we crossed through the newsroom, Viv said—entirely too loudly— "Is he the one you didn't sleep with?"

"Shhh!" I hissed. Viv being my best friend and all, I had told her of the time I had been drunk and thought I'd spent the night in my best friend's fiance's bed. Well, I actually *had* spent the night in his bed, but nothing of a...*conjugal* nature...had happened.

Still, Trisha had thought it had, and I still felt guilty about it. This was the first time I'd seen Scott since then, and it felt tremendously awkward. "As a matter of fact," I said, "there are quite a few guys I didn't sleep with."

I didn't even bother with the pretense of offering Viv the chance to drive. I climbed into the passenger seat and pulled out my phone. "Windy, call Tony."

The command app on my phone was called Windy, and she was voiced by the phone developer's aunt from Sundown, Texas. Windy with an "I" from Sundown. If you ever wondered what West Texas was like, that sums it up right there.

"Gettin' him now, honey," Windy said. The icon was a little cloud with wavy trails that stirred in a digital breeze while she worked. The phone rang.

"Is Stump doing okay?" I asked Tony.

"She's great," he said. "She's parked beside me in the recliner and hasn't budged since you left."

"Good." Thankfully, Stump seemed to have taken to Tony. When she was comfortable, Stump was basically a slug covered with fur. She rarely moved unless it was to get her belly into better position for rubbing. When she was uncomfortable, she screamed a loud unholy-sounding cry and destroyed things. And she was highly uncomfortable whenever I left her home alone, which was why I had to find babysitters for her. There was precious little in my trailer house in Trailertopia, and I couldn't afford to replace what I did have. It was an immense relief that Stump was comfortable with Tony, as long as he was comfortable with her. "Do you mind if I stay out a while longer and go to the press conference with Viv?"

"Daddy, can I play with my friend?" Viv mocked as she pulled out of the Channel 11 parking lot.

I swatted the seat beside her. "It's common courtesy," I insisted.

"No problem," Tony said. "Like I said, she hasn't moved all night. Just stay out of trouble."

"You keep saying that."

"Because you keep getting shot at."

"*At* being the operative word," I said. "We will be the very image of carefulness," I promised.

Bobby Sloan, one of Lubbock PD's homicide detectives, was in the press conference room talking to some other cop-looking people when Viv and I came in. I nodded to him as we took our seats.

He rolled his eyes.

After he'd wrapped up his conversation, he strolled over to us. "Since when did you two become media? Oh wait, I know. You've started your own YouTube channel."

Viv pointed at him. "That's a smashing idea, actually. I know because I had it myself earlier today."

"No, it's not," I said. "Don't encourage her."

Bobby put one booted foot on the chair in front of me, leaning on his knee. "You're going to be disappointed this time. Nothing to see here but a guy who apparently wanted out."

"Out? Of what?"

Bobby shrugged.

So, suicide? "Why are they holding a press conference for that?"

"Maybe this isn't such a sad day for the PD, considering all the grief Peter Browning had given you guys this year." Viv arched an eyebrow.

"Come on." Bobby frowned. "He wasn't a favorite, but nobody around is happy to have him dead."

"No?" Viv motioned with her head toward the back of the room where a group of uniformed officers were gathered, talking and grinning.

Bobby's frown deepened. "We decided to make the statement because a few thousand people have been looking for the guy, and we thought it best that they know they can stop." He straightened and dropped his foot. "Stay out of trouble, Salem." He clapped a hand down on my shoulder as he walked away.

I tried very hard to be unaffected by that hand on my shoulder. I was a somewhat-married woman, after all, and I was most definitely in love with my husband. But Bobby Sloan...well, I'd had a crush on him since the fourth grade, and he was still ridiculously handsome. Old habits die hard.

He joined the group at the back of the room and said something low. All the smiles immediately vanished, and the officers—all of them looking suddenly like middle schoolers playing dress up—became a silent, respectful group.

The room filled quickly, the mood again somber as it had been at the side of that dirt road. Almost everyone in the room knew Peter Browning, and the ones who didn't know him knew of him.

The new police chief stepped up to the microphone, looking nervous. He was the most boyish-looking grown man I think I'd ever seen—tow-headed, good-natured features, easy smile. I thought he was likely the same age as Bobby, and I wondered briefly if Bobby had been disappointed he wasn't picked for the position. I had heard he'd been in the running.

Chief Patterson cleared his throat. He looked at the cameras and started.

"This afternoon at around 4:00, two juveniles in east Lubbock were riding motorbikes west of the Lubbock city limits and found the remains of a deceased male. They immediately contacted their parents, who called police. The remains have been tentatively identified as 29-year-old Peter James Browning of Lubbock."

A hushed murmur went through the crowd, and I glanced around to see if Misty Monahan was one of them. I saw that Channel 11 was represented by another young reporter, though, a new guy I didn't recognize.

"Tentatively identified," Viv murmured. "What does that mean?"

"They're covering their butts," I said. "They wouldn't have said this much if they weren't positive it was him."

"Police secured the scene and gathered evidence from the surrounding area. The remains have been taken to the Lubbock County Medical Examiner's office, where they will be analyzed to determine cause of death." He looked up, straight at the cameras. "At this time," he said firmly, "we are collecting and analyzing evidence. We do not have a cause of death and we will not speculate."

Five or six hands shot up, and reporters started shouting questions.

The chief pointed at one of them.

"You say you won't speculate on cause of death. But can you say if you suspect anyone else of being involved in his death?"

The chief chewed his lip. "I can say that we have no suspects, no persons of interest at this time."

Viv and I looked at each other. I heard whispers of "suicide" from the small crowd.

CHAPTER TWO

Nigel the Brit

Back at Tony's, I entered the house without knocking. He rose from his chair in front of the news and came to greet me. Stump kept her seat.

The sight of him made my breath catch, as it always did. Broad shoulders, warm brown eyes, nice smile. Check that—not nice. A dazzling, dreamy smile.

I sat on the sofa and he joined me. "I saw the press conference. So it's definitely him."

Stump, annoyed that Tony had moved from the recliner, grumbled, wobbled to the edge of the chair, and dropped to the floor with a thump. She stumbled over to us and backed up so I could pick her up.

"It was definitely him."

"That's too bad. They sure didn't give a lot of information at the press conference. What happened?"

"Who knows? Viv was going to pump her source at the Medical Examiner's office to see what she could find out." I stretched my legs out in front of me, a trifle concerned that my hamstrings seemed sore. Didn't soreness usually hit the next day? "Oh, guess what?" I said, remembering. "Viv has a new love interest. A British guy at Belle Court named Nigel."

"Nigel?"

"I know, right? I mean, that's the most British name I think I've ever heard. Viv is besotted. I think she's actually trying to convert herself to British. Tonight she said *crikey, smashing,* and she said *jolly good,* like, three times."

"Sounds like she's got it bad." He lifted my legs up into his lap and leaned close to me.

I winced as his hand closed around my calf.

He pulled away. "I told you, I don't care if you haven't shaved."

"It's not that this time. It's just that my muscles are already kind of sore from the yoga. I thought yoga was supposed to make muscles feel better."

"You'll probably feel better tomorrow." He massaged my calf gently.

I leaned my head back against the sofa and closed my eyes. "That feels very nice."

He murmured and massaged a little more.

Very nice indeed...

After a few minutes, I said, "What does *crikey* mean, anyway? I thought it was that weird game they play with the flat bats, but it didn't make sense, given the context."

"I think it's like...*dang*." He laughed and leaned over me, his face close to mine and drew the word out. "*Daaang*." He kissed me.

"Crikey," I said, when I could breathe again.

"I'd like for you to spend the night," he whispered, his forehead to mine, his brown eyes deep and dark.

"I could spend the night," I whispered. This would be the first time I'd actually spent the entire night at his place. It felt...momentous. Which was scary. "I'd need to be home early so I could get ready for work."

"Nope," he said. "Last time I was at your place, I wrote down the name of every beauty and personal hygiene product I could find, so you now have a matching set of everything here. Plus, I had Flo order some of those scrub outfits you wear to work. So you're good to go."

I snuggled into the crook of his arm. "Well, *dang*," I said, kissing him. "I can't think of a single reason to say no."

"Which was my plan all along."

Later, as we lay spooned together, our heads on one pillow, Tony said softly into my ear, "I'm glad Viv has a new boyfriend. Maybe now she'll settle down and you two can quit chasing after people with guns."

I was silent, unsure what to say.

"She can be like we are and not need the thrill of chasing after bad guys anymore."

"Mmmmm," I said. I had to admit, tonight had been pretty thrilling and a lot more fun in general than having a gun pointed at me.

"You don't sound convinced," Tony said, lowering his head to kiss my shoulder.

"It's just that I'm not sure this guy is as into Viv as she is into him. She didn't mention anything except that he was charming and fascinating and talked with a British accent."

"You could play matchmaker. Get them together. Then maybe he can get her to take up canasta or something. Then I can quit worrying that you two are going to end up dead in a back alley somewhere."

I rolled over and kissed him. "I don't even know what canasta is, but it's probably no guarantee that we won't still end up dead in a back alley somewhere."

He brushed a thumb over my lower lip. A smile played on his lips, but it was a sad smile. "I'm serious, Salem," he whispered. "We're just getting back on track, you and me. The thought of something happening to you now is just...." He kissed my forehead, then brought his gaze back down to mine. "Doesn't it sound like one of those heartbreaking, ironic stories? The soldier killed on the last day of his tour of duty? The couple in the plane crash, taking the dream trip they saved for all their lives?"

I swallowed and didn't answer, the thoughts in my head spinning too fast to choose just one. I wanted to joke. *"It would have made a much better story if I had died when your aunt tried to kill me,"* but I couldn't because now was clearly not the time. And these analogies he was making—our separation like a soldier surviving a tour of duty in a war zone. Our reunion like a dream trip we'd saved for. It all made a hard lump in my throat that I couldn't speak around.

I kissed him and snuggled into the crook of his shoulder. I wanted to assure him, but I didn't know what to say. I could definitely say that every single time a gun had been pointed at me—without exception—it had not been my idea.

I could understand how Tony would like for that to stop, though. It seemed reasonable to expect that your wife—who groomed dogs for a living and had no real reason to go chasing down killers—would not be repeatedly held at gunpoint.

Still. Viv, playing canasta? I couldn't imagine it.

I woke to Stump whining to be let out. I slid out from under Tony's arm and hurried to let her out the back door, wearing nothing but one of Tony's t-shirts. It was still full dark out, the early morning air chilly on my bare legs.

I went into the kitchen and pushed the start button on the coffee maker, doing my best not to wake Tony. I was touched that he'd set everything up for me to spend the night, but also a little freaked out. Okay, a lot freaked out.

In my colorful past (aka: when I was drinking every day), a freak-out would have me searching for things to support my freaked-out-edness. Like now, when I felt uncomfortable and uneasy in Tony's house, I would look for all the reasons I didn't belong there. Wonder of wonders, that kind of thinking led me into one conflict after another.

Now when I felt uneasy, I dug out my Bible. At the moment, though, my Bible was back in the tiny spare bedroom in my place in Trailertopia.

The truth was, I often woke up feeling out of sorts. Overwhelmed by the day ahead. Sometimes even depressed before I started the day. But over the past year and a half, I'd created a routine of a morning prayer time and devotional reading. God spoke to me through those readings. Every day, there was something in what I read that either spoke to something I was experiencing already, or that came up as I went through the day. My devotional and my candle were also back in Trailertopia, but it was a safe bet that Tony had a Bible I could read.

While the coffee brewed, I let Stump back in and grabbed a throw off the back of the sofa. I wrapped up in it and studied Tony's bookshelves. Six Bibles, actually, plus commentaries and a bunch of books about the Bible. I pulled out a Bible marked New International Version, poured a cup of coffee, and curled up in the corner of the sofa by the lamp and let it fall open. Bible roulette. Whatever verse I landed on would be the one I read today.

Romans 12:4

For just as each of us has one body with many members, and these members do not all have the same function, so in Christ we, though many, form one body, and each member belongs to all the others. We have different gifts, according to the grace given to each of us. If your gift is prophesying, then prophesy in accordance with your faith; if it is serving, then serve; if it is teaching, then teach; if it is to encourage, then give encouragement; if it is giving, then give generously; if it is to lead, do it diligently; if it is to show mercy, do it cheerfully.

I contemplated that for a while. I knew the Apostle Paul probably meant his analogy to be a comfort. We all have our part to play. Everyone has a job and heaven on earth is when we all do our job. That's probably very encouraging if you know what your job is.

In my more cynical times, I've honestly felt like my job was to screw things up. There is purpose in every pain, right? Some way for God to be glorified no matter what we're going through? There was a time when I believed that my purpose was for things to go wrong so that others could look at me and be thankful for what went right. I didn't even realize that's what I believed until I had a conversation with Les, my AA sponsor, about this very passage.

Les was confident that his part of the body of Christ was to be a hug for those who were down. He didn't care how a person came to be down, either. In fact, if it was a self-inflicted downing, he was even more the hugger. "When your life has gone off the rails because of something out of your control—a crime committed against you, a serious illness, a natural disaster—there are lots of people willing to step in and help you out. When you've done it to yourself, you're on your own. Everyone wants to let you stew in your own juices for a while. And I get that. But I was off the rails one time, from choices I made, and someone reached out to me. It made all the difference. Now that's my job. To reach out to those no one else wants to touch."

He'd done that for me. And it made all the difference.

He'd laughed when I said I thought perhaps I was born to be a cautionary tale.

"I think God has bigger plans for you than that, Salem. It's good to learn from your mistakes, and it's good to share what you've learned with others. But there's more to your purpose than just to be the example of what not to do."

I hadn't even wanted to admit it to him, because it was just silly, but part of me had secretly come to hope maybe my gift was solving crimes. No, I wasn't great at it. And, no, I wasn't the least bit qualified. But since Viv and I had started hanging around together, we did seem to have a knack for asking the right questions and insinuating ourselves into situations where we ferreted out the truth.

Viv had no qualms about it. After we had solved the murder of Tony's former girlfriend—a murder he'd been suspected of committing—she'd had PI business cards printed up for us. Horrible things with dangling handcuffs and lipstick font that read "Discreet Investigations" across the top. Those horrible cards made it look like we might be in the business of providing something both immoral and, perhaps, painful as well. I was mortified every time she pulled one of those awful cards out of her pocket. I didn't think we were actual private detectives. I didn't particularly like chasing down bad guys, and I definitely didn't care for being on the receiving end of a gun.

But I did like helping people. I liked solving problems. I liked being useful.

If it is serving, then serve.

Did this count as service? Surely it did. Did that mean this particular service was my gift, given according to the grace given me?

I lay down, resting my head against the arm of the sofa and remembering what Tony had said last night. He assumed that Viv was just bored and that I was only going along with her because I had nothing better to do. But we both had better things to do now. So it made sense that—Peter Browning's suspicious death or not—we would steer clear of trouble now.

It shouldn't have made me sad. Probably I just felt sad because it was early in the morning and I was out of my comfort zone. It wasn't the idea that I couldn't go chasing after trouble with Viv anymore. That would be silly.

But...what was my gift? If it wasn't being a living, breathing, cautionary tale, and it wasn't chasing down bad guys, what was it?

Stump chose that moment to root her nose under my hand, and she scootched and flopped around until I could rub her fat belly. Maybe my purpose was to love Stump. There were worse fates, I decided.

I heard Tony stir in his room. He went to the bathroom, then walked slowly down the hallway, stopping near the entryway. He stood, motionless, not saying anything for so long that I started to wonder if he was sleep walking.

"I hope we didn't wake you," I said from the sofa.

He jumped, whirling on me with bug eyes.

I couldn't help but giggle. I rose and walked to him, still carrying the throw around me. I wrapped it and my arms around his shoulders. "I'm sorry," I said.

"Well, I'm awake now," he murmured into my hair, snuggling under the blanket with me. His heart was thudding a bit.

"I started the coffee." I pulled away and poured two cups, carrying one to him. He still looked shell shocked, and it dawned on me why he'd jumped when I spoke.

He thought I'd left. He woke and found me and Stump gone from the bedroom and assumed I'd left while he was asleep. Despite all the trouble he'd gone through to get me to stay.

I would have liked to react with righteous indignation, but the fact was, I had left him before. I'd left him and he had no reason—other than my word, which, historically speaking, wasn't worth much—that I wouldn't leave again.

All I could do was put down my cup and wrap myself around him again. I could tell him a million times that I was different now. I could tell myself that, too. But neither one of us were going to believe it without proof.

I kissed the side of his neck and laid my head against his shoulder. "I need to get in the shower," I said.

"Me, too."

"I'll hurry."

"We could save time. Shower together."

"You," I stood on tiptoe and kissed his forehead, "are so practical."

I had to admit, it was nice staying at Tony's house instead of my trailer. For one thing, everything worked. When I turned the hot water knob in the shower, hot water came out. At my trailer, I had learned the complicated sequences of turning the knob to exactly 17 minutes past the hour—not fifteen, not twenty—and then tilting the wobbly knob forward to get almost enough hot water to wash my hair and shave both legs before icy spray started shooting out.

Plus, Tony was there. Tony, who had looked to see what kind of shampoo I used and bought the exact brand for me to use in his shower. Tony, who made sure I had healthy stuff to eat and even stocked the freezer with special Fat Fighters frozen breakfast sandwiches and fresh fruit.

I remembered what he'd said the night before, about me and Viv no longer chasing bad guys, and in the light of day, it sounded like a highly sensible idea. I could have all this. A nice, normal life. Why would I go chasing after trouble? Surely Viv and I could find something else to do.

I poured a cup of coffee and filled up Tony's cup. He sat at the bar, reading the newspaper. "Help me think of something Viv and I can do together that's not chasing bad guys," I said. "I really don't think she's the canasta type, but I want to think of something to keep her busy."

"How about this?" He folded the paper over and slid it to me, tapping an announcement surrounded by a thick border.

Volunteers needed at Lubbock Arboretum. No gardening experience necessary—you provide the muscles, we'll show you what to do with them.

"Gardening," I said. "Wow."

"Yeah, it could be great. My aunt always has a garden, and she grows the best tomatoes you've ever tasted. How cool would it be to have dinner picked from our very own garden?"

"I'm fairly sure I have a black thumb," I said.

"It's okay." He nodded toward the paper. "They'll show you what to do. And since it's fall, there's no real growing involved. This is probably all about cleaning out the beds, getting things prepared for the next growing season."

That sounded like something even I couldn't mess up. And he had wanted me to stay badly enough that he replicated everything he could find and even bought me breakfast sandwiches so I would have something to eat before work. It's hard not to fall completely in love with a gesture like that.

"I'll put it to Viv today. And I'll see what I can do to encourage this thing with Nigel the Brit. Maybe by this time next year we'll all be playing canasta over a plate of sliced tomatoes and cucumbers that Viv and I grew ourselves."

Each member belongs to all the others.

As I groomed dogs at my job at Flo's Bow-Wow Barbers, that verse kept running through my head. I had to admit, I didn't care for it. I didn't like to think of myself as being obligated to anyone else—and certainly not to everyone else. To be honest, the Apostle Paul and I don't always get along.

That didn't mean that I necessarily thought he was wrong. He did, after all, write half the New Testament. That had to give him some credibility right there. I just didn't like it. The truth was, though, that everything we did affected those around us. I had learned that lesson a million hard ways when I was drinking. No one lived in a vacuum.

It was a slow day at Flo's, and one of the great things about working there was that we didn't have to stay until closing time. If we got done with our dogs, we could leave. So when I realized I was going to be through with work by two o'clock, I decided to use whatever gifts I had to help Viv.

"Windy, call Viv."

Viv didn't even say hello. She must have seen it was me, because she answered with, "What time are you getting off?"

"I'll be done in about fifteen minutes," I said.

"Ooooh, that's perfect! Come straight over. I have a job for you."

"Does this involve Nigel?"

"It does! I had a fantastic idea but I need someone to help me play it out." She hung up.

I frowned at the phone. She needed someone to help play it out? What mortifying scene was she getting me into? I swept up and cleaned my tools, thinking that this could help pay back some of the shampoo and breakfast sandwiches Tony had bought.

That was a thought I immediately checked, though. Tony would never owe me. I would forever be in Tony's debt. I decided that while I was helping Viv capture Nigel the Brit, I would also bring up the volunteer thing at the arboretum. It was the least I could do.

When Stump and I got to Viv's apartment at Belle Court, she was in a tizzy. She had written out a scene for us to act out as Nigel walked by.

Although my part was crucial, I wasn't exactly playing Lady Macbeth. Viv rushed us to one of Belle Court's numerous hallways and positioned me and Stump, then stood back and surveyed the effect.

"Bend your knee a little."

I bent my knee.

"No, the other one. More. No, not that much."

"What look are you going for here? Tell me that, and I can bring my own interpretation."

"We're just two friends engaged in casual conversation. Do you remember your line?" She checked her lipstick in the mirror that hung above a huge flower arrangement on the hall table. We were in one of the many byzantine hallways in Belle Court's main building, where an alcove held two floral print wingback chairs for a chance to sit and watch the world go by.

"But Winston Churchill was Prime Minister during World War II," I stated. Again. I mentally tried to force my body into the stance of someone engaged in casual conversation about World War II.

"You're not selling it," Viv said. She leaned forward and ran a thumbnail along her lip to edge away a stray lipstick smear. "Say it like you're honestly confused."

I was honestly confused. I wanted to help Viv, but I couldn't believe she was working so hard to get this guy's attention. She had, after all, already had as many husbands as Elizabeth Taylor. Wasn't that enough? I hefted Stump to my other side, trying to be supportive but also trying to figure out what the urgency was. "What do you hope is going to happen? What is it about this guy that has you working so hard to impress him?"

"I'm not working that hard," Viv said. She turned and stood on tiptoe, checking her butt out in the mirror. "I'm just...he's..." She stopped and frowned. "He's British."

"And?"

"And it's so cool. You need to hear him talk—*Oh*! Here he comes!"

I turned to look down the hall.

"Don't *look*! For crying out loud!" She whirled around and visibly tried to catch her breath.

I could hear Nigel's group—consisting of himself and what sounded like four or five "old widder women" as G-Ma called them—coming down the hall toward us. Viv took a deep breath, squared her shoulders, then held a hand up to me in a wait-for-my-signal gesture.

The women were all talking at once, though. I could see why Viv had named them The Gaggle. It was bizarrely like a group of tweens walking through the mall. One of the ladies was Anne, one of my favorite people at Belle Court. Privately I thought of her as Apple Annie because of her round red cheeks. She was every sweet little old lady you've ever seen—Mrs. Santa Claus, the lady who owned Tweety Bird, etc.

Behind Anne was Imogene, a gruff old bear of a woman who was like the opposite of Apple Annie. My nickname for her was Intimidating Imogene. I never knew if I had somehow, at some point, managed to disappoint Imogene without knowing it, or if she just went through life looking like that, but every time I saw her I felt like slinking away with my tail between my legs.

"Shut up, Anne," Viv hissed through her lips. "For once in your life, just shut up!"

They were on us, then, and the moment was about to be lost. With a frown, Viv signaled to me and whispered, "Loud!"

"But Winston Churchill was the Prime Minister during World War II," I shouted.

"Oh, Salem! Hahahahaha!" Viv threw her head back and laughed hugely. She slapped her leg. She checked the mirror to see if the group passing behind her had noticed. "That's all anyone remembers. The good ol' British Bulldog! But he became Prime Minister halfway through the war. Neville Chamberlain was Prime Minister when war broke out—" She started as if she'd just realize we weren't alone in the hallway. "Well, hello there, Nigel." She smiled brilliantly. Then her mouth went flat. "Ladies."

The snub was lost on Anne. She stood at Nigel's side, smiling
her cherubic smile. "You should join us at the pool, Viv. We're
about to do water aerobics." She reached out and rubbed
Stump's ears with her soft little-old-lady fingers. "Right, Nigel?
Viv would enjoy water aerobics, don't you think?"

"That's right," Nigel said. "The more the merrier."

I had to admit, for an old guy he was kind of hot. His silver
hair swept back from his high forehead. He had the requisite old
man bushy eyebrows, but they were still somewhat dark. He
sported a mustache and a very narrow goatee, both darker like
his eyebrows instead of full silver like the hair on his head. The
effect reminded me of a rakish riverboat gambler, except with a
British accent.

"I fear we're not able," Viv said.

I looked at her. *I fear we're not able?*

"We're working a new case. Got to catch the baddies, you
know. Gotta...crack on."

"That's right!" Anne said. She beamed up at Nigel. "Viv and
Salem are private detectives."

"He knows, Anne. You've told him at least five times that I
know of," Imogene said.

"Yes, well, we'd best be on our way or we'll miss the class."
Nigel turned to Viv and me with a bow. "Perhaps another time."
He took Anne by the elbow and steered her back toward the
pool area.

Viv and I watched him go in silence. She frowned. "Did you
see the way he was holding Anne's elbow?"

"Probably just trying to make sure she didn't fall."

She latched on to that. "He is very considerate."

"Viv, what is it about this guy that has you so bowled over?"

She looked at me like I was crazy. "Did you see him? Did you hear him speak? The more the merrier," she parroted in a sad imitation of his accent. "I mean, he really meant that, I could tell. That was sincere."

"Do you think he's impressed by your knowledge of British history?"

"Of course! He's a war hero—did I tell you that? He flew Spitfires in World War II."

"That is impressive."

"And you should hear him read poetry." She turned back toward her apartment, lost in the memory of Nigel's voice. "It's like...you know that feeling you get after a nice brandy? Warm in the center of your body, relaxed, content? Nigel reading poetry is like that." She swanned around the hallway like someone in a half-swoon.

I remembered the way Nigel had taken Anne's elbow. I didn't want to say anything to Viv, but that hadn't looked merely considerate to me. He'd been almost proprietary. I could imagine that sweet Apple Annie would bring out the masculine nature of a retired war hero.

Poor Viv. She wasn't the kind of person who dealt graciously with not getting what she wanted. She told me one time that she'd keyed the car of a romantic rival. Not exactly blood sport, but still, I was starting to become a trifle concerned for Anne.

My phone bleeped as I followed Viv back to her place. It was the sound I'd set for G-Ma.

"How's it going, G-Ma?" I said in answer.

"Serena had a vision about that reporter fella and wants you to tell the police."

Five questions immediately began to clamor for top billing. I chose the most obvious one first. "Who's Serena?"

"She's the new card reader in room 6, with all the crystals and stuff. She had a vision."

G-Ma had recently converted her rundown strip motel to a cute little shopping center full of individually owned and unique shops. All the former motel rooms were now small businesses—a coffee shop, a nail salon, a used book store-and, of course, the yoga place Viv and I had been to on Tuesday night. This was G-Ma's innovation after her regular clientele of prostitutes—which she still swears she knew nothing about—were forced to either find other operating quarters or change lines of work. G-Ma made the offer to help any of the girls who were willing, get training and small business loans, and started advertising the place big time. A few of the girls took her up on the offer, and although the place was still undergoing some renovations, the shops that were open were getting by.

I had seen Serena's shop when Viv and I had been there for yoga, but I hadn't met her. I liked her shop, though—she'd had a big blue and silver swirl painted on the front window that spiraled out into what looked like a starry sky.

So anyway—that was question number one out of the way. On to question two. "What kind of vision?"

"She said it was more of a feeling, actually. Not like a clear vision. She doesn't get them like tuning into a TV show or something." She said this with a tone that told me these were the exact words Serena had said to G-Ma. "They're more like just feelings. Like when you're watching a movie and a bad guy comes on the screen, and you know he's a bad guy because the music changes. It's like all that, without the visual, though. You just hear the music and get the sense that there's a bad guy. It's subtle like that."

"What kind of feeling did she get?"

"She said that fellow had been wrestling with demons."

I waited, but nothing else was forthcoming.

"Demons?"

"Right."

"Like...what kind of demons?" Since we were in Viv's hallway by now, I let Stump down to trot alongside us. The other residents on her floor were used to Stump and didn't freak out that she would pee on the carpet or anything.

"Just demons. But she thinks it's important that the police know this."

"Okay, well..." *Does Serena not have a phone?* I wanted to ask.

"I told her you had that boyfriend who was the cop and that you would tell him."

"G-Ma! Bobby is not my boyfriend. You do remember that I'm married, right?" Somewhat.

"Colleague, then."

I let that one slide, but I couldn't help but grin at what Bobby would think about me and him being colleagues. "Why doesn't she want to tell the police herself? I think police work with psychics sometimes. They would probably want to hear about her having a vision about Peter Browning's death."

At this, Viv whipped her head around. "Psychic vision? Peter Browning's death?"

I took Viv's key from her—because she'd suddenly lost interest in unlocking the door and was focused on my phone call—and opened the door. "I can give her Bobby's number."

Viv took the phone from me. "We'll be happy to pass on the information. Now give me all the details."

I knew how G-Ma was going to react to that. G-Ma did not like Viv. She thought Viv was a snobby old biddie who'd had nothing but good luck and thought she was better than everyone—'everyone' meaning G-Ma specifically, who'd had to work her own fingers to the bone and never had a break from anyone. To her credit, G-Ma was right about parts of that assessment, but dead wrong about other parts. It was true that G-Ma worked like nobody's business and always had. She'd had to make her own breaks, and it made me happy to see how well the motel was doing now, after years of mere subsistence on the side of a highway that people rarely used anymore. And it was true that Viv had seen some good fortune in the last couple of husbands, in that they'd had fortunes to see, and left it all to Viv. But Viv had also had her share of bad breaks in life before that, and she wasn't a snob. She most definitely didn't think she was better than anyone. She just really enjoyed annoying my G-Ma. Nothing made her happier than winning a point in the Battle of Viv vs. G-Ma.

"No, I think you should give me the information so I can convey it to the proper authorities," Viv was saying. "Yes, give it to me. What is her phone number, then? I'll call her myself. Just tell me!" Viv frowned and dropped her Jimmy Choo handbag on the floor. "Lady, do you want to be cited for obstruction of justice?"

I could hear G-Ma laughing from the other end of the line.

Viv scowled and jabbed the End Call button, then thrust the phone back at me. "She won't tell me."

"It's okay, we can go see Serena ourselves."

Viv picked her handbag back up. "I'll drive."

"Right now?" I suddenly remembered that I was supposed to be steering Viv away from murder investigations and onto less dangerous territory.

"Of course, right now. Come on. We're taking your car and I'm driving." Apparently, the point loss to G-Ma needed to be made up somehow.

Fine by me. I was still not comfortable driving that bus. But I wasn't sure about the whole psychic thing. Would Tony consider this dangerous? Was it okay for a Christian to talk to a psychic? Plus, I hadn't even mentioned the cleanup at the arboretum yet.

But Viv was already headed out the door.

"Hang on," I said. Stump grunted as I picked her up and chased Viv down the hall to the elevator.

On the elevator I said, "Listen, I need to talk to you about this whole private investigator stuff." Might as well just be honest. "Tony isn't comfortable with this."

"That's fine. Tony isn't doing it." Viv pushed the first-floor button.

"He's not comfortable with me doing it, as I'm sure you understand. What with all the guns being pointed at me and stuff. He doesn't care for that."

"Has that man forbidden you from conducting investigations?" She put her hand on her hip and glared.

Viv liked Tony—I mean, everyone liked Tony. He was a great guy. In fact, Viv had worked hard to help me prove him innocent of murder, in fact, when his aunt had tried to frame him. But that didn't mean she would hesitate to go full feminist on his butt if she thought he was exercising overbearing male authority over me.

"Of course not. But I think I owe it to him to try and stay out of trouble."

"No problem. We're going to see a psychic. What's the worst that could happen?"

I shrugged. "I'm sure nothing will happen. I just...the thing is..." I grimaced. "I kind of told him I would encourage you on to other endeavors that aren't so...rife with bad guys."

"Such as?"

"Such as...gardening."

Viv drew her head back. "Gardening?" She wrinkled her nose.

"The arboretum put out a call for volunteers to help clean up the place. You know, rake up dead leaves and clear out underbrush and stuff. I promised him I'd talk to you about it."

"Okay, well, check that one off your list. We talked." The elevator dinged and the doors slid open. Viv perched designer sunglasses on her nose and waltzed out the door, a woman who would not be denied her mission.

I handed her the keys and loaded Stump into the passenger seat. I didn't bother locking the doors anymore. No one wanted a 1974 Monte Carlo, except to marvel that it was still running.

I studied Viv as she swung the Monster Carlo out of the Belle Court parking lot, her chin set. It was clear I needed to take another tactic with this.

"You know, it was his idea that I help things along with Nigel," I said casually. "That's why I called today."

"Whose idea? Tony's?"

"Yes. He really liked the idea of you being in a relationship with such a distinguished man." Or any man. Any person. Anything that would burn off some of her energy without involving gunfire.

"Nigel is very distinguished."

"Exactly. I think Tony is hoping you and Nigel could become our couple friends. You know, hang out on weekends and stuff."

"We could go skiing together!" Viv said. "Weekend trips to Santa Fe!"

"Exactly!" Never mind that I didn't ski, and it was somewhat debatable whether Viv and Nigel should ski. Tony was back on Viv's nice list, so I could now strike while the iron was hot. "Like I said, he didn't forbid me from doing investigations. He's just uncomfortable with it, so I think I need to lie low, kind of, until he gets used to the idea." Or until you find a new hobby. I sent up a silent prayer that Viv would discover a heretofore untapped love of gardening. It would take a miracle of Biblical proportions.

She chewed on her lower lip and seemed to consider it. "Well, okay. I could do some volunteer hours at the arboretum. It would look good on my resume for Nigel, anyway. Last night I saw a documentary about land girls—the women who worked the fields during World War II while the men were gone."

"That's fantastic! That would give you a great talking point for him."

"Well, I didn't actually watch the documentary. I read the description, though."

"Well, that's a starting place. You can watch it tonight, and there's a work session at the arboretum tomorrow afternoon. I think I can get off in time to make it. I'll meet you there."

"Nope, we're taking your car and I'm driving. That's the plan. For now, though, I want to hear what this psychic has to say."

That reminded me of another question I had. "Is this okay for us? I mean, talking to a psychic? Can Christians do that?"

"Sure. Why not?"

"I don't know. It feels like dabbling in the occult or something."

"Nonsense. The Bible said God gives some the spirit of prophecy."

I gasped. "Hey! I read that verse just this morning!" That had to be a sign, right? If God had not wanted me to go see a psychic, He would not have given me that verse two times in the same day, surely.

That reminded me of my own low spirits that morning, though. I rubbed Stump's belly. "Do you ever think about what your gift is, Viv? That verse I read said that we're all part of the body and we all have our parts to play. Do you know what your part is?"

Viv looked at me with a crooked grin. "We have been friends for over a year now. I should think that would be obvious."

I ran through the what I could remember – prophesying, obviously. Giving – well, I couldn't honestly say I'd seen much of that. Teaching – maybe. Encouraging – when she felt like it.

"I give up," I finally said.

"Salem. Clearly, I have *all* the gifts."

CHAPTER THREE

Bridled Enthusiasm

The changes to G-Ma's motel, although still in process, were impressive. Gone was the sad, seedy-looking motel and in its place was a cute, quirky place where you actually wanted to hang out. The place was shaped like a huge V, with Mario's tamale factory and the old swimming pool in the center. G-Ma had had the sidewalks widened and the old overhang taken down and replaced with a pergola that ran the length of both sidewalks. Trumpet vines grew in large pots and had already begun to climb the pergolas to create the beginnings of shade. What had been the pool area was now a quaint, tiny park, with grassy little hills, a koi pond with a footbridge and waterfall, and iron chairs and tables with striped umbrellas for people to sit and enjoy their pastries, smoothies, and coffees. It was encircled with another pergola that would undoubtedly also be covered in trumpet vines soon.

As we pulled into the motel parking lot, my phone made a siren noise.

Viv frowned, more annoyed than scared, and looked in the rear view mirror. "I really didn't do anything this time," she grumbled.

"It's okay, that's my phone. That's the ring tone I set for calls from my mom."

Mom was planning her wedding and being a bit of a bridezilla about it. I debated ignoring the call, but I felt guilty. Just last week my morning Bible study time had included the commandment "Honor thy father and mother." If I was going to take the verse on prophecy as a green light for visiting Serena, I probably ought to take the commandment reminder, too. Picking and choosing surely lessened the effectiveness of trying to live by scripture.

"Hi, Mom," I said.

"Wait until you see the brochures for our honeymoon. It's like something out of a movie! I am so excited, I just went out and bought three new bikinis. Gerry is going to kill me."

She laughed because of course he wasn't going to kill her. He adored her. At least, that was the story. Plus, he was loaded so he could afford it, and she would probably look dynamite in a bikini. Mom had kept all the hot body genes and selfishly refused to pass any on to me.

"Where is the honeymoon again?" I asked, to keep the conversation off the bikinis. Honoring your mother probably didn't include envying her tiny waist.

"Costa Rica! For the first time in my life, I'm getting a passport!"

"Woohoo!" I was proud of how not-envious I sounded.

"Oh, please," Viv said, and I realized she could hear everything Mom was saying. "Come on, I'll bet that's her."

I looked where Viv pointed, to the psychic's place across the parking lot. Two women stood chatting on the sidewalk in front of the swirly blue window. Both wore jeans and tennis shoes. I didn't think either one was Serena. With a name like Serena and a job like psychic, she had to wear a flowing caftan and have a wide streak of snow white hair, didn't she?

Mom was going on about what an ordeal it was to get the passport. I inserted an occasional "Uh-huh" and "Wow" to keep things going.

"Wrap it up," Viv said. She opened her door. "We have an interview to conduct."

"That's crazy, Mom," I said. "Listen—"

"Not to mention the complication with the flights. You would think if we can put a man on the moon we could get a man from Lubbock to South America without going through Dallas. But no!"

Viv rolled her eyes, and I gave her an apologetic smile.

"Tell your mother she's going to Central America, not South America." She gave up on me and left me there. The rat.

She crossed the parking lot, already pulling out another one of those horrible cards.

I figured, though, that anyone who carried a card for being a psychic probably didn't throw stones at anyone else's business cards, so I decided to skip my usual mortification over the cards. The two women finished their conversation and one walked off.

The other one, a petite woman with big eyes and cropped short brown hair, smiled and took Viv's card with one hand, closing the other hand over Viv's and holding it. She kept her hands there while Viv talked—presumably explaining who she was and what she was there for. The girl listened, nodding, smiling. She leaned forward, still holding Viv's hands, and said a few things. She appeared to be around my age—28.

"I mean, right?" Mom said with a laugh.

"Seriously," I said, having no clue what I was agreeing to.

Viv cocked her head, then nodded briskly. Whatever the girl had just said, Viv had liked.

It went back and forth like that a few more times. The woman never let go of Viv's hands. She never stopped smiling that wide smile. Her eyes never left Viv's face. She talked, Viv talked, she talked again, and then they were done.

And I had missed the whole thing.

When Viv recrossed the parking lot, it was as if she was walking down a runway. Shoulders back, chin high, arms swinging.

G-Ma came out of her office, and Viv waved at her. "Virgie! Hello!" as if they were old friends.

As for G-Ma, she apparently didn't have time to waste on Viv; she had an empire to rebuild. She gave a short wave to us both and power walked down the sidewalk.

"Well, I guess I need to let you go, I have to finalize the menu with the caterer because today is the drop-dead deadline. I told Gerry if I ever get married again, I'm going to elope!" She laughed, apparently not seeing the irony of someone saying this while planning their sixth wedding.

"Good luck," I said. "Talk to you later." I ended the call.

Viv dropped into the seat. "Well. That was most helpful."

"What did she say? Wait, is she leaving?" I had hoped to get to talk to her, but Serena was locking the door from the outside.

"She said she was just about to leave and would be gone already except she found that woman's—the one she was talking to when we walked up?—Serena found that woman's wallet on the sidewalk and was holding it until the owner came back. If that hadn't happened, we would have missed her. We just barely caught her! Synchronicity, right?" Viv leaned back and shook her head as if stunned by the miracle she'd just encountered.

"Wow," I said, dutifully. "What did she say about Peter Browning?"

"Oh, that. Yes, we did talk about that, too."

"Too? I thought that was why we were meeting her in the first place."

"We were, of course. It's just...messages are more complicated than that, Salem. She passes on everything she gets, so it's all a package. It's not just about Peter Browning, it's about the entire situation. Which, frankly, is pretty awesome."

I nodded as if a young man dead before his time being "pretty awesome" made perfect sense and started the Monster Carlo. "Sounds great. What did she have to say about the entire situation?"

"Well, first I told her who I was—"

"Who *we* were," I corrected.

"Exactly, who we were. I gave her the card. I told her we had heard she'd received a message on Peter Browning's death and I was prepared to hear it so I could pass it on to the proper authorities."

"Great," I said, pulling onto the Clovis Highway. "What did she say?"

"That she could tell I was just the person for her to go through, because she could see I was a person who was open to everything. I did not put up barriers the way most people do."

I nodded. I thought of it more along the lines of "no boundaries," but po-tay-to/po-tah-to.

"In fact, she said she could see along my entire time stream, and one thing stood out—one color ran like a bold thread throughout the entire length of it. Do you want to know what it was?"

I nodded. "I do. I also want to know what a time stream is."

"Well, it's your life, of course. But maybe not just the dates between your birth and your death, but your entire, you know...soul existence."

"You got all that while I was talking to my mother?"

"Well, she didn't explain the time stream thing, that's just my take on it. Anyway, guess what color I am?"

"You've got me."

"Yellow! Yellow, for enthusiasm! I mean, isn't that just hitting the nail on the head?"

I had to admit that, as enthusiasm went, Viv was a major player.

"She said it was the brightest yellow, in fact, that she'd ever seen. She said I'd lived my life with unbridled enthusiasm and exuberance." She shook her head again. "I mean, wow, right? Such wisdom and keen insight in someone so young." She tapped her fingers against her knee. "Isn't it great when you meet someone who just gets you? Just clicks with you immediately?"

"That's pretty amazing," I said. I wasn't sure if what I was feeling was residual envy from the phone call with Mom, or fresh envy for Viv's soul-to-soul encounter. "I wish I'd been able to talk to her." Maybe she could give me some insight. Although to be honest, I was less than bowled over by her assessment of Viv. Anyone could see that Viv had the energy of ten men. But if she could give me enough insight to even point me in the general direction of my own strengths, it would be an improvement. I brought the conversation back around. "What did she say about Peter Browning?"

"Oh, that he'd been struggling with demons."

I waited. But that was it.

"But, we already knew that."

"Yes. She is quite certain the man had been struggling with demons. She thought it was a demon of vengeance, but she couldn't be sure."

"But...what does that even mean?"

"I don't know, but we are definitely going to find out. She said I was the perfect person to get to the bottom of it and bring about reconciliation and healing, because she knew I would not give up until a sense of peace had descended over the situation."

I couldn't help but think this was all about Viv and not nearly enough about Browning.

I got lucky two days in a row and finished my dogs early. I wasn't sure if I was happy about that or not—I wouldn't have been very upset to have a good excuse to miss the work day at the arboretum. I decided I would take getting off early as another sign that God approved of me doing this, although it could have just been a sign that business was kind of slow, as it was every year in early November, especially with all the rain we'd had. Nobody wanted to drop a fifty on getting their dog clean just to see it roll around in the mud immediately after. Still, it was what it was, so I took Stump home to sit in the recliner with my neighbor, Frank, changed into my grubbiest clothes, and drove up to Belle Court to get Viv.

My shabby attire earned me a couple of looks by the people at Belle Court.

"Viv and I are helping out at the arboretum," I started saying to everyone who got within earshot. "Gonna go get our hands dirty." This got me more looks, unfortunately.

I knocked on Viv's door, then opened it and said, "Ready to rumble?"

"Be there in a second," Viv called from the bedroom. "Make yourself comfortable."

I already had. I lounged on her sofa and thought about the afternoon ahead. Maybe God was putting this garden thing in my path because growing things was my "gift." I mean, it could be. I'd never tried my hand at it. Maybe I would be fantastic at it and Tony's vision of eating from our very own garden was spot-on.

Completely unbidden came the image of me, blithely yanking up some rare, pride-of-the-entire-Lubbock-gardening-community plant, thinking it was a weed, throwing it onto a burning pile of garden rubbish as horrified onlookers screamed in anguish.

I gnawed my lower lip. By the time Viv called out, "Okay, I'm ready," I had resigned myself to supermarket produce for life.

She hurried in, not wearing grubby working-in-the-garden clothes, but a sharp new pantsuit. She stood before the hall mirror and adjusted her collar and belt, then fluffed her hair.

I stood in my baggy jeans and ripped shoes. "What did I miss?"

"Change of plans. There's a meeting this afternoon of the planning committee for the Veterans Day thing on Sunday. Now, don't freak out, but we're kind of going to crash this meeting. Just follow my lead and act like we belong there."

I nodded. I wasn't necessarily upset, since I could now quit worrying about pulling up a precious flower. But I was confused. "Okay, sure. Lots of questions, though. One, there's a celebration committee for wars? And two, we're crashing a committee meeting? Why?"

"It's for Veterans Day, actually, November 11. Belle Court always has a big to-do for the residents who are veterans. Mostly they're World War II—some Korea and some VietNam."

"But Nigel's World War II."

"Exactly. The committee is meeting today to finalize all the details. They did ask for volunteers," she added, with a 'they have only themselves to blame' air.

"They're kind of leaving it until the last minute, aren't they?"

"Oh, no, they asked months ago. I just didn't volunteer then."

"But you're volunteering now?"

"Yep. How does this look?" She unbuttoned her jacket to show a dazzling Union Jack t-shirt, with red, white and blue sequins that danced in the light.

"Classy," I said. "So, Nigel is on this committee?"

"Would I have bought this otherwise?" She picked up a leather portfolio and unzipped it to check inside. I saw a pad of legal paper and four lipsticks. No pen.

She turned sideways again and checked her butt in the mirror, rolled her lips together and said, "Okay, let's go."

I tagged after her, mentally debating whether I should just bail now. I looked like...well, like the gardener tagging along after the owner of the mansion.

"I'll need you to back me up with Imogene Hall, okay? She's the chairperson and already said I couldn't come to the meeting today because I hadn't participated before now. But we're going anyway."

I stopped in the middle of the hallway. "Nope. Uh-uh." I shook my head.

"Come on. She's not that scary."

"She is, too! You said yourself she made your blood run cold."

Viv and I had accidentally attended one of the Belle Court luncheons where Imogene spoke on her career working as an architect for a big firm in Houston and all the battles she'd fought for her gender. We were only there because we got the dates mixed up—we had meant to go to the one the week before, which was about how to make money speculating on futures. That interested us because Viv had money and I enjoyed watching her do stuff with it. But we ended up at Imogene's instead, and she'd glared at me through the entire presentation, especially when she talked about the debt today's generation of women owed her and her counterparts, as we "walked through our workdays on the shoulders of those women who had gone before and paved our way."

I felt really uncomfortable about the whole thing and kind of guilty for being a lowly dog groomer. I didn't think I was standing on anyone's shoulders at Flo's Bow Wow Barbers, but I hadn't exactly thought about it before, so how would I know?

I briefly considered getting a degree in architecture to make it up to Imogene, but I was pretty sure you had to be smart for that. So I just smiled apologetically every time I saw her, and then tried to see her as little as possible.

"Don't let her get to you. She can't hurt you."

"She hates me."

"So? She hates me, too. I don't let it bother me." Viv pushed the button for the elevator. "Besides, this gives me more time with Nigel, and we've all agreed I need more time with Nigel if we're ever going to be couple friends and buy that boat together."

"Boat?"

"Sure. Summer weekends on the lake. What could be better?"

I decided it must be so much fun living in Viv's fantasy world. I'd like to take a weekend trip there sometime. "I'm not dressed for committee meetings," I said. I stuck my foot out. My shoe had an actual hole in it. "I'm dressed for gardening."

"We'll garden after," Viv promised. She moved into the elevator and pushed the button for the top floor. "I swear. We'll garden our bums off. I just need to show Nigel what a..." She frowned at her reflection as the doors slid closed. She bared her teeth and checked for stuff in her teeth.

"Show Nigel what a what?" I prompted.

"What a clever dick I am."

"Viv!" I said, shocked into laughter.

"No, it's okay," Viv said. "Brits say that all the time. I mean, you could say that on Sesame Street over there and get away with it."

"They have Sesame Street there?" I was confused.

"Oh, I don't know. Probably not. But you get my meaning. That's not considered foul language there."

I wasn't sure I did get her meaning, but I felt fairly certain she ought to keep that one in her pocket around Imogene Hall. "Just remember that you're not over there, you're over here."

Viv groaned and shook her head. "Don't remind me."

The doors slid open and Viv marched down the hall, me hurrying in her wake to keep up.

The meeting appeared to be already in progress, but Viv marched in and slid into a seat like she belonged there, nodding to me to take an empty chair across from her. "Sorry, we had to take the lift to get down here on time. Cock-up at the front office."

I couldn't help it, I yelped a little laughter again.

Viv looked at me. "I know, right? That one isn't as bad as it sounds, either." She slid her portfolio onto the table. "Okay now, where were we?"

Imogene Hall frowned at her. "We weren't anywhere. We—" She circled the table with her hand, indicating the entire Nigel fan club. "—were putting the finishing touches on a project we've been working on for months. Then you two walked in."

"I told you," Viv said with exaggerated patience, "there was a cock-up at the front office. Now, what kind of refreshments are there? Because I know some people who make a smashing red punch and a spread of finger foods that will put a smile on anyone's face. Perhaps even a tray of biscuits." She smirked. "And of course, by biscuits I mean the kind that are actually cookies, not the kind with gravy. And, I would be happy to underwrite that expense."

I lifted an eyebrow. Not that I didn't know it already, but Viv was clearly smitten. She didn't volunteer to underwrite very much.

"The refreshments are covered," Imogene said.

"Excellent. Speakers?"

"Covered."

"Press? Advertisement?"

"Covered. Now if you would please let us get back to work..."

"Actually," Anne said, raising a tentative hand. "We were still working out the details about press coverage." She turned to Viv. "Bea Nance used to always have her nephew cover the story, but since she died and he moved away, we are in need of some promotional assistance."

Viv slapped a hand on the table. "Done! I have a very good friend who happens to be an anchor at Channel 11. I'll give her a call." She glanced over to Nigel to see if he was suitably impressed.

He appeared to have tuned out of the entire meeting.

Not to be deterred, Viv turned to him. "Nigel, I heard you were making a presentation. How exciting! I am fascinated by stories of our heroes in the sky." She batted her false eyelashes.

"Yes, well, I intend to do my best, of course. I'm just one man out of thousands who served."

"You're very humble." Viv gave him a beneficent nod. *"Per ardua, ad astra!"* She saluted and said, "That's the RAF motto. Did y'all know that?"

The Gaggle remained silent. Nigel cleared his throat.

"What about the Baucum Local Hero award?" one of the Nigel fans asked. "Does anyone know yet who it's going to be?"

One of The Gaggle gave a delicate snort and another said, "Nobody this year."

"Maybe nobody next year, too, or ever again."

Anne looked confused. "But why? It's such a great tradition." She turned to Nigel. "It really does your heart good to hear about the wonderful things being done in our community."

"Good luck with that now," the one who had snorted said. "Just mention the name Baucum and people fall immediately into a battle stance. Either they're horrified that the grandson destroyed the Baucum name, or they're incensed at that young reporter for—"

As if this was a cue in a play, the table erupted.

"Well, he did drag everything Donald Baucum built for years right down to the ground in one—"

"That reporter was out for blood and he didn't care where it came from—"

"It's heartbreaking, no matter whose side you're on. I heard the poor woman would have to move out—"

"Enough!" Imogene slapped her leather planner on the table with a loud whap! "We are here to plan an event! I will not allow this time to degenerate into a hysterical gossip session!" She glared at Viv.

Viv, making no attempt to hide her self-satisfied smile, drew her head back and lifted her hands in a "Who, me?" gesture. In her defense, she hadn't said or done anything to set this particular frenzy in motion.

Collectively, The Gaggle shrank back into their chairs and gave Imogene looks that vacillated between fear and resentment. Anne looked confused. Imogene looked annoyed. Viv looked happy.

Nigel looked like he wanted to get out of there. "Sounds like we're ready to wrap this up, then?" He stood with a half bow toward Imogene.

Imogene frowned again—or maybe it was just that she never stopped—but even she didn't contradict Nigel. She pointed at Viv. "I want the plans for media coverage in writing, in my hands by the close of business on Wednesday."

Viv saluted her sharply. "Tally ho!" Then she stood and nodded to the table at large. "Cheers, mates!"

As we filed out, I said—perhaps more loudly than strictly necessary, but I did want to get it out there— "Okay, now we're going to garden, right? I mean, I put on my grubbiest clothes for this." Although that wasn't precisely true. I had way grubbier clothes than what I was wearing.

"Are you kidding? You just heard the Govnah, right? We're going by Channel 11 and lining up our media coverage, or else I'll be court martialed."

"And then we'll garden?"

"And then we'll garden. You're very keen on this gardening, aren't you? Very keen, indeed."

"What's that from?"

"I heard it on Downton Abbey. One of the below-stairs group. I like it, don't you?"

I nodded. "Yeah, it's cool."

CHAPTER FOUR

The Fascinator

The receptionist at the Channel 11 studio gave me a quick up-and-down look as Viv and I walked through, taking in my getup. Then she looked over to Viv's polished shoes and sharp suit.

"Oooh, snazzy," she said, with a nod toward Viv's sparkly Union Jack shirt.

Viv struck a model pose, tucking the jacket back with one hand on her thrust-out hip, nose in the air, and her cheeks sucked in.

"Y'all here to see Patrice?"

"That's right." Viv straightened.

"She's in her office. You can only stay a few minutes, though. Her husband has asked me to limit her disruptions."

"No problem. Cheers."

The receptionist wrinkled her brow and checked Viv's hand for a glass she'd missed.

"That's British for thanks," I said as I followed Viv through the swinging door.

"Oh, okay. Well...cheers!" She waved.

Trisha was back in her office with her feet propped up, reading from typed pages. "Hey, you two," she said when I tapped on her door. "Come in."

"I'm in charge of making sure we have media coverage of the Veterans Day ceremony at Belle Court," Viv said without preamble, plopping down in the chair across from Tri-Patrice's desk. "Can you take care of that for me?"

"I can put someone on it."

"Thanks. The drill sergeant who's heading up the committee wants it in writing. I assume she doesn't need it notarized." She rolled her eyes.

"I can have them put something on station letterhead if that helps." She picked up her phone and spoke into it. By the time she put it down, everything appeared to be on its way to being taken care of.

"Can you be there?" Viv asked. "And interview me?"

"Sorry, I can't be there myself. But I can ask Misty to interview you. What's your connection to the war?"

"I want to impress a bloke at Belle Court."

Trisha cast a quick raised-eyebrow glance at me.

"It's true," I said. "It's that British guy I was telling you about. He flew Spitwads in the war."

"That's not funny." Viv game me a disgusted look. "Spit*fires*. Little planes. He was a war hero. You need to show some respect."

"Sorry," I said, feeling kind of sorry for the disrespect but happy that I'd gotten Viv's goat, since it was her fault I was walking around looking like a vagrant while she looked like she'd just stepped out of *Retired British Model Magazine.* "Spitfires. He is handsome," I allowed.

Tri-Patrice appeared to be trying to frame a question to mitigate its rudeness. "He lives at Belle Court?"

"That's right," Viv said. "In the new cottages, on the north side of the complex."

"Aren't those independent living? He must be doing really well if he's old enough to be a Spitfire pilot and still able to live independently."

"Oh, believe me, he's still got everything going on."

I looked at her. "Everything? And you know this for a fact?"

"Indubitably," she said.

"And *how* do you know this for a fact?"

"A woman knows, Salem," Viv said. She rolled her eyes. Clearly, she'd had enough of my attitude.

"I see." I raised my eyebrows at Trisha, and she hid a smile.

"Just for your information, he actually lied about his age and his ability to fly. He was so keen on becoming a pilot that he ran away from home at fourteen and pretended to be a janitor on the base where they trained the pilots. He listened and snuck in after dark to read their textbooks. He hid behind corners and listened to the lectures, and he snuck into the planes while everyone was asleep and learned where all the controls were."

"Wow," Tri-Patrice said. "That is a story. I'll ask Misty to interview him."

"Just make sure he knows that I'm the one who got you to do it. I'll introduce Misty to him, in fact. Set up some face time."

Tri-Patrice nodded. "You do that." She picked up the phone and told whoever was on the other end to add Misty Monahan to the story on Sunday.

Someone tapped on her door and it opened a crack. It was the camera girl we'd seen with Misty Monahan on Tuesday night.

"Yes, Jessica?" Trisha asked.

"The video's ready, they're just changing up some of the music."

"Go ahead and upload it to the server. I want to look at it."

Jessica closed the door and Trisha gave us a flat smile. "They're working on the tribute video to Peter."

She waited a few seconds, then clicked on the video file. She turned the monitors and scooted her chair so Viv and I could stand behind her and watch it.

The video opened with Peter sitting at the anchor desk, talking to Trisha and Tom, his white teeth flashing in a slow-motion laugh. Pictures slid slowly one by one: Peter holding a microphone out to an interview subject. Peter laughing with a group of school kids on a field trip to the station. Peter with his pregnant wife, holding a black and white sonogram photo. Peter, somber and contemplative as the sun set behind him. The entire KBST news team at a picnic somewhere, wearing their matching blue polo shirts. Lots of slow-motion laughing, hugging, a tug-of-war game, Peter holding up a plate filled with hot dogs, grinning triumphantly. Another picture of him and his wife at a gender reveal party. Fade to black as the music fades out.

"That's so sad," I said.

Trisha cleared her throat and reached for a tissue. "I still can't believe it. It's just...it doesn't feel real."

"Have they said yet what happened to him?" Viv asked.

"They're not saying. But it's very suspicious. I mean, he was young and healthy. What reason could there be for him to lie down under a mesquite tree and die?"

"We have it on good authority that he was wrestling with demons," Viv said.

Tri-Patrice looked at her. "What? Where did you hear that?"

"Come on, Patrice. We share a code of ethics. We can't reveal our sources."

"There's a psychic out at G-Ma's new shopping center that had a vision," I told her.

Viv glared at me.

"You're the one who has me running all over town in my very shabbiest clothes while you look like Rich Retiree Barbie," I said, lifting my shoe to show Trisha. "You have only yourself to blame."

"The thing is," Viv said through gritted teeth, turning back to Trisha. "we just don't know, do we? What demons, exactly, could he have been wrestling with?"

"You know that could mean anything, right? I mean, they weren't actual demons. She probably meant demons like we wrestle with."

Viv and I had met at AA. We knew from demons.

"Or, it could mean an actual bad guy. Or bad guys. Don't underestimate the power of the prophetic vision, Salem. There are things in this world we're not meant to fully understand."

"Well, I'm leaning toward the actual bad guy theory, to be honest." Trisha shifted in her chair and put her feet up. "Peter Browning was at the top of his game. He had job interviews scheduled with stations in big markets: Houston, Atlanta, Chicago. He was getting all kinds of attention for the reports he was doing on the fracking-related earthquakes. His star was on the rise, for sure. And you know his wife is pregnant. He was all excited about the baby. He had no reason to be wrestling with inner demons."

"That's all about how stuff looks from the outside, though. You never know what's going on in a person's private life. Some people are good at presenting the perfect facade when their life is quietly going off the rails."

Not me, of course. Anybody could spot my own personal train wreck from forty paces. But that was one of the things that surprised me most from my AA meetings—some people really had the outside figured out.

"Well, I know there were some police officers who didn't seem exactly sad about Browning's death."

Trisha frowned. "That doesn't surprise me. He made some enemies with that Space Cop story."

"The Lubbock PD are not demons Peter was wrestling with," I insisted. "Seriously."

Trisha sighed and shook her head. "I'm sure you're right. The truth is, he had quite a few enemies. After David Baucum's death, his popularity took a real hit. There was even some talk that Baucum's death should be laid at Peter's feet, but that's just..." She waved a hand. "That's just stuff people say. Monday morning quarterbacking. Everyone has an opinion."

"That's true," Viv said, giving an 'utterance of wisdom' nod of her silver curls.

"Wait, what? Who's Baucum?"

"David Baucum, the architect who designed that elementary school that collapsed." Viv looked at me. "Where have you been?"

"He was actually an engineer," Trisha corrected to my instant satisfaction. "He didn't design the building, he did the soil report that the architects and engineers based the building design on. Salem, we ran parts of that interview five or six different times. You never saw any of it?"

"Oh, *that* Baucum," I said. I vaguely remembered a middle-aged guy's leering face imposed over a collage of a collapsed building and ambulance pictures.

"Anyway, after Baucum died, some people said that Peter had been too hard on him, but that's just how people are—everyone knows how everyone else should be doing their jobs. The vast majority of comments I read were that Peter was a hero who exposed corruption, and Baucum got exactly what he deserved. I can promise, whatever demons Peter was wrestling with, regret over those stories was not among them. He was getting ready to ride that train to the big time."

"So, jog my memory. How did Baucum die? Did they ever say?"

"Overdose. Accidental, supposedly. I heard it was alcohol and Ambien. He'd been drinking a lot since the firm closed. I heard several stories of him being berated in public, attacked practically, for that little girl being crippled."

Now that part of the story I did remember. When the earthquake hit, a little girl had been crushed by a falling wall in the new cafeteria. She'd survived, but would never walk again. I'd read all about it online. I'd even given to her GoFundMe campaign.

"That reminds me," Trisha said, turning to Viv. "They always present the Baucum Local Hero award at that Veterans Day ceremony. What's going on with that?"

"Nothing, apparently," I said, happy to have something to contribute to the conversation, thanks to The Gaggle.

"They're just going to skip it?" Trisha raised her eyebrows. "Wow."

I shrugged. "Looks like."

"That's the talk, anyway," Viv said. "But I'll see if I can get confirmation on that."

"Please do. I'd like to give Misty a heads-up if there's a scoop she needs to be watching out for."

Fortunately, Veterans Day was on a Sunday so there were a couple of things I didn't have to worry about. One was that we would get a rush of dogs to groom and I would miss the ceremony entirely. The second was that I would have to go in my grooming clothes. Since I was already dressed nice for church, I was all set. I wore my current best dress to church and gave another little prayer of gratitude for the fifteen-pound weight loss. The last time I'd worn this dress, my ample hips had been uncomfortably emphasized by the chevron pattern. Now the thing draped a little more like it should.

At Belle Court, I opened Viv's door and said, "Knock knock."

"It's open, obviously."

She wasn't in the living room or dining room, so I sat and prepared to wait. "The room is filling up down there," I called toward the bedroom, where I assumed she was primping. "You'd better hurry if you want to get a seat."

"Almost done."

A few seconds later, she came out wearing a lavender pencil skirt with a black satin button-down shirt and black pumps. Pinned to the side of her white head was a black and lavender...hat? I supposed it was a hat. It was a small purple box with black ribbons and black mesh ruffling out from it.

"What do you think?" she asked with a wide grin, tilting the hat in my direction. "It's called a fascinator. It's an exact replica of one Princess Kate wore to the Royal Ascot races last year." She dropped into a curtsy, then winked at her reflection.

"You know what? That's actually pretty awesome." I stepped close and looked at it. It did look rather fetching against her silver hair. So what if she was going to be the only person within two thousand miles to wear a "fascinator?"

"I know, right?!" She grinned and spun, her arms out. "I've ordered seven more in different color combinations."

Downstairs, the Fireside Room—named for the giant stone fireplace that took up an entire cathedral height wall—was filling up fast. Misty Monahan and some guy from KLBC were both there. "I didn't realize this was such a big deal," I murmured to Viv as we scootched down a row to two empty seats.

"It's usually not," Viv said, sitting up tall in her chair and glancing queenly around. She nodded once as if to confirm that hers was, in fact, the only fascinator in attendance. "It's Nigel. He's a big draw."

The ceremony came to order then and we hushed. First, a man from the Belle Court Board of Directors stood and spoke about his father and what he would think about the day. His dad had been a WWII vet, and he himself had done a tour of Vietnam. He was a vice-president of a bank or something and was probably used to getting the respect his position normally garnered, but the air was thick with a "so what?" kind of attitude.

He sat, and a different man stood and thanked everyone for coming. The crowd perked up a bit at this.

"Cecil Turnbull!" I whispered to Viv.

"Shhh!" She hissed.

Unlike with Nigel, Viv didn't have to try to get Cecil Turnbull's attention. Cecil volunteered at the prison ministry that my friend and mentor Les ran, and every time Viv and I went up there, Cecil was all over her like a golden retriever puppy.

Viv was having none of it, since Cecil had both a wife and a history of embezzlement. Also, she just didn't like him.

"I didn't know they'd moved into Belle Court," I whispered. I looked around the room and spotted Janine, Cecil's wife. Janine was nice. She'd stuck by Cecil through the scandal of his embezzlement from the bank and subsequent prison term, and through losing their family home and all their society friends. When Cecil was released, she joined him in volunteering at Exodus as if it was just another one of her Junior League charities, although Janine was always the only one there wearing pearls. Personally, I thought she deserved better than Cecil Turnbull.

"They moved in three months ago, and look at him. He's already practically running the place."

Cecil nodded toward Nigel, who sat looking regal in his sport coat and ascot, his white hair particularly leonine and his goatee groomed to a sharp point, and Nigel nodded solemnly back. I had to admit, he and Viv would make a very handsome couple. Together they could probably do commercials for fancy European river cruises or reverse mortgages.

"But I'm afraid I have some disappointing news. As many of you know, Belle Court has recently welcomed a new resident who is also a World War II hero from across the pond. Nigel Frost has been a resident here for the past several weeks, and when I learned that he had flown Spitfires in World War II and was involved in some of the major battles in the war, I asked him to speak about his experience. He graciously agreed, but unfortunately, over the last few days he's suffered from laryngitis, and he's not able to speak. His friend Anne has agreed to read his presentation, and Nigel is here for moral support, but he won't be able to speak or answer any questions today."

Viv frowned. "What? Blimey."

"Shhh," I said. "I think that means something pretty bad."

Anne stood and smiled nervously, her red cheeks flushed. "I want y'all to know that I haven't spoken in front of a group since I retired from teaching twenty years ago. I'm out of practice!"

She laughed and then fiddled with the presentation clicker until Imogene Hall stood and helped her advance to the first slide.

"I'm going to read directly from Nigel's presentation, because he's done such a good job of laying everything out. I'm sure you'll agree that he has a fascinating story."

She clicked through the slides and, if it wasn't what I would call fascinating, at least it wasn't boring. Nigel had included pictures of his plane, group pictures of his troop, some in-air pictures that he said were taken from Life magazine. There were maps of where he flew and a few anecdotes of his misadventures. Once, his plane stalled over open water and, just before he was about to crash, he was able to get it started again. On a slide about the lengthy post-flight procedure the pilots had to go through, Anne read the same line three times and never seemed to realize it. It took Imogene standing and encouraging her to go to the next slide before the whole thing moved forward.

Anne kept looking out at Nigel for reassurance, and he smiled back warmly and nodded each time, even through the needless repetition bit. He had kind eyes, I thought. And he really seemed to care for Anne. I hated to think that Viv was going to miss out on her next Mr. Right, but from everything I saw, this couple was pretty solidly established.

Once it was over, the crowd clapped and Anne turned to sit down.

Viv stood. "If you don't mind, I know Nigel said he couldn't answer questions, but maybe just one yes or no question? I've been reading up on the different planes that were flown by the British pilots, and from what I understand, most Spitfire pilots also flew Hurricanes." She turned to Nigel and gave him a flirtatious smile. "I wondered which you preferred—Hurricanes or...Spitfires?" She waggled a brow.

Nigel blinked a few times, then smiled, his own eyes a little frustrated. He pulled a notepad from his jacket pocket and scribbled quickly, then tore off the paper and handed it to Anne.

"He says that's too complicated to go into briefly, so he'd like to answer at a later time."

"Of course," Viv said, with a gracious nod of her own. "I'll look forward to that." She sat and whispered, "Bloody hell."

"Viv! Language!" I whispered back.

"Bloody heck, then."

I leaned toward her and whispered, "He was impressed by your knowledge. I could tell."

"I guess. Maybe he's really into that whole helpless female act that Anne puts on. Maybe brainy isn't the new sexy." She frowned, then slap at her thigh in frustration. "Golly gumdrop!"

I raised an eyebrow at her.

"You're the one who won't let me say bloody hell," she said in a you-have-only-yourself-to-blame kind of way.

Everyone milled around with their cake and punch, taking surreptitious looks at Viv's fascinator. Both Misty Monahan and the KLBC guy had cornered Cecil Turnbull and wrangled a few questions out of him. He seemed happy enough to comply. I made a mental note to avoid the comments section of this news story. People got all bent out of shape when someone refused to slink away in shame when they made mistakes.

Cecil cast a glance Viv's way every few minutes, but she didn't notice because she was too busy keeping an eye on Nigel.

Nigel kept one hand on Anne's elbow as they slowly circled the room, looking at the different pictures that people had brought. Every time someone spoke to them, he would touch his hand to his throat and give an apologetic smile.

Viv held a plate with an untouched piece of cake on it, scowled and tapped her foot.

"You know what?" I leaned closed and said in a low voice. "Who needs that guy anyway? You don't. You're a hot, exciting red-blooded female who has a lot to offer a red-blooded male. You don't need to look farther than your own doorstep to find a man who'd be thrilled to get a second glance from you."

"Oh, I know," Viv said, and clunked her plate on the closest tray. She sighed gustily. "He's not even going to be interviewed, though. I was looking forward to recording it so I could listen to his accent over and over." Then she straightened. "I could at least get a picture."

She fished in her handbag and brought out her phone. "Get a picture of me and my fascinator."

I pulled up the camera and pointed it at her.

She smiled and said through her teeth, "Is he in the background?"

Nigel and Anne were still walking slowly through the room.

Holding the phone up, I took Viv's elbow and gently moved her so Nigel would be in the background. He turned his back.

"Do you want one of his back?" I asked softly.

She frowned and shook her head. "His jacket is too long for that to be any good. Wait until he's turned around."

Finally, after I had kept turning Viv in almost a complete circle, Nigel looked in our general direction. I snapped three quick pictures.

Viv took the phone back and flipped through them. "That will have to do," she said with a sigh.

I looked around for something to cheer her up.

"Let's see if we can talk to Misty Monahan and get some info on the Browning thing. You're good at leading people to believe you feel sympathy for them. Let's mention how upset she looked when we saw her the other night and see if you can get her to talk." I made a silent apology to Tony, but I was sure he would understand if he could see how dejected Viv looked. Besides, we were in the Fireside Room at a retirement home. What danger could I be in here?

Viv sighed again, still looking unhappy. "Hush. I am sympathetic. Usually."

"Well, then. Come on, let's go use your power for good."

She dragged after me, but she turned on her charm when we reached Misty.

"Hello, Miss Monahan, do you remember us?"

Misty was packing away her microphone, but she stopped when she saw us. "Of course, Patrice's friends. How are you?" She cast a cautious eye up to Viv's fascinator, but didn't say anything about it.

"We're doing very well, thank you. What we really want to know, though, is how are you? We were at the scene when Peter Browning's body was found." Her voice dropped into a smooth cadence and she tilted her head. "You seemed so distraught, Love. How are you?" she asked again, placing a soothing hand just above Misty's elbow.

I crinkled my own brow in concern and did the head tilt thing, too. I did feel bad for her, that much was true. I just didn't have people skills like Viv did.

Misty swallowed and nodded, her mouth tightened in a flat smile. "That was really hard," she said. "I worked with Peter for a year, and it was...well, it was hard. For him to be found like that."

I sensed Viv's antennae going up the same as mine. Like that. Like what? Did she mean just the fact that he'd been a young man who was found dead? Or did her choice of words indicate something more?

Viv shook her head. "Such a shame. And such a shock. You don't expect someone like that to...end up like that." She rubbed Misty's arm and waited for her to drop another hint.

But the movement seemed to bring Misty back to the present. She frowned and moved away from Viv's touch. "Of course, it's a shock."

Viv gave it another go. "I heard the Medical Examiner's report will be released sometime this week. And then it will all be out in the open."

Misty's eyes snapped to Viv, but she said nothing.

Viv waited a couple of beats. Then she said, "I mean, they'll have determined the exact cause of death, at least."

Misty nodded and her shoulders dropped a fraction of an inch. "Yes, of course."

"Weird, isn't it, that they aren't saying anything about how he died?"

She gave a slight shrug and "Not really, no. When there are no obvious injuries, it takes a full autopsy and sometimes a toxicology report to determine exact cause of death. It's not like on TV, when you find out at the scene."

Viv blinked. "Yes, well..."

"Was there anything else? No? Okay, well, have a good day." She shouldered her bag and walked away.

Viv and I watched her go.

"Son of a biscuit," Viv said.

"Right," I said. "The cookie kind again?"

"Shut up." She sighed and frowned. "Well, that was a big ol' ball of useless."

"She's kind of scary," I said. "She reminds me of a much younger Imogene Hall."

"Me, too." She snorted. "Thinks she's too smart for us. But did you see that moment of sheer panic in her eyes when I said it'll all be out in the open? I got one over on her."

"I don't know that I'd call it sheer panic."

"It was definitely sheer panic. She has something to hide," Viv insisted.

"Maybe."

"And what about the way she said, 'Like that.' Like what, Love?"

"That could have been something. Then again, she also said there were no obvious injuries."

"True." She frowned again, apparently realizing we hadn't actually gained any information. I felt guilty for taking what she'd seen as a win after being disappointed by Nigel.

"Oh, I forgot about the Baucum Local Hero thing," I remembered. "We told Tri-Patrice we would find out. Should we ask Cecil about it?"

The look she gave me has no polite word to describe it.

"No? Okay," I said, not bothering to hide my grin.

"Let's ask that girl."

I looked back the way Misty Monahan had gone, but she was nowhere to be seen. The same camera girl who'd been with her at the scene Tuesday night was there, though, packing away her camera. I took Viv by the elbow and moved through the crowd to talk to her. We caught her just as she was about to follow after Misty.

"Hi," I said, standing in front of her to keep her from leaving. Viv needed a new thread to pull on, and if it was a non-scandal, then so be it. "I'm not sure if we met. We're friends with Patrice Watson."

She lifted her chin. "Oh, yeah, I've seen you at the station before."

"We were just talking about the thing they usually do here on Veterans Day, the Baucum Local Hero thing. What's going on with that, do you know?"

"Oh, that. They said it was postponed on account of the weather."

We all looked at each other for a beat.

"Seriously?" I asked.

"I know, right?" Jessica said. "As if they couldn't move the ceremony indoors, like they've done on several occasions." She shrugged, then peered around my shoulder.

Probably looking for Misty, I thought. "Do you think they're hiding something?" I asked, kind of desperate to find a string to latch onto, if for no other reason than to cheer Viv up with a new lead to follow.

She shrugged again. "I mean, who knows? My theory would be more along the lines of they just weren't prepared. Baucum Engineering always coordinated the whole thing, from what I understand. No Baucum Engineering, no Baucum Local Hero award. Everybody's just standing around waiting for someone else to either take up the responsibility or pull the plug."

She took a half step sideways, again looking past me.

"I'm sorry," I said. This wasn't going to give Viv anything to work with, so I might as well let her go. "I don't want to make you miss your ride." I stepped aside.

She smiled, but her brows twitched. "Misty would never leave me," she said as she walked away.

Viv and I stood silently, both feeling kind of bummed. I fought the urge to cheer myself with sugar-laden red punch and saucer-size cookies. "Come on. Let's head to the outlet mall and find some new shoes that will make Nigel sit up and take notice." Because I wanted to get her into a better mood, I said, "Do you want to drive the Monster Carlo?"

She didn't even feign disinterest this time. She took the key from me wordlessly and headed across the parking lot. She was so lost in her funk that she barely watched where she was going and nearly stepped into the path of an oncoming pickup.

The horn blared, and I grabbed Viv's elbow, pulling her back. The pickup slowed almost to a stop, past us by this point, and I lifted a hand in apology. After another second or two, the guy drove on.

"Do I have to put one of those leashes on you like they do toddlers? Get your head out of the Nigel cloud."

"I'll have you know I am thinking about the case." She unlocked the Monster Carlo door and dropped into the seat with a sigh. "I'm thinking about Nigel, too. Maybe I'm a bit too CSI Miami, and he's really more into Miss Marple."

"Miss Marple? Is that—"

"Agatha Christie. Little old woman who knitted and solved the case by eavesdropping."

"I haven't read those."

"Me either, but I've seen a few episodes of the TV show, and if that's what he's into, he may be a lost cause. Mousy hair, little old lady clothes, polite type who's seen and not heard."

"Nope," I said. "I can't see you pulling that off."

She pointed the Monster Carlo for the outlet mall.

At the mall, Viv not only found three pairs of shoes, but two handbags and three scarves. That lifted her mood considerably, enough so that she offered to spring for an early dinner at the steakhouse.

I slid the basket of rolls over toward her, dutifully ordered a grilled chicken breast and steamed vegetables, and spent the rest of the time half listening to Viv talk about how maybe she didn't want Nigel anyway and half remembering what those warm yeast rolls with melted butter tasted like. When my chicken came I kind of wanted to slap the plate to the floor.

I cut into it with determination, though, and at that moment a thought popped into my head. "Hey!" I looked up at Viv.

She froze, eyes wide, a buttered roll halfway to her mouth.

"The guy who almost ran over you in the Belle Court parking lot. He was driving an Eagle Construction truck." I remembered the sign on the tailgate of the pickup.

"Yes. And?"

"And the guy out at the crime scene the other night? He was wearing an Eagle Construction shirt. Remember? He called Misty Monahan something. A rat. No...a vulture."

"I remember him. Are you sure he had on an Eagle shirt?"

"Pretty sure. I remember the logo with the eagle in the circle."

Viv bit her roll, then tilted her head. "I suppose it's worth following up on. But that company must have a hundred employees. It's not hard to imagine that two of them would be at two different high-profile events."

I raised an eyebrow over the concept of the Belle Court Veterans Day Ceremony being "high profile" to anyone living outside the Belle Court campus, but didn't say anything.

"After dinner we'll head over there and see if we see anything unusual."

At that moment, I remembered I was supposed to be discouraging this kind of activity, not encouraging it.

"It probably wasn't him."

"Probably not. But we're near there, so we might as well check it out."

Crud. "Actually, I really need to get back to Tony's so I can pick up Stump."

"What's happened to Frank?" Viv asked.

"I think he must have a girlfriend," I said. "I hardly see him anymore."

"Good for him. It's about time. Handsome, virile man like that needs a woman."

I was so stunned at the idea of Frank being handsome—not to mention virile—that for a second I forgot I was trying to talk

Viv out of hunting down clues to a mystery that might not even
be a mystery.

"In any case, I'm sure Tony won't mind hanging on to Stump
for another half hour while we check out this construction guy."

I chewed my steamed broccoli and thought. Talking to Misty
Monahan in the safety of the Belle Court Fireside Lounge had
felt safe. Going to a construction company felt infinitely less so.
If we did happen to be following a murderer, there could be all
kinds of ways to get into trouble. He'd have...tools and stuff.
Hammers, crowbars, probably even nail guns. Yikes.

On the other hand, there was the fact that we didn't even
know if there was a murder to begin with. So it wasn't like we
had compelling reason not to hunt the guy down
and...hmmm...apologize for walking in front of his truck? That
sounded like a decent straw to grasp at.

"We'll need to make it quick," I warned. "Maybe just swing
through the parking lot to see if it's the same guy. We won't
even get out of the car."

"Whatever. You stay in the car if you want to. If I see him,
I'm talking to him." She signaled for the check.

Eagle Construction was a couple of miles from the outlet
mall, and I insisted on driving this time. If things went south, I
didn't want to rely on Viv to get us out of there.

"There he is! Don't let him get away."

"Would you chill out?" I said, annoyed that she'd made my
heart race for no reason. "He's not going to flee the interview."

"He will if you don't hurry up." She was out the door before I
killed the engine.

It was definitely the same guy from Tuesday night. Whether it was the same guy as at Belle Court, I couldn't say. What I could say—and didn't care for—was that he carried a tool box in one hand.

"God, if this guy is a murderer, please don't let him kill us, or else Tony will be so mad at me."

"Excuse me," Viv called to the guy, the ribbons on her fascinator flouncing with each step. She reached into her jacket pocket and pulled out one of those mortifying business cards.

Jeez-o-Friggin-Peet. I killed the engine and wondered what could be going through his mind—one old woman and one chubby girl in a forty-year-old Monte Carlo, handing out bondage cards.

"First, I wanted to apologize for stepping in front of you at Belle Court. That was you, wasn't it?"

He looked at the card, then looked from Viv, her hat, then to me.

I tried not to look embarrassed.

"I'm sorry...what?"

"At Belle Court, after the ceremony."

"Ceremony?"

"The Veterans Day ceremony this afternoon. Were you there? After it was over, we were walking to our car and I accidentally stepped in front of your truck." She nodded toward the pickup he'd been about to get into. It looked like eight other white pickups in the parking lot.

"Oh, yeah...that. Yes, that was me."

I got a little thrill of fear. One pickup out of nine happens to belong to the same guy we were looking for. We happen to see him twice in less than a week, at two totally unrelated events. We happen to find him here on a Sunday evening, when the place was closed. It all had to add up to something, right?

"I wanted to apologize for that. I get a little preoccupied in my thoughts."

I eyed the well-muscled arm that still held the tool box. Could he just...whip out something and bash us over the head with it? Just in case he got any ideas, I thought I'd better make sure he knew we were no danger to him. I put my arm through Viv's and patted her. "She gets confused sometimes. Forgets to watch where she's going." I hunched my shoulders and giggled. "Sometimes it's all I can do to keep her from wandering onto the Loop in her nightgown."

Viv gave me the stink eye, but turned back to the guy. "Anyway. Were you at the ceremony?"

He took a moment to turn and slide the tool box into the pickup seat. He turned back to us and stuck his hands in his pockets. "No, I didn't know there was a ceremony, actually. My mom's up there in the Alzheimer's unit. I was visiting her."

We were silent for a moment. "I'm sorry," I finally said.

He took a deep breath and nodded in a *What can you do?* kind of way.

"I'm sorry to hear that," Viv said. "Belle Court does have the best Alzheimer's treatment available, though. She's in good hands."

"I know." He nodded again. For a second his face flashed with anger, and I was reminded of the way he'd muttered, "Vultures," at the reporters Tuesday night.

Now that we'd bumbled our way into this situation, I wasn't sure how to proceed, though.

Luckily, Viv had no such problem. "We also saw you on Tuesday night, when Peter Browning's body was found."

"Oh, yeah." He looked from Viv to me and back again. "Yes, I remember you. That was something else, huh?"

"Shocking," Viv said.

"I was driving by there on my way home and saw all the commotion. I had to stop." He ducked his head and gave us a sheepish look. "I hate to be a sightseer, but I had to stop. You know." He shrugged. "All the lights. You have to wonder what's going on."

"Did you know Peter Browning?" I asked.

He tilted his head forward. "Who? Oh, the reporter guy?" He shook his head. "No, not really. I mean, I knew who he was, from the television. And I'd seen all the stories about him going missing. But I didn't know him. I've only lived here a few months." He frowned and shifted, as if something had just occurred to him. "Now, what did you say you were doing here? You're..." He looked at the card. "Private investigators?"

"That's right," Viv said. She lifted her chin. "We're investigating the death of Peter Browning."

He drew his brow down, confused. "But...I heard it was suicide."

"The ME report isn't in yet," Viv said. "It's not like on TV when you know the cause of death within half a day, you know."

"Of course, I'd just heard, you know, there was a note or something."

Viv and I looked at each other. We hadn't heard about any note!

"Yes, well...what does a note prove?" Viv crossed her arms over her chest.

He shrugged again. "I guess that depends on what is in the note."

"Yes, and what was in the note?"

"Exactly. I mean—umm. What?"

"What was in that note?" Viv leaned toward him, her eyes flashing. "Come on. What did it say?"

"How should I know?" He took a step back, eyes widening.

"You're the one who said there was a note."

He looked lost. "That's just...that's the rumor I heard." His confusion was quickly turning to annoyance.

"Where? Who told you?"

"Look, lady—"

Clearly it was time for me to intervene. We certainly didn't want to annoy someone into becoming a murderer if they weren't already.

I put my hand out. "Please excuse our...overzealousness."

"It's actually unbridled enthusiasm," Viv said.

"We just hadn't heard about the note, so this is a bit of a surprise to us."

He frowned, but gave a slight nod. "I guess if there's no crime, there's no need for an investigation."

Viv did not look happy about that. "Bloody heck."

I apologized again, and we got back into the car silently. Viv sat with her arms crossed and her chin stuck out, looking like an 80-year-old toddler who'd been sent to bed without her supper.

"Your enthusiasm is admirable," I offered as I pulled onto the loop.

"Fat lot of good it's doing me."

I decided not to continue. Truth be told, I wasn't exactly feeling energized by the way that had gone, either. I felt stupid for bothering the guy and reminding him about the mother with Alzheimer's. It was probably a good thing Tony didn't want me to investigate anymore. I wasn't exactly good at it.

But what was I good at? What were my gifts?

I went through the list I'd read in Romans the other morning. Teaching? No. Prophecy? Clearly not. There was something about contributing with generosity, but since I had to get by on my salary as a dog groomer, it was difficult to see how that could be my God-given gift.

Exhortation. Wasn't that kind of like enthusiasm?

That was not my gift, either, but thinking of it did remind me of how excited Viv had been after leaving the psychic the day before, all jazzed up because she'd been told she had lived a life of unbridled enthusiasm.

Personally, I could use something encouraging like that, and it looked like Viv could use a fresh shot. Maybe Serena could give me some insight into myself that would help me figure out why I was here.

"How about we go back to Serena's and see if she's had anymore visions?"

Viv shrugged. "Might as well."

The new lease on the motel's life had given G-Ma a new lease on life, too. She seemed to have aged backwards a good fifteen years. At least her hair had. The solid red football helmet style she had worn for years was replaced by a soft auburn with blond and brown streaks and a soft, wispy fringe of bangs around her forehead.

She met me and Viv on the sidewalk, turning this way and that to give us a chance to fully admire the new 'do. Sometimes it was easy to see where my mom had gotten her confidence.

"What do you think? Elma did it just this morning."

"It's great!" I said and meant it. "Who's Elma?"

"You knew her as Felicia.

"Oh," I said, and immediately changed my mind about going to her for my own updated new look. Felicia had expressed a desire to kill me one time when I'd accidentally gotten us all arrested for prostitution. I didn't know if "Elma" held the same views, but I wasn't keen on finding out.

"We're here to see Serena," I said. "Get some more information about her visions."

"That's a great idea." G-Ma clapped her hands together. "Fantastic!"

My dour, grumpy G-Ma, clapping her hands together and declaring things "fantastic!"

"She has a new collection of crystals, just in today. You have to see them!"

I drew my head back. My G-Ma, who scoffed at anything she couldn't see, hear, taste, or feel, excited about crystals. Who was this woman?

"Have her read your aura," G-Ma said. "She just told me mine was purple. Purple is a sign of financial gain. She said the universe is telling me to keep striving, that all my hard work is about to pay off."

It all made sense now. Nothing excited G-Ma more than the idea of "financial gain." I could certainly understand that. That would probably make me happy, too.

"Come here and rub some of your purple off on me," I said, closing in for a hug.

Across the parking lot, Viv was already inside Serena's shop. The place was lighter than I expected, but still had plenty of shiny, spinny, dangly things hanging around the room—dream catchers, spinning crystals, other unidentifiables. Something like music played in the background—a humming, moaning kind of thing. Whales, maybe?

"We actually haven't had a chance to talk to the police yet."

"That's great," Serena said. "The opportunity will present itself when the time is right for it to be received." She smiled with serenity.

She turned to me, still smiling. As soon as she saw me, though, her smile vanished. She drew her head back, her brow suddenly furrowed.

Uh-oh. My heart started to pound, and I immediately ran through the list of possible explanations for this reaction. Back when I was drinking, I'd had quite a talent for mouthing off and offending people. Okay, the truth was I wasn't too shabby at it now. But when I was drinking, it was as if I *looked* for ways to offend people. They weren't hard to find.

I studied Serena's face, trying to trigger a memory so I could know what I should be apologizing for. Did I flirt with her boyfriend? Spill a beer on her? Insult her to her face?

Nothing came to mind. After a few seconds, I realized she and I were staring at each other.

"Sorry," I said. "I was trying to jog my memory—your face looks familiar to me." It didn't, but that seemed like a good enough opening.

Serena shook her head. "We've never met." Not a trace of doubt.

"Oh." Soooo...the sight of me made her frown for no real reason? I looked over at Viv, who was busy studying a crystal.

"I'm sorry," Serena finally said. "I've just...I've never seen such a deep blue before."

I looked down at my dress.

"No, your aura." She looked at the area just a few inches above my head.

"Oh?" I stood there feeling self-conscious. "Umm, well. Thank you." I gave a tiny curtsy.

"Seriously." As if in a daze, she waved her hands lightly above my head, as if trying to touch it. "It's so dark it's almost black."

I remembered what G-Ma had said about her purple aura. Purple meant financial gain. Blue and purple were right next to each other on the color spectrum, right? My heart rate ticked up another notch.

"That's great," I said.

"No, it's bad," she said.

"Bad?" Good grief. Financial *loss*, then? But I had nothing to lose!

"Well, I mean...nothing is good or bad, right? It just...is what it is."

"If it is what it is, why is your face all like this?" I pulled my own mouth down in an exaggerated frown. Suddenly, she was kind of getting on my nerves.

She shook her head and gave a flat smile. "It's not...it's just...I feel bad for you."

"But why? I'm going to be hit by a bus or something?"

"No, it's not like that. Auras don't predict the future or anything like that. Auras reflect the state of our spirits, the state of our energy."

"So, what does dark blue mean, then?"

"It's the color of blockage. The color of..." She frowned again and put her hands on her hips. She tilted her head. She put her hand to her chin, studying me. "It's the color of repression. You, my friend, are harboring an enormous fear of self-expression."

Then she straightened and smiled, satisfied.

I waited a couple of beats. Then, "That's it?"

She nodded. "Absolutely. You have the biggest fear of self-expression I've ever seen."

"Well, give me a smiley-face sticker!" I said sourly.

She laughed. "I get that it's not exactly the thing someone would want to hear unless—"

"No kidding," I interrupted. "You told Viv she was a bright ray of sunlight or something and told G-Ma she was about to come into great wealth."

"Not precisely true on either count," she said. The serene smile was back in full force.

"I need to hear something good," I said.

"Nothing is good or bad. It simply is what it is."

I sighed. Did I really need this? No. No, I did not. I turned to Viv. "You ready?"

"If you want to change the color of your aura, all you have to do is start expressing yourself." Still with that smile.

I wondered what color my aura would turn if I, say, bounced one of those crystals off the side of her head. "I can't," I said. "I've taken a vow of nonviolence."

She laughed. I hated that she had such a nice laugh, light and bubbly.

"Just be you. That's all. Let the world see you. You deserve to be seen."

"I am me," I snapped. "I'm me every blessed day. If I knew how to be someone else, believe me, I would have made the switch long ago."

She drew her head back again. "Whoa."

"What?"

"It actually just turned darker."

I held my hands out, game show hostess style. "Get me, I'm a wonder of spiritual constipation. Viv, are you ready?"

"Sure, let me just get a couple of these." She handed over a handful of shiny things to Serena. Then she looked at me. "Jeez-O-Peet . What are you frowning about?"

I hooked a thumb at Serena. "I came here hoping she would say something to cheer me up, and she made me feel worse." Something about that smile made me want to smash it.

To me, Serena said, "Why do you need cheering up?" Then to Viv, "That'll be $39.74."

I opened my mouth to explain about Tony and chasing bad guys with guns and about Paul pointing out the different jobs in the body of Christ and about how I had no idea what part of the body I was.

But I didn't want to talk about Tony in front of Viv. It would seem a bigger deal than it was. Viv would go all feminist commando on me, and I wasn't emotionally prepared for that. Not with my navy blue aura and all.

"Nothing," I finally mumbled. "It's just that Viv and G-Ma were encouraged by what you said to them."

"You could be encouraged, as well."

I felt my eyes bug. "Encouraged?"

"Yes! Encouraged to let open the floodgates, be who you are, express your deepest self, and walk out of this small world you've locked yourself in." She handed Viv the paper bag of her goodies.

I shook my head. "Nope. When I open the floodgates, entire villages are wiped out."

"Hmmm...must not have been your true floodgates you were opening, then."

I stared at her. I blinked. I opened my mouth to say something, but couldn't think of a thing. "What?"

She nodded serenely. "Yes."

I sputtered a few attempts at words, then said. "Look. I came in here hoping you could help me—I don't know. Tell me why I'm here. What my purpose is. I feel lost and pointless and..."

I drifted off because she'd lifted her hands to her mouth, opened in a fond smile. The smile you would give your five-year-old who has just learned to ride a bike without training wheels.

"What?" My heart thudded. This was good, right?

"You are!" Serena said. She clapped her hands. "You really are!"

"I really am what?"

"You really are seeking!"

"Well, that...yeah. That's what I'm saying."

She nodded, grinning. I wasn't sure, but I thought there might be the faintest hint of a tear in her eye.

I lifted my palms. "Okay, so...?"

"Oh, I can't give you the answers."

I gritted my teeth. "I'll pay you $39.74."

"No, I mean...I don't know. The journey is for you to find out."

"Find out what?"

"Exactly." She nodded, still with that same grin.

"Ugh!" I sighed and spun on my heel.

Serena laughed. "The universe is telling you something. That's why you have this feeling that something is missing, this uneasiness. That's why you feel that hole."

"Okay, great," I said, turning back to her. "Let's fill that puppy up."

"Oh, no." She shook her head, her smile turning sad. "Trying to fill that hole with anything except your true purpose only leads to heartache and disaster."

"Addiction," Viv said.

"Exactly," Serena said again.

I shook my head. "Been there, done that."

"So, be patient, but be excited!" Her grin widened. "The universe is telling you something," she said again. "Once you find it—once you're in the flow of your true purpose—all other problems will simply fade away."

CHAPTER FIVE

To The Rescue

Viv called me at work the next morning. "What time are you getting off?"

I checked my list of dogs. "Barring any unforeseen standard poodles, probably around two."

"Perfect. I've been thinking about what Serena said all night, and I think I know what to do about it."

"My navy blue aura? Fantastic! What are we doing?"

"Not your aura. Nigel's."

"What color is Nigel's aura?"

"How should I know? But the point is, he needs to get back into the flow of his purpose. Then all my problems will fade away."

I sighed. "I honestly don't think that's what she said."

"Of course it is. And I have a plan. Come up here as soon as you get off work." She hung up.

By 2:30, I was sitting on Viv's sofa, watching her fluff her hair and frown in the mirror. "This had better work. That cap is going to do a number on my hair."

"What exactly are you doing?"

"I'm giving him a chance to rescue me. You know what a hero he is. I'm going to give him a chance to relive his glory days. Tap back into that part of him that wants to save the day." She turned and gave me a confident nod. "Get him back into the flow of his purpose."

It actually sounded like a half-decent idea. But execution, of course, was everything. "And how are you going to accomplish that?"

She applied a fresh coat of clear lip gloss and smacked her lips. "I'm going to get a cramp while I'm swimming laps and flail around so he can save me." She waggled her eyebrows. "In a bathing suit. Just the two of us, locked in a life-saving embrace. I will, of course, show him my sincerest gratitude."

"Gag," I said. "What is my part in all this melodrama?"

"Okay." She turned to me and put her hands together, old-school prayer style. "You are crucial. First, you have to make sure the "Pool Closed" sign stays up until Nigel heads for the pool. Then you rip the sign off and get out of there."

"The pool is closed? How are you going to—" The look in her eye had a light bulb going off in my head. "You got the pool closed? How did you manage that?"

"I put up a "closed for repairs" sign." She shrugged.

"Okay, in the first place, that is outright deceit and I want it known—" I looked at Viv's ceiling "—that I had no part in this charade. And in the second place, won't anyone think it's a problem if you go into the pool while it's closed?"

"That is also your part. You are going to create a diversion so I can slip in unnoticed."

"I already don't like this."

"Oh, come on. It's not going to be a big deal. Cecil Turnbull is on activity desk duty. We're timing it so we go in right before Cecil goes off duty, and then Glen Baker comes on. Glen won't know about the pool closure so it won't be a problem."

I did actually feel better when I found out Cecil was on duty. We could probably talk him into anything.

"So, I'm creating a diversion to keep Cecil and all other residents—"

"I can handle Cecil. I'll get me in the door. Your part is just to get the sign down once I'm in and keep everyone else out."

I nodded, mentally gauging whether my conscience would allow me to do this. I would be taking down a sign that's not supposed to be there anyway. I could do that. And I would be engaging in conversation, hopefully for only a few minutes, with anyone headed toward the pool so the fateful events could unfold. I didn't see any problem with that either. In my experience, most Belle Court residents were open to a nice hallway chat when the opportunity arose.

"So what we're going to do is, we'll walk through like we're headed to the car. You'll stop and chat with him, get him to go back into the office for something, and I'll slip into the pool. When he comes back, just tell him I went on to the car. Easy peasy."

"So how is Nigel going to get in?"

"Once you see him coming, rip the Closed sign off and hightail it out of there."

"What if someone else is with him?"

"I did think of that. If anyone is with him, stop them. Start a conversation. Ask about their grandkids or their cat or something. That should give me enough time to get him engaged."

"So you're going to launch into the drowning bit as soon as he comes through the door?"

"The very moment. I don't want to take the chance of someone else coming in and taking over. So make sure he comes in alone."

I saluted her, thinking that Tony was going to owe me a back rub or something for this.

As promised, Cecil was manning the activities desk, where residents went to check out ping-pong paddles, chess boards, and pool noodles.

"Morning, ladies. How are you this fine day?" He stood as he usually did, with the back of his hands on his waist, elbows out. He reminded me of a toddler in their first dance class, preparing for their first recital. Any moment I expected him to start singing "The Good Ship Lollipop."

"We are in excellent health, Mr. Turnbull." Viv declared. "We are headed out for brunch and shopping, but first I wanted to stop by and reserve the bridge table for 4:00 pm tomorrow."

"Vivian Kennedy." He leaned from the waist, wrists still on his hips. "How many times am I going to have to tell you. Call me Cecil."

Viv gave him a flat smile. "Of course. Cecil. Will you please get the appointment book from the office in the back and reserve the table for me?"

Cecil reached under the counter and pulled out a calendar.

"What's that doing here?" Viv asked with a frown. "Glen always keeps that book in the office. By the phone." She nodded toward the office behind the desk.

"I know, and it's inconvenient if you ask me. I have made some changes since I took over this shift. Okay, 4:00 pm tomorrow? I've got you down." Cecil smiled.

"Did I say bridge? I meant ping-pong."

"No trouble, no trouble at all. That's why I do this in pencil." He scrubbed away with the eraser, then flipped to another page in the book. "Ping-pong for Viv Kennedy at 4:00 pm on Tuesday."

"You keep both calendars in one book?" Viv was starting to look put out.

"We are becoming the very model of efficiency around here." Cecil closed the book with a satisfied smile and folded his hands on top of it. "Will there be anything else?"

Viv pursed her lips, thinking. She craned her neck to see the pool door down the hallway.

"The pool is closed," Cecil said. "Must be cleaning it or something."

"I see." She took a deep breath, still frowning. Finally, she turned back to him. "Listen, Cecil. Last time I played ping-pong, I think I lost a ring. It's..." She stopped, slowly dropping her hands beneath the counter. "A sapphire ring. Gold." As she talked, she slowly slid her sapphire ring off her pinky finger. It hung on a knuckle and she bit back a grimace as she tugged. "We looked all over the floor, but didn't find it." Finally, she got the ring off and smiled, dropping her hands into her pockets. "Later, I realized that it probably fell into one of the boxes with the paddles. I asked Glen Baker if he would look, but he refused. You know, I don't think Glen cares for me." She looked sad.

"Seriously?" Cecil drew his head back, mouth slightly agape.

I shrugged.

"Why, that old grump," Cecil declared.

"I'm sure he has a lot on his mind with the..." She waved a hand, as if it wouldn't be decent to mention what, exactly, Glen had on his mind. "Would you be a dear, Cecil, and look through them for me?"

"I would be happy to." He leaned over the counter and smiled. "Why don't you come back there with me? Help me go through those boxes."

Viv's smile grew brittle. "Cecil Turnbull. I do believe you are flirting with me."

Cecil waggled his eyebrows a little.

"This is becoming awkward," I said.

"And how is Janine?" Viv asked. "Please tell her I love the way she's wearing her hair nowadays."

Cecil got the hint. He shook a finger at Viv. "Okay, okay. You wait right here and I'll see what I can find."

We stood, smiling and nodding, until he'd passed through the office and into the storeroom behind.

"Ick," I said as he passed out of sight. "I wasn't happy about being part of your deceit, but when you two start flirting with each other—b""

I broke off because she was heading down the hallway toward the pool.

Once inside the humid room, she immediately began to unbutton her shirt.

"Don't you feel kind of bad for lying to Cecil?"

"Kind of. Until he wanted to get me into the back room with the ping-pong paddles, and then—" She flicked her hand in the air. "Poof. Guilt gone."

She ripped her blouse off. She wore her bathing suit underneath.

"Still. I'm concerned about what kind of seeds you're sowing and how I could possibly be nearby when you begin to reap."

She kicked off her shoes and unbuttoned her trousers. "Salem, you need to keep your eye on what we're really sowing here. Not a minor, harmless deceit with Cecil Turnbull. What we're sowing here is bringing a man—a war hero, Salem—back into the flow of his purpose." She tossed her slacks onto the chair and grabbed a swim cap. "Think of it. He's a strong, virile man, but he's been put out to pasture. He feels unnecessary. He feels emasculated. We are giving him a chance to get his mojo back. Be a hero again. That is huge."

"It's still deceitful. Thou shall not bear false witness is in God's top ten."

"Salem, think about God's chosen people during that time. Remember Abraham? Tried to pass his wife off as his sister. Remember Jacob? Stole his brother's birthright. God sees the heart, Salem."

She tugged the swim cap onto her head and began tucking strands of white hair inside.

Is it bad to admit that it was rather satisfying to see that Viv's thighs were a bit baggy? She still had a knockout of a figure, and I was dying to ask what kind of bra and swimsuit she wore to keep the girls looking so... uplifted. But her thighs proved that even Viv Kennedy wasn't completely impervious to aging. Almost, but not completely.

She faced me, hands on her hips. "Is it all in? I don't want any straggly hairs hanging out."

For one horrified moment I stood and gaped, then realized she was talking about the swim cap. I shoved some white hairs behind her ear into the cap. "Okay, you're good."

"Be sure and take that sign down on your way out!" Viv called after me.

I ripped the sign off the door and headed back to the reception desk. Turns out I hadn't needed to rush. It was a full two minutes later before Cecil came back, dusting his hands and frowning. "I'm sorry, I emptied all three boxes, and didn't find a—b" He looked around. "Where's Viv?"

"She forgot her sunglasses," I said. "She went back to her room to get them." See? Five minutes in Viv's lying company and I was making up my own tales with ease. I silently repented.

"Oh. Okay." He looked down the other hallway toward Viv's wing. "Well, tell her I looked very carefully in all the boxes."

"No, man, you tell her. When she comes in to play ping-pong tomorrow at 4:00."

He grinned. "Yes, well. I will do that, then."

"Oooh, here comes Glen!" I looked quickly away and back to give Cecil a conspiratorial wink. He winked back solemnly.

"I'm going to pull around to Viv's side of the building and pick her up there," I said, as if I'd just decided it.

Cecil winked at me again, then threw Glen a baleful look, and left.

Just in the nick of time. Because down the hall, towel wrapped around his neck, came Nigel.

Alone, I was happy to see. Now I didn't have to worry about distracting any of the old widder women. I gave him a polite nod, then backed toward the outside door.

But, oh no. Was that...? Jeez-O-Peet , yes it was. Imogene Walker was coming down the hall with her swimsuit cover up and beach bag.

Why couldn't it have been Anne? Anne I could handle. Or any of the other sweet little old ladies. Why did it have to be Intimidating Imogene, who was already mad at me for not living up to my potential?

"Ummm, hi," I stammered, stepping into her path.

She scowled at me. Her mouth said, "Hello," but her eyes said, "What do you want?"

"That's a lovely...cover up." I reached out to touch the edge of the sleeve but drew back quickly when she looked down her nose at my hand.

"It's a robe," she said shortly. "I don't see a reason to make up a different word for something just because it's used in a different setting."

"Oh, of course not." I laughed. "Silly, isn't it?" I strained to hear whether Viv had launched into her damsel in distress act yet. *Hurry up*, I commanded silently and furiously. "Silly how we do that." I racked my brain for another example to draw the conversation out. "I always say 'pee' unless I'm at the doctor's office, when suddenly I'm all 'urinate.'"

I actually did jazz hands. I tried to laugh, but I kind of choked on it.

I should have racked harder.

Was that a cry I heard? Yes! Thank goodness. Any second now Nigel would come running out with a dripping wet Viv in his arms—

"Help!"

Imogene and I turned to see Nigel, alone, screaming in the pool room door. "She's drowning! Someone help!"

Glen and Imogene both took off running.

For a big girl, that Imogene was fleet on her feet. She shoved past Nigel, who stood stupid and mute in the doorway, and leapt into the pool.

Glen was right after her, but he didn't need to be. Imogene had things firmly in hand. She had Viv firmly in hand, in fact. Imogene flipped Viv onto her back, wrapped an arm under Viv's armpit and began swimming backward.

"Let go of me!" Viv shouted, slapping at Imogene's arm.

"Stop struggling!" Imogene shouted back. "You need to save your strength."

"My strength is fine!" She spit out pool water and kicked her legs. "I just got a cramp!"

"A *cramp*? You were flailing around like you were being attacked by a shark!" Nigel shouted from where he stood, safely away from the edge of the pool.

Imogene reached the edge and handily lifted Viv up. "Lie down," she ordered.

Viv ignored her, sitting up and sputtering. "I am fine." She glared from Imogene to Nigel. Then she glared at me.

I shrugged. "Are you okay?"

Glen was already calling an ambulance, though.

Things got kind of ugly after that. The ambulance came, and despite her loud and energetic protests, they stuck an oxygen mask on Viv and began to check her out. Half the population of Belle Court seemed to congregate in the activities area, trying to figure out what was going on. I heard a couple of rumors that I didn't dispute. One was that the pool had been closed because of a chemical issue and Viv now had chemical burns that were going to require reconstructive surgery. I made a mental note to tell her about that one. I could see her wanting to capitalize on this by wearing lots of flowing scarves and huge sunglasses.

I stepped outside and pulled out my phone.

"Windy, call Tony."

"Gettin' him now, honey."

When Tony answered, I said, "First of all, everything is fine."

"What did you do?"

"Nothing. I swear. Viv and I were chasing a good guy, for once, and we still caused a scene. Ambulances and everything."

I gave him a quick run-through.

He made a sound that was not quite a word, but then stopped.

"I know, right?" I said. "We manage to get into trouble no matter what we're doing."

"If you're trying to make a case for continuing this private eye thing, you're taking the wrong approach." I could hear a smile in his voice, though, so I didn't take it too hard.

"I need to work late tonight," he said. "I'm having issues with one of the teams and I need to supervise."

"No problem," I said. "Stump and I will play nursemaid to Viv, if she's allowed to stay home."

I hung up and went back to check on Viv.

The EMTs had finally agreed that Viv was no worse the wear for her experience, although they did insist on getting her back to her apartment in a wheelchair. Someone had taken her swim cap off and her hair was in a matted mess on top of her head.

I patted her shoulder as I followed her down the hallway.

She jerked away and glared up at me.

"Are you okay" I asked loudly enough for those around us to hear. Then I leaned closed and whispered. "Reaping and sowing."

Genesis 25:26

After this, his brother came out, with his hand grasping Esau's heel; so he was named Jacob. Isaac was sixty years old when Rebekah gave birth to them.

When I read the Bible verse for my prayer time the next morning, I smiled and wondered if I should text Viv to let her know. What did it mean to get this verse the day after Viv had talked about Jacob just yesterday? Was it a warning, or a confirmation that Viv had been on track yesterday? Given the outcome, I had a hard time believing the second one, but I flat didn't want to believe the first. That was kind of scary.

I decided to read the devotional part before I jumped to any freaked-out conclusions.

Because his hand grasped his brother's heel as he was born, he was named Jacob, which literally meant 'heel-grabber.'

I wrinkled my nose. Well, now. That seemed kind of mean. He was a newborn, for crying out loud. Maybe he was scared in there and hanging on to his brother for comfort. They were twins, after all. They'd spent every moment of their lives together up to that point. Maybe he just didn't want to be separated from his brother. So the poor guy gets labeled a 'heel-grabber.' It was as if they thought Jacob wanted to be first, so he was trying to pull Esau back in and shove his way to the front. Somehow, I doubted newborns thought that way.

I was so sleepy. I curled up on the floor and put the pillow under my head, wondering what it did to a person to be labeled a *heel-grabber* for their entire lives. I had read the story of Jacob and Esau before, and always felt bad for Esau. He got the shaft. I couldn't remember what happened to Jacob after the whole stealing-of-the-blessing thing, but I thought it was something good.

I closed my eyes, thinking about dysfunctional families and labels; what would that kind of upbringing do to a person's ability to make good choices?

Maybe being called a heel-grabber was why Jacob turned out to be such a hot mess. He thought of himself as a heel-grabber. He came to self-identify with the label.

Had he become a deceiver because he'd been named one? Or had his parents somehow been able to see that side of him the moment he was born?

Unfortunately, I thought about this for too long. So long that I fell back to sleep and dreamed that I was trying to wash my aura but I kept making the stain darker. Then I realized I had gotten my aura confused with the comforter on my bed, which wasn't supposed to go into the washing machine anyway, and now it was ruined and my aura was still jacked up beyond all repair.

On that happy note, I woke with a start, looked at the clock, and jumped up to head for the shower.

As I was tugging on my shoes, my phone dinged. I didn't recognize the number, and I almost didn't answer it. It always feels a little too much like Russian roulette to me, answering an unknown number. But sometimes I like living dangerously, so...

"Hello?"

"Salem, it's Scott. Watson."

Instantly, my heart began to hammer. I almost dropped the phone. There was no good scenario for Scott Watson to be calling me.

"What?" I blurted, because I was too shaken to remember my manners. "Is Trisha okay?"

"Yes. Well. No, not exactly. But she's no worse than she has been. It's just...that's still not good. And I wondered if maybe you could...I don't know. Help me."

"I...what?" I said again. Because this was just too weird.

He sighed. "This thing with Peter Browning. I don't know if it's the hormones or what, but it's like she's obsessed. I mean, she was upset about his death, obviously. But now people are saying it was suicide."

"I heard that, too. I heard there was a note."

"Right. That's what Trish said. But she's convinced it couldn't possibly be suicide."

"Yeah, that's a hard thing to wrap your head around."

"No, I mean..." He broke off, and I heard him sigh—he sounded very frustrated. "It's like she's taking it personally. She talks about him all the time, talks about Bitsy all the time. How heartbroken she must be. How betrayed she must feel. She talks constantly about how many different scenarios—mostly murder, but sometimes even accidents—I could have been, and is obsessed with each of them. The police aren't helping, either—they won't say a thing. I'm sure they're conducting their investigation, but since they won't tell her anything and aren't keeping her in the loop, she thinks they're not actually doing anything. She thinks they've just written it off as suicide. Or even that they're in on it—like, they're covering for someone."

"That can't be good for her pregnancy," I said.

"I know!" He went silent again, but I heard in those two short words just how distraught he was. "It's not good for her. It's not good for the baby. She shouldn't be working at all. She shouldn't be stressed right now. But she can't let this go."

"Do you want me to have a talk with her?" For the life of me, I couldn't imagine what I could say that would convince her to chill the heck out. Nothing that she didn't know good and well already, that her doctor and Scott hadn't already told her. But I could try.

"No, I want you to see if you can find out anything. She usually has a lot of respect for the police, but she feels like on this case they're blowing it off because of Browning's past stories about the department. You remember all that stuff last year about the toy drive."

I did remember that—there was some unbelievable scandal about the police department Christmas toy drive, and a couple of people actually lost their jobs over it. Peter Browning had been in the middle of the whole thing, acting like he'd uncovered the scandal of the century. I could imagine how the LPD might not feel too fond of the guy.

But I knew Bobby Sloan fairly well. He could be a pain in the neck, but he was earnest about his job. He wouldn't *not* follow through on an investigation because of a personal vendetta. "I have a hard time believing that," I told Scott.

"Me, too. But she keeps typing stuff into her phone, and I found out she was keeping all these notes on different stories Browning was working on, different calls to the station, different groups he'd offended. She's got a whole file that she can access from her phone and her computers, and she's adding to it all the time. When she's not looking at baby stuff, I mean, she's looking at all these conspiracy theories about Browning. I even found a search on our computer about how to murder someone and make it look like suicide. Maybe you and your— your, you know—partner—could look into it."

For a moment, I was too stunned to think of a reply. Viv considered us actual private detectives. My G-Ma had come to think of us as actual private detectives. But most sane people understood what I did—that we were two people with too much time on our hands who had gotten lucky a few times and accidentally solved a few crimes.

"Well, sure," I said. "We'd be happy to."

"I can pay you," he said. "I don't know what your rate is, but—"

"No!" I blurted, still shocked. Rate? Viv and I had never even discussed rate for our "services" because we were happy just getting away with asking people nosy questions. "I mean, this is Trisha. It'd be...what do you call it? Pro bono."

"Well, thanks. But I am happy to pay. I mean it. At least I could pay your expenses. You know, gas and supplies or whatever."

I quickly wracked my brain, but couldn't think of anything I could legitimately call "supplies."

"I'll let you know," I said. "Is it okay for me to tell Trish we talked?"

"No," he said flatly. "Absolutely not. Her hormones are all over the place. One moment she's perfectly normal and the next she's crying—I mean, full-on sobbing—because I bought the wrong brand of ketchup. I'm not even making that up. If she knows I called you, she'll think we're ganging up on her."

Poor guy. He sounded shell-shocked.

"How about this? How about I come to her office, tell her Viv and I have a feeling the police aren't seeing the whole picture, and ask her thoughts on the matter? Ask if she has any ideas who might have wanted to kill Peter and make it look like suicide? Maybe she'll just turn over her notes to us."

"That would be fantastic," he said. He let out a deep breath. "Yes, that sounds really good."

My heart squeezed in my chest. Seriously, the poor guy! How bad off did he have to be to look to me and Viv for his salvation?

"That's what we'll do, then. Right after work tomorrow. Viv and I will meet with her and try to convince her—we'll be subtle, I promise—convince her to turn over her notes to us and we'll take it from there."

"I hope it works."

"Me, too. I just...Scott? What's the good news we're looking for here? Would it be so much better to find out he was murdered?"

"I know it sounds crazy, but yes, I think that will give her some comfort. I mean, you should see the way she looks at me when she thinks I'm not looking. I think, in her head, her pregnancy and Bitsy's pregnancy are getting kind of tangled up. She talked to Bitsy and, I don't know...the enormity of the betrayal, I guess, is what knocked her for a loop. That Peter would rather end his life than spend it with Bitsy and their child. Then she looks at me like...like she's wondering what secrets I'm keeping."

"But she knows you're not Peter. And you two have a solid foundation."

"That's what I keep trying to tell her. But...this is going to sound weird, but did you ever have a superstition about something? Like, if this happens, everything will be okay? If I make it all the way to the loop without hitting a red light, it's going to be a good day? When that has nothing, really, to do with what's going to happen when I get to the office. But it feels like an omen. You know?"

"Sure, I know."

"It's like that. It's as if, if she can make some sense of this thing with Browning, she can relax about our own situation. And man, would it be good if she could relax about our situation. She's freaked out about everything. It's as if we have to already know every single word we're ever going to say to this kid, and it's not even born yet. We have to make a lifetime of decisions, today. Gender-neutral toys. Church or no church. What kind of discipline for what kind of infraction. Nicknames.

I mean, we're not even sure if it's a boy or a girl, and I have to know for sure what age we're going to let them date. And if I don't know, or I say I need to think about it, she freaks out and says we're not prepared for this. We're going to screw it all up."

That was weird. Trisha was the type to face everything head on, make a plan, work the plan, and then dust her hands and move on to the next challenge without skipping a beat. It really must be the hormones. I kind of remembered those fears from my own pregnancy. Trisha did not have the benefit of youthful ignorance that I had, but I had known enough to know that I had no clue what I was doing. When I panicked, I turned to G-Ma, and she assured me that no one knew what they were doing. The best you could do was pretend you did and then stick to your guns.

Trisha spent roughly half her work day talking about people who had made bad decisions, so her level of awareness of bad people was different than mine.

"I'll go see her tomorrow afternoon," I promised, then hung up.

Immediately, I felt guilty. Had what I'd just done violated what Tony wanted me to do? I mean, this one was kind of iffy, because general consensus was that there was no murder. Ergo, I was in no danger from confronting a murderer.

Still. Did I really want a letter-of-the-law kind of relationship with Tony?

No. No, I did not.

On the other hand, I didn't think I had it in me to tell Scott Watson no to anything. I owed him too much. I would just...have to make Tony understand that.

CHAPTER SIX

The Best-Laid Plans

During a break that morning, I stepped out and called Viv to tell her about Scott's phone call.

"I told him I would go see her tomorrow. You'll come with me, right?"

"Of course. And tomorrow is better for me, anyway. I couldn't go today. I'm grounded."

"Grounded?"

"They're calling it *observation*," she said with a sneer. "Because of the *trauma* I experienced yesterday."

"Are you making air quotes right now?"

"Maybe."

"Well," I said. "You did get a very special hug from Imogene. That's got to have an effect on a person."

"Don't make me gag!" Viv said. "That woman is being hailed a hero all over this blessed place. Can you believe that?"

"Well, yeah. That was the intention, wasn't it?"

"Shut up. You know what my intentions were. And they sure as heck weren't for Imogene Walker to suddenly find herself back in the flow of her purpose."

Poor Viv. I could certainly understand the frustration of having one's plans go completely off the rails.

"I'm making the best of it, though," she said. "Miss Marple marathon on Amazon. If that is what Nigel's into, surely I can find a way to make it work."

"You're still into him, even when he stood by like a scared little old woman while an actual old woman saved you?"

"I don't appreciate you talking about my boyfriend that way," Viv said with a sniff. "He was only calling for help, as any sensible person would do. Imogene was the one who barged in and took over, like she always does. You're still going to yoga tonight, right?"

I had forgotten about yoga. I considered for a moment. The yoga studio was right beside Serena's little shop. I was still kind of mad at her for giving me a weird dream this morning.

"Actually, I'm going to skip, too. Everyone will just ask me about you the whole time. It'll get annoying."

It was true that yoga would be less fun without Viv. But tonight, I had a different set of awkward positions I needed to tackle.

I pulled out of Flo's parking lot that afternoon with a knot of anxiety in my stomach. Schemes kept going through my head—schemes of how to get Tony on my side.

Schemes were quickly replaced by guilt. I honestly did not want the kind of marriage where I schemed to get my husband to do stuff. Tony was always straight with me. I wanted to be straight with him. Whatever my role was, I didn't want it to be manipulator.

But...would it be so wrong to just...make sure he was in a good mood when I did talk to him?

I sighed and pulled into the grocery store parking lot.

"Windy, call Juanita."

Juanita was one of Tony's many sisters, and she seemed pretty okay with me. I mean, basically everyone in his family took a better view of me since I helped prove Tony innocent of murder, but Juanita had liked me when we first got married and not many of the sisters had.

When she answered, I said, "Juanita, I want to cook something nice for Tony. What's his favorite dish?"

"Do you mean I wrecked the car nice, or I spent too much at the mall nice?"

I scoffed. "Neither." Good grief. Was I fighting a losing battle with this manipulator thing? "I just...want to do something nice for him."

"I forget you two are newlyweds, kind of."

"I use the term somewhat. Does he have a particular favorite that's not too complicated and doesn't require a lot of ingredients?"

"You're in luck. Tony is notoriously easy to please when it comes to homemade cooking. Make him some tortillas, put some butter and honey on them, and he'll do anything you want him to."

"I'm not trying to get him to do anything," I protested.

"Well, I'd think of something if I were you. Because if you give him warm tortillas he's going to be ready to do something impressive. I'm just saying."

I chewed on that one for a second, but couldn't think of anything appropriate to say. "I guess. Let's just see if I can pull it off, first."

"No sweat. Tortillas are literally the easiest thing you can make. If you manage to mess them up, I'll be impressed."

"Remember, you grew up with a family that cooks. It's in your genes. I grew up in a family where cooking meant reheating in the microwave."

"I'll text you the recipe. Don't worry. Follow the directions and you'll be fine."

My phone dinged with the text from Juanita as I was pulling the shopping basket out of the corral. She wasn't kidding—it was ridiculously simple. Corn flour and water. Don't be afraid to adjust the amounts to get the right consistency. Mix it up, roll it into balls, press it out in the tortilla press, grill it on a hot cast iron pan.

My anxiety lifted. This was something I could definitely handle.

I grabbed a bag of cornmeal, a jar of cooking oil, a package of wax paper, a pound of butter, and a jar of honey and headed home to pick up Stump.

Back at Tony's, I found the key he kept hidden and let myself in. While I unloaded the few items I'd bought onto the counter, Stump busied herself dragging the bed Tony had bought her from the living room to the kitchen. I rummaged in the cabinets and found the tortilla press, a bowl for mixing, and a cast iron pan. I stood back and surveyed everything. Surely it couldn't be this easy.

I measured everything out like Juanita had instructed. At first the mixture looked too lumpy. I divided it up and rolled it into balls, but they kept falling apart.

I dumped everything back into the bowl and added a little bit more water. I grabbed a handful and tried to roll it into a ball. It mushed and stuck to my hands.

"You will not panic," I ordered myself, because I was starting to feel defeated already. "These are literally the easiest things you could make. You've made harder stuff before and it was fine." That was true. Just the week before I had made a baked cod recipe from my Fat Fighters book that had looked beautiful on the plate. It hadn't tasted very good, but I think that was the cod's fault, not mine.

I elbowed on the water faucet and washed the gritty, sticky gunk off my hands, took a deep breath, and headed back into the fray.

I added more cornmeal. Too stiff. Then more water. Too mushy. Then more cornmeal. I decided that, even if the little balls fell apart, they would stick together once I smushed them in the tortilla press. That thing was solid cast iron and as heavy as an anvil. I thought—and then looked guiltily around in case there was a mind-reader in the room—that it would probably make a good murder weapon, should one need such a thing. I got the cast iron pan hot, added a little oil, and gently peeled the first tortilla off the wax paper. It ripped in two, but I put both halves in the pan anyway, feeling that if I didn't get *something* cooked, I was going to cry.

The two jagged halves sizzled away on the pan and I started to gain a glimmer of hope. They smelled okay. I bent over the stove and studied them carefully, watching for signs that it was time to turn them. Then the warm corn smell turned to a suspiciously burnt smell. I used the spatula to lift an edge of one, but it didn't look burnt. I sniffed again, lifting the other one. Both were just turning golden brown. But something definitely smelled burnt.

Too late, I realized that while I studied the tortillas, I had laid the crumpled wax paper too close to the burner. As I watched, the red ashy edge along one side flamed to life and the whole ball went up. I screamed and threw the burning wad into the sink, then stood for a moment too long, chest heaving in fear that I would hit the curtains and burn Tony's house down, even as I saw with my own eyes that it was in the sink. I leaped over, turned the water on full blast and the flames sputtered out. I was dismayed, though, at the scorch marks that now marred Tony's white sink. Would that come out? I checked under the counter and found some powdered cleaner—a brand I hadn't seen before. Probably something from Tony's cleaning business—something only businesses had access to or something. I shoved the burned wax paper down the disposal and sprinkled the powder onto the burns.

I checked the clock. Still an hour before Tony would be home. I had time to erase the evidence of my clumsiness. I sniffed. The room still had a decidedly burnt smell, though.

I leaned over to open the kitchen window to let in some fresh air. The mid-November air rushed in with a gusty chill and the curtains blew into my face. I pushed them back, annoyed, but I thought I would only need to leave the window open a few minutes to air things out enough to be presentable again. If Tony noticed a smell, I could always pass it off as a burned tortilla. Those black marks, though—I had to get rid of them.

I found a scrub brush in a jar beside the sink and scrubbed the powder, encouraged that I could tell a difference almost immediately. Unfortunately, it smelled even more burnt, though. How porous were porcelain sinks? Could the smell be, like...baked into it?

I scrubbed some more and sniffed. Jeez-O-Peet . Had I done something to permanently stink up his sink? Would I end up having to replace the thing? How much did sinks cost?

I scrubbed some more, but it wasn't helping. In fact, it was making things worse—the air was acrid. I felt a moment of panic as I wondered if maybe this cleaner was something that reacted to the material of the sink in a harmful way. Tony had told me that you had to be careful with mixing cleaning chemicals. What if I had just created a toxic concoction and Tony would come home to find both me and Stump, dead on the kitchen floor?

But Tony was a very safety conscious guy, I reminded myself. If it wasn't supposed to be used on the sink, he wouldn't have had it under the sink.

The smell was getting worse, though—there was no denying it. I leaned forward and put my nose right to it. No, not bad. I straightened, then sniffed again. Yes. Bad. What the—

At that moment, several things happened in quick succession.

Tony pulled into the driveway.

Stump began to bark like crazy.

I turned to see what she was barking at, and instead saw a rather large conflagration in the cast iron pan on the stove.

I hadn't turned the "tortillas" off, and they were now in full blaze.

"Oh no!" I grabbed the handle of the pan with both hands and jerked it off the stove. I turned back to the sink.

The curtains blew in the wind. If I got near them with this pan, they would go up.

I spun around, looking frantically for something to do with this portable bonfire. The freezer? No. The fire climbed higher. Stump decided she would help by dancing around between my feet and barking furiously. Jeez-o-friggin'-Peet, it was one tiny ball of cornmeal, how could it be creating such a big fire?

Also, the pan was heavy. Heavier because I couldn't help but carry it at the very length of my arms. It's not as if I wanted to snuggle up to the thing. I was afraid if I took one hand off to open a door, I would drop it onto the floor and Stump.

So basically, here's what it was: me, spinning like a demented top in the middle of Tony's kitchen, holding a foot-high fire at arm's length, screaming "What? What? What?" because I was too freaked out to form coherent thoughts. All of this was accompanied by Stump's frantic agitation.

The front door opened.

Outside! I thought. I corrected course and set off for the entryway. I stumbled over Stump and almost dumped the entire thing in the middle of the dining room floor, but I managed to stay upright long enough to lunge, arms outstretched, into the entryway.

Tony, one foot in and one foot out of the front door, froze when he saw me, his eyes wide.

"Outside!" I shouted, because it was the only word my mind could form. I barreled toward him.

He leaped back outside, one hand on the screen door to keep it open, and I rushed past. I ran to the middle of the sidewalk, not sure what to do now. The wind was high. Would it carry a spark to the nearby trees, full of dead and dry fall leaves, and set Tony's entire neighborhood on fire?

I stood in the middle of the sidewalk and repeated my spinning performance from the kitchen.

"What is it?" Tony shouted.

"Fire!" I shouted back.

"I know! But...what *was* it?"

"Homemade tortillas!" I tried to say. But the word choked off with the tears suddenly clogging my throat. If you manage to mess them up...

He must have understood well enough, though, because he turned, pulled a water hose from a nearby pot, and turned the water on. "Put it down, Salem. In the middle of the sidewalk. Just put it down."

The fire that had raged just seconds before was now visibly smaller. As I bent to lower it to the sidewalk, a black crumb rolled over and the flame went out. A second later, water splashed into the pan with a loud, steamy hiss.

Tony turned the water off, silently wound the hose back into the pot, and turned to me.

I chewed my lip. Finally, I said, "Your sister is going to be so impressed with me."

Inside, Tony silently surveyed the kitchen. Now that the fire was gone, it didn't look too bad. I'd made a bit of a mess with the cornmeal and everything, but it wasn't the post-apocalyptic disaster it could have been.

"I wanted to surprise you by making one of your favorite things," I said. "Juanita sent me her recipe for homemade tortillas and she said it was literally the easiest thing I could make."

He nodded. Turned the bag of cornmeal and studied it, then the bottle of oil. Nodded again. Then, "She told you to get cornmeal?"

"Yeah, she said you preferred the corn kind to the white kind, so..." Something about that sounded funny, though. I pulled my phone out of my pocket and reread what Juanita had texted. I raised my head. "Corn *flour*. Which is the same thing as cornmeal, right?"

The corners of his mouth tipped up. "It's very, very close."

My shoulders slumped. "Ugh. I didn't read it closely enough. No wonder they wouldn't behave."

"It's okay. Salem, I'm a Hispanic man with five sisters. If I need tortillas, I can find tortillas. I promise." He laughed and slid his arms around my waist, kissing the top of my head. "I just wanted to make sure she hadn't given you the wrong information."

"No, this one is all on me." I sighed.

"How about instead of making one of my favorites, you make one of your favorites?"

"My favorites are all take out," I said.

"Then make something on your favorite things to make list."

I leaned my head against his chest. Everything I'd made lately had been bland at best. My forays into Fat Fighter recipes hadn't been exactly mind-blowing gastric delights. What was my favorite thing to make?

"Cinnamon toast," I finally said.

He drew back. "That sounds delicious, actually."

"Really?"

"Really. It's been years since I've had cinnamon toast. I have some sausages, and I think I have milk and orange juice."

"Breakfast for dinner," I said, leaning up to kiss him lightly.

"Breakfast for dinner," he repeated, pulling me in for a deeper kiss.

We worked side by side in the kitchen, the window now closed, the acrid smell almost gone, and I was finally able to let the clench in my stomach ease a bit. I still needed to talk to Tony about Scott's phone call. But as we laid the table for our simple meal and sat, side by side, enjoying the juicy sausages and the crisp caramelized sugar and cinnamon, I felt such a strong, stable foundation under me that I could believe whatever lay ahead of us was something we could handle.

As we polished off the toast, I said, "Okay, confession time. I wanted to cook something special because I need to have a serious talk with you."

He stopped in mid-chew.

Instantly, I felt the urge to backpedal. It had been such a lovely meal, even with the pandemonium that preceded it. Springing this on him now didn't feel like I'd been preparing him. It felt like I was sucker-punching him.

But I needed to be honest with him, and I didn't know how else to get to the truth without the whole truth.

"It's not that bad. But, it is about something that happened when we were apart."

Tony swallowed and sat back in his chair. I could see him steel himself for what was coming.

I hated that he found that necessary.

"You have to listen all the way through, because I think once I've said everything, you're going to see that it's not as bad as it could be." Good grief. That didn't sound the least bit comforting. I took a deep breath. "I'm just going to spit it out. You know Trisha and Scott Watson?"

"Of course."

Of course he did. We'd all grown up together in the tiny town of Idalou, Texas, and it just wasn't possible to live in a town that size and not know someone the same age as you.

"I mean, you remember that they were together in high school and got married after they got out of college?"

He nodded.

"Well, here's what happened. The night before their wedding day—the day that was supposed to be their wedding—Scott's friends gave him a bachelor party. I showed up there. To be honest, I have no memory of how I got there. I'm sure we heard from somewhere that there was a party, and...and anyway."

Tony remained frozen and my heart pounded. Things were going to sound a lot worse before they sounded better.

"You remember Rick Barlow? He was there. And he didn't really care for Trisha. He wanted to play a trick on her. A mean trick. So he got me and Scott into bed together and let her find us that way the next morning." I reached across the table, not quite touching his hand, but almost. "Tony, nothing happened. I was very drunk, Scott was very drunk, we both passed out. Rick was there and he knew for a fact that nothing happened, but he let Trisha and Scott both believe that it had. She came in the next morning—apparently, he was late for his own wedding—and found us like that and assumed what anyone would naturally assume."

Tony shook his head. "What an awful thing to do to someone."

"She was devastated. They broke up. She moved away and cut off all contact with him. Eventually, they got back together because he just refused to let her go. He just...loved her too much to let her walk away. He followed after her and kept hounding her until she let him back in. They reconciled and got married, but it took two years of him pursuing her relentlessly."

Tony was staring at the table now, his jaw clenched. He didn't say anything.

It hit me suddenly that maybe he'd heard that last bit as a condemnation of him. I had left him, and he'd let me go. He waited for me, but he didn't chase after me. The me of many years and many lessons ago had found fault with that, but I understood now and even admired what he'd done—or not done. It took a lot of faith to put an important part of your life on hold and wait for someone else to grow up, with no real indication that they ever would.

I reached further and took his hand. "Do you remember when Lucinda Cruz was found, and they used that horrible picture of me in the news story?"

He nodded, coming out of his reverie. "Sure. I thought that was weird."

"That's how Trisha and I came back into contact. She saw on the video that I was the one who found the body, and she dug up an old arrest photo of me and ran the story with it. Which was awful, by the way. She managed to make it sound like I was under some kind of suspicion for Lucinda's murder. That's what people kept thinking—that I'd been arrested for murder."

Again, I cringed. He knew firsthand what that was like, because he had been the one arrested and charged, in fact. Viv and I had been able to prove that he hadn't done it, which was when I found out that Tony and I weren't as divorced as I thought we were.

"I could have sued her and the station ten different ways for that, and I went up to the station to tell her just that, but in that confrontation, I learned about the whole nightmare with Scott. I had blocked out the entire thing. Even after she reminded me, only bits and pieces came back. I remembered vaguely being at the party, and I remembered the next morning when she found us in that bed. Her screaming and crying, throwing my shoes at me and pushing me down the sidewalk. The few years before and after that were so alcohol soaked that it didn't even stand out to me. Not until I sobered up, and it was years later, and I could see how much it still hurt Trisha."

Tony took a deep breath and squeezed my hand, but he kept silent and let me finish.

"She forgave Scott, but she had no desire to forgive me, even though I was sincerely sorry and told her so. It wasn't until that night when Thomas and Rey had us in that car, with Rick, that he told me that nothing had happened. Everyone, including me, assumed the worst. But it hadn't happened. He was quite sure."

Tony breathed then, and I realized he'd been holding his breath. Tony knew that I had not been faithful to him in the time we were apart. I thought we were divorced and hadn't considered it adultery. So, he knew on one level, of course. But the idea of my adultery and the fact of it—having a face to put it on, an exact time—those two things were worlds apart.

My heart caved into my chest and I wanted suddenly and fervently to be able to tell him that none of it had happened—none of the other guys, none of those years had been spent with me drinking my way through one relationship after another. I would have given everything I had to be able to say that.

But I couldn't. All I could do was squeeze his hand and let him know that I was with him, that I loved him, that I was his completely.

"The only reason I'm telling you this now, Tony, is that I need you to understand why it's so important to me to help Trisha and Scott. I kept them apart for two years."

"Rick Barlow did that."

"I was part of it. I know it wasn't my idea, but drunk or not, I went along with it." My throat closed and I had to squeeze out the last part. "I didn't say no, Tony." I remembered that I had actually protested, half-heartedly. But I was drunk, and Rick said it would be funny. I was all about the funny. Hey, get me! I slept with your fiancé. Ha-freaking-ha.

"Trisha and I have talked about this a few times. She's told me the hell she went through during those two years. She was destroyed. Her heart broken. Just imagine how awful that was— It was her wedding day. She'd planned for months and then had to call it all off at the last second. It took her two years to forgive him and trust him again. That kind of experience, Tony—it has an effect on a person."

"I know that."

Of course, he knew that.

Now it was time for me to take a deep breath. "So, you understand that when Scott asked me to do something for Trisha, I really wanted to do it."

"What has he asked you to do?"

"Trisha is convinced that Peter Browning could not have committed suicide. She's offended by the very idea, in fact. It's as if the concept of Peter Browning choosing to kill himself is some kind of betrayal that she can't get past. Scott says she's become obsessed by this suspicion that Peter was murdered, and the case isn't going to be fully investigated because the police are writing it off as suicide. Scott asked us—me and Viv—to look into it so maybe she would stop worrying about it so much. He's afraid she's going to harm the baby with all her worry."

He sighed and remained silent, his dark eyes on mine.

"Tony, here's the thing. Scott said this morning that sometimes he'll catch Trisha looking at him like she's wondering what secrets he's hiding. This..." I shrugged, unsure on how to put into words what my concern was. "This fear that people are hiding things from her..." I felt my throat catch. "Maybe she's not thinking this on a conscious level, but I have to think that fear goes back to that awful bachelor party."

He took another deep breath, frowning, but still didn't say anything.

"Look, you haven't come right out and asked me to stop doing these crazy little—investigations or whatever you would call them—with Viv. But I know you don't want me to do it."

"I don't want you to do it."

"Right." Actually, I had kind of hoped that when push came to shove he would say something more along the lines of, 'No, it's your life, I'm fully supportive of whatever makes you happy.' But...

"But Scott is seriously worried about her. He would have to be for him to even call me. And I still feel some kind of...I don't know. Like I owe them."

"That's guilt talking, Salem."

"Well, yeah." Of course, it was.

"You're not guilty. You didn't plan that."

"No, but I was there. I was part of something that hurt her tremendously."

"Salem, did you ask Trisha for forgiveness?"

"Of course."

"And did you ask God for forgiveness?"

"Yes, Tony, but—"

"Then you're forgiven. This isn't on you anymore. You've made atonement."

"Have I? Tony, seriously, if you could have seen how she still agonized over it." I would never forget the day I'd met Trisha again after ten years. The pain in her eyes was still so raw.

"But nothing happened."

"A lot happened. She faced an entire wedding party, with guests and everything, and told them the wedding was off. How awful must that have been?"

"Salem, I understand that you have so much sympathy for Trisha. That's admirable. But you should be clear on your motives."

"I want to help Trisha. I want to make up for—"

He lifted his hand and stopped me. "You want to *make up for.*"

I studied him for a moment. "But...why is that bad, Tony?"

"It's not bad. It's just...Salem, it's an exercise in futility. For one thing, nothing you could do would ever make up for that. I think you know that. You can't undo what was done. You could work for the rest of your life and it wouldn't undo whatever Trisha and Scott felt that day. That year." He took my hand back and touched my cheek with his other hand. "And for another, you're forgiven. It's washed clean. Not because of something you did, but because of grace."

I didn't say anything, but my frustration must have shown on my face, because he smiled and kissed the tip of my nose. "Salem. You're a Christian."

"I know that."

"Every Sunday you say the Apostle's Creed. Come on. Say it with me. I believe in the forgiveness of sins. Come on. Say it."

I rolled my eyes, then grudgingly said, "I believe in the forgiveness of sins."

"What's that? Did you say you believe in the forgiveness of sins, except for Salem's?"

"Tony, stop. You sound like a hip high school Sunday school teacher."

He laughed. "No, this is taking it out of Sunday school. This is it, where the rubber meets the road. Do you believe what you said or not?"

"Sure, but..."

"But what? It doesn't count if you just say it and don't live it."

"I am living it. Did I not just this very day talk to my mother on the phone for fifteen whole minutes? I practice forgiveness."

"Not for yourself."

I opened my mouth, then closed it again. Turns out I had nothing to say to that.

He kissed me again. He put his hands on both sides of my face, his nose less than an inch from mine. "You asked me one time if I could forgive you. I can. I have. It doesn't mean that memory of the time we spent apart doesn't hurt. But when I look at you, there's no doubt in my mind. I forgive you."

Not much I could do except sniff back tears and hope my nose didn't start pouring snot.

"But Salem, I don't see how we're going to make this work if you can't forgive yourself."

"I have."

"Bull."

"Okay, but I know I should. That's a first step, right?"

He was right. I knew he was right. From the perspective of hindsight, I could see how so many of my crazy actions had been motivated by guilt. Guilt for conceiving the baby that had made Tony and me a teenage bride and groom, meaning he had to forfeit his bright future. Resentment when that guilt welled up. Anger that he insisted that we were still married and could still make it work, after my car was t-boned and I lost the baby. Guilt that I hadn't been strong enough to keep that baby alive in me. Guilt that his heart was broken, too, that I'd ripped his future away, then ripped his family away, even though by the time of the accident, I was also half in love with that still-nameless baby.

I dealt with it the only way I knew how. When he pushed for us to stay close, to help each other heal, I pushed him away. I did everything I could to make him angry, make him hate me the way I knew I should be hated. When he refused, I left, and set about burning every bridge I could find.

Guilt had created a lot of destruction in my life, so I knew he was speaking wisdom. I did have to forgive myself. But how?

"I don't know how," I finally whispered.

"I know," he said. He kissed me, once on the lips, then softly on each eyelid, now wet with tears. "But promise me, we'll figure it out, okay?"

"Okay." More sniffing.

"One thing I know, it's not going to happen with you running around devoting your life to making up for stuff."

"You do know I kept you out of jail by trying to make up for what I'd done to you?"

He gave me a flat look that made me laugh.

"Okay, yes, I'll give you that one," he said.

I giggled and sniffed again, drawing back to swipe at my nose, then reached behind me for a box of tissues on the bar.

He studied me while I wiped away tears. "Look, Salem. I worry about you chasing after bad guys. I don't like the idea of you facing down another guy with a gun and only Viv there for protection."

"Viv carries a gun, too."

"That's not supposed to give me comfort, is it?"

"It doesn't comfort me," I admitted.

"But you're a grown woman and you can make your own decisions. I mean, it's not like I'm going to forbid you from doing it or anything."

"Oh, come on. You're not?"

"Mmmm, of course not. What exactly would you do if I did forbid it?"

"Use your unreasonable authoritarianism as an excuse to do it anyway." I swatted at him. "You've totally messed up my plan."

He grabbed my hand and brought my fingers to his lips. "I worry about you. How much danger do you think there is in this thing with Browning?"

I shrugged. "Probably none. The odds are on suicide, so there's no other bad guy with a gun to find. But apparently, Trisha has a whole list of possible suspects we can go through. Scott said he found a bunch of files and searches on her computer."

"This is starting to sound like a lot more than none."

"I tell you what. We'll look through the notes Trisha has collected. It's probably nothing—just Trisha trying to process something very difficult at a time when her hormones are out of whack. We might talk to some people, but only in open spaces in broad daylight. We won't meet anyone in dark alleys."

"Or abandoned houses."

"That was one time, and I learned my lesson." I held my palm up. "Promise."

Viv was recovered enough from her 'near-drowning' experience to be raring to go by noon the next day.

"I have four more dogs to finish," I said. I'll be done around 3:00."

"Shoot. Well, I guess I'll have to just do more research while I wait."

"Did you get ungrounded?"

She made a noise that could have meant anything, but actually indicated nothing. "Pick me up behind the miniature golf course."

"You're sneaking out?"

"Salem, a woman's life is at stake here, and the life of her child. This is no time to worry about what these medical professionals are going to say."

She was making air quotes again, I could tell. "So you're sneaking out."

"I'm sneaking out. Text me when you're close and I'll meet you there."

I swung by Trailertopia to drop Stump off with Frank, then headed to Belle Court. The miniature golf course was on the back side of the campus, deserted in the mid-November chill. I slowed the Monster Carlo and looked for Viv.

Nobody I knew had a more beautiful "obviously incognito" look than Viv Kennedy. I pulled into the miniature golf lot and didn't see her. But as I circled the lot, she came running out from behind the big windmill. She had tied a scarf around her hair and wore sunglasses with lenses as big as coffee cans. She high-step ran toward the Monster Carlo, darting glances behind her as she went, giggling.

She threw herself into the passenger seat and shouted, "*Go go go!*"

I went.

On the ride to Channel 11, I briefed Viv on the important points while she got her act together. "Scott doesn't want her to know he talked to me."

Viv nodded, her face set. "Totally on the down low. Got it."

"We need to make it seem like this is her idea."

"Right-o."

"She's convinced Peter Browning was murdered, so we need to find out exactly why she thinks that, and we need to reassure her that we're going to get to the bottom of things."

"He was, and we will."

I glanced over at her. She'd taken off the scarf. "You're wearing a fascinator under your scarf?"

"Yep. Change in costume, you know. Mix things up a bit. Keep people on their toes."

"Nigel?" I asked.

"He was coming in from the miniature golf course as I was getting ready to go out. I don't think he even saw me, though. Too busy acting all concerned for Anne, who apparently forgot how to play miniature golf."

"Anyway. What makes you so sure Browning was murdered?"

"Demons, Salem," she said. "The man was wrestling with demons."

"Okay. And what makes you so sure we'll get to the bottom of things?"

"We always do."

I had to allow that. So what if we'd had less than half a dozen "things" to get to the bottom of? We did, indeed, have a 100 percent success rate.

The receptionist at Channel 11 didn't even bother asking why we were there. She looked up from her phone long enough to take in the fascinator, then motioned toward the offices with a tilt of her head.

Tri-Patrice was in her office with her feet up, issuing orders over the phone and in person to one employee after another. Viv and I took a seat.

Viv didn't waste any time getting to the point as soon as Trisha didn't have a phone to her ear or an intern at her door.

"Listen, you're obviously busy, so we won't keep you. It's just that Salem and I have been talking about this Peter Browning thing, and something seems very...chalk and cheese about it all."

"Chalk and cheese?" I drew my head back. "Is that another one of your British things? What does that even mean?"

Viv looked at her lap and frowned. "I don't actually know."

Trisha threw me an amused look. "Like, things don't add up?" she offered.

"Exactly! Do you get the feeling the Lubbock PD isn't really investigating this as thoroughly as they could?"

Trisha's feet dropped to the floor and she said, "Yes! Right? I mean, they find a note, and it's not even a full note, it's one sentence that could have meant anything. And immediately they're like, 'Case closed!' and move on."

"We keep hearing about this note," Viv said. "Where did they find a note?"

"Bitsy said they told her it was in the car. And it said almost nothing. *I didn't mean it to turn out like this.* I mean, come on. That could mean anything."

"You said the police have moved on. But, have they? Have they said the case was closed?"

"Who knows?" Trisha said with evident scorn. "I call every day and I get no information. They asked a few questions at first, but then nothing. It's as if it didn't even happen." She shook her head. "Poor Bitsy."

Viv and I waited in silence for a few seconds, waiting for her to realize there were two somewhat seasoned investigators sitting immediately across from her.

Finally, I said, "So the police are saying nothing? Even though you guys worked with Peter and knew his schedule and everything?"

"Exactly. I mean, most of us spend more time at work than we do at home, and we know all about each other's lives. But all they'll tell me is they're waiting for the report from the medical examiner. Which could take weeks. And in the meantime, whoever did this has plenty of time to destroy evidence and get away." She shook her head in disgust. "I gave them a list of messages I had taken in the last few months, people who'd called in or emailed to complain about a story Peter had done. I don't think they've followed up on any of them." She parked her feet back up on the box beside her desk and settled her hands over her stomach.

I couldn't help myself—I had to come to Bobby Sloan's defense. "It could just be that they don't want to share that information with you. They might be doing all kinds of interviews."

"Maybe, but I doubt it. They didn't even ask me for the list, you know. I volunteered it. And I added a couple of ringers—my hairdresser, for one. I said she'd called to complain about a story Peter had done about that police toy drive at Christmas—you remember that whole mess with the Space Cop toy? I thought they might follow up on that, but they never called her."

"Maybe they just haven't gotten to her yet. I mean, doing the kinds of stories he did, he had to have a lot of enemies," I said.

"He did." Trisha nodded. "People hated him. I know. I got to handle a lot of the complaint calls."

"You definitely don't need to be dealing with stuff like that. Not in your condition. And you shouldn't be worrying about Peter Browning, either."

"You sound like my husband."

I hid my cringe.

"It's true," Viv said. "Besides, Salem and I are in a better position to look into this a little more. We could follow up on those names, if you want."

I gave her the side-eye. So much for letting Trisha think it was her idea. I supposed the main thing was, though, that she not know Scott had put us up to it, and there was very little chance she'd even think of that.

Trisha leaned back and looked at the ceiling. Then she turned back to us, her eyes intense. "I suppose you could. I mean, the police haven't asked me not to share the information I have. Would you conduct a whole investigation, like you did with CJ Hardin and Lucinda Cruz?"

"And the High Point Bandits," Viv reminded her.

"And the Braswell Maltese kidnapping," I added, for good measure. What's the point in having a 100 percent success rate if you can't brag about it?

Trisha twisted her mouth like she was thinking about it, then she turned to her computer and clicked a few things. Behind her, a printer began to whirr.

"I'm going to print up what I have. It's probably a mess, but it made sense to me. The first file is all transcripts of stories that Peter did that were somewhat controversial. Basically, it comes down to two events, though—the Space Cop thing and the school collapse. Well, the school collapse and all the fracking earthquake stories. That all kind of ties together."

I watched with a faint sense of trepidation as the stack of printer paper grew. She clicked a few things. The printer beeped and kept going.

"Okay, I'm sending some instructions to your phones," she said, her fingers clicking away at the keys. "This will explain things as you're looking through the notes."

Viv and I watched silently, and I realized that this was what it must be like to be one of Trisha's co-workers. Those junior reporters probably sat just like this while she handed down their instructions. No, they probably stood at full attention.

Trisha sat back and studied her screen, her brow creased. She clicked a few things and scrolled her mouse, then picked up her phone.

"Jessica, will you come in here, please?"

Before I could have counted to three, the door opened and the camera girl who had been at the Veterans Day ceremony entered. "Yes?"

"I sent you that list of names and notes to organize and send to the Lubbock PD, right?"

She nodded. "Yes. Monday, I think."

"Can you send that back to me, please? I can't seem to find it."

Jessica nodded. "Sure. No problem." She left without appearing to notice that Viv and I were even there.

Trisha stood and pulled the papers out of the printer, tamped them together and then slid them into a manila folder. Her computer dinged softly, and she bent to look at the email she'd just received. She studied it for a second, then printed it as well.

"Okay, I'm putting the list of names on top. Here's the thing. We rarely take down messages from disgruntled viewers because we get disgruntled viewers all the time. People are mad because they want us to cover their kid's school event and we don't. They're mad when we release names that they don't think should be released, or when we don't release names that they think we should. Sometimes, I swear to you, sometimes they're mad at us when the news is bad, and sometimes they call up here and want to talk to Matt Lauer."

"Seriously?" Viv said. "What do you do then? Ask them to look out their window and ask if they're looking at skyscrapers or wind turbines?"

"If they're nice, we give them the number to the NBC studio in New York. If they're rude, we put them on hold, and eventually they give up. My point is, there were probably calls we should have noted and didn't. Hindsight, you know. But when things get especially hairy, I try to take as many notes as I can, just in case. Those two events were two of the hairier ones I can remember in the recent past, so I started asking for contact information when people called about those two events. Sometimes they won't give it to you, of course, and I don't always have time to write everything down anyway. Even when I do write it down, I can't always read it or understand what it means when I'm typing up notes later. So it's entirely possible that I missed something significant because I didn't recognize it at the time." She frowned.

I took the folder from her. "No problem. We'll start with this, and we'll see what floats to the top. Maybe if we can narrow down a few leads, we'll meet with you again and see if that triggers any more memories."

She sat down with a sigh, looking a little relieved. "I'm so glad you guys came by. I think everyone thinks I'm crazy. I know Scott does."

"I'm sure he doesn't think you're crazy," Vi said. "He's probably just concerned about your health and the baby's health. Now that we're on the case, promise me, Love, that you'll relax about this and take care of yourself."

Trisha raised her eyebrows at me. *Love?*

Then I remembered how Viv had spent the past few days. "Miss Marple?"

"Oh, I love those!" Trisha said, grinning. Then she gave Viv a look. "You make an awfully hip Miss Marple, though."

"I know," Viv said, looking unhappy.

"Well, I mean...you have the detective skills, obviously."

"Obviously," Viv agreed.

"But the little old lady frumpy stuff...you're going to have a hard time pulling that off," Trish said.

"I know," Viv said again, looking even unhappier. "I don't think I even pulled off the 'Love' bit."

"Sure you did," I said, rubbing her arm. "I bought it." That probably fell under the heading of "bearing false witness," but I felt God would understand I was doing it to lift up a friend in need.

"Oh!" Trisha said, as if she'd just remembered something. "I forgot about the videos. I'm going to send you a link to the videos I saved on our server. Wait. No, I can't give you access to that." She stopped and stared down at her desk for a moment, thinking. "I'll copy them to my personal cloud storage and give you a link to that."

Viv and I looked at each other. Whatever else fell under the heading of our "area of expertise," servers and cloud storages most definitely did not. I was the least tech-savvy twenty-something in the civilized world.

Trisha clicked a couple more things, then turned back to us. She correctly interpreted the looks on our faces. "They're just videos. All you have to do is click the link I send you, and then play the videos." She nodded toward the folder in my hands. "Those are the printed transcripts, and the videos are what we showed on the newscast, plus some links to surveillance videos from different spots around town. Nothing major."

I stood, a bit overwhelmed at the job ahead of us. But Trisha really did look relieved, and that made me feel better. Whether we deserved it or not, she clearly thought of me as something other than a "heel-grabber," as did Scott. Otherwise he wouldn't have called, and Trisha wouldn't have handed over all of her notes.

Now all I had to do was prove their faith wasn't misplaced. And not get myself shot at in the process, or Tony would be so mad.

Back at the Monster Carlo, I tossed Viv the keys so she could drive while I sifted through the folder. By the time we were back on the loop, I was overwhelmed again. "What in the world are we supposed to do with all this?"

"What we always do," Viv said. "Investigate."

"Yeah, but..." This looked an awful lot like a haystack that probably had no needle in it. "All we really do is go around and ask people nosy questions."

"You act like that's not investigating. Let's go get a cuppa and decide what nosy questions we need to ask."

Viv pulled into a little coffee shop on 34th Street and we carried our notes in and found a booth. A waitress came over.

"I'll have a cup of Earl Grey, hot," Viv said.

The waitress looked confused.

"It's tea, Love. Hot tea."

Her face cleared. "We have Lipton, I think."

"Hot?"

She looked at Viv like she was crazy. "Um, no. It's iced."

Viv sighed.

"I'll have coffee," I said. "Black."

"I guess I'll have coffee, too," Viv said with a put-upon look.

I skimmed through the notebook. I had to hand it to Trisha. Even her borderline-paranoid ravings were organized. The stories fell under two headings, just as she'd said. The first was the Lubbock PD/Space Cop scandal, and the other was related to the earthquake and school collapse in March.

"Do you think it's weird that both stories are almost a year old?" I asked Viv.

She shrugged. "Cheers, Love," she said as the waitress placed our coffee cups at the table. Then to me, "Not really. I mean, the earthquake was a while ago, but the fallout is still going on. That architecture firm just closed down, what—three months ago? And then Baucum's death two months ago."

"Trisha has 'Baucum Engineering employees' on the list. I guess a lot of people were laid off when it closed."

"It might take a couple of months for things to go off the rails for them. Picture it—trouble finding a new job, savings dwindling, the family is facing possible bankruptcy, maybe a move to a new town. Have to sell the house—the dream home they planned to retire in. The teenager who just made the cheerleading squad has to give it up, start over with a bunch of new kids she doesn't know."

"Or he," I said. "Don't be sexist."

"So you can see how a desperate architect father—"

"Or engineer mother," I interrupted, "Since it's an engineering firm, and women go to college now. Don't be sexist," I said to the least sexist person I knew.

She went on as if I hadn't said a word, "—could get so beaten down he—or she—traces the whole disaster back to Peter Browning's investigative reports."

"Not the guy who helped design the building that collapsed in a relatively low-level earthquake?" I asked.

She shrugged again. "For one thing, he's already gone by this time. For another, that's someone our baddie knew—"

"*If* there is a baddie, and *if* the baddie is from Baucum Engineering." I sipped my coffee. "The Baucum Baddie. I like it."

"It has a nice ring. The point is, I don't see anything off about the time line." She thumbed through the papers. "Heavens. This is a lot of paper."

"I know. Want to watch the videos first?"

"Absolutely." She pulled out her phone and I joined her on that side of the booth.

"Let's look at the surveillance videos first. I've seen all of Peter Browning's reports, but I haven't seen all of those."

Unfortunately, we couldn't get any of those links to work. After several false starts, we eventually asked the waitress for help. She tried for a few minutes, then pulled her son from the back office where he was doing his homework.

He was maybe thirteen years old and in need of a haircut. He also seemed a little annoyed to be bothered, but eventually we were able to explain to him what we wanted and he took over.

"You don't need links for that," he said. "You can type in a search for webcams and then find what you're looking for."

"Those would just be live feeds, though, right? We're looking at history."

He nodded, typing something new into the browser. "Lots of places store their surveillance history in the cloud, so you just have to know..." He tucked his tongue over his bottom lip as his thumbs danced over the keyboard. "Not all of them, but a lot of them. You just have to know where to find them." He looked at me from under his shaggy hair and said, "I'm bookmarking it for you so you can find it again. Go to the camera you want to see, then type in the date, and it'll bring up everything recorded on that day."

"And how do you know about all this?" his mother asked.

He rolled his eyes. "It's common knowledge, Mom."

"It's not common to me. What kind of things are you looking at through these webcams?"

"They're out in the open. It's not like there are any webcams in a girl's bedroom on this site."

She frowned but said, "Okay, you. Get back to your homework."

He turned to follow her back to the office, then turned back and whispered, "The bedroom cams are on a different site. Let me know if you want to see them."

The surveillance videos were interesting for about eight minutes. Basically, though, it was just watching people live their normal lives, which we could do by looking out the window. We watched the footage of the school collapse, but it was exactly like it was in the news story, so we figured we might as well get started on that.

We clicked the first link to Browning's stories, then Viv clicked the big sideways triangle to play the video.

The first video was the story right after the earthquake. I didn't need to be reminded of that—we had all watched the footage over and over again, as one does after a huge event. But this was the report put together a few days afterward, with video from different cameras around town, and words scrolled onto the screen between videos.

Browning's somber voice began the voice-over: *It began like any other afternoon.*

Trisha—or Patrice, of course—sits beside the news desk, talking to the little camera girl, the one Trisha had called Jessica. Browning is behind her, talking to the sports guy.

Then the camera begins to shake. All four of them straighten, look around. Trisha and Jessica both grab the news desk. The men end their conversation, step apart, look beyond the camera.

The camera shifts, points at nothing, then at the lights on a bar across the high ceiling. The lights shake noticeably, but not wildly.

Then everything shakes. In the background, people scream.

The scene changes to the roll of a seismograph. The paper crawls across the screen and the blue line jumps, low at first, then spikes a little. Then low again. Then spikes, much larger this time. The screen pans in with a tight focus on that spike as it jumps wildly up and down.

Six-point-two on the Richter scale. The largest earthquake ever recorded in the southwest.

The scene then switches to various security cameras around town. A convenience store counter, where a man stands looking out the front window. Suddenly, he grabs the counter, trying to save overtoppling displays before he's thrown to the ground.

A used car lot, a salesman walking in the distance, two guys looking at a pickup in the foreground. They all stop, look at the sky. The salesman stumbles. The two guys crouch beside the pickup, hanging on to it.

We had never felt anything like it before.

A teenage girl's video of her and her friend showing off their new sunglasses and giggling. They stop, clutch each other, still giggling as they felt the first tremors, but then shrieking in terror as the ground quakes hard beneath them.

A mom, recording her young daughter and a grown man, as the man holds the back of the little girl's bicycle seat, encouraging her to keep peddling, keep peddling, she had it. Suddenly the bike wobbles and he stumbles. The girl doesn't catch on at first, thinks she is just falling, but the dad grabs the bike, drags it to a stop, and looks at the camera, eyes wide. "Was that...?" the woman says. Then the ground shakes, the girl falls, the dad falls, the camera falls, pointing at blue sky and bare tree branches shaking. The girl cries while the mom tries to her reassure her, her own voice verging on panic.

Then back to Peter Browning, walking down a sidewalk on a cloudy day. An empty field spread behind him, and as he slowly walked, the corner of a building came into view, then a curb behind his feet.

"Just last year, News Channel 11 did a special report on the 45th anniversary of the EF5 tornado that struck Lubbock in 1970. I had the privilege of talking to many people who shared with me their personal stories of where they were and what they were doing when the tornado hit. I was struck by what a pivotal event that was to so many people. All those years later, they still remembered it as if it had happened the day before."

"Little tool," Viv said. "Forty-five years isn't that long." She sipped her coffee.

"I could sympathize," Browning went on. "but I couldn't relate. At least, not until March 11."

The scene went back to the Channel 11 studio, where Patrice Watson and Tom Timmons were now at their desks, Browning standing beside them. Tri-Patrice was calm but alert, Tom was calm but alert, and Browning looked serious and thrilled at the same time.

"For those of you just tuning in, we have confirmed with the United States Geological Survey that what we experienced at 4:24 this afternoon was, in fact, an earthquake. What you just felt was an earthquake."

Back to Browning on the sidewalk on the cloudy day, where the scene behind him is now fully revealed. NorthStar Elementary. The only building in the area to sustain major damage from the quake.

"I'll never forget the experience of my first major earthquake. Nothing can prepare you for the feeling of the very world around you falling apart. But as powerful as that experience was for me, it will never compare to the experience of one local family."

The camera rose, away from Browning, taking in the front of the school building, pristine and new, the ground still bare of grass, a few little twig trees surrounded by their round water moats. We saw the flat roof of the long, wide school building, where it was easy to imagine hundreds of noisy kids running around inside, moving between classrooms, school bells ringing, teachers herding kindergartners.

Then, with a rise in perspective of a degree or two, the scene took in the devastation at the back of the building—the gym wall collapsed, a pile of rubble, a gaping hole where a gymnasium roof should have been.

"Camera drone," Viv said. "Fancy."

The scene switched once again: the same location from a slightly different perspective, ambulance and police car lights flashing brightly against the darkening night. A small crowd gathered behind the police car. Stretchers being rolled down the new sidewalk. A man, face and head bloody and covered with white dust, the lower part of his body draped by a white sheet. He was looking back, though, twisting on the gurney even as one of the women pushing it was trying to get him to straighten and face forward.

A second gurney enters the scene now, the body on it much smaller. Half covered. Not fully covered, thankfully. A small blond head showed, dusty and still, streaked with blood, above the blanket.

As the camera closed in, the second gurney drew even with the first, and the man reached out, grappled with the blanket on the second stretcher, and took hold of the small hand he found there.

Browning came back to tell about Matthew Logan, the foreman of the construction company that built the school. He'd been the man on that first stretcher, and his daughter was the small blonde on the second one. They'd both been crushed under the collapsed gymnasium wall. He had a broken leg, broken ribs and collar bone, but expected to recover fully. His daughter's recovery was not quite as easy to predict, Browning said.

"Hmm," Viv said. We both knew now what Browning had not when this video was made: the girl lived, but would never walk again.

That video ended and Viv clicked the next one. In it, Browning interviewed the man and his wife in their home, a few weeks after the quake. The man wore a cast on his lower leg, and the cuts on his face and head were mostly healed. He was the foreman for the construction company that had built the school, which was scheduled to open the week after spring break. He and his family had been in the school building when the earthquake hit. His wife and two other children were in the hallway of the school and had been safe. He and his eight-year-old daughter had gone into the gym and were buried under the rubble of the collapsed roof and wall.

Viv and I were both holding back tears by the time it was over. The man choked up when he told about how proud he was to be able to show his family the building he'd been working on for the past year, the building they would attend school in for the last part of the year.

Why was it so much more awful when men cried than when women did? Viv sniffed hard, blew her nose into a napkin from the dispenser on the table, and clicked the next link.

This time, Peter Browning was interviewing a USGS expert who said that earthquakes were certainly rare in our area, but the possibility shouldn't be ruled out, especially considering the increase in hydraulic fracturing, injection wells, and tremor incidents in and around Texas.

Another interview with the same USGS guy, who talked about the increase in small earthquakes and how we need to accept that tremors and injection wells go hand in hand, and either adapt to that or ban the use of injection wells.

"What are injection wells?" I asked.

Viv shrugged. "Something to do with fracking," Viv said.

But as she said it, Browning went into a description of the wells.

"Hydraulic fracturing—or fracking, as it's widely known—is the process of shooting water, sand, and chemicals into shale beneath the earth's surface in order to break up and extract petroleum from the shale layers deep underground."

In the background, an animation ran of a pipe drilling into the ground, past different colored layers of earth, deep under a thick blue layer marked with the words "ground water," through a few more layers, and then sideways. Blue dots representing water then shot down the pipe and out of what must be tiny holes in the end of the pipe. Tiny cracks appeared in the rock layer. Fractures. The tiny blue dots were then joined by black and brown dots, and the process reversed itself, back up to above ground. The dots then separated, with the black going into one tank and the blue and brown ones into another.

"Back above ground, the oil is separated from the water and sand, which is either used again on more fracking, or disposed of according to EPA regulations."

"That seems like an awful lot of trouble," I said.

"Getting oil has never been the easiest job in the world," Viv said. "Jed Clampett made it look too easy."

On screen, Browning gestured with his hands as he tried, emphatically, to educate his audience.

"For several years, as you probably know, there has been speculation about the link between fracking and increased earthquake incidents. Scientists now believe it's not the actual fracking process that is causing the quakes, but rather the process of injecting the waste water from the drilling back underground. In other words, the use of injection wells."

On screen, the black dots were pumped into a little cartoon tanker truck, which drove away as the blue and brown dots were once again pumped down to rest below the ground water table.

"The EPA has determined that the disposal of this waste water is not a threat to our drinking water, but what is coming to light now is that this process—this practice of pumping that water back underground—is actually lubricating these layers of rock that have, for thousands and millions of years—"

"Thousands and millions," Viv scoffed.

"Rested against each other." He pointed out the layers in the picture. "The pressure of these enormous layers of rock, stacked so far below the earth's surface, has kept them from shifting." In front of him, Browning held his hands flat, palm to palm. His upper arms stiffened as he increased the pressure. "What scientists are saying is that these layers of water between rock are decreasing that pressure –" He drew his hands slightly apart. "and making it easier for them to –" He slid his hands apart. "slide against each other. As they did the afternoon NorthStar Elementary collapsed."

"Good lord, you are boring," Viv said. She ended that video and clicked the next one.

The next story began with a map of the United States, with bubbles popping up all over the country, then individual pictures of structural failings. A shopping center, another school, several highway retaining walls, a bridge collapse. A stack of papers labeled "Engineering Report" dropped onto a desk, with a dramatic red stamp that read "SAFE." On top of that, another stack, titled "Earthquake Risk" landed, stamped "HIGH RISK."

"Drama queen," Viv pronounced, and clicked the next link. I sipped my coffee and didn't comment. It seemed bad form to be disrespectful of the guy just a week or so after he died, but I had to agree. He seemed to relish this all to an unseemly degree. I guess that kind of excitement was what made him good at his job, though.

On Viv's phone screen, the drama queen was back.

"Unless you're new to the area, you will probably recognize the Baucum name. Baucum Engineering has been involved in such jobs as the new Texas Tech football stadium, the four new elementary school campuses for Lubbock ISD, and a host of other high-profile projects. Not only that, but locally the Baucum name is synonymous with heroism. David Baucum's grandfather was one of the first soldiers on the beaches of Normandy, before D-Day. Interestingly enough, that mission also involved geotechnical engineering. Take a look at this Channel 11 footage from almost forty years ago."

The screen switched to a black and white film of hundreds of boats heading toward a beach. "Sword Beach in France, 1944. The D-Day invasion, when thousands of allied soldiers braved rough waters and enemy fire to liberate a nation under Nazi occupation. Among these thousands, however, two soldiers had the distinction of having been there before."

The scene cut again to a man in an office, wearing a red collared shirt and a bad '70s comb-over. He was talking and pointing to a certificate. "For valuable and honorable service to the cause of freedom," he read proudly. He turned and smiled at the camera.

"Before the powers that be could decide where to invade, they had to consider a lot of factors. One of the many things they had to consider was whether the beaches we landed on could hold us. Could it hold all that heavy equipment? Could we get our boats in there, get the men offloaded, without sinking into the sand and making everyone sitting ducks? They needed some volunteers to go in and take samples of the ground there, to determine whether it was a viable plan.

"I mean, that's the level of thought that went into this mission. They did their best to leave no stone unturned. Would you have thought of that?" He laughed. "I sure wouldn't have. I mean, I would now," he laughed. "I would after spending the last thirty-something years in the field. But back then, that's the first time I learned that digging around in the dirt could give you such important, practical information. When I got out of the service and came back home and knew I needed to pick a career, well...I remembered that, and I thought that sounded like a pretty good career. And here we are." He laughed.

"Here we are," the reporter echoed. He looked around the office. "A pretty good career, as you say."

Switch to the narrator voice as the screen showed Baucum and the 70s reporter studying a map on the wall of the office.

"Baucum's mission: to join other allied troops in a covert mission to obtain soil samples from the very beaches where they would land for the D-Day invasion. In the middle of the night, without the aid and protection of their fellow soldiers."

Back to the men talking, still at the map. The reporter points to a jagged line where the sea met the sand.

"And so you snuck ashore and took soil samples from the beach?"

"That's right. We had our wet suits on, we got off the boat a mile or so off shore, and swam in during the night."

"That must have been scary."

"Oh, it was terrifying, let me tell you. We knew there were jerrys all over that place, just itching for something to shoot at. But we got on the beach, and they had given us these little metal tubes to poke down." He made a motion with his hand, of prodding something into the sand. "We had to push it down, then turn it so the thing would seal up around our sample, and then pull it out again. And of course, cover up the hole and our tracks as best we could."

"So how long was this tube?"

"Oh..." He held his hands about a foot apart. "About yay big."

"So this entire mission hinged on something about—" The reporter held his hands apart. "About yay big."

"That's right. Well, that and a bunch of other things. Weather, of course, and whether it was in reach of allied fighter planes, how far away was the nearest port, and a bunch of other unanswerable questions. We were able to answer one of those unanswerables, though, and that made us happy. We made a contribution, and that contribution helped turn the tide of the war."

The screen switched to the reporter, this time standing on a sidewalk outside a stone building, a low, curving stone wall at his back. As he walked slowly down the sidewalk, the scene widened to reveal that the low wall was actually a circle, freshly laid and ready to commemorate a special occasion. He talked about his visit with Baucum, then said, "and that's why Dan Baucum is being honored this Saturday, November 11, as the nation pauses to remember our veterans."

"Is that Belle Court?" Viv asked, tapping pause. "It is, look! There's the bell tower. Wow. They've added on a lot since then."

"They have to," I said. "They have to have enough room to house all those rich old widder women."

"Pensioners," Viv said with a sigh, shaking her head. "This is brilliant, though! I can talk about this mission with Nigel." She dragged the little dot at the bottom of the screen back to the left, and the thumbnails flipped past: the old Belle Court, the now-tranquil Sword Beach, the flashes of gunfire and pandemonium of D-Day.

Viv paused the video again and pulled her little notebook and gold pen out of her handbag. As '70s Baucum talked again, I watched as she made notes. *Sword Beach! 28-thousand soldiers! Secret mission authorized by Churchill himself!!*

The scene changed to the modern day sidewalk in the same spot where the '70s reporter had stood, but this time the stone facade of the building was replaced with red brick walls and white plantation shutters. There were four-story buildings looming on the other side of the bell tower, and the 70s reporter was replaced by Peter Browning. "For almost forty years, the Baucum name has been honored, along with the names of the other veterans from the South Plains, during the annual Veterans Day remembrance ceremony. For the first time since the first Baucum Local Hero was awarded in 1978, people are questioning whether it might be time to change that."

The stone circle was the same, with an upgrade of black lamp posts hung with flower pots flanking either side. Trees that had been sticks at the time of the '70s story were now solid and stately.

As he talked, the camera panned around inside the stone circle, to the names inscribed on the stones along the wall. *The Local Hero Award, sponsored by Baucum Engineering*, the stone in the center read. Dan Baucum's name was first on the list. The camera panned to the side, taking in name after name around the circle.

"It's a disgrace. A disgrace to the name of that great man." The shaky voice of an old lady came on now. "I'm not saying we should not honor Dan Baucum. We should. His courage and sacrifice must always be remembered. But it's a shame that now the name is tarnished. From now on, when that name is spoken, what people are going to think of is tragedy. Not heroism."

Viv tapped the screen and the woman's face froze in mid-tirade. "Barbara Hale, you are a tragedy. I swear all that woman does is gripe."

"Were you there when Browning was filming this?"

"No, I didn't see any of it. Too bad he didn't ask to interview me. I could have done better than that."

"That camera girl, Jessica, said they didn't issue the award this year because they didn't get it organized in time. Do you think they just used that as an excuse, though—that people were really thinking about David Baucum and the school collapse and decided to skip the award this year because of that?"

"Maybe, but I doubt it. I haven't heard any talk about changing the award. I find Jessica's story a lot more plausible."

She tapped play again, and the video continued through Barbara Hale's tirade, then moved once again to the pile of rubble at NorthStar, the red and blue ambulance lights flashing, the dad, reaching from one gurney to grab the hand of his daughter, lying still on the next gurney.

"Ugh," I said, hitting the pause button again. "I don't know how many more times I can watch that. Of course, everyone is going to think of tragedy now because every time the Baucum name is uttered, we see this same footage."

"We'll switch to something else. Patrice said there were some interviews with the oil company, right?" She scrolled through the list of links. "Here."

This video opened in the inside of a wood-paneled office. A middle-aged man with a white fringe of hair and a big mole on top of his head sat behind a large desk and smiled at Browning with exaggerated patience.

"Everything we do is completely above board and in line with the regulations of the EPA. We are very careful to follow protocol. Believe me, we have to be. When something goes wrong, we're the first ones everyone looks at. That's okay, we're happy to do it. All the companies I know are doing the same thing. No one is interested in ruining our planet in the name of making a profit."

"Which is exactly what someone would say if they were ruining the planet in the name of making a profit," Viv said. "And you ought to have that mole biopsied."

Peter Browning kept pushing. "You mentioned the EPA, but that's only one regulatory agency. We've talked to the United States Geological Survey—"

"Oh, believe me, we're familiar with USGS," the oilman said.

Browning smiled. "Excellent. Then you know that they believe that the earthquakes could be caused by the use of injection wells, which are the wells used—"

"I know what injection wells are, young man."

Peter gave an uncomfortable smile. "Yes, I'm sure—"

"Listen. Here's the truth. Nobody knows for sure what causes the earthquakes. One scientist says one thing, another one says another. Unfortunately, nobody really knows, and nobody even thinks to ask until something has already happened. People want affordable fuel for their cars, they want the cost of living to stay low. This is what we do. We provide that."

"In the case of NorthStar Elementary—"

"In the case of NorthStar Elementary, a natural disaster occurred and people did what they always do when something horrible happens—they looked for someone to blame."

"Nobody is blaming—"

"No? Let's just get honest, shall we? You're here with your little pen and pad, your camera going, trying to get a good story for your viewers. Here's the story." He lifted a folder from the top of his desk and held it up. "I tried to give it to you and you're more interested in creating a sound bite." He slapped the folder down on top of the desk. "Dorsett Oil and all of our subsidiaries do everything by the book. When the EPA writes a new book, we follow that. We're not interested in being the bad guys, and you're not going to come in here and lay what happened at NorthStar on us. Period. I won't let it happen."

Browning opened his mouth, then shut it again. He shifted in his seat. The room grew completely silent. The camera shifted a little.

"This is weird," I said. "I don't remember this on the news."

"They must have edited it," Viv said. "This story would have been news in itself."

Browning looked at his lap, then put his pen and paper on the desk. "We're on the wrong track here," he said.

The oil man nodded. "Damn straight."

"How about this? How about if you just tell me what you'd like for the people to know? I know you must feel attacked—"

The oil man laughed. "Son, I can handle your questions. I'm just not going to let you run me down a road I have no reason to be on."

Browning lifted his hands. "No, no, of course, I'm not saying—"

"Wow," I said. "He's backpedaling as hard as he can."

"Crikey. The lad folded like a house of cards, didn't he?"

"Here is what I'll say," the oil man said. "We get oil out of the ground. That's what we do. We use the best, most efficient methods we can, and we play by the rules. We respect the rules. The rules are there for a reason. We're playing the short game—getting the resources out for people to use, and staying on the right side of the law—and the long game. Namely, making sure our grandkids and their grandkids get to enjoy this planet like we have." He sat back and spread his hands. "Now, from time to time the smart guys come along and say that we need to change the rules. We've learned something new. Now everything has to be done like this instead of like that." He shrugged. "Okay. So we change how we do it. That's the way it's always been done, and that's the way it always will be done."

"Fair enough." Browning chewed his bottom lip for just a moment. "Now. Okay. If you don't mind, I would like to ask a question about what you just said." His head was ducked into his shoulders a bit, and the confident smile of five minutes ago was significantly subdued.

Oil Man nodded sagely.

"You said, from time to time the smart guys come along and say we need to change the rules. Do you believe, based on your years of experience in this industry, that a change in those rules is coming? That it's needed?"

Oil Man shrugged. "I wouldn't be surprised. Maybe, though, it's not our rules that need to be changed. If that earthquake we had would have happened in California, it wouldn't even have made the news."

"My contact at the USGS said that we either need to eliminate the use of injection wells, or adapt to the effects."

"Well, we're back to assuming that the injection wells cause the earthquakes, and I think we've established that I'm not even going to slow down and wave to that."

Peter gave a sickly smile. "But if it's shown there's something to adapt to..."

"If it's shown that there's something to adapt to, of course we will. But in my experience, the regulators don't wait until something's proven. If they decide we need to adapt, they'll let us know." He grinned widely.

Browning nodded, then turned toward the camera. "Okay, you can cut it now."

"Okay," a disembodied voice said. The video ended.

"Was that Jessica?" I asked Viv.

"It sounded like her."

"Maybe we should talk to her. If she was there during Browning's interviews, she might have some inside information."

"Like what?"

"I don't know—like, how the mood of the interview was, before it was all edited and put to music. See, I don't remember this interview on television very well, but it seemed like it was pretty straightforward. Two guys talking, congenial. If we could get a handle on how all the interviews actually were, it might point to something."

"The only thing this one points to is that Peter Browning was a chicken-weasel." Viv downed the rest of her coffee and scrolled through the remaining links. "It looks like these are all interviews with Baucum. At least, his name is in the title."

"Here's one about a quake in North Texas."

The story was fairly short, less than two minutes. A family's newly built dream home was so badly damaged, they were in the process of deciding whether it would be better to repair it or tear it down and start over. Fracking had increased in that area around the same time they signed the contract to build. At the end of the story, Browning wrapped it up from the news desk by reminding everyone of the similar incident in Lubbock. Behind him, a still picture of the collapsed NorthStar Elementary and another one of David Baucum's smiling face sat in the background.

In the next video, Browning went further afield, into Oklahoma and points north. On a map of the United States, red dots radiating pulsing, concentric circles popped up one by one. Pictures spun from off camera and landed on the map. A collapsed roof. A failed highway embankment. A gash in the earth that a crowd of people gathered around.

David Baucum's face spun and landed in the center of all those disasters.

Viv sighed. "It's no wonder the poor man drank himself to death. Watching all this kind of makes me want to jump off a tall building, and it's not even my fault."

I shook my head. "I'm still not convinced it's *Baucum's* fault that this happened. I mean, it was an earthquake. An act of God or, like the man said, a natural disaster."

I leaned back in my seat. "I can't watch anymore. This is exhausting." I reached for my purse. "I'm going to go home and cuddle with my dog for a while."

"You sure you don't need to check in with the hubs first?" Viv asked, fishing my keys from her purse.

"I'll text him that I've survived our first official day of investigation," I said, taking the keys from her.

She frowned. "I can drive."

"You have to sneak back in, right? Or else you'll get grounded again?"

She scowled, but didn't argue.

I patted her on the arm. "Careful, Viv. Your aura's looking a bit brownish."

Back at Trailertopia, Frank and Stump were waiting patiently for me to get home and fix dinner. I stood in front of the fridge for so long that I forgot what I was doing.

I kept thinking about the "gripey" Barbara Hale, who had proclaimed the Baucum name such a disgrace now. I wondered what it would be like to be David Baucum. Growing up in a town where everyone knew your name. Where everyone thinks the best of you and expects the best from you.

It was a far cry from the way I'd grown up. As I'd reflected yesterday, my own personal bar was set pretty low.

And a far cry, of course, from Jacob-the-heel-grabber.

Someone with the Baucum name would be expected to do great things. Be a hero, even.

What would it do to someone like that, to fail so publicly? And then to lose the family business, on top of everything else? The business his war-hero grandfather had started and passed down to him. A fall like that would be difficult for anyone, but when you're falling from an even higher platform...

"Ummm," Frank said.

I looked up to see him and Stump both looking at me from their spot in the recliner, and realized I'd done nothing but stare at the open fridge for the past several minutes.

"Should I get the peanut butter and jelly?" Frank offered.

I shook my head and laughed. "Sorry, no."

Frank wasn't trying to be critical. He would honestly be fine with PB&J, and to be honest, it didn't sound half bad to me, either. But I was cold and kind of depressed from the afternoon. I wanted comfort food.

I had grilled chicken, which according to the unrealistically ambitious plan I'd made for myself on grocery shopping day, was to be paired with acorn squash and roasted brussel sprouts. I could not—nor did I want to—imagine the circumstances wherein brussel sprouts would be considered comfort food.

I pulled the chicken from the fridge, mentally ordered the crisper to keep those veggies crisp for a few more days, and added cheese, butter, tortillas and salsa to the counter.

I toasted the tortillas with the chicken and cheese, slapped them together and cut them into wedges, set a plate full on the coffee table with a bowl of salsa—which I reminded myself was, after all, a vegetable, and collapsed onto the sofa with Stump.

"Hard day?" Frank asked. This, for Frank, was the very height of sympathy and concern.

I shrugged. "I think the universe is telling me I suck."

CHAPTER SEVEN

Smashing

Between dogs the next day, I tried to watch the rest of the videos on my phone, but I was having trouble finding the links Trisha sent us. Finally, I just Googled Peter's name and came up with a video we hadn't seen yesterday—an interview he'd done with the Dallas NBC affiliate about earthquakes in the North Texas area.

I had to hand it to the guy—whatever that *it* thing was that made some people attract attention, Peter Browning had it. He was professional, the kind of person who would be deemed 'trustworthy' by viewer polls.

A far cry from the weasel who had caved to the oil man in yesterday's video.

At the end of that story, too, he brought the video back around to the NorthStar building collapse and David Baucum's leering face.

"Jeez-O-Peet ," I said. Why did he keep bringing everything back to Baucum Engineering? Things that clearly weren't associated in any way? It was starting to look personal.

A thought struck me. What if Browning had been on to something with Baucum, and this was his way of trying to hammer home that message, or that suspicion?

I texted Viv: *I'll be done by 3. Pick us up to go to Trisha's office?*

She answered immediately: *Smashing.*

I hoped that meant she was ungrounded, but as I went back to shaving poodle feet (on a schnauzer, of all things!) I decided that it really didn't matter. Viv would find a way to stay on the case.

Once we got to the station, Viv and I decided to divide and conquer. She was going to talk to Jessica about Peter's interview with the oil guy, and Stump and I would talk to Tri-Patrice.

As she'd been yesterday, Tri-Patrice was in her office with the door closed but seemed happy enough to take a break when I came in carrying Stump.

"What did you think of that interview with Baucum?" she asked.

"We didn't get that far," I admitted.

"Seriously? That was the most powerful one."

I must have had a funny look on my face, because she laughed and said, "What?"

"I have to admit...it's been hard to watch. Maybe because it was so...concentrated? With us watching one after the other about the same thing? But I was really uncomfortable with the way Peter handled the whole Baucum angle."

"What do you mean? Baucum Engineering was a big player in the collapse. That'll be more apparent when you watch his interview."

"But it's not just the school collapse. It's all of them. Oklahoma, Kansas, Colorado, South Dakota. I mean, they go all over the place, but every time he brought it back to Baucum and the NorthStar collapse. He kept showing that same horrible graphic in every story."

"What horrible picture?"

"The one with the school all in rubble with Baucum's leering face plastered over it. Looking at it like that, it's as if the poor man is gleeful about the disaster. Why do that?"

"Well, I'm sure Peter wanted to make it apparent why he's showing events that happened in other places—he wanted viewers to make the connection that this isn't just one of those things that happen elsewhere. I mean, if there's no connection to here, there's no reason for us to be doing the story, right?"

"I guess." I sat silently for a minute, rubbing Stump's ear. I wasn't sure if I should bring this up, with Trisha in her delicate condition and her concerns about Peter's cause of death.

"What?" she asked.

"I just...do you think all those stories could have been part of what drove Baucum to do what he did?"

Trisha shrugged. "How would we ever know? We don't know that he even meant to overdose. I mean, the ME classified it as accidental. Maybe he was self-medicating to deal with the fallout, and he went too far. But Peter didn't say anything that wasn't true."

"I know that. I just wonder if maybe Browning took things a little further than he needed to. He jumped on something that looked sensational and ran with it, not caring about the fallout."

"Salem," Trisha said patiently. "Peter was an investigative reporter. So, he investigated. He found something to be concerned about, and he reported on it. Baucum was under a lot of strain, but that strain was in large part his own fault. He should have been more diligent than he was, and people were hurt because he wasn't. Watch Peter's interview—you'll see. Baucum knew he was at least partially responsible, and the guilt that was rightfully his is probably what drove him to do what he did, whether he meant for it to cause his death or not."

"But..." I frowned, then nodded. I was here mainly to ease Trisha's mind, not contribute to her anxiety.

I decided to switch topics a bit. "I also wondered if, perhaps, Peter was onto something more with Baucum. Something he wasn't able to share just yet, and this hyper focus was his way of keeping a bead on Baucum while he worked it out?"

Trisha drew in a breath, her eyes wide. "I don't know. Maybe."

She looked so instantly hopeful that I immediately wanted to backpedal. "I mean, that's just a wild guess. It could be nothing."

"It could be something, though."

Despite my moment of panic, I felt kind of proud of myself. Maybe I had a knack for this after all. "Did he say anything along those lines?"

She shook her head. "No, not really."

"Any hints that he was working on something bigger?"

She thought for a second. "Actually, yes. The whole fracking and earthquake scene had kind of become Peter's area of expertise, and you saw by the list of videos I gave you that he was active in pursuing more stories. He did say, though, that he was investigating a new angle. I asked what it was, but he just shook his head and said he didn't have enough to share just yet but would let me know." She bit her lip and shook her head. "Wow. I'll bet that's it. I'll bet it's got something to do with that. I should have followed up on this sooner." She scribbled on a notepad. "I'll tell Bobby Sloan. They need to be checking his computer. If he was talking to someone about a new angle, there would be some record of it on there."

For Trisha, who—God bless her, I loved her, I really did, but still—was a bit of a control freak, this seemed oddly hands off. "Is that how you guys normally handle stuff? They're kind of their own agents and bring you the stories once they're ready?"

"Honestly, no. But Peter was bringing in big stories. He'd proved he had good judgment. I figured I could trust him to follow up what needed to be followed up."

"If Baucum wasn't dead, I would suspect him," I said. "Revenge, you know." I decided to skirt around the question I really wanted to ask. "After Baucum died, did Peter ever express any remorse? Have second thoughts about the way he'd handled the stories?"

Trisha shook her head. "No. Listen, Salem, you have always had a tender heart for the underdog and I admire that in you. But Baucum wasn't the underdog here. He had a huge responsibility and didn't take it seriously enough. He brought himself down."

"I guess I need to watch that interview," I said.

"You do. You'll see why Peter probably didn't lose one second of sleep about the way things turned out. Baucum's hubris. I mean, seriously, Salem. The guy was unbelievably cold about the whole thing. And Peter was thrilled with the attention the stories were getting. Everything was going his way. He had job interviews in Dallas, Houston, and Memphis. He was leapfrogging over two market sizes, and he was looking forward to getting a shot at the big leagues. I didn't see anything that would make me think he was second-guessing the work at all."

Hmmm...cashing in on a tragedy to work his way up the ladder. I decided that, dead or not, I didn't care much for Peter Browning. "Does it feel slimy to you that he dogged so much on Baucum, when the poor guy clearly had suffered? He lost his business, he lost his reputation—"

"And a little girl who dreamed of being a prima ballerina has lost that. Along with any hope of walking across the stage at high school graduation or dancing at her own wedding. It's a horrible, horrible situation. Calling it a horrible situation doesn't seem slimy to me, no."

"I guess you're right." Although it still seemed slimy to me. I stood and hefted Stump onto my hip, remembering how Misty Monahan had appeared that night at the side of the dirt road when Peter's body had been found. I set aside my discomfort with the man. People who worked with him and knew him well were obviously devastated by his death. Maybe I just didn't understand the news business that well.

"Is Misty Monahan working today? I'd like to talk to her while we're here. Maybe see if she knows anything about that new angle Peter was working on."

Trisha frowned. "She's supposed to be here, but she called earlier and said she wasn't feeling well. That's the third time this week, which is weird because before this she never called in sick once. Remember that fire out at the cotton gin? She covered that with a 102 degree fever."

"Wow. Impressive," I said, but I was thinking, *Good lord, why? There were three other TV news teams, a newspaper, and countless radio stations. Why drag yourself out of your sickbed to say what a dozen other people are also saying?*

"This whole thing with Peter has really taken a toll on her. They were very close."

Trisha's door flew open and Viv popped her head in. "Salem, come see what I just found out!"

I followed after Viv, who quick-stepped through the news room back to where Jessica, the camera girl, stood, looking slightly confused.

Viv planted herself beside Jessica and gestured toward her like a game show hostess. "She's British! Another Brit! Can you believe that?"

"No," I said. "I can't." I had only talked to Jessica once, but she clearly was not British.

"What about the white cliffs of Dover? Breathtaking, right?"

"We moved from there before I was two years old," Jessica said, with the thin patience of someone who had already tried to say this at least three times.

"But you were born there?"

"On a US Air Force base, yes."

"Do you have dual citizenship, then? Oh, don't you miss it?"

"No," Jessica said, not specifying which question she was answering.

Clearly it was time for me to step in. "Has Patrice told you that we're investigating the death of Peter Browning?"

Jessica blinked at this sudden change in topic, but seemed relieved. "Ummm, no, she didn't."

"Yes, yes, we need to get down to business," Viv said, reaching into her pocket.

Don't give her a card, I prayed silently. She's young. She'll be traumatized.

In an effort to push the conversation forward before Viv had a chance to pull the cards out, I said, "We've been going through some of Peter's interview tapes. Some of the more notable stories he did. Were you with him for those interviews? It's hard to tell from watching the video."

"Hopefully it's impossible to tell," Jessica said. "Misty and I are kind of a team on most stories, but yeah, I worked with Peter, too."

"Good. We wondered if maybe you would be willing to talk with us and give us your take on some of the different stories."

She looked between us again, then gave the slightest of shrugs. "Sure, I guess so."

"Nothing major," I assured her. "We don't really know what we're looking for. But maybe just your general impression of the way people reacted to him."

"For instance, can you remember any instances of people getting angry with him over an interview."

Jessica gave a short laugh. "Of course. People got mad at him all the time. He was kind of annoying."

Viv and I glanced at each other.

"Not a fan, huh?" Viv said.

"Oh, he was okay. I mean, he was trying to do something, right? Trying to get noticed, trying to get a bigger piece of the pie. Tell a bigger story. If that means you get annoying sometimes..." She shrugged again.

"So, do you remember specific instances when he was so annoying that he would actually cause someone to want him dead?"

She rolled her eyes slightly and shook her head once. "Not one that stands out, no. I mean, hindsight, right? I was a little nervous about the whole Space Cop thing. Nobody wants to make the cops mad, you know?"

"Right." I had actually been there and done that. She was right. You don't want to do that.

"But then that all kind of blew over and things went back to normal."

"Did it?" Viv asked. "Tell us about that interview with the chief of police."

"It was tense. He made it clear that he didn't care for what Peter was doing. He felt like it could have been handled a lot better if they'd kept it private. There was no need to create a big stink."

"How did Peter react to that?"

"Peter loved it. He seemed to be excited by it, honestly. I mean, look around." She cast her own glance around the news room. "We're all here because we like to be in the thick of it, right? We like it when stuff happens. We want to be a part of it. Peter was no different."

"You said you didn't want to make the cops mad. Did they get mad, with all those stories about the Space Cop toy thing?"

Jessica sighed. "Oh, there was some pushback, for sure. We got lots of calls. People would scream "Back the Blue!" at us when we drove by in the station van. Or when we were standing out by the road somewhere giving a traffic report or a weather report. But that was just people around town. Not the police, necessarily."

"So they were professional about it?"

"Sure. I mean, like I said, the police chief was mad about the whole thing, but when it came down to it, he knew that Peter was just telling a story about a thing that happened. The thing that happened—that was the real problem. He would have chosen for it to be handled differently, but he couldn't exactly fault us for reporting it."

"There is a theory that Peter was murdered and it was made to look like a suicide." I didn't tell her it was Trisha's theory, of course. " And, of course, a policeman would know ways to murder someone and make it look like a suicide."

"I mean, I guess. It could have happened."

"But not Chief Simon?"

"I'd be really surprised. Shocked. He seemed more like he was ready to chuck the whole thing and be done with it, if you ask me. It takes a lot of passion to sustain a grudge for almost a full year, and that guy just didn't have it in him. He was beyond burned out."

"What about one of his officers? Or the one who was fired? What was his name—Brownlow? Or his wife?"

Jessica shook her head. "You're completely out of my sphere. I was there for the wife's interview, but if she was going to kill anyone, it would have been her husband. She was furious with him."

We all digested that for a moment. Then Viv said, "Okay, moving away from the police. We watched the unedited video of Peter's interview with Dorsett Oil. That was our first experience with an unedited video, and I have to say, we were a little surprised."

"Oh. Why?"

"Well, surprised by Browning's demeanor, I guess. We've seen him as the hard-nosed investigative reporter, going after the facts. But he kind of..." I didn't know a polite way to phrase it.

"Rolled over," Viv said.

Jessica lifted her chin as if remembering, then smiled. "Oh, yeah. I do remember that. He was so mad after that."

"Mad?"

"Mad at himself, I guess. Embarrassed that he'd let the old guy bulldoze him like that." She nodded again, looking off with a smile, remembering. "Yeah. I remember thinking that, too, that he just caved on the guy. Suddenly he was Mr. Deferential."

"Did he say why? I mean, this was after his big showdown, expose thing with the police. He has a few months more experience, and by all accounts, a big win under his belt. You would think he would have had the backbone to stand up to Dorsett."

"I thought so, too. Okay, it's coming back to me now. He was very silent, kind of stompy, you know, when we were loading the stuff back in the car and heading back to the station. Then, when he got in the editing bay and started editing the footage, he got really mad, but...an embarrassed mad, I guess I'd call it. Stomping around, muttering under his breath. I steer clear of people when they get that way. But Misty watched the video and asked him why he'd rolled over like that—just like you said, he rolled over—and he said he just felt suddenly really uncomfortable there. Like he got a bad vibe or something. A really threatening vibe. And he wanted to get out of there."

I wondered what Serena would think of that. A bad vibe. Huh.

"You were there, too. Did you get a bad vibe?" Viv asked.

She shrugged. "Not any more than I always get when we're doing an interview with someone who doesn't really want us there. But, I mean...I'm behind the camera, right? People just look at the camera. Never the person behind it. So even when things get tense, I don't feel that same level of exposure that the reporters experience. Misty talked about that sometimes, about how she felt like she was the point person for everything people hated about news media."

I thought about that for a moment.

"Anyway," Jessica went on, "Once he got outside, and then especially back at the station when he played it back, he was really embarrassed. He had to edit out a lot of it just to get a decent interview for the broadcast."

"Did you do a lot of interviews with him?"

Again with the little shrug. "I mean, sure. We have four photogs and four reporters, so there's just so much rotation you can go through. But like I said, Misty and I are pretty much a team. We work together as much as we can."

"How typical was that for him? To be cowed by someone he's interviewing?"

"That's the only time I saw it. After that he seemed to be even more determined to get whatever story he wanted."

I thought about that for a second. "Do you remember which story he did first—the Dorsett Oil or the Baucum interviews?"

She thought for a second. "I don't really remember. But the dates should be on the videos, in the bottom corner."

I made a mental note to check the dates.

"Now, one last question. Patrice said Peter was working on something but hadn't told her yet what it was. A new angle, I think she said. So I assume it had something to do with the fracking and earthquake connection. Did he tell you anything about that?"

She shook her head. "No. Nothing like that."

I switched Stump to my other hip and chewed my lip. "Do you think he would have said something to Misty?"

She frowned. "I doubt it. I mean, they were kind of competitors, you know."

I nodded as if I did, indeed, know that, but of course I didn't. They worked for the same station. One would think they were collaborators, not competitors.

But what did I know?

"I would like to talk to her, too, but Tri-Patrice said she was out sick today."

"Oh, she's coming in. She texted me and said she felt better, so she's going to go ahead and come in."

"That's good. Trisha—Patrice, I mean—said Misty had been sick quite a bit lately, and she thought it was because she was taking Browning's death particularly hard. Since they were so close, you know."

Jessica raised her eyebrows. "Hardly. I mean, yeah, sure, she's been kind of sick lately, but most of the time it's pretty short-lived and she's back to work as soon as she can be."

"So, she's not particularly bothered by Peter's death?"

Jessica gave a short laugh. "I mean, of course she's upset about it. We all are. It's a sad thing. But Peter was no closer to Misty than any of the other of these guys are."

I nodded as if this was exactly what I expected.

"She texted you, though, that she was feeling better and planned to come in?"

"Well, yeah, we are pretty close," she said with a short laugh. "Much more than she and Peter ever were."

"Will she be here soon?"

"Should be any minute."

"Smashing," Viv said. "We'll wait outside and see if we can catch her on her way in. It shouldn't take but a tick."

"A tick?" Jessica and I both asked.

"Like a tick of the clock, sillies," Viv explained.

"I am a dog groomer," I reminded her. "Tick means something completely different to me."

"Well, I would expect that from you, but not from a fellow Brit," Viv announced over her shoulder as she headed for the parking lot.

"You know that you can't actually, like, convert to being British," I said as I tagged behind. "You do get that, right?"

She sighed. "You know, I rather think I can, if I want to. I mean, if I moved there and took up their customs. Learned their ways. Eventually the culture would have to...permeate, right?"

"Eventually," I conceded. This was not the time to remind her that she was upwards of 80 years old and there was just so much "eventually" left for her.

I decided to change topics, since some of the responses we'd gotten this afternoon were not meshing. "I wonder how Jessica and Trisha can both work with these people and have such different views on them?"

"Like how?"

"Trisha specifically said that Misty and Peter were close. But Jessica seems to think they're more like competitors and not real friends at all."

"That's odd. But my money is probably more on what Jessica says. She's their age, she's more of a peer. Patrice is in a supervisory role, so they probably act different around her than they do around Jessica."

We reached the parking lot just as Misty was pulling into her space.

"Since I did most of the talking with Jessica, I'm going to let you take the lead on Misty," I said. I remembered the swift way Misty had handled us at the Veterans Day event, and how she had visibly pulled herself together before she had to report on the finding of Browning's body. She was obviously upset, but she found some inner reserve of strength somewhere to do what needed to be done. She struck me as a decent person, but someone not to be trifled with. Someone who might possibly see right through our nonsense.

"Driven career women intimidate me," I admitted. "Young people who so clearly have their act together. I can't relate to that."

"We don't have to relate, we just have to get information from her." Viv slid her sunglasses on and took off across the lot.

"We have to create some kind of connection if we want her to open up to us. Make sure you ask about that new angle Peter was talking about."

"You ask her, chicken."

"No, it's your turn. I've already faced down one intimidating woman this week, trying to help you land Nigel. I need some recovery time."

"Well, don't worry. I'm not intimidated by Misty Monahan. I've got knickers older than she is. Miss Monahan!" she called. "Please. If you have a minute."

Misty closed her car door and slung her handbag over her shoulder. She raised an eyebrow in question. "Sure. What is it?"

Viv pulled a business card from the inside pocket of her jacket. I cringed inside, but let it go. I waited for the usual look of unsettled confusion to appear on Misty's face.

But Viv didn't give her time to ponder the graphics. "We are investigating the death of Peter Browning," she announced.

"Weren't you doing that at the Veterans Day thing?"

"Unofficially," Viv said. "It's official now. Do you have time for a few questions?"

Something I had discovered in Viv's and my interviews is that people tend to think they have to let you ask them questions. As if we're some kind of pseudo-police. They don't, of course. They could tell us to go take a hike and be well within their rights. They rarely do, though.

Misty was going to be the exception, I could see immediately.

"No, I don't. I'm late already, in fact."

"It'll only take a few minutes. There are people who believe Peter was murdered, but the police have written it off as a suicide and won't investigate further. Any information you can give us is going to help get to the truth."

She hesitated, then turned her phone to check the time.

"Peter told Patrice that he was chasing down a new angle," Viv forged on, bless her relentless heart.

"A new angle on what?"

Viv shrugged. "No one appears to know. But if he was onto something dangerous, that could come into play here."

Misty just frowned, but didn't say anything.

"He didn't say anything to you about a new angle?"

"No."

"Nothing? Patrice says you two were very close."

Misty drew her head back, looking borderline offended. "We weren't very close. I mean, we were co-workers. We spent a lot of time together, but only what was needed to get the job done."

"Well, I think Patrice is going to turn his computer over to the police, so they can find out if there's anything worth following up on."

"Yes, well," Misty said. She opened her mouth to say something, but then stopped and frowned hard at the ground, as if something had just occurred to her. She chewed her lip. "Is that all you needed? Because I have to get—"

Viv reached out and touched her arm. "Listen, Love, we're just looking for what happened to Peter Browning." She patted Misty's arm. "That's all. We're not here to throw stones or muddy the water with things that don't pertain to his death.

We're just trying to get to the truth. Now, we already know about some of the, let's say, poor decisions you've made lately."

Misty's and my jaws dropped at the same time.

"I'm just saying," Viv said. "It's true, isn't it? You and Peter Browning had an affair? And now you're pregnant with his child?"

Misty's eyes blazed. "Who told you that?"

"Don't worry, it's not common knowledge or anything."

"At all," I reassured her, seeing as how this was the first time I was hearing it. How in the world had Viv figured that out? And why hadn't she told me?

"Of course, it's not common knowledge. I haven't told anyone yet except Peter. How did you know?"

Viv ignored the question. "As I said, we are aware of that situation, but we're not going to dwell on that unless it appears that it's germane to the case."

I nodded my agreement, because there were no words I could say. What had I missed?

"But I'll be honest. You don't seem like the hook-up type to me. I would imagine that you had more than just an affair with Peter Browning. I imagine you two had a relationship. Something beyond the superficial."

Misty's mouth worked, but she didn't say anything. Her eyes became hard, and she stared Viv down.

"You know nothing about me. If you did, you would know that I'm also not the type to be manipulated into spilling my guts to you with a little tenderness and flattery. Now if you'll please step back, I have a job to do."

She hitched her purse higher on her shoulder and stalked into the building.

"Well," Viv said as we watched her go. "I guess she told me."

"I told you she was intimidating," I said. "How did you figure out she was pregnant with Peter Browning's baby?"

"You see, but you do not observe, Watson. That's what that hot guy on Sherlock says. Anyway, all the clues were there. She's sick a lot lately, but just for short periods of time. They either had a close relationship, or they had a combative one, depending on who you ask. Sounds like romance to me."

It actually kind of did.

"Plus, you saw how defensive she got when I called them very close. Clearly something up with that."

I pondered that for a while. "If Peter Browning was expecting two babies from two different mamas, that could be a lot of pressure for a guy."

Viv nodded. "What did Patrice say that note said? I didn't want it to turn out like this?"

"Something like that," I said. "That could fit this situation, I guess."

I wondered if knowing this new bit of information might sway Trisha's theory that Peter couldn't possibly have committed suicide. "Where did Trisha say that note was found?"

"In his car, I think."

"Was his car found where the body was found?"

Viv shrugged. "Let's go ask her."

I grabbed her arm. "No. Misty is in there. I'll call her."

"You'll call her from the parking lot?" She looked at me like I was stupid or something.

"Yep. Windy, call Trisha." Hard to believe, but I used to be the kind of person who actually looked for trouble. Turns out that backbone had been made mostly of tequila. Sober me could be a real wimp. In general, this was a trade-off I was okay with.

Trisha confirmed that Browning's car was found not far from his body, all a few yards off the road on that stand of mesquite trees we'd seen behind the ambulance that Tuesday night.

"I think it's still impounded by the police, but you might check with Bitsy on that."

I ended the call and told Viv.

"Let's go out there."

"To the impound lot? They won't let us see it," I said.

Viv frowned. "Bloody obstruction," she groused. "Let's go back to the scene of the crime, then."

I checked the time. It would be dark soon, but if we were just going to drive through there... "Might as well. Are you okay with taking your car out on the dirt roads?"

Viv frowned at her car. "Hmmmm." She did not like that car.

I said, "Maybe we should drop by Flo's and switch to mine. I'd hate to mess up your new car on those back—"

"Great idea," she said, before I could finish. "It's on the way, anyway."

This was fine with me. Viv had had her car in the shop a dozen times in the few months since she'd bought it. It would not do to get out on a dirt road and have it break down. That's how horror movies started.

So, we left Viv's Caddy at Flo's and piled into the Monster Carlo, with Viv behind the wheel. She drove us over to the south side of town. We swooped off the loop, following the roads back to the area where Browning's body was found. While Viv bounced us along dirt roads, I thought some more about what we'd just learned, trying to put together a picture of Peter Browning.

Hotshot reporter, getting major attention from bigger news markets. A star on the rise.

Family man with a baby on the way.

Adulterer, with *two* babies on the way.

If and when that came to light, his fall from grace was going to be public, at least in local eyes. Browning would then add the phrase "sex scandal" to his other labels.

If I had only seen Browning's reports that included Baucum Engineering, NorthStar Elementary, and the Space Cop toy scandal, I would have tagged Browning with the word 'relentless.' But his work also included that uncut interview with Dorsett Oil, where he had shown a notable—and somewhat confusing—lack of courage.

Thinking of labels put me in mind of Jacob the Heel-Grabber and David Disgrace-to-the-Family-Name Baucum.

As I had done with Baucum, I wondered what all this would do to a person like Peter Browning. He was thrilled with the attention he was getting on the earthquake stories, Trisha had said. Jessica had painted a picture of an ambitious person. He must have seen all these reports as his ticket to a better career.

And then, along comes the threat of a scandal. Would something like that hurt the career of someone in the news business? If he was facing that kind of fall just as he'd been getting started, would it be enough to drive him to the brink?

I also had to consider that Browning was considering something more personal than just a failed career—if his affair with Monahan came to light, of course, his marriage could very well fail, too. Although his treatment of Baucum made me slightly nauseous, there was no reason to think Browning didn't love his wife and want his marriage to succeed. I mean, apart from his infidelity to it, of course.

Viv stopped in the middle of the road, then looked behind us, shifted into reverse, and swung the car so that it was pointed diagonally toward the trees.

The dead branches looked stark and ghostly, lit by the Monster Carlo's headlights. I shivered. "What if someone drives by?"

"On this road? At this time of day? Highly unlikely."

"Still. Maybe we should pull off to the side a little, just in case."

She rose in her seat and craned to see the edge of the road. "Those ditches look deep, and might still be muddy. We'd probably get stuck."

I sighed. I did not want to have to call Tony to come help me get unstuck from what could be a murder scene. "You're right. If someone comes we'll just hop in and pull to the side. You do have your gun, right?" I asked.

"Are you thinking this is going to turn into some kind of dirt-road-rage thing?"

"No, I was just thinking that Tony wouldn't be very happy with me being out here unprotected."

"Well, don't you worry." She stretched and leaned over the back of the seat, tugging her handbag over with a groan. "You are protected." She dug through the bag. "Wait. Where is it?" She pulled out her wallet, her phone and a small notebook she carried for notes she rarely made. After that came a makeup case, a planner, a coupon book, and two sets of keys.

"Why do you have so many keys?"

She shook her head. "I don't even know anymore. I'm just afraid to throw them away." She kept rummaging. Three more lipsticks followed the original makeup case. "Blast. Where is it?"

I turned on the flashlight app on my Smart Enuff phone and held it over her purse.

"There it is!" She pulled out a small handgun. "Look at it. Isn't it cute?"

"Adorable." I reached out and gently pushed the barrel away from my general direction.

Viv slid forward in her seat, tucking the gun into the back of her waistband. "If I had needed to, I could have found it quicker. Besides, I haven't let you get shot yet, have I?"

"True," I said. I opened the door and checked the ground for rattlesnakes—I'm Texan, I can't help myself—before I stepped out. "In fact, you beaned the last guy who tried with a toilet tank lid."

I looked at Stump, pondering whether I should leave her in the car. She would pitch a deafening howling fit if I did, and sound carried out here. Someone might call the cops, and I didn't want to explain to anyone (again) that I hadn't been torturing my dog, that she just had major issues with separation anxiety.

I was hesitant to let her roam around the place where Browning's body had been found, though. I had promised her I would never put her in another dangerous situation after she'd almost been shot at a stakeout one time. I looked around us. We were in the very middle of nowhere. Nothing but dirt road and stripped cotton fields until a row of houses started about a mile away to the west, and town half a mile to the north. I wasn't sure what, if any, hunting season we were in, but there would be no chance for dove or deer in these open fields, so I didn't really have to worry about hunters, either.

"She'll be fine," Viv said.

"It's dark." There was only a faint tinge of pale blue in the center of the sky, and it wouldn't take long for that to fade to dark, too.

"Is she afraid of the dark?" Viv asked. "Or are you?"

"I'm only afraid of snakes and of murderers returning to the scene of the crime," I said.

"All the snakes are hibernating right now. Come on. Let's just go walk through and see what we can find." No mention of a returning murderer, of course.

I sighed and hefted Stump out of the car. I could just hold her. I was more convinced all the time that there was no murderer to return to this scene.

Silently, Viv and I approached the mesquite trees. Four stood, each about fifteen feet tall, in a loose clump. I pointed my flashlight at the base of the trees. Browning's body had been found resting against one of them, but we didn't know which one.

I moved to the side and angled my light down, and things became clearer. The ground around the third tree was noticeably more disturbed than the other three. The dirt was rutted with boot prints dried in the mud and the grass was trampled. I thought I could even make out a faint depression in the dirt, where a body could have lain for three days of rainy weather, sinking slowly into the mud.

Stump grunted, and I shifted her to my other hip, trying to focus my flashlight on the ground. I wasn't sure what I was looking for, but I supposed if I found something besides a dirt clod or a stray cotton boll, I could take it to Bobby. Not that he would take it seriously, but I could at least know I'd done my duty.

"So many footprints," Viv said. She had her own phone out and was using the flashlight to do the same thing I had. It was pretty cool, actually. The lights were very bright and very focused, so the eye could fully concentrate on one small area at a time.

Stump grunted again, and I finally set her down. There was clearly nothing to worry about out here. "I guess Bobby's group kept track of these footprints," I said. "Still. Maybe we should take pictures."

"Good idea." She focused and snapped. "This is one. And here's a different one, smaller." Another snap. "I can't tell if this is the same one or not. Oh well." She snapped it anyway. "Look." She pointed at the ground. "These don't have any sole markings. They're probably from the police, wearing those blue bootie things. The people on CSI wears those at crime scenes."

Every time she snapped, the flash strobed and lit up the night, and it made the loud fake-camera snap sound.

"You know, you can turn off that sound," I said.

"Now, why would I want to do that?" She snapped busily away, filling her phone with pictures that we would not know what to do with.

I studied the ground. There was a fairly definite difference between some of the prints—rounded toe work boots with a waffle sole, more pointed-toe cowboy boots with the square heel, and the ones Viv was talking about, which were just foot-sized depressions in the ground.

"What about the two kids who found the body? I guess some of these could be from them."

"We'll need to get a list of people who were at this scene so we can account for all these prints," Viv said.

"Yeah, I'm sure Detective Sloan will get right on that," I said. I straightened and watched Stump busily sniff the area. I supposed it couldn't hurt for us to have a catalog of different shoe prints out here, but the truth was, we didn't know what we were looking for. I kept looking for something unusual, but was hampered by the fact that I didn't know what unusual meant, in this context.

Stump froze, staring at a spot of high weeds a few yards away.

She growled.

I froze, every nerve pointed toward the direction she was pointing. The dark, dark direction she was pointing.

Without moving one iota, I cut my eyes over to Viv. She'd heard it, too. She was also frozen, her hand pointed toward the ground at the end of the circle of light cast by the phone.

Something rustled in the weeds.

Stump barked once, loudly.

The sound made Viv jerk and the camera went off. The sky lit up, revealing a possum. Its white face and beady little rodent eyes flashed in the brilliant light.

It hissed.

Viv and I both screamed.

I grabbed Stump and took off running for the car. Viv was already halfway there.

I kept screaming, in fact, because that nasty little varmint had given me the heebie-jeebies. "Ewwww!" I screamed as I ran. "Ewwww! Yuck! Ewww!"

"It hissed at me!" Viv shouted over her shoulder. "It's probably rabid!"

We jerked open the car doors, slammed them behind us, and sat, breathing hard. Viv reached behind her and slammed the door lock down, and I did the same, even though I knew not even a rabid possum was going to be able to open the door of a '74 Monte Carlo.

"Did you see it?" Viv asked, peering over the hood of the car.

"Yes, I saw it," I said. "Why do you think I kept saying 'Eww?'" I shivered. "Those things give me the full-on creeps! Nasty little pointy-nosed rodents!"

"Did you see its little hands? It was waving its nasty little hairless hands at me." Her voice sounded haunted. Suddenly she jumped up and peered over the back of the seat. "It didn't follow us back here, did it?"

"Viv, it couldn't possibly have run that fast." Still, I had the overwhelming urge to lift my feet off the floorboards. I looked back the way we'd come, but I couldn't see anything except the trees. The possum was probably far away by now, as scared of us as we were of it.

"Let's get out of here," I said, still struck by the occasional shiver at the memory of that hiss.

"Absolutely." Viv started the car and maneuvered a rough three-point turn in the dirt road.

I shivered again. I looked back over my shoulder, terrified that I was going to see the red beady eyes of a rabid possum looking back at me.

Nothing. Even the trees were too dark to make out now that the headlights were pointed the other way.

I faced forward and adjusted my seatbelt.

"Wait," I said, leaning forward. "What's that?"

Viv peered through the windshield. "Tail lights?"

We looked at each other. "Tail lights?" we said at the same time.

How could that happen? We'd been blocking the entire road.

"Did someone come down the road and turn around?" Viv asked.

"Not that I saw. But I was busy looking at the ground. And the possum."

It was certainly weird, though. The trees weren't that far from the road—forty yards or so? If someone had come by and tried to get by the car, we would have noticed. If someone had come by and turned around, we would have noticed.

Viv looked at me, then floored it. "Let's see who it is."

I slammed against the back of the seat. I hissed in a breath and pulled Stump into my lap. "I don't think whoever it is is trying to get away."

"No?" She leaned forward. "It looks like they're getting further away, not closer."

The lights did seem to be getting further away, but it was hard to tell. I squinted. Was it a pickup? Were there lights along the back of a cab? We were too far away to tell.

We bounced hard over a rut and the car fishtailed a bit on the soft dirt.

"Slow down!" I shouted. "What are we going to do if we catch them? Apologize for being in the middle of the road?"

She hunched over the wheel. "What if it's Browning's killer? You said yourself, the killer always returns to the scene of the crime."

"And what if it is the killer? What are we going to do?"

Viv frowned, and for a second her foot lifted off the pedal. She shifted in her seat. "Reach back there and pull out my gun."

"Umm, no." The car veered toward the right side of the road. "Keep to the middle." We dipped into the ditch and weeds slapped hard against the undercarriage. "Keep to the middle, please."

She sighed and focused on keeping us on the road. "Look. He's gone."

I looked up. Sure enough, the lights were gone.

She frowned at me and sat back in her seat, her shoulders slumped.

"Sorry I was so focused on keeping us from dying in a ditch that I let an unknown person who was probably nobody get away." I pulled out my phone.

"Who are you calling?"

"Bobby. I'm going to tell him we were at the scene of the crime and someone else was there but we don't know who or why."

"He'll love that."

Fortunately, Bobby didn't answer. He probably saw it was me and let it go to voicemail. That was fine by me, I was just doing my duty anyway. This way I could do my duty and report what little I knew without having to listen to him laugh at me.

"Bobby, it's Salem. Viv and I just went to the scene where Browning's body was found. We took a bunch of pictures of different footprints. We were also attacked by a rabid possum."

Viv nodded. "That happened."

"Anyway, an interesting thing happened and I am being careful and reporting it, even though it was probably nothing."

"Probably something." Viv leaned over and shouted into the phone. "Probably the killer."

"So we had my huge cruise ship of a car parked diagonally in the middle of the road. We were the only ones around, of course. But if someone had come by, we would have seen them. We would have been in their way. No one came by. But still, when we left, we could see taillights down the road."

As soon as the words came out of my mouth, a thought occurred to me. I pulled the phone away from my mouth. "There wasn't a cross road, was there?"

"No," Viv said. Then she tilted her head. "Was there?"

We looked at each other. I ended the phone call.

"Do you think we should go back and check?" I asked.

Viv shook her head. "Nah. I'm hungry now."

I started to point out that this was crazy, then noticed the time.

"I could eat," I said. I chalked my hunger up to the near-death-by-rabid-possum experience. Probably life needing to reassert itself after all that trauma.

We reached a Road Ends sign and turned left, back toward town. I looked carefully both ways but saw no more taillights, or headlights, or any lights.

Viv sighed and shrugged. "Oh, well. Let's get some Chinese food and go back to your place to plan our strategy from here."

After a trip through Little Ling's drive-thru, Viv and I carried bags of cardboard cartons up the steps of the wooden deck to my trailer in Trailertopia. I set Stump on the ground and let her sniff around our little yard and take care of her business, relieved that we were all safe at home again.

Stump, basically, was my life. I felt guilty that I had let her, once again, get caught in a potentially deadly situation, but I told myself that she might have saved us from a deadly rabid possum attack. Maybe that was a stretch, but it was possible. She was an excellent sidekick.

She was also my baby, a true companion that I'd found early in the days of my sobriety when I was clinging by a very tenuous thread, and we'd rescued each other.

Although the sight of her always squeezed my heart, Stump could not be called attractive in the traditional sense. Her legs were ridiculously short, and her body was very wide and solid as a brick. The width of her nose and the length of her legs were exactly the same. She was black, with a sprinkling of white on her muzzle. Her tail had a tiny screw tip with three or four red hairs at the very end. It was as if she'd been put together from leftover parts of three or four different dogs and a metal toolbox.

But she was my world, and I loved her. I felt guilty because, until a few months ago, I took her everywhere with me. Then Viv and I got caught in a wild shootout in an alley, and I was certain she would be hit. After that, I vowed to never put her in danger like that again, and I probably shouldn't have taken her with us tonight. I missed having her with me, though.

CHAPTER EIGHT

The Grenade

Frank must have smelled the mushu from his trailer next door. He had his butt in my recliner before I got the sacks unloaded. I grabbed forks and plates from the dish drainer and we all dug into the food around the coffee table.

We tried to take stock, we really did. We kept saying that we were going to make a list of all the facts we knew, once we got some food in our bellies.

But as soon as the food hit my belly, it was as if every bit of energy got diverted into digestion or something.

Viv seemed to have the same problem.

"I think I've hit a wall," she said, leaning back in my saggy sofa.

"Me, too." I was having difficulty stringing two thoughts together. It was either sucking down the Chinese food too fast or a crash from the adrenaline rush.

Frank looked back and forth between the two of us. For the most part, Frank didn't speak unless spoken to, and even then his answers were mostly one word and were as likely to be in Spanish as in English.

He stood and walked to the door, then back.

"Where's your car?" he asked Viv.

"Oh, blast," she said. She lolled her head in my direction. "We left it at Flo's."

"Ugh," I said. I shifted to rise. I would have to take her to Flo's to get her car so she could get back to Belle Court.

"I'll take you."

Viv and I both looked at Frank.

"What?"

"I'll take you back to your place," he said.

I was too tired to hide my shock. "You're volunteering?" I immediately felt guilty, but if Frank was easily offended, he would have not been my friend.

"You're in no shape to drive," he said. "Neither one of you."

Viv looked touched. "No one's said that to me since I got sober."

For some reason, this struck me as hilarious. They left me cackling on the sofa, with Frank looking not entirely sure I was sober at all.

Stump and I made it to bed, and I fell asleep almost immediately. Unfortunately, I woke up way too early the next morning and couldn't go back to sleep.

I decided to make up for lost time from the night before and jotted down a list of all the facts I knew. It added up to precious little.

I thought about Trisha's insistence that I watch Peter's interview with David Baucum, so I decided to pull that up. Again, I wasn't able to find the links she'd sent us, but I kept searching until I found some stuff on Donald Baucum, the grandfather war hero who had started Baucum Engineering. I turned on the lamp beside my bed and jotted down notes on the back of an envelope my utility bill had come in.

Donald Baucum was, indeed, a World War II hero. I read an entire scholarly paper on his mission to gather soil samples at Sword Beach, and I could understand almost all of it. On the face of it, it doesn't sound like it would be that scary to swim to a beach, stick a thing in the sand and then swim back out, but when you factor in German soldiers who would have been quite happy to shoot first and ask questions later, it made the danger a bit more apparent. Add that to the fact that just the two of them went ashore, *and* they couldn't carry any weapons for defense in their wetsuits, and I became sure that I wouldn't have been able to do it.

Baucum came home from the war and went to college and said he chose the major he did because he had begun to see what an interesting field it would be. He liked the world of building, but he didn't necessarily want to work in construction. He married and had a son and a daughter.

Donald Junior, or DJ, followed in his father's footsteps. He worked in the firm and helped make it even more successful. He married and had a son, David. (Apparently, he was loyal enough to keep the same letter, but not enough to carry through to Donald the Third.) Unfortunately, DJ also smoked a lot, and liked his bourbon. He was playing golf on a beautiful March afternoon and dropped dead of a heart attack.

His wife remarried and had another son, and soon after that David followed granddad—who was still alive for a few more years—into the fold of Baucum Engineering and grew the firm with jobs from the highway department, major shopping centers, and, of course, schools. David never married and had no off-spring, so there was no other D. Baucum to take over. Which I supposed was just as well, since there appeared to be nothing left to take over now.

Once the story broke about the soil report, he lost a couple of big jobs. That was news, but only because of the earthquake school connection. I checked the comments on that story. In typical Internet comment style, they were horrible. "Good," people said. "They deserve it after what they did to that little girl." As if the entire Baucum firm stood there and shook that building until it fell on her.

More jobs were lost, and a civil lawsuit was filed. More clients fled. Before the suit even went to trial, Baucum closed the company. Within a week, he was dead of an overdose of alcohol and Ambien. The speculation is that it wasn't an accident, but no one really knew for sure.

I checked the clock. Still an hour before I needed to get in the shower. I clicked another link for a story about the family who'd been injured when the building failed.

Peter began by holding up a framed family portrait of a young family – Mom and Dad, two boys and a girl between them. The scene switched to the family in the backyard, with Dad at the grill, Mom and little sister sitting at the picnic table, laughing at the boys who ran around the back yard throwing a ball and chasing the dog.

Matthew Logan was the head of construction, and the building of the school was a family event. He had three kids who would attend NorthStar Elementary the day it opened. His son was in fifth grade, his only daughter going into third, and another son who would begin kindergarten there.

The scene switched to Peter sitting across from Matthew Logan and his wife in their living room.

"Macon has been hounding me every day for the past six months. He wants to make sure the school is going to be ready in time. He doesn't want these other two to go there and him not have his chance. He was real upset with me when we didn't meet the original deadline."

Every time dad had come home with a story about a delay or a problem on the site, all three kids were up in arms.

"Macon and Meredith knew that if it wasn't finished in time, they'd be doing school in the portable buildings, but Marcus was under the impression that we were just going to make him go to school on a working construction site. And he was okay with that."

The Logan family are used to construction sites. Mr. Logan has worked construction all his life. He often took the family onto job sites.

"If we could do it safely," he said. "After the crew was gone and I knew we wouldn't be in anybody's way. When I knew the site was stable enough for them to walk around. So, they learned early on the environment, got to see firsthand everything that goes into a project, everything that's behind the walls you see and under the floors you walk on."

"They have a perspective a lot of kids don't have," Peter said.

"They do. I'd slap a hard hat on them and we'd take a look."

"It wouldn't bother you any if your kids decided to follow you into the business?"

"Wouldn't bother me a bit." He grinned.

"I want to go back to what you said before. You said, 'If we could do it safely.' March 11 was a day when, by all indications, you could let your kids visit the school safely."

"March 11 was definitely a day when we should have been able to do it safely. It was finished. All the inspections had been done. It was done."

"A brand new building, ready to go."

"Ready to go. The next day, the teachers were going to come in and tour their rooms. They had hired people to move stuff in over Spring break, and when the kids came back from Spring break, it was going to be all new stuff. The kids were excited. Everyone was excited."

"So, you took them all up there. Just the five of you?"

"No, it was the five of us—my wife and I, and the three kids, along with the principal and a couple of the teachers."

"The ribbon cutting was scheduled for the next day."

"That's right. The superintendent and school board were all going to be there, news cameras and everything. This was just a sneak preview."

"And then..."

"And then." He shifted in his chair, his mouth set grimly.

"Describe what happened."

"Meredith wanted to see the cafeteria, and Macon wanted to see the gym. They're side by side, so we were down there. I'd just opened the cafeteria door and Meredith ran inside, when we felt the first rumbling."

"Did you know immediately what it was?"

"No. The first thought that went through my mind was that a pipe had blown somewhere. A small explosion. Meredith turned to me—she was scared and shocked, it was all over her face—but then it stopped. Got real quiet. I thought, "Was that an earthquake?" I couldn't believe it. I had been hearing, of course, about earthquakes around the area, but I'd never felt one before. And I thought, "Well, that wasn't so bad." I started walking toward her to reassure her."

"And then it hit."

"And then it hit."

The screen switched to a shot of the graph that showed the quake's intensity. The first tremor they'd felt was a small red hump. Then the red line spiked.

The wall in the cafeteria collapsed on Logan and his daughter. Out in the hallway, the rest of the family was okay. But under that wall, Matthew and Meredith Logan were trapped and hurt.

"What do you remember from that time under the rubble?"

"Oh, I remember all of it. I never did pass out. I had a blow to my head, my legs were stuck, and my right arm was trapped. But I could hear everything and still see some things."

"Could you hear Meredith?"

"I—" He stopped. Breathed deep through his nose. His face contorted. He looked at the floor in front of him, biting his

lower lip. He shifted in his chair. "I could hear her. She was
calling me. "Daddy, Daddy." I called back to her, told her it was
okay, I would get her out. She said she was stuck. She was
scared. "I want to go home," she said."

"I want to go home."

The scene switched to video of the rescue workers who pulled
the Logans out of the rubble. Some walls of the school stood, but
the gym and cafeteria were open to bright blue sky. Mrs. Logan
and the boys stood at the side of the collapse, looking shocked.

A series of images followed. Meredith, dusty and
unconscious, lying under the white sheet of a gurney, her left
hand dangling off the edge. Matthew, beside her. A close-up of
his hand, reaching out to take her much smaller one across the
space between them, before they were loaded onto the
ambulance.

"The doctors said pretty early on that Meredith wasn't going
to walk again. The kind of injury she had, it just wasn't possible.
With what they were able to do now, they said that she would
never walk again."

"Never walk again. Never dance again."

"Never dance again."

The screen filled with shots of Meredith Logan in her various
dance outfits. White blonde hair, and pink, gap-toothed grin.
Meredith in a pink tutu and white tights; Meredith in a spangly,
fringy flapper dress, wearing a huge red lipsticked smile;
Meredith in a black leotard, the background dark, her young
face in somber profile, the light soft on her tender features.

"She lived to dance."

"Always dancing. Always. We'd be walking down the aisle in
the grocery store and she's waltzing along behind me, listening

to the music in her head. All over the house. At the park. I mean, she would just tune everything out and dance wherever she was."

"Does she understand what's happened? The permanence of it?"

The parents looked at each other. The mom ducked her head quickly. Her shoulders jerked slightly as she sniffed.

"We've been talking about that," Matthew Logan said. "We've told her, of course. And sometimes it seems like she does understand it. When we first told her, she just..." He broke off.

"She acted like she just didn't hear it. She just—" The mom brought a hand down in front of her face. "Shut it completely out. No acknowledgment at all." She sniffed and cleared her throat. "I felt like...she must have overheard some of the hospital staff or someone talking about it. Because she didn't seem shocked or upset, just...completely ignoring it."

"So, we decided we had to give her time to process it." He shrugged. "We didn't need to push it. She had plenty of time."

"The rest of her life."

That hung heavy in the air.

After a few painful moments, Peter went on. "So, tell us about those first days after the earthquake. There were things going through your mind as a father, of course. And as someone who'd also been injured. What about as a construction foreman? What was going through your head as the person who'd been in charge of constructing the very wall that had fallen on you?"

He shook his head slowly as he relived those days. "Lying in that hospital bed, I went over and over those plans in my mind. Had we followed them right? Had we screwed up somewhere? I mean, an earthquake is an act of God and you can't design for every disaster like that. You just can't. But we certainly try. We try to build things that will withstand what we know is a high risk. In this area, that's usually wind. Wind is the biggest threat to our structures. So we build with that in mind."

"Everyone knows we're here in tornado alley. Lubbock has had devastating tornadoes before."

"Right. The engineers and architects who design the plans— they design with the wind in mind. How deep do our foundations need to be to withstand 120 mile-per-hour winds? How thick do our supports have to be? What kind of connections do we use?"

"So, I'm going to go back to something you said earlier. You said you'd heard about earthquakes in the area."

His mouth flattened and he nodded.

"This area has seen a fairly dramatic uptick in tremors over the past several years."

"That's right."

"So, it might be reasonable to assume that—" Peter shrugged, spreading his hands. "That it's time to work that into the calculations."

"It would be reasonable to assume that. Because that's exactly what the professionals who work in this area have been talking about."

"That they need to consider the possibility of earthquake now, along with the possibility of high wind?"

"Exactly."

"So...did this plan include those considerations?"

Matthew Logan shook his head. "No."

The scene cut to the front of Baucum Engineering, then shrank to the corner so that we now saw Peter at the news desk with Trisha and Tom Timmons.

"Patrice and Dan, I talked to the engineering firm that designed the NorthStar Elementary building, and tomorrow night we'll see that interview, right here on News Channel 11."

"All right, Peter. Interesting stuff. We look forward to learning more. Switching gears now to weather..."

I clicked the link for the interview with David Baucum.

The story opened with Baucum sitting behind a large desk, and I realized this was the same office—even the same desk, I was fairly sure—that had been in the elder Baucum's interview, thirty-something years before.

"Yesterday we talked to the Logan family. As you remember, they're the ones who—"

"I know who they are, yes." Baucum's mouth was a thin line.

"Good. One of the things we discussed—one of several things, in fact—was the design of the school. For the benefit of our viewers who might not be familiar with architecture or engineering and building design, could you give us a layman's idea of what goes into making a building safe?"

Baucum's expression didn't shift one iota. "No. I can't sum up years of education and experience in one pithy statement. What I can say is that there are very detailed, very considered guidelines and requirements in place, strict building codes dictated by years of experience in building design and usage, that we and every other engineering firm, architecture firm, every city government that enforces building codes, all go by. It all exists."

"And it's all followed?"

Clearly holding back an eye roll, Baucum said, "Of course it's followed."

Peter nodded. He opened his mouth to say something, then closed it again. He took a breath. Then he said, "Let's get right to NorthStar Elementary."

Baucum lifted a hand in a *"Be my guest"* gesture.

"In my conversation with Matthew Logan, he mentioned that buildings in this area are typically designed to stand up to heavy winds, because, well, that's what buildings in this area usually have to do. Stand up to heavy winds."

He stopped and waited for a response.

"Was that a question?" Baucum asked.

"Well, is that correct? You're the engineer."

"That is correct. The building code in this area stipulates that buildings such as NorthStar Elementary be reinforced to resist wind loads."

"Okay," Peter said. He took another breath.

I felt for the guy. Baucum wasn't making it easy for him, that was for sure. I wondered if he would fold the way he had at Dorsett Oil.

"So, can we assume that NorthStar Elementary was built to withstand—what did you call them? Wind loads?"

"You don't need to assume anything. The school was designed to withstand wind loads of 120 miles per hour."

Peter nodded. "That's kind of a worst-case scenario for this area?"

Baucum shrugged. "The most likely worst-case scenario, yes."

"The most likely."

"Sure. For instance, a worst-case scenario might be a 747 crashing into the building, but nobody designs for that, because that's not likely to happen."

Peter nodded and smiled as if the guy wasn't being a complete jerk. "So you take whatever is the most-likely event to occur and design for the worst-case scenario for that event?"

"To a reasonable extent, yes. For instance, if that school was being built in Minnesota, we would have considered what kind of load a significant snowfall accumulation would put on the roof. We don't have to worry about that much here."

"And if you were building a school in say, California?"

Baucum eyed Peter for a second. He knew a gotcha question when he saw it coming.

"We would design for seismic loads."

"Seismic loads. Like earthquakes."

"In layman's terms, yes." His smile was chilly.

"But you didn't consider seismic loads in the design of this school?"

"No, because that's not the most-likely event to—"

"But isn't it true that seismic activity has become more common in this area, with the increase in fracking and injection wells?"

I had to admit, I felt pretty proud of myself for knowing what he was talking about.

"To an extent, yes. Seismic activity is more common, but it's not been of an intensity strong enough to take into consideration—"

"But isn't it true that we don't, in fact, know for sure that buildings in this area are designed to withstand this—this increased seismic activity, even if it isn't, as you say, of significant intensity?"

"No, that isn't necessarily true. We do know that structures built to the current code will withstand up to—"

"And isn't it true that architects and engineers were, quietly, out of the public eye, discussing amongst themselves the very real possibility that what happened at NorthStar Elementary could happen here, before it did happen?"

"You make it sound like we were skulking around in the shadows, with secret handshakes and—"

"But this wasn't public knowledge, was it?"

Baucum shook his head, his mouth growing even thinner. "That would depend on your definition of "public knowledge." We formed a committee to study the issue. We invited people we thought could contribute." His eyes flashed anger. "We did not invite investigative reporters because it wasn't immediately apparent what their contribution would be."

Peter grinned, and I wondered how he would feel if he knew how apparent it was that he got a kick out of goading the guy. I mean, Baucum was a bit of a jerk, but Peter Browning suddenly looked like that horrible middle school boy who loved to torture you until you cried.

"Hey, no hard feelings," Peter said. "And what did this committee find?"

"Nothing. At least nothing conclusive. We were still in the middle of it when the—when the building failed."

"Isn't it true, Mr. Baucum, that you had concerns over the design of NorthStar before it failed?"

Baucum sighed. "Look, there are things you just don't know until they present themselves. We designed that building—"

"Isn't it true that you had concerns, specifically, about NorthStar Elementary?"

Baucum frowned again. "It's true that I thought the situation bore further investigation. The school was built on soils that are subject to—"

"Subject to liquefaction," Peter interrupted. He pulled a white page off his lap and slid it across the desk toward Baucum, with the air of someone who had just dealt the death blow to a sworn enemy.

Baucum stared at the paper, then at Peter. "Where did you get that?"

"This is your email, isn't it?"

"Yes, it's my email. I wrote it—"

"You wrote it to another member of the committee regarding concerns you had about the increase in injection wells in the area. Here you say, and I'm quoting you directly, 'Some areas that weren't even red flags a few years ago could be ripe for a disaster now that we see the possibility of everything coming together the way it has—a kind of 'perfect storm' of conditions that weren't considered ten years ago or even two years ago, when the site was chosen for NorthStar. That whole neighborhood is built on land reclaimed from a dried riverbed. I would definitely consider that soil susceptible to liquefaction. Something that can be designed for, unless we're bringing seismic into the mix. Now that we are bringing seismic into the mix...'"

Baucum opened his mouth to speak, but Peter held up a finger.

I paused the video.

"Liquefaction?" I asked Stump. She looked as clueless as I was.

I searched 'soils subject to liquefaction' and ended up losing half an hour looking at bizarre videos of water that seeped up through the earth and dirt that rippled like water when it was jumped on. It was pretty freaky stuff.

"Okay," I said to Stump. "We learned something today." I flipped back to Browning's interview with Baucum.

"The person you were corresponding with here responds, 'Who's going to be the one to tell Daniels that his school is going to be delayed again? Because it sure as'—and here I'll just say blank— 'it sure as blank isn't going to be me.' Then you respond, 'I don't want to do it, either. And I don't know that a delay—at least not a significant delay—is necessary. But I'm beginning to think we do need to hit the pause button and study the situation a little closer, especially with the school.'"

Peter laid the paper on the desk and looked at Baucum. "Did you hit the pause button?"

"No." Subdued now, Baucum shook his head and stared at the desk. "No, we..." He trailed off.

"By Daniels, in that message, of course, you were referring to Michael Daniels, the LISD School Board President."

Baucum gave a slight nod.

"Did you alert him?"

Baucum took a deep breath, then shook his head. "No, we hadn't really had time to—" Peter leaned forward. "This was written on December 28th. The earthquake happened on March 11. That's..." He looked up like he was calculating in his head. "Nine weeks, give or take?"

Baucum didn't answer.

"No communication with the school board during that time? With the parents of the kids who would be attending the school?"

"Look," Baucum said, clearly tired of feeling railroaded. "It's not responsible conduct to go around saying the sky is falling if you don't have clear evidence that the sky could be, in fact, falling. Obviously, we were looking into the matter. We were performing due diligence. We felt we had reason to look into the matter further, but not reason to bring—"

"Some people have asked if there could, possibly, be a conflict of interests here."

Baucum drew his head back. "What? No. Why?"

"Well, your company was part of the design team on the building. And here you are, on the committee investigating whether the design of this building is adequate to the environment it's being placed in."

"It wasn't just this building. We were looking at the entirety of the area, whether we need to change actual building codes and specifications to match this—this new reality."

"And yet you mentioned NorthStar Elementary by name."

"Well, yes. Because that's the one I was most familiar with, since it was recent and I had been directly involved in it. But we weren't—"

"You mentioned NorthStar Elementary by name," Peter said again.

Baucum stopped. He ran a hand over his mouth. "It takes time to conduct a thorough investigation like this. I thought...we needed more time to..."

Peter let him sit in silence for a moment. Then he laid a picture of Meredith on the table. She held her hand up in a weak wave from her hospital bed, her leg raised in a plaster cast. It was the picture shown on her GoFundMe page.

"Meredith Logan has time. She's facing a future full of nothing but time. A future when she's not able to do the one thing she loves most—dancing."

Music kicked in, and I hit the pause button. They were about to show little Meredith dancing before the accident, and I wasn't sure I could handle that.

I checked the clock again and decided I would just go to work early.

My early morning caught up with me around 11:00 am. Unfortunately, I still had dogs to finish and then a biting Scotty came in and put me in a foul mood. By the time I got off work at 4:00 pm, I was in an even fouler mood and decided I needed some TLC.

I texted Tony before I left Flo's. *"Warning: grumpy wife headed your way."*

"There," I said to Stump as I lowered her onto the seat. "He can't say he hasn't been warned."

My phone began playing the siren as soon as I walked through Tony's door.

Tony looked at me, brow raised, and then at my pants pocket. "Where's the fire?" He waggled his brows.

I laughed. "That's my mom's ring tone. I'll check it later." I had to be emotionally prepared to talk to my mother, and right now I did not have the reserves to pull it off.

He let me put my lunch box on the counter and toe off my shoes by the sofa, then he gathered me in his arms.

He'd kissed me once when his own phone buzzed.

He groaned, pulled it from his pocket and looked at the screen, then gave me an apologetic look. "Sorry."

I shrugged. "No problem. I will put the time to good use by going into a near-vegetative state on your sofa."

He kissed me and headed back to his office.

I stretched out on the sofa, but my mind was in that frenzied, exhausted state where it refuses to stop running. I picked up my phone and found the interview with Baucum again.

Trisha had said he was unbelievably cold, but he hadn't seemed cold to me. He'd seemed defensive and rude, but by the end of the interview, he'd seemed beaten.

I rose and paced, waiting for Tony to finish. To be honest, I'd expected him to drop everything and tend to me once he knew I was having a bad day.

It was childish to assume he would be able to do that, though. Tony had built a successful building services business through hard work and long hours, and I loved that about him. If it meant I had to be a big girl and let him put it before me once in a while, that seemed a small price to pay.

Or it would have if I hadn't been in such a mood. As things stood at the moment, I had to lecture myself not to be a big baby, but even then it was a struggle not to feel sorry for myself.

I sighed and ordered myself to really put the time to good use. I thought about Peter and the string of interviews I'd watched. What did they have in common?

I stood and walked slowly through Tony's living room, dining room, and kitchen, then back again. The truth was, there didn't seem to be a shortage of people who could have had it in for him. We needed to get a list of Baucum Engineering employees who had been laid off. Maybe I could cross-reference those names with anyone who had recently filed for bankruptcy or for divorce. How did one go about cross-referencing things, I wondered.

I tripped over something and stumbled. I looked down. My tennis shoes.

I cringed and picked them up, carrying them to the bedroom to tuck into the closet. I didn't have much at Tony's house, so the least I could do was keep my stuff picked up.

I went back to the living room and noticed my lunch box on the counter, ready to be cleaned out. My keys on the hallway table, not on the key rack by the back door where Tony kept his. My magazine on his coffee table.

I looked around. It was as if my stuff were the artfully placed items meant to make a model home look "lived in."

I picked up my magazine and carried it to the rack beside the sofa. I was sliding it in beside Tony's books and magazines, when the spine of a book caught my eye.

Alcoholic.

I tugged the book out from where it was wedged between two other paperbacks and a stack of folded newspaper.

Living With An Alcoholic.

I stared at the title.

Surviving and Thriving with a Loved One Who Drinks read the subtitle.

I stared at the book for a long time. Eventually, I became aware of a buzzing in my ears.

This was good, I told myself. Tony wanted to know how to help. I needed help. We all needed to be on the same page.

This was good.

So why did I suddenly burn with shame?

I stood and paced a bit. There was no legitimate reason that I should feel so suddenly exposed. I knew I was an alcoholic. Tony knew I was an alcoholic. It was all out there. What's more, I knew—Jeez-O-Peet , how could I not know?—that addiction of any kind made life complicated. For everyone.

I sat on the edge of the sofa, then with a quick shove, put the book back where I'd found it.

I stood and paced some more.

I told myself to calm down. After all, it was silly to feel resentment or shame or even panic—all emotions that had been running through me, one after another.

Surviving a loved one who drinks.

I felt like a live grenade. Like a walking open-sore highly infectious disease.

I felt like an EF-5 tornado. Like the earthquake that had taken Meredith Logan's ability to dance.

I picked the book up again, thumbed it open, then slapped it closed.

No. This wasn't going to help me, not right now. Tony was facing truth. He was seeking knowledge on how to live with that truth. I, as well as anyone, should be able to appreciate the value of that.

Facts were facts. I needed to focus on them and get my focus off my feelings. My feelings were obviously leading me to a bottomless swirly that could only result in something disastrous.

I took a deep breath. I started to list facts.

I was an alcoholic.

I was in recovery.

I had not had a drink in 421 days.

I was experiencing an uncomfortable feeling, but I was familiar with this feeling. This feeling said I wanted something, desperately needed something, in fact. It said that something fundamental was hanging out there, needful and unsatisfied, awkward and uncomfortable and screaming for something to be done. There was a hole that had to be filled.

It was just feeling. I had gotten through it before.

This feeling wasn't an indication that I did, in fact, have to fill the hole. I could, instead, just sit with that hole for a moment. Feel the edges. Gauge the depth.

Tony had to figure out how to survive me.

I made myself re-read the entire subtitle.

Surviving and Thriving with a Loved One Who Drinks.

I made myself focus on the good words. *Thrive. Loved One. With.*

I tucked the book back in the rack and stood, taking more deep breaths.

I had asked Tony if he could really appreciate what he was getting into, staying married to me. He'd said he did. He made the choice. He was a grownup, he knew what he was doing, we were both adults and were going through this with eyes wide open.

Okay. So if Tony could do this, so could I.

I walked into the hallway and looked at the closed office door. It was quiet in there.

I made the circuit of the living room, dining room, kitchen, hallway again.

We were grownups. We did what grownups do.

Grownups call their parents back, I remembered.

That was one thing I could do that would be simple enough. Mom was so excited now about her wedding, phone calls with her were mostly one sided and simple. I usually just kept up a revolving commentary of the words, "Wow," "Cool," and "That sounds great," until she got ready to hang up. It cost me nothing and seemed to make her happy.

I called her.

"Salem!" she said when she answered. "I'm glad you called me back. I need to talk about wedding plans."

For the next few minutes, I "wowed" and "cooled" my way through the call, but I had to make myself focus when her tone shifted just slightly.

"Because this is Gerry's fourth wedding, we can't have it at a church, of course."

"Of course," I said. No mention that their tally of previous marriages was equal. Or was Mom's number higher? I couldn't remember. There had been a number of false starts for a couple of the fiancés (What was the plural of fiancé? my frazzled brain wondered. Fianc*i*?) and I had a hard time remembering which ones made it all the way to signing on the dotted line. At least four, though.

She went on about the backyard wedding they were planning at Gerry's parents' house. They were incorporating a fall theme, of course, using orange and teal for colors (which sounded hideous, but I held my tongue on that) and pumpkins, mums. The cake was a big horn of plenty.

"Neely describes it as rustic, but not country."

I had been in Neely Bates's backyard, and her house. She could pull off a classy version of "rustic" if anyone could.

"And we've decided not to have any attendants," she said, a little rushed. In fact, it was almost with the air of someone ripping off a Band-Aid.

Jeez-O-Peet . I hadn't even considered that she might have asked me to be her bridesmaid or anything. Now I wouldn't have to make up an excuse. Whew.

"But I do get to be your flower girl, right?" I had been her flower girl three times. The last time I'd been fifteen, sulky and resentful in what I considered a baby dress, and already assuming this was just another man I would have to fight off.

Awkward silence.

"Just kidding," I said. "No worries from me, I'll be happy to take my place on the bride's side." Then, to change the subject, I said, "Okay, I know you and Neely have this well in hand, but I have to ask—aren't you concerned about rain? Even if it doesn't rain, it will surely be chilly."

"Neely has it all figured out. They have fifteen of those outdoor patio heaters, plus they're renting a big tent that will be heated. We'll have the ceremony out by the fountain if it doesn't rain and inside the tent if it does. They're providing throws and heated gloves for the guests, just in case. And there will be plenty of alcohol flowing, of course. It's going to be fun!"

Actually, it did sound fun, in a very loud, obnoxious kind of way. For some reason the "fun with alcohol" attitude when she knew I was in recovery, coupled with the lack of a role for me in the event, had become extremely annoying to me.

Definitely time to take the high road. "I know I'm not in the wedding, but I'd love some suggestions on what to wear," I said.

"I'll email you some ideas," she said. "Or you could come up here and we could shop together. Girls weekend!"

She actually squealed. My mom. Squealing. I developed an instant migraine. And by migraine, I mean an even crummier attitude.

"Sure," I said. "If I can get the time. But send me some suggestions, just in case." Because nope.

I hung up and promised myself that if Viv ended up marrying Nigel, she was going to let me be her bridesmaid. If I had to threaten her with her own gun, I would.

I curled up on the sofa and stared into nothingness. Stump, ever sensing my moods, crawled into my lap and rooted at my hand until I petted her. This morphed into a full-out belly rub.

Tony came in and looked at the two of us on the sofa.

"She looks ecstatic and you look miserable."

I told you I was grumpy, I thought. Instead of complaining, though, I raised my head. "Do I?"

He sat beside me. "The phone call go badly?"

I shrugged. "Not really. She's all excited. She's going to send me some suggestions for what to wear."

"Excellent. We'll go shopping."

"You want to go shopping with me?" I shifted until I could lay my head on his shoulder.

"Maybe just once." He kissed the top of my head. "Why do you look sad?"

"I'm not sad." Was I? I did a gut check. I wasn't happy, that was for sure. The thing about no attendants was bugging me, but I didn't want it to. I didn't want to be her bridesmaid.

I want her to want me to be a bridesmaid, so I can tell her no.

I groaned and rubbed my face. Did I want to admit that to Tony? No. No, I did not. I didn't even want to admit it to myself.

"I'm being silly," I finally said. "I forgave my mother weeks ago, but the silly, childish part of me wants to hold a grudge. That's all."

I tried to remember what Les had told me. Forgiveness is an over and over kind of thing.

Then a new thought occurred to me. Weeks back, when Mom and I had a huge argument, I had told her that she should warn her friend Susan not to talk to me at the wedding. Susan, who had been Mom's drinking buddy throughout my unstable childhood. Susan, whose teenage son had molested me when I was seven years old.

She couldn't have both me and Susan as attendants—I'd pretty much guaranteed to wreck the whole thing if she did. So, rather than tell Susan that she'd chosen me as a bridesmaid over her, she'd chosen to have no attendants at all.

I didn't know why this caught me off guard. Mom had chosen Susan over me a million times. She'd chosen Susan over me, men over me, any good time that presented itself over me. This one time when she could have chosen me over Susan, she elected to choose no one at all.

It all added up much better than the "no attendants just because" line had. She was making a big deal about this wedding. She had never once failed to expect everyone around her to jump on whatever drama train she was conducting. It didn't make sense that she wouldn't want attendants. Unless she couldn't bring herself to tell Susan no.

I stood so suddenly I startled Tony and Stump grumbled. "What?"

I shook my head, suddenly antsy. "Nothing. I'm just..." I looked around, searching for the term. Antsy was the only way to describe it. "I'm just antsy."

"Talking with your mom?"

I nodded. "Yeah. Wedding plans. Mom." I rubbed hands palms together in fast, frantic circles. "Bringing up stuff I don't really want to think about."

"Let's talk about it."

I shook my head. "No. Not now." I walked to the edge of the room and back.

"Yes. Come on, Salem." He patted the sofa beside him. "Sit down. Let's talk it out."

I felt a spurt of impatience with him. I had warned him I was grumpy, and half an hour ago I would have been glad to have his attention. He'd gone off to work instead. Now it was too late.

I paced in front of the coffee table. "No. Not now."

He took a breath and picked up my phone, I think just to have something for his hands to do. He scooted forward on the sofa, his elbows on his knees. "Salem, you're getting yourself worked up. Calm down."

I stopped and stared at him. "Has anyone in the history of the world ever calmed down because someone told them to calm down?"

I had spoken more sharply than I meant to. I began to pace again, the urge to move too strong to resist. "I'm sorry," I said. "I just...I feel anxious and I think I need to get out for a while."

"I think you need to sit down and just talk it out. I think that will help."

"I can't."

"Of course you can. Don't be afraid of me, Salem. You can trust—"

"I'm not afraid of you!" I snapped. I gritted my teeth. "I just feel anxious and I feel like I need to get out. Get some air."

He stood and tried to gather me in his arms. "Come here."

I just couldn't do it. I pulled away. "I'm sorry, but I need some space."

"Look." He frowned and dipped his head to meet my eyes. "I don't think you should go."

"I'm just going back to my place. I'm sorry, but I can't think."

"Salem, I don't think you should go."

"I have to get out of here!" I shouted. I didn't mean to shout. But for some reason I felt panicked, trapped, desperate. "I'm just going back to my place for a breather."

The look on his face told me all I needed to know.

He thought I was going to drink.

"Don't look at me like that," I said through clenched teeth. I pointed at him. "You do not look at me like that."

He held his hands out in the universal symbol for 'simmer down.' "I think you should stay here while you're upset. I can stay in my office or something. I don't mean to crowd you. But I think you should stay here."

"And I think you should trust me! But you don't, do you?"

A fleeting look crossed his face. A kind of *seriously?!* look that he managed to smother almost immediately.

But I saw it. And something inside me burst into flame. It was here—the moment I had known was coming—the moment when I couldn't push it down anymore. The moment I knew I would explode and ruin absolutely everything. That look. That look that told me he had been waiting for this moment, too.

This was the moment he needed to survive.

I lost it. I narrowed my eyes at him and said, "Don't give me that look! Don't give me the look that says you would have to be crazy to trust me! Despite everything I've said and done over the last year, you're still waiting for me to run off at the slightest provocation and guzzle down a bottle of rum!"

I bent and ripped the book from the magazine rack. "Here!" I held it out to him, then jerked it back. "No, let me look. Where's the chapter on keeping your alcoholic at home where you can keep an eye on her? Let's see how this works."

I slapped the book shut again and shoved it at him.

My anger made him mad. He threw the book on the sofa and crossed his arms over his chest. "How stupid would I have to be to think that a recovering alcoholic is not going to want to drink after talking to the person who always triggered her the most?"

"And here you are, Sir Galla-Freaking-Had riding in on your white horse to save the day! Oh, you love being the hero, don't you, Tony?" I sneered at him. In the back of my mind, I thought, *See, Serena, you strip mall psychic! This is what happens when I open the floodgates.*

But it was too late now - the gates were open and all kinds of awful was pouring out. "You know what this is called, don't you?

Codependency! You're codependent and just waiting for me to
screw up so you can rescue me again. So you can lord your
superior coping skills over me. So you can prove how patient
and forgiving you are! So you can be perfect, again! Saint
Anthony!"

I grabbed my purse off the sofa and tossed my phone into it
before I slung it over my shoulder. I stooped to pick up Stump,
who grunted as I lifted her onto my hip.

"Does it ever get old, Tony? Being everyone's knight in
shining armor? Of course not. You get to be adored by your
entire family, your staff, everyone you know. You know what I
think? I think *that's* why you never divorced me! So everyone
could see what a pious saint you are. I mean, what tops staying
married to a slutty alcoholic? You win, Tony!"

He looked like I'd slapped him.

I felt like an elephant had stepped on my chest. I wished the
words back.

At the same time, I was a little relieved. I had been delusional
to ever hope this moment wasn't inevitable, and so had Tony. It
served us both right for living in such a dream world.

I slammed out the door.

Fury raged through me as I jerked open the door to the
Monster Carlo, dumped Stump and my purse inside, and then
slammed into the seat. I was so furious that my mind was hyper-
focused.

He expected me to drink. Fine. I would drink.

CHAPTER NINE

Heel-Grabber

I clenched my jaw, turned the key in the ignition, looked carefully behind me, and pulled out of the driveway. All of my senses were on high alert. I could see everything with perfect clarity. The nearest liquor store was three blocks away. I planned each step in my head. One block to the main street. Turn right. Two blocks north. I would park the car, go in, get a bottle, drive to my trailer, and drink the whole thing. Why not? It was the very thing everyone was holding their breath waiting for. Why not just get it over with?

I rehearsed the steps over and over in my head. This was happening. Of course, it was happening. It was inevitable and always had been.

I made the right turn. Drove the two blocks. I could see the liquor store on the corner. What kind of bottle? Vodka? Rum?

Something good. Heck, I hadn't had a drop of alcohol in over a year now. I deserved a splurge. Do it big. A bottle of Chivas.

I drove past the liquor store.

I pulled into a parking lot down the block, swung the car around, and drove back.

I drove past the liquor store.

I drove down, turned left, made the block.

I pulled into the liquor store parking lot. I put the car in park. I stared at the door.

Here's the thing. I had known from the first day of my sobriety that this day would eventually come. So I had planned ahead. When the time came that I couldn't white-knuckle it anymore, I would remind myself of all the mistakes I had made while I was drinking.

The times I had embarrassed myself.

The times I had hurt others.

The times I had said things I regretted.

The times I had driven drunk.

The times I had been with a man I didn't particularly want to be with, but was caught up in the need to be the carefree, careless daredevil.

Those memories I carried around with me like a talisman, a list of private, personal horrors to have available to ward off the urge to drink. I had told myself that I would remember how it felt. The memory of the consuming regret would be enough to steer me away, when the moment came that my willpower had played out. Those stories would remind me of why I had to stay away.

All those bad memories, though...they withered and died as soon as I pulled them up. Because the fact was, I knew none of those things were going to happen. Not tonight. Tonight, I was going to get a bottle, I was going to drive home, and I was going to drink. That's all. I was going to go numb for a while.

No one else would even have to know.

Frank was gone. Tony wouldn't come after me. Les thought I was at Tony's and wouldn't bother to check unless I called him.

I stared at the liquor store door. All I had to do was pick up my purse, open the car door, and walk in.

Things seemed so clear now. I had used a boogeyman to keep myself in line, but when the moment came to really look at that boogeyman, he was just a bunch of fabric stitched together and stuffed with cotton. He had no power.

I could drink. The world wouldn't end. Blood wouldn't run in the streets. Sirens wouldn't even go off. I could drink, and the only thing that would happen is, I would fail. And hadn't I been doing that all my life? Wasn't that the one thing I was really, really good at?

I turned my head to look at the seat beside me, where my purse waited with plenty of money for one bottle.

Stump sat with her chin resting on my purse, her brown eyes on me, her brows raised in concern.

I stared back, feeling a kind of tug at my heart.

You're not seriously going to use this dog as an excuse to not drink, are you? a snarky voice in my head asked. *You're not seriously going to act like this is one of those Jesus-freak God moments your sanctified friends like to talk about, are you? She's a dog. She has no idea what's going on. She doesn't care if you drink or don't drink. She's a dog.*

I took a breath, turned the key in the ignition, and backed the car onto the street.

I made it to the end of the street before I burst into tears. I kept going. For another half a block. Then I was crying too hard to see and had to pull into a church parking lot so I wouldn't take out a light pole or something with the Monster Carlo. I made sure I wasn't in anyone's way, put the car into park, killed the motor, put my head against the steering wheel, and cried.

I cried out of anger—anger at Tony and at myself. I cried out of sorrow that I wasn't able to do this thing right. I cried out of fear and frustration. What had I done? What kind of person got mad at someone for being good?

I was such a jerk.

I cried more when I realized that I wasn't mad at Tony. I was mad at my mom for something I was not supposed to care about. Which made me madder at myself.

What sucked perhaps most of all was that I couldn't blame the hateful words on alcohol. I had spewed all that bull hockey while stone cold sober.

I wanted to go back and scream at Serena-Wow-look-how-blue-your-aura-is, "See! This is what happens when I open the floodgates!"

I rooted around in the glove box and under the seats until I finally found a couple of crumpled Subway napkins stuffed between the seats. I wiped my eyes and tried to blow my nose, but it was clear these sad napkins weren't equal to the task. I sniffed and started the car.

"Okay, Stump, let's go home."

I made it to Trailertopia and into my house, all the way to the back where my bedroom was, dropped my purse, and fell face first onto the bed. I felt so horribly wretched. For the first time in weeks, I wished I could go to sleep and not wake up again for weeks. Months. Maybe ever.

The hurt look on Tony's face haunted me. I wanted to go to sleep and shut it out.

I lay for a while, exhausted, my eyes burning, my throat sore. I wanted to sleep and block it out for a while.

But, exhausted as I felt, I was too tortured to sleep.

I rolled to my side and pulled my knees up. Stump curled into the curve of my body and laid her head on my arm.

Her brow was wrinkled in what honestly did look like concern. She might have been concerned for me. Then again, she might have been concerned that we were back at my crummy trailer in Trailertopia and not in Tony's nice big house with the thick carpet and the perfectly manicured lawn.

I petted her until I felt like I might be able to speak without losing it again. Then I rolled over, fished around on the floor to find my purse, dug in it until I found my phone, and said, "Windy, call Les."

"What is that, honey? I didn't understand you."

Windy didn't understand my thick-with-tears voice. Maybe this wasn't the time to call Les.

I hit the text app.

"I had a fight with Tony. I was mean. I feel awful. I drove to the liquor store but then Stump looked at me and I couldn't go in so I came home but I still feel awful and I don't know what to do."

I read over it. That about summed it up. I hit send.

I laid back on the bed, still thinking about that look on Tony's face. Suddenly desperate to undo what couldn't be undone, I pulled up his name and started and deleted half a dozen messages. Finally, I wrote, "*I'm sorry. You didn't deserve that. I was mad about my mom and took it out on you, and I regret it so much. I'm not drinking. I'm sorry.*"

I read through it, but it seemed pitifully little against the enormity of what I'd said. I hit send anyway.

Then I stared at it and waited for him to respond. Nothing.

My phone beeped the sound I'd assigned to Les.

I answered. "I called him Sir Galla-Freaking-Had and Saint Anthony. But, that doesn't even...I was mean. I said it in a mean way. I said it like an insult, and he knew it. He was hurt by it."

"Where are you?"

"At home. At Trailertopia."

"Alone?"

"Stump is here."

He made a noise that might have meant anything. "I'm on my way."

Frank came in while I was in the bathroom washing my face. I came into the living room to find him sitting in his usual spot in my recliner, watching TV, Stump at his side.

He looked up and kind of blanched when he saw me.

"Still pretty bad, huh?" I asked. I had looked absolutely scary in my bathroom mirror, but I had hoped splashing cold water on my face and blowing my nose would have brought some improvement.

"Was it...worse, before?" he asked, studying my puffy face.

I shrugged. "Marginally. Les is coming over."

He looked enormously relieved. We all knew Les was much better equipped to deal with a crying woman than Frank was.

"You need me to watch Stump?"

I nodded. "Yeah. Les and I can go get some coffee or something." I still felt antsy, like I needed to keep moving. "I'll bring back dinner," I promised.

I grabbed my purse again and waited for Les on the front deck of my trailer.

We drove to a little breakfast place that was mostly deserted at this time of day. He ordered coffee for us both, but when it came he looked at the cups, frowned, and said, "Milkshake?"

I nodded. I had skipped on the bottle of Chivas. I deserved a milkshake for that if nothing else.

After the shakes came, Les listened as I poured out everything that had happened that afternoon.

"It's crazy, because before those words came out of my mouth, I never thought that. I never thought Tony was with me out of some self-righteous desire to lord it over me. But now I can't stop thinking about it." I looked at Les. "What if I'm right? What if he's somehow dependent on me screwing up because it creates this—this hero role for him to play?"

Les leaned forward, his elbows on the table. "What if it does?"

"Don't do that now, okay?"

"No, we're doing it. Once you say 'what if,' you have to follow it all the way through. What if he's codependent?"

"Then...that means he doesn't love me for me. He's invested in my dysfunction."

"And what's bad about that?"

"He might not want me to get better. He might subconsciously undermine my progress."

"Has he done anything to make you think he would do that?"

"Not yet, no."

"But?"

"But he might."

Les shrugged. "He might. What can you do about it?"

"What can I do about it?"

His lips tilted just a bit. "Nope. I ask the questions, you give the answers."

"I don't know!"

He sat back and shrugged.

"There's nothing I can do about that, is there?"

He shook his head.

I sat back and tapped my straw against the glass. "You know what else? I wasn't even mad at Tony to start out. I was mad at my mother because she didn't want me as a bridesmaid in the wedding I don't even want to be a bridesmaid in." I groaned and dropped my arms to the table and buried my head in them. "Seriously. I don't want to be her bridesmaid. But she didn't ask, so I didn't get to reject her."

"You're making terrific progress, Salem." Les reached over and patted the top of my head awkwardly.

"I am a self-involved, childish fool," I mumbled against my arm.

"You're human. Understanding why you were mad in the first place is huge. It brings you one step closer to not letting that anger get misdirected."

"One step. I'm still at least three football fields away, though. Do you remember what Bonnie was talking about in the meeting last week? About wearing the world like a loose garment?"

That was actually a fairly common phrase heard in recovery circles. It meant not being too invested in the outcome of anything. Just relaxing and letting whatever was going to happen, happen. So easy to say. So difficult to execute.

"I want to be like that. I want to not be bothered by the world. I want to be so—so content and at peace that I barely even notice what's going on around me. And when I do notice, I want it to be just like noticing something in a movie. It's not me. It doesn't mean anything to me. It doesn't change anything." I frowned and took a pull on my straw. "But I feel like the world is actually a big static sticker that I push off one hand and it just sticks to the other one."

"Oh, I hate those," Les said.

I raised my head and looked at him. Then I burst out laughing.

He smiled and slurped on his milkshake.

I waited for more words of wisdom, but they weren't forthcoming.

I dipped my straw in my milkshake, scooped up a bit on the end and then put it in my mouth. "I feel like he's just waiting for me to fail."

"I know."

"I feel like I'm just waiting for me to fail."

"I know."

"If you know so much, tell me what to do about it."

He gave me a you're-not-going-to-like-this smile and said, "One day at a time."

I sighed. "Does it ever seem inevitable, though? I mean, like the one day at a time is really just marking time until the inevitable happens."

"Every day is a choice, Salem."

"I know," it was my turn to say. Although my "I know" sounded much less sure than Les's "I know."

Les lifted his brow.

I sighed. "It doesn't feel like there's much choice, though, does there? I mean, in theory, yes the world is wide open. But it feels more like there's a lot of...predestination, I guess? I mean, we're all born into certain circumstances that play a huge role in what kind of life we have."

I frowned because I knew it sounded like I was deflecting responsibility. I remembered the verse about Jacob. "Like, look at Jacob. Did you know his name actually means 'heel-grabber'?"

He nodded. "Sure."

"Of course, you did. Well, I didn't. I mean, what kind of thing is that to do to a kid? Give him a name like that?"

"People gave names based on the events or circumstances of their birth."

"I know, but...doesn't it seem unfair to you? He was an infant, literally. It's not like he was already a schemer at birth, right? But with a name like that..." I shook my head. "What would that do to your self-esteem? The way you saw yourself?"

"Don't forget, his mother was a real piece of work herself."

I nodded, although to be honest, I had to think for a moment to remember what Les was talking about. I got my Old

Testament guys mixed up sometimes and got Jacob and Abraham confused the most.

"She's the one who sold out the older son so the younger one could get the inheritance or whatever?"

"The birthright, yes. She clearly favored one son above the other."

"Between the dysfunctional mom and the negative label for a name, it's not like he was going to turn out to be some upstanding citizen."

"Everyone has free will, Salem. Even the heel-grabber."

"But don't you see how that kind of label could totally skew the way you looked at the world? The way you looked at yourself?"

"Sure."

"I mean, your entire life you would know that people were just waiting for you to live down to your name. *You* would be waiting for you to live down to your name."

"Is that what you're doing?"

I chewed my lip. "Yeah, I think so."

He studied me for a moment. "You didn't go into that liquor store, Salem. You made that choice."

"You don't know how close it was, though."

"Doesn't matter. Not really. A miss is definitely as good as a mile, in this case." He leaned forward and clasped his hands together on the tabletop. "No, that's wrong. It does matter how close it was. Temptations come in all sizes, and you stared down a big one. Size does matter." He winked at me.

I rolled my eyes.

"I've told you, you can't expect the day to come when you never want to drink again. It's not going to happen."

"I know. But what if it happens again and Stump is not there? I mean, if I hadn't been looking right at her and feeling like I had to stay sober for her..."

He put his hand over mine. "You'll face that moment when you get to it. It's not going to do you any good to fight your battles in advance."

I sighed and leaned back, staring at the melting milkshake in the bottom of my glass.

"You know, he got a new name. Jacob."

I frowned, thinking. "Is that why I keep getting him mixed up with Abraham? Did he become Abraham?"

"No, Abram became Abraham. Jacob became *Israel*. Remember, he wrestled all night with the angel until God gave him a new name? *Israel*."

I tried to picture what that would be like and couldn't, but it did remind me of what Serena had said about Peter Browning—he was wrestling with demons.

"Maybe I should wrestle with an angel until God gives me a new name," I said. I stretched.

"Maybe you should, if that's what you want." He put a tip on the table and got to his feet with a groan. "You could just stick with 'heal-grabber', though. Grabbing your healing. Get it?"

I rolled my eyes again, but I couldn't help but smile. I slid my arm through Les's and put my head on his shoulder as we walked back to his car.

It turned out that while Les was feeding me a milkshake, his wife Bonnie was talking to Tony. On the surface, that seemed like a good idea. Bonnie knew what it was like, living with someone in recovery. Tony needed someone who could understand what he was going through.

It made me uneasy, though. I wanted to know what they were saying. I hated the idea that they were discussing me. I hated the idea that they were coming up with a plan to *manage* me, even though I had no trouble admitting that I needed to be managed.

"Should I call Tony?" I asked Les as he dropped me back at Trailertopia.

"What do you think?"

Dread bloomed in the pit of my stomach. "Do you think he needs some time?"

Les shrugged.

"Would it be cowardly for me to just text him and tell him he can call when he's ready to talk to me?"

Again with the shrug.

"It's a good thing you buy me milkshakes," I said.

"How about this? Call him, tell him you'll be happy to talk when he's ready, and then leave it to him."

That sounded like a decent plan, so I did that—and breathed a sigh of relief when I got Tony's voicemail.

"I'm sorry," I said first. "Really. I'm sorry for what I said. I've been with Les, and I didn't drink. I'm just...I wanted you to know that, and to say that I'll leave it to you to decide when we talk again."

I hung up and tried not to envision him sitting, staring at his phone and refusing to answer because he knew it was me.

He didn't call back until right before I fell asleep.

"Are you okay?" he asked.

"I am. I'm sorry."

"I'm sorry, too, Salem. I didn't mean to crowd you."

He didn't say anything about the hateful words I'd spoken. But I couldn't let it go unsaid.

"You were concerned about me. You have every reason to be. Tony, I'm so sorry for saying what I did. I didn't mean it."

He made a sound—not a sigh, but not a word, either. More like the sound he was making if he didn't know what to say.

"Listen, Salem." He breathed deep on the other end of the line. "I shouldn't have pushed. I should have given you space. Space would be...would be good right now."

My heart thudded. I didn't really care for the sound of that. "I just needed a few hours to myself, you know. I wasn't—" I bit my lip, afraid. *Space would be good right now.* "I wasn't even mad at you. I was mad at my mother and took it out on you."

"I know."

"I don't want to do that. I don't want to be like that."

His voice was tender. "I know, Salem."

"I keep thinking about what I said."

"Me, too."

"I wish I could erase it from your mind."

"Maybe it doesn't need to be. You're not the first one to call me Saint Anthony, you know."

"I'm sure I'm not. I mean, you really are such a good—"

"You're not the only one to call me that and mean it in a...not complimentary way. Rey used to say that, too."

Rey! That freak. "Everyone looks like a saint next to Rey. I look like a saint next to Rey." Since Rey was currently serving prison time for participating in the murder of one of Tony's employees and helping frame Tony for that murder, I could legitimately claim the higher ground here.

"The point is, there is a part of me—a part I'm not proud of—that does need to feel superior. I like being the hero. I like being the good guy, and I like knowing that people see me as the good guy."

"As personal faults go, Tony, that's not such a huge one."

"It was big enough to make you feel small, Salem." He waited a beat. "Wasn't it?"

He sounded so truly remorseful that my nose began to burn. I couldn't answer.

"The thing is, I've been talking to Bonnie. I have to admit, I don't think I really grasped what I was getting into here. With your addiction. With all the...there's just so much out of my control."

He sounded so overwhelmed that I wanted to hug him. Welcome to my world, I wanted to say, but just said, "There is, yes."

"The more I think about what you said, and what Bonnie said, the more I see the danger for someone like me—someone with savior behavior." He gave a short, humorless laugh. "That's what Bonnie called it. This could...this could be very bad for both of us."

My throat was too tight to speak, and I didn't know what to say. I wanted to reach through the phone and grab onto him, but I was afraid to make a sound.

He waited a few interminable seconds, then said, "You know what I realized? You...you're the first thing I ever failed at. You and me, I mean. Us. The baby. Fixing you."

"Tony, it was never your job to fix me. It was never within your power to fix me."

"I know that, now, of course. And I don't think I ever really thought of it on a conscious level like that. But after talking to Bonnie, and looking back at it now, with the benefit of hindsight...that's definitely how I saw it. That I had failed. And I had no experience with that. I didn't know how to handle that."

I chewed my lip. I was terrified to ask the next question, but I had to know. "Is that why you stayed married to me? Because you couldn't admit that you'd failed?"

He was silent, and the silence sent daggers of ice into the pit of my stomach.

"I don't know," he finally whispered. "Maybe partly. Maybe I hung on because letting go would be an admission of defeat. And I couldn't handle that."

I didn't know what to say to that. The silence on the line was huge, all encompassing.

It seemed like pitifully little to build a marriage on.

"But we have to be honest," I said. "With ourselves and with each other."

"Exactly. Maybe we were moving too fast."

"Maybe." My heart began to thud again. Maybe he was saying 'too fast' but what he meant was 'in the wrong direction.'

"Can I have a few days, Salem? Just to think? Go to a few meetings? Bonnie gave me this schedule of Al-Anon meetings and I'd like to—"

"Of course. Of course. Take all the time you need."

"Just a few days."

"Sure."

He breathed deeply, and I realized he'd been at least partially holding his breath. "It's going to be okay, Tony," I said, but it was as much for me as it was for him.

"It is." He waited a beat. "I do love you, Salem—"

"I love you, too," I said quickly. "I'll talk to you...well, you just let me know, okay?"

I hung up and sat clutching the phone in silence for a long time, staring at nothing. The trailer was silent.

I do love you, Salem...

There had been a 'but' coming. I had sensed it coming, so I had cut him off. He'd been about to say, "I do love you, Salem, but..."

The enormity of what I hadn't allowed him to say grew like a black hole, its inky darkness threatening to swallow me. I curled up on the bed, Stump tucked into my side, and eventually fell asleep.

I woke the next morning with that sense you have when something important has happened but you can't quite remember what.

It took only seconds before it all came flooding back, of course. I trudged to the front door to let Stump out, and wondered if I was really in any shape to go to work. It wasn't like I could call in worried, though. Flo would have dogs ready to be groomed, and I would need to be there to help her do it.

I looked at the sky, though, and felt somewhat relieved to see dark clouds forming. More rain. That would keep the numbers of dogs down and might mean I could get done early. I would definitely not mind that.

After Stump came back in, I headed to the second bedroom of my trailer, where I did my morning quiet time. I lit the candle and sat back, settling my mind for the daily Bible verse and prayer time.

My mind wouldn't settle, though. I finally sighed and picked up my daily devotional book.

A thought occurred to me as I was flipping through the pages to find today's date.

Good Lord. What if today's verse is from Proverbs 31?

I slapped the book closed.

Proverbs 31 is all about the ideal woman, and I'm reasonably sure it was written to be an encouragement. At least, I'd like to think that. Usually when I read it, though, I felt wholly inadequate. It was like looking at a list of all the good things I wasn't.

I chewed my lip. On the whole, I had begun to trust that God would speak to me through whatever verse happened to be in the devotional that day. Many times—many times!—it felt like God had selected that verse just for me, because something in it pertained to something I was thinking, something I was struggling with, something specific to what was going on in my life at the moment. But even when that wasn't the case, there was almost always a time later in the day when I thought about the verse, when I saw how it related to my life.

I just did not think I could handle a Proverbs 31 moment like that. Not today. Not with that unsaid "but" hanging in the air.

I chewed my lip some more. Did I just...skip it for today?

I stared at the candle. I tried to remember if I had skipped a single day of my quiet time since I began it. I know there were days when I felt distracted, when I was frustrated with God because my prayers weren't being answered the way I wanted them to be, but I couldn't think of a time when I didn't at least go through the motions of reading a verse.

I frowned and grabbed my Bible. Better not start today.

As I flipped it open, I remembered what Les had said about Jacob getting his new name. Wrestling with an angel.

That's what I wanted to read about, I decided. Jacob getting his new name. Maybe I could get some pointers.

Genesis 32:

That night Jacob got up and took his two wives, his two female servants and his eleven sons and crossed the ford of the Jabbok. After he had sent them across the stream, he sent over all his possessions. So Jacob was left alone, and a man wrestled with him till daybreak. When the man saw that he could not overpower him, he touched the socket of Jacob's hip so that his hip was wrenched as he wrestled with the man. Then the man said, "Let me go, for it is daybreak."

But Jacob replied, "I will not let you go unless you bless me."

The man asked him, "What is your name?"

"Jacob," he answered.

Then the man said, "Your name will no longer be Jacob, but Israel,[a] because you have struggled with God and with humans and have overcome."

Jacob said, "Please tell me your name."

But he replied, "Why do you ask my name?" Then he blessed

him there.

I closed my Bible and watched the candle for a while, trying to get some comfort from this. Finally, I sighed and gave up.

I knew Jacob was one of the big patriarchs of the Old Testament and everything, but that guy was a piece of work! First stealing his brother's blessing (my heart broke a little bit every time I read about poor hairy, smelly Esau's anguish that there was only the one crummy blessing left for him) then running like a complete chicken-booty to his uncle's, where he had the unmitigated gall to be successful and prosperous, when by all rights he should have ended up starved and feverish and covered in oozing sores. Everything the man did turned to gold. Frigging heel-grabber.

I went through the verses again, thinking there had to be some lesson in there for me somewhere.

I had originally pictured Jacob coming upon the angel and jumping him. Like a car thief spotting a shiny new Mercedes and being unable to resist. But reading it again, it didn't seem that way. The verse said that Jacob was alone, and a man wrestled with him "until the breaking of the day." The angel. It was as if the angel had come to take Jacob, but when it came down to it, he just couldn't defeat the guy. So he touched his hip socket and put it out of joint.

I wrinkled my nose. What the actual heck? He could put his hip out of joint (ouch, by the way) with a touch, but he couldn't overcome him in wrestling? How did that even make sense?

And right away, Jacob was back to demanding blessings. Even after the huge one his father gave, even after the years of prosperity with his uncle, this greedy guts is demanding more. He was like a spoiled toddler. I'll hold my breath until you give me candy!

And why did the angel ask Jacob's name? Surely he knew it already, unless he was some kind of fallen angel who just roamed the earth, looking for guys on their own so he could show off his divine half-Nelson.

To rub it in his face? To say, "What are you, a heel-grabber or something? Okay, fine. Now you're a God-wrestler."

You have striven with God and with man, and have prevailed.

He didn't just wrestle with God and man. He *prevailed.*

It was like an Internet meme. "One does not simply...*prevail* against God and man."

And why, when Jacob asked the angel's name, did the angel say, "Why do you ask?" and then bless him instead? I thought the name change was the blessing, but no. He got the name change and the blessing.

I sighed and sat back again. So was that the secret? Don't bother being Mrs. Nice Guy? Wrestle. Demand what you want. Go for it!

And if that was it...did I have it in me? Did I have the...well, we'll be polite and say "inner fortitude" Jacob had, to wrestle an angel to change my name?

CHAPTER TEN

Itsy Bitsy Spider

I had lots of questions about the labels that had been put on me during my lifetime. Trouble. Hot Mess. Drunk. Slut. Failure. Those had either been put on me, or I'd put them on myself—I wasn't even sure anymore. But I very much liked the idea of being given a new label. I didn't want to be a heel-grabber anymore.

What was my new label, though? The first hopeful thought that popped into my head was Helper. I thought of Tony, when he was suspected of the murder of Lucinda Cruz. Of CJ Hardin's parents, not knowing what had happened to their son. G-Ma, certain that the High Point Bandits were going to rob her blind. I helped those people. I had liked helping those people.

But one label I definitely had was Wife. And I didn't think that was compatible with Helper—at least not in the way I wanted to be a Helper.

And although I could not say I was completely down with the idea of being submissive to my husband, the facts were plain. Tony had stood by me. He was my husband. He was concerned for my safety. That deserved at least some of my consideration.

As I showered and got ready for work, I thought of other ways I could be a helper. I was becoming a fairly decent dog groomer. That wasn't nothing. The dogs seemed comfortable with me and maybe hated coming to the grooming shop a little bit less because they knew I would rub their tummy for them and might sneak them a treat. That sounded like a pitifully small way to make the world a better place, but I didn't mind that much. The truth was, I loved dogs. I loved Stump so much that if I had to justify the existence of a person just because they were good to Stump, I would do it in a heartbeat.

And speaking of people who were good to Stump—I helped Frank, via a comfortable recliner and free food. He helped me right back by making sure Stump didn't get caught up in one of her separation-anxiety fueled meltdowns and destroy my trailer. So, this was a shared endeavor, but still...

I could just be a normal person, I thought as I tugged on my clothes. There were lots of people in the world who went around not solving crimes, and they did just fine. They were still good people.

Maybe I could perfect my lemon pound cake recipe. Or learn to knit, maybe knit blankets and hats for the babies in NICU. Or be the best wife Tony could possibly hope for. Those were all worthwhile endeavors.

I wrinkled my nose. God made Jacob into Israel, father of the twelve tribes of Israel. Personally, I would have preferred something that came with a cape, but whatever. As long as I wasn't a heel-grabber anymore, I would learn to be happy with it.

Viv texted me around noon. *"What time are you getting off? I have booked two appointments for us today—Dorsett Oil and Bitsy Browning."*

I checked my list. *"Should be done by 2."*

"Be ready by 1:45," she replied. *"Dorsett Oil is at 2."*

I frowned and put the phone down. Maybe she needed a reminder that the British were known for being polite.

Before she got there, I had second thoughts, though. We still didn't know if Browning had been murdered, but if he had...a powerful oil company would be a good suspect, right? Browning's reports on earthquakes related to fracking had been getting a lot of attention.

On the one hand, it wouldn't have made a lot of sense for Dorsett Oil to be behind a murder like that. Peter was one reporter. It wasn't as if someone else couldn't have taken up the thread. For all I knew other reporters were already doing it—I hadn't looked for any other reports. So it would be foolish to kill someone to silence them when someone else could easily start where Peter left off. Like a high-stakes game of whack-a-mole.

On the other hand, I was a big chicken. Powerful men scared me.

When Viv picked me up in her Crystal Frost Caddy, I told her as much.

"Salem, men are men. A few well-placed compliments and meaningful looks, and they all fold."

I bit my lip on that. Viv was 80-something, and I was still too overweight to believe anyone would fall for my wiles, Tony being the exception. "Maybe it would be a good idea to let someone know where we are, just in case. Where is the office?"

"In the Metro Tower building. That's where Browning did his interviews, too."

"Oooh! That's the tall building downtown!"

I hadn't been inside that building, but I'd always wanted to go. Forty-something years before, a tornado had torn through downtown Lubbock and demolished a bunch of buildings. The Metro Tower building, then (and now) the tallest building in town, had been damaged but not destroyed. I had heard that if you looked closely, you could tell that the building was slightly twisted.

Although I had stood at the corner of that building no less than five times, peering up along the brick line, I had never been able to discern any twist. Maybe I could see a slight curve. Maybe it just seemed that way because I was looking straight up and my equilibrium got a bit woozy. I wondered if I would be able to tell any better from inside the building, looking down.

"Are you sure your hubby's going to be okay with this?"

I thought about that, but wasn't sure how to answer. I had told him I would be careful. Was this being careful?

"It's a downtown office in the middle of the day," I finally said. "It's not like we're going to be combing back alleys. Again."

Viv shrugged.

"Seriously, nothing is going to happen inside some oil baron's office in the middle of the day. Come on."

"You're the one who was worried about them bumping us off."

"Well, yeah, but that was before I knew their offices were in the death-defying-tornado building. Besides, how many opportunities do we have to even go in a skyscraper around here."

"Honey, you need to get out of Lubbock if you think that's a skyscraper."

"One, yes. Yes, I do. And two, it's close enough to a skyscraper for me. I want to try and see the twist."

Viv flapped a hand. "It's nothing, barely even noticeable."

"You've seen it?"

"Yes, I've seen it. It's just a slight curve near the top of the building."

She said it as if it wasn't a super-amazing freaky fact.

"Seriously? I need to see that."

"Why?"

"A tornado turned an entire brick building."

"Just a little bit."

"A tornado turned an entire brick building!" I repeated for emphasis. "Come on! Like, it twisted an entire building." I held my hands out, twisting them in opposite directions as you'd do if you were demonstrating how to twist open a jar of face cream. "Admit it, that's pretty freaky."

"I guess."

"Can we pretend like I'm your granddaughter and I'm going to inherit your wealth?"

"Granddaughter?!"

"I meant daughter," I said quickly. "Or sister. Maybe your sister who will inherit your millions."

"Sure. If I were you, though, I'd rather pretend I had my own millions to invest."

I hadn't thought of that. Even in my wildest imagination I was mooching off someone else.

I tried again to see the twist in the building, but it still didn't look like anything but a plain old tall building to me.

"Maybe the whole thing is just urban legend," I said as Viv pushed the elevator button for the 20th floor. "Like the lights at Marfa."

"Oh, the lights at Marfa are real," Viv said. She straightened her collar in the reflection of the elevator door.

"You've seen them?"

"A couple of times, actually."

I frowned and kept my mouth shut. I would complain that I'd led a sheltered life, but it hadn't really been that sheltered. Just kind of boring and highly localized. Here I was excited about going up in a 20-story building.

I swatted at my pants and top again to knock away any lingering dog hair. The elevator came to a gentle stop and dinged softly before the doors slid open.

The elevator opened onto a short hallway, flanked by one metal door to the right that led to the stairwell, and one glass door to the left that led to the office of Dorsett Oil. Viv strode through the door like she already owned the place. I followed, trying and probably failing to take on an air of nonchalance.

"Vivian Kennedy," Viv told the middle-aged woman at the desk.

"Good afternoon, Mrs. Kennedy." She smiled brightly. The smile faded just a fraction when she took me in.

"This is my niece, Salem," Viv said. "My much older sister's daughter."

The woman gave a noncommittal smile and nodded. "I believe Mr. Dorsett is ready for you. Have a seat and I'll let him know you're here. Would you like something to drink? A bottled water or soda?"

I took a look around and decided this place could afford to spring for a soda. "Do you have Diet Coke?"

"Of course." She smiled like I shouldn't have to ask that. Viv asked for a bottled water.

We had a seat. Viv looked around like she was judging the decorating and finding it wanting. I tried to sit as lightly as I could, in case the scent of Furr-Ever Lovely Dog Cologne lingered on my clothes.

Mr. Dorsett followed the receptionist back to the waiting area.

"Vivian!" he said, holding out a hand to be shaken.

They shook hands and greeted each other like old friends. I stood and smiled a flat, don't-mind-me-I'm-just-the-deadbeat-niece smile. The receptionist handed us our bottles and went back to her desk.

We followed Dorsett back to his office, which looked exactly the way I expected an oilman's office to look—dark wood paneling, one wall of books that probably nobody read, and a painting of a longhorn standing in bluebonnets behind his desk.

Dorsett got right to the point. "So, your lawyer tells me you're interested in getting into the oil business."

"I'm thinking of expanding my interests in the oil business," Viv clarified. "I've been in the oil business since I married Hoss. But I'm hearing a lot of good things about newer techniques that Hoss wasn't involved in, and I wondered if it might be a good idea to investigate them further, see if it might be a good idea to venture into some other areas and diversify my portfolio." She smiled and leaned on her cane. "You could call this a bit of exploratory drilling." She laughed at her own joke.

Dorsett laughed back. "I understand completely. And you're right, traditional drilling is a safe bet for the conservative investor. Somewhat safe, at any rate. Getting less safe every year, though, as oil is getting harder to find and more expensive to bring up. That's why we've included fracking in our processes. It's not even really new anymore. We've been doing it for fifteen years, and we only got in after we saw other companies work out the logistics." He smiled broadly. "My motto is, it's a lot easier to learn from other people's mistakes than to go through them yourself."

He gave me a look that I interpreted as "Are you listening, loser?" but I could have been wrong.

"I heard that," Viv said.

"And now is the time to buy, since our stock is down from all the stuff in the news." He moved his hand like he was waving away a particularly ineffective gnat. "It'll go back up, believe me. Here. My sales team would give me heck if I don't give you a prospectus. So here." He handed her a folder emblazoned with a serene picture of an open prairie at sunset, the oranges, reds, and yellows of the sky contrasting with the dark purple of the prairie. A weathered windmill stood in the foreground, and a cowboy father and his grade school daughter—wearing a set of pink cowboy boots and her own cowboy hat—walked toward a white farmhouse cozily lit against the oncoming dusk. A pump jack stood in the mid-right of the picture, unobtrusively pumping away to provide this picture perfect world for these picture perfect people.

"But I can summarize everything in that folder in a few sentences. If you trust us with your money, we'll put it to work. We'll use it to put men to work, to harvest our country's natural resources, and we'll do it in a responsible, ethical way. And you'll get a return on your investment that's a lot prettier than what you're getting from traditional drilling."

"Let's talk about that responsible, ethical thing you just mentioned." Viv leaned back in her chair and tapped the bottom of her cane on the carpet. "I'm getting conflicting information about the practice of hydro-fracking in general, and about injection wells and earthquakes in particular."

"Of course, you are," Dorsett said without skipping a beat. "That's the nature of the world we're living in, isn't it? Everybody's got a subject matter expert, and no two of them agree on a single point."

"True, but still. I want to put my money to work making more money. I'm not interested in funding the poisoning of our water or creating earthquakes."

"Yeah," I said, mostly just because I hadn't uttered a single word since we walked in and I was getting annoyed with that.

Dorsett shook his head and frowned a little sadly, as if he couldn't believe we'd be so gullible.

I wondered if he'd practiced that look in the mirror.

"I don't know what reports you've been hearing—"

"Peter Browning's," I said. I studied his face to see what reaction he had to the name.

His frown deepened, but I really had no idea if that indicated more sadness at Browning's passing, or mere annoyance that he was still having to deal with the guy after his death.

"Peter Browning was a good man and obviously passionate about his job. The problem is his passion got the better of his brain. He was looking for any scandal he could find in order to make a name for himself, and to be honest, I don't think it mattered one bit to him what the actual truth was. He had to be David to somebody's Goliath." Dorsett shrugged. "And it's a shame, what he did. I wonder if in his heart he knew the truth and couldn't live with what he'd done."

"There are some reports that perhaps his death wasn't a suicide after all," I said.

"What reports?" Dorsett said, barely holding back a scoff.

My turn to shrug. "I've heard rumors."

"Well, I guess that'll ultimately be for someone else to decide. I know I wasn't there. I assume you weren't, either?" He gave me a pointed look and I had to allow that I had not, in fact, been there.

"But whatever comes out from that doesn't change a few hard facts. Browning skewed his report. I gave him all kinds of sources—" He waved a hand. "All kinds of sources. Geology reports, industry reports, unbiased, scientific studies that all said there was no proven connection between hydro-fracking and earthquakes. Did he mention one of those, ever? No, he did not."

"I think he did," I said.

Viv gave me the side-eye. We probably didn't want to reveal that we'd spent several hours two days before re-watching every single one of Peter Browning's "Special Reports" on the oil industry. That might be hard to explain.

"I think," I stressed. Lame.

I remembered the little Diet Coke in my hands. I twisted off the top and took a swig.

Immediately, I felt my diaphragm constrict. Hiccups. Crud.

"Well, if he mentioned them, it was only in passing. He stressed over and over again a 'connection'—" Air quotes. His lips tightened and he shook his head, like 'Can you believe it?' "The *connection* between injection wells and earthquakes until it looked like Dorsett Oil had personally crippled that little girl. Or David Baucum had."

"Is that what you mean by 'what he'd done?'" I asked. Or tried to ask. In the middle of "done," I hiccuped. It was *so* loud. "Sorry," I said. "What I mean is, do you think he felt some kind of responsibility for David Baucum's death and killed himself out of remorse?"

Dorsett shrugged. He didn't smile or otherwise noticeably change his expression. Still, he managed to look chillingly smug.

"Could be. I guess we might not ever know. But I know how I'd feel if I'd vilified a man for something that was an act of God. Hounded him until he lost his family's business, until he had nothing left to live for. I'd feel pretty bad about that, let me tell you." He shook his head in an *"ain't-it-a-shame"* kind of way. Then he lifted his hands, took a deep breath, brought his elbows onto the desk, and faced Viv. "Anyway, we're completely off track here. What Peter Browning did or didn't do isn't why you're here."

My heart raced a tiny bit at that. "Of course no-*OT*," I couldn't help but say. And hiccup.

"Of course not," Viv echoed, giving me a scathing look. "I just like to know what I'm mixed up in."

"Well, I can put your mind at ease about that. In that prospectus is a copy of all our reports. Our industry is regulated like no other, and you can read through our entire clean bill of health if you need something to put you to sleep at night. It's all in there, every time we dotted an I or crossed a T."

I nodded toward the folder and hiccuped again.

The problem was, it was funny. And when I try not to laugh, I get semi-hysterical. In fact, nothing in the world is funnier than trying not to laugh.

I felt the hysteria bubbling in me and decided I had to get out of there. I slid to the front of my seat. "Well, we appreciate yo-*UR* time." I clamped my lips together, but some bubbles of laughter escaped out my nose.

Viv gave me another withering look as I stood, but she stood, too, and held out her hand. "I'll be getting back to you," she said.

Back in the reception area, I smiled and nodded at the receptionist, hurrying through as quickly as I could while also trying to look like I was not hurrying.

Viv, not ready to let go of her role as Wealthy Investor just yet, swanned through the room holding the prospectus folder with her nose in the air. She joined me in the hallway as I pushed the elevator button.

"What is your deal?" she asked, irritated.

"Hicc-*UPS*," I said. Then giggled.

"I know that." She sighed and pursed her lips. "You act like a ten-year-old boy who's just seen his first nudie. How are we ever going to be taken seriously if—"

"Oh, my gosh!" I cut her off. Exiting another office down the hallway was Imogene Walker.

I grabbed Viv's arm and pulled her toward the stairs.

The stairwell door slammed behind us. "Imogene!" I hissed. Then hiccuped. The sound echoed off the concrete walls.

Viv frowned and looked through the window. "What in the world is she doing here?"

"I don't know, but I don't want to ta-*ALK* to her." I giggled, collapsing against the stair rail.

"Not in the state you're in," Viv agreed. She narrowed her eyes at me, which made me laugh even harder. "Get a grip on yourself, for crying out loud."

I took a deep breath and tried to do just that. "Come on," I said, heading down the stairs.

"Well, I'm not going to climb twenty flights of stairs," Viv said behind me. "We'll go down one and then get the elevator there."

"But what if she's coming down and we ca-*ATCH* her there?" I asked. I couldn't help it—I pictured the elevator door sliding open, me letting a roaring hiccup loose into the confines of the small space, and Imogene unleashing the full force of her disapproval in one eye-burning glare.

This sent me into a fresh gale of giggles. I staggered down the steps, holding onto the rail and fighting for breath. The more I laughed, the more I hiccupped. The sound reverberated against the walls and made me laugh harder.

"Stop it!" Viv smacked me on the shoulder. "You look like a lunatic."

I nodded and swallowed, fighting for breath. "Sorry," I said. I stopped on the landing for the 19th floor and wiped tears of laughter from my eyes. I took a deep breath, feeling the tightness in my chest ease a bit. Maybe I was done. I tentatively took a few more breaths. Yes, I was done. I was almost sure of it.

Okay. One more deep breath. I swallowed, determined to move forward like a rational, sane person.

In mid-swallow, though, I hiccuped again. The spasm jerked my tongue back. For a second I felt like I was going to swallow my own tongue.

I gasped and grabbed my throat. "Oh my gosh!"

Aaaand, I was off again. Giggling, hiccuping, staggering down steps, clinging to the stair rail, bent over as tears streamed down my face. I made it to the eighteenth floor landing and sat on the bottom stair, helpless and weak.

When I was finally able to get myself back under control, I wiped my eyes again and looked around for Viv. She was standing beside the stairwell window, silently scrolling through something on her phone.

I drew a few test breaths. Yes, I was definitely done now. No more hiccups. No more giggles. "What are you looking at?" I croaked.

"I'm searching for what is wrong with you."

"Well, let me know what you find out," I said. "Whew." I drew another breath and wiped my hands on my pants. "That was fun."

"According to this, you might have emotional incontinence." She held a warning finger up. "Do. Not. Start again."

I laughed, but it was just normal laughter now, somewhat controlled. "How am I not supposed to laugh at that?" I stood and looked over her shoulder. "Emotional incontinence sounds like—y ikes. That's a real thing?"

"A neurological disorder, usually caused by head trauma."

I skimmed through the Google description. "Uncontrollable crying and laughing. Wow. How awful."

Viv narrowed her eyes at me again, studying. "No, I don't think this is what you have."

I shook my head. "No, thank goodness."

"I think what you have is just..."

"A bad case of immaturity?" I offered.

Viv nodded. "Exactly. Okay, can we go now? Imogene left five minutes ago." She tilted her head toward the window.

I stood on tiptoe and peered down at the parking lot, far below. I took one more deep breath and squared my shoulders. "Absolutely. Let's do this."

Viv opened the door and headed toward the elevator. "Finally."

I followed her into the elevator and concentrated on breathing normally, not wanting to set myself off again. As the elevator stopped with a soft ding and the doors slid open, I said, "Where are we going now?"

"To talk to Bitsy Browning, the young pregnant widow. Do try to keep it together, won't you?"

As we passed through the lobby, I looked at the row of portraits along one wall. I stopped with a gasp. "Viv, look! It's Imogene Walker!"

"Would you give it a rest! I told you, she left."

"No, look. On the wall."

I approached the portrait of Imogene, in line with other portraits of men. Judging by the hairstyle, the portrait was forty years old, but it was definitely Imogene. Her skin was smoother but her expression was just as severe. I stood back and found a plaque that described what all these 1970s faces were doing there.

"Cool," I said. "Imogene was one of the architects who studied the building after the tornado and helped get it back into shape for occupation."

"Would you look at that hair," Viv said.

"Well, it was the '70s," I said.

"There were a couple of good hairstyles from the '70s. She could have chosen one of them."

"She was too busy being a high-powered architect," I said. "Moving and shaking, you know." I studied the row of pictures alongside her. There was the original architect from the '50s, the real estate developer who'd had the place built, and a couple of other men who had been involved in getting the building back into usable shape. Imogene was the only female. I wondered how they had treated her. Maybe that's why she was so grumpy. She was tired from fighting for her gender for so many years.

I chewed my lip. "I'm about to suggest something, and I want you to tell me no," I said.

"Got it."

"Remember Browning's interviews with Baucum, where he talked about how they design buildings for worst-case scenarios? Imogene would probably know something about that. We could talk to her about it."

"Nope."

I nodded. "Yes, I know, but..."

"Nope. Not happening.

"But what if...what if Browning had the wrong end of the stick, somehow? What if he latched onto this one thread to explain that disaster, but that wasn't really the whole picture? Imogene would probably know something about it."

"So what if she did? What would that have to do with Browning's death?"

I didn't really know how to answer that one. It probably had nothing to do it with it. But I still felt like I needed to talk to Imogene and get her take on Browning's interviews with Baucum.

I shrugged. "Probably nothing," I allowed, turning to go.

"Besides, you would probably get nervous and giggle your fool head off."

"Mmmm, you're right." I shuddered. Nobody needed that.

By the time we got to Bitsy Browning's place, I had fully recovered. Although I did have *Itsy Bitsy Spider* stuck in my head.

Viv killed the motor and sat back in her seat.

"You ready?" I grabbed my purse off the floorboard.

"Hang on." She was staring straight ahead, breathing in a weird way.

My heart lurched. It was easy to forget that Viv was 80-something—I didn't really know because she refused to say, so even that was a guess based on some of her drunkalogue stories—but at times she would take on a look that reminded me. One of my worst and most secret fears was losing Viv. "Are you okay?"

She shook her head. "I just remembered we're about to go talk to a brand new widow who's almost nine months pregnant. I'm trying to figure out what to say to her."

I tried to remember a time when Viv had appeared to care one bit how anyone reacted to her. "Wow, Viv," I said. "That's surprisingly thoughtful of you."

"I know," she said. "I think that yoga did something to me."

"Does that mean we're not going back?" I asked, trying not to sound hopeful.

"Oh, we're going back," she said. "I look dynamite in my leotard. Okay, we're going to tread carefully here," she said.

"Are you thinking like Trisha does, that she couldn't possibly be responsible because she's pregnant?"

"Not necessarily. I just feel like the odds are against it. I mean, just going by our list, she's at best got a 25 percent chance of being our guy."

"Yes, but going by larger statistics—society at large, I mean—the first person the police look at in a crime is always the spouse. So we have to bump her up to at least 50 percent."

Viv sighed. "I know you're right. But let's just tread carefully on this one."

She didn't have to tell me. She was the one without a filter. But still, I said, "Okay, I'll follow your lead."

Viv rapped lightly on the door, and Bitsy answered almost immediately.

"Come in," she said, stepping back to let us in.

"Thank you for agreeing to see us," Viv said.

"Patrice told me it would be a good idea to talk to you."

Viv and I looked at each other. That helped.

I wasn't sure what I had expected from someone newly widowed—maybe that she'd be still in her pajamas in the middle of the afternoon, with dark circles under bloodshot eyes. But Bitsy looked fairly well put together. She only had light makeup on, but I was pretty sure she was wearing some. Her dark curly hair was held back by a purple headband, and she wore a purple and black maternity smock.

She led us into a small living room, tastefully decorated, and indicated chairs for us. She sat and folded her legs under her. She was the daintiest pregnant woman I had ever seen.

"It's sweet of you to be taking on this case," Bitsy said.

I experienced the now-familiar moment of resistance to the idea of anyone thinking of me and Viv as actual detectives. But we had been involved in some fairly high-profile events, so I supposed it had come to appear we knew what we were doing, anyway. Maybe if you acted enough like you knew what you were doing, people treated you like you did, and eventually you just did. Self-actualization.

Maybe I should try that with being skinny. Being a good wife. Being a fully-functioning, responsible adult.

"Patrice told us how frustrated she is with the police. She thinks they are writing Peter's death off as—self-inflicted—" Viv left just the merest hint of a pause. "She's afraid they're not investigating it as thoroughly as they should be. Is that your opinion as well?"

Bitsy nodded with a brave smile and tears pooled in her big amber eyes. "I know what it looks like. I understand that they're doing their job, and they're going by the evidence they see. I know it appears he was alone, and I know they found that note. But I know Peter." Her voice broke, and she swallowed. "I know him. He wouldn't have done that. He was excited about the future. He was excited about our baby." She shook her head. "I don't believe it. I'm sorry. I just don't believe it."

Viv and I exchanged a brief look.

Viv said, "What I'd really like to do is get your thoughts. You were privy to his thoughts and fears. I don't want to be too intrusive, but I think it would be most helpful if you could share some of your thoughts on who might have wanted to harm Peter and make it look self-inflicted? Was there someone he was particularly fearful of? Someone who had made threats?"

"Well, you can imagine. He did that story on the police last year and that made him pretty unpopular. Both of us, actually." She shook her head, her fat curls bouncing, then stared at the ceiling and blinked back more tears. "I was threatened at a Junior League meeting, for heaven's sake." She laughed through tears. "Three of the policemen's wives cornered me in the ladies room and told me I'd better get my husband to shut his mouth or we were both going to regret it. They said pictures would turn up of him in a compromising position. He would become the laughingstock of the entire town, and he could kiss his career goodbye."

"Jeez," I said. "The Junior League, really?" I knew I was right to be intimidated by those women.

"Seriously. It was so...ridiculous, but still so scary. Peter said they were all talk, they couldn't actually do anything, but it was terrifying. Every time I passed a police car, I would have a panic attack. Imagine, if the people in power really are corrupt? I mean, who do you turn to? Who do you trust?"

"From what I remember, the officer who was implicated in that case resigned and moved away. Is that right?"

Bitsy nodded. "He was from Colorado, and last we heard he lives there. He's not a cop—he can't be, legally. He can't even be a security guard. I think he was selling cars at a friend's dealership in Denver or somewhere around there, although I'm not entirely sure about that. That's just what I heard."

"Did he threaten Peter?"

Bitsy shook her head. "I really don't know. After the thing with the Junior League, Peter stopped talking to me about it. He didn't want me to worry. He wanted to convince me that everything was fine."

"Did he seem afraid, though?"

"Honestly, no. He seemed excited. I think he really got into the idea of being a crusader, you know? He was energized by it. And once that whole thing was cleared, he really seemed a bit bummed by it." She laughed, then sniffed back tears.

Viv and I looked at each other. That lined up with what Dorsett had said. He needed to be the David to someone's Goliath.

"And once that officer resigned, was it over? I don't remember hearing much more about it."

"Peter was pretty upset that no charges were filed. He didn't like the brush-it-under-the-rug aspect of everything. But the guy lost his career, he wouldn't be able to be in a position of authority like that, a position of power. So Peter said that had to be justice enough."

"He was a believer in justice."

"He was definitely a believer in justice. Like I said, a crusader."

"How was his relationship with the police after all that?"

Bitsy shrugged. "Like I said, he stopped talking to me about stuff like that. From what I saw, though, it was okay. Maybe Patrice would be the one to ask about that."

"Do you think that the whole scandal has anything to do with how they're handling this case now? That maybe they're not investigating as hard as they could, because they're holding a grudge?"

She took a deep breath. She thought for a moment. "I don't know. I hate to think that, but..."

"Well, I guess it's one possibility that we ought to keep in mind," Viv said. "What other stories come to mind, when you think of people who could possibly want to harm him?"

"This whole thing with NorthStar and Baucum Engineering, of course. Dorsett Oil. All the stories he pulled together with the earthquakes and other failed buildings. I mean, he talked to a lot of people, and several of them didn't come off looking too good."

"How did he react to David Baucum's death?" I blurted the question without thinking. Viv gave me a look. Possibly this was the kind of question she had been trying to avoid asking.

"He was really upset by it, of course. I mean, it was so sad and so senseless." She shook her head. "Tragic."

I wondered if she would say anything about the irony of the two men's deaths. The connection to the events at NorthStar. That event had been the end of one man's career and looked to be the catalyst for another man's rise. Both had died by what appeared to be self-inflicted means, and both conclusions were questionable. Did Baucum intend to kill himself, or had he just become careless? Did Browning kill himself, or had someone made it look like he had?

I studied her face to see if there was anything else there— resentment toward Baucum, for example. Anger. Remorse.

I couldn't see much, but it did seem like she was holding something back. Her mouth tightened and she drew back into her chair just the tiniest bit. But she just shook her head again and repeated, "Tragic."

"Bitsy, Patrice told us about the note that was found in Peter's car. She said it said something like, 'I never meant for this to happen.' Do you think he was talking about David Baucum?"

"The note said, 'I didn't mean for it to turn out this way.' And I know that's what the police think, that it was a suicide note speaking to David Baucum's death. And I can understand that, to a point. I mean, the fallout from David Baucum's mistakes has been enormous, and a lot of people have used Peter as the lightning rod for all that fallout, because he was a visible entity. He put a face to the entire debacle coming to light. But it's not as if Peter caused any of that to happen. And it's not as if anyone else couldn't and wouldn't have asked the same questions Peter did. It's not as if the same conclusions would not have been reached, should someone else have been the one to grab that ball and run with it. Peter did an excellent job of ferreting out the truth and bringing a real problem to light, but it's not as if he caused the problem."

"I understand," Viv assured her. "But did Peter understand that? What I'm asking is, is there any possibility that he carried remorse—"

"No." The word was spat out, and Bitsy's once-friendly eyes turned bitter. "I know what you're asking, and the answer is no. He was sympathetic to the tragedy that David Baucum's decisions caused, and he was sympathetic to a man who had to live with knowing he'd caused so much damage. But he felt no ownership in that man's decisions. David Baucum is the one who decided to drink half a bottle of vodka and take a bottle of Ambien."

"What do you think the note meant?" I asked.

Bitsy shrugged. "It could be anything, right? I mean, maybe he was writing a note about Baucum. Maybe he felt some—some sadness about what Baucum did and wanted to communicate that to the family. But it could have been something as simple as he hadn't intended for a story to be produced or edited differently from the way it was. It was scribbled on a notepad that he kept on his desk, and it could have meant anything. Anything at all."

Viv gave me a side-eye, and I knew what we were both thinking, but we silently agreed not to say it. The note could have referred to Misty Monahan, of course. That he'd never intended to have an affair with her. That he'd never intended to have a child with her.

"I know you've already addressed this, but I feel like we need to ask again," I said. "Just in case. Did he seem fearful at all about retaliation from Baucum Engineering or Dorsett Oil? Any of their employees? Shareholders?"

Bitsy sighed again and shook her head. She seemed a little sad now, or maybe just very tired. "No. I keep going over and over it in my mind. The thing is, the last several months I've been totally wrapped up in my own world, you know?" She ran a hand over her rounded belly. "All I've talked about is baby. What she looks like now, what's developed, how I want to decorate the nursery, all the things I want to do with her as a mom. All the things I wanted us to do as a—" She stopped and swallowed. "As a family. So maybe he was concerned and I just didn't notice. But he was also excited. He loved that he was getting attention from the bigger stations. He was so excited about that. We were already planning where we'd move next. He wanted to go to Dallas or Houston, or maybe even out of state. He had talked to a station in Atlanta. He was looking forward to the future. I honestly never remember anything that seemed fearful."

"Fair enough," Viv said. "We'd like to conduct some more interviews, of course. Would it be okay with you if we make it known that we have your permission? That helps sometimes."

"Of course," Bitsy said. "Feel free to have them call me. I appreciate everything you can do."

We stood to go, and there was an awkward moment when I felt like she should do something else—shake hands, or hug, even. But we all just nodded and then she turned toward the door.

We were on the front porch when she said, "Oh, hey. I just thought of something I was going to ask you. The police asked me if Peter had been in a fight or had injured himself somehow, before he died. But they wouldn't tell me why. Do you know anything about that?"

Viv and I looked at each other, then we both shook our heads.

"I keep thinking about it, because he said it a couple of times—like, did he injure himself that day, or the day before?" She sniffed back more tears. "They wouldn't let me see him, you know. When they found him. He'd been lying in that mud for three days, and apparently some...animal had been at him." She looked at the ceiling and blinked, her voice shaking. "I wanted to see him, but they just would not let me. So it must have been bad, right? But even with...all that...he asked about a fight or injury during his last few days. So that's something. Right? It means something?" She shook her head. "I just don't know what."

We could only shrug and shake our heads. "We'll definitely let you know if we find out," Viv promised.

I checked my phone again when we left Bitsy's. Nothing.

Suddenly tired, I invited Viv over for dinner, secretly hoping she would offer to buy takeout.

No such luck. "I'm going home to do some research."

"That thing she said about an injury?" I was curious about that, too.

"What? Oh, no. I've watched the entire first two seasons of Marple and I have yet to find anything remotely attractive about that woman. It might be time to move on."

"From Nigel?" Indeed it might, I thought.

She looked at me like I was crazy. "No, not from Nigel. From Marple. There's got to be an attractive female detective in a great nation like Great Britain."

"Well, good luck with that," I said as she dropped me off. It was just as well. My mind was about done in, thinking about Peter Browning, Bitsy Browning, Dorsett Oil, Imogene Walker.

Tony.

I grilled some chicken breasts, onions and peppers for dinner, and Frank brought over some flour tortillas. We settled with our fajitas in front of the TV to watch Frank's favorite Spanish soap opera. I couldn't tell much of what was going on, but Frank filled me in. Just after ten o'clock, my phone rang.

It was G-Ma. "Turn on Channel 13."

"Why? Did the Cowboys announce a new quarterback?" The only time G-Ma felt compelled to call about the news, it was related to the Dallas Cowboys.

"No, that reporter friend of yours was arrested."

"Trisha?!" I jumped up to switch on the TV.

"Not her, that other girl."

I flipped through to Channel 13 and gasped when I saw Misty Monahan being led away from Channel 11 in handcuffs. Bobby and another detective walked behind her, and two uniform cops walked in front of her. I was too freaked out to listen to the voice- over, but a picture of Peter Browning popped up in the bottom corner of the screen.

"No way!" I said. "Misty Monahan?"

"That's what they said," G-Ma said. "She was arrested for the murder."

"I need to call Bobby," I said to G-Ma. "I'll call you back in a minute." I pushed the *end* button, then said, "Windy, call Bobby."

"I'm gettin' him right now, Sweetie," Windy said, her little wind streams waving in a digital breeze.

I got his voicemail. "This is Detective Sloan. Leave a message."

"Bobby, why did you arrest Misty Monahan? What do you have on her? Call me back."

I hung up. Would Tony consider that being careful?

"Call Viv," I said to Windy, just as the phone rang and Viv's face popped up on the screen.

"Misty Monahan got arrested!" she said as soon as I picked up.

"I know! I kind of freaked out and didn't hear what they said."

"They said obstruction in the investigation of the death of Peter Browning."

"Obstruction. Hmmm..." I had no idea what to say about that. That could mean almost anything. We needed more information. "I saw it on 13. Where did you see it?"

"Channel 13 for me, too."

"What are you doing watching Channel 13? Tri-Patrice is going to be mad."

"Then don't tell her," Viv said. "Why were you watching Channel 13?"

"G-Ma called me and told me about the arrest."

"Channel 11 isn't running it," Viv said. "I'm looking at it right now, and they're talking about a cold front moving in over the weekend."

"I guess they're in a bad spot. An arrest has been made in their star reporter's death, but the arrest is another one of their star reporters. How do you spin that?"

"By focusing on the weather. Apparently this is the rainiest November since 1990-something."

Viv and I fell silent, both watching as the newscast went on to a high school football, then college football, then national football. Because this was Texas; if all else fails—football.

When the camera moved back to Trisha, I studied her face. She wasn't big enough yet to really look pregnant, but her eyes did look tired. Had she been crying? It was hard to tell.

The sports guy, the requisite "color" personality of the show, was noticeably subdued, although he said all the right things. They went to a national story about the upcoming election, then one about a development in driverless cars. Then a commercial.

"Are they just going to pretend like it didn't happen?" Viv asked. "Unbelievable."

But in the last two minutes of the newscast, the station manager did one of his "In My Opinion" segments, where the rest of the news desk went dark, and he stood to the side in a spotlight and...well, gave his opinion. Sometimes he would use the segment to endorse a candidate in an election, or to complain about a lack of transparency on utility rates, or how Lubbock needed and deserved a minor-league baseball team.

"Tonight, I want to address something that many of you have already heard about, and we're already seeing mention of it on our social media. As you know, Channel 11 and all of our counterparts around the world, in fact, are tasked with reporting facts. We bring to you the stories that affect our lives and the world around us, both locally and far from home. Oftentimes, those stories become much more than just stark facts—they become intensely personal. Even in those times, it is still our job to be objective and fair in our reporting. But nothing has been more personal to this station than the death last week of Peter Browning or the arrest today of Misty Monahan on charges of obstruction in the investigation into Peter's death."

The man stopped and cleared his throat. He took a deep breath.

"In a team meeting this afternoon, we reached a consensus that we would not—that we simply could not—treat this as any other story. This is our family, and we are all staggered both by Peter's death and by Misty's arrest. We don't even know what to say, except that we are grateful for the outpouring of support that we've received over the last week, and we continue to place the utmost faith in the Lubbock Police Department and in our justice system. As we go through the next few days and weeks, we will do our best to stay on task, to report on the news that matters to you, and to continue to work with the LPD as they discover the truth about what happened to Peter. We ask that you remember that there is a place for justice, and it is time for us to take a step back and let that justice happen. We ask for your patience and your continued prayers and support. We ask for your prayers to continue for the family of Peter Browning. And—" Another deep breath. "And on a personal note, I ask also for the prayers and support of Misty Monahan and her family. I understand the gravity of the situation that she's in, and I know that it might be hard for some of you to even consider what I'm saying. But I would remind you of this fact: in our country, one is considered innocent until proven guilty. Nothing has been proven yet, so at this point Misty Monahan is an innocent woman, and she and her family need your support. Thank you."

The soft music started and the lights slowly faded as he turned and walked, head bowed, out of the now-empty studio.

"Whoa," Viv said. "I told you she was hiding something."

"Literally, if she's been charged with obstruction. Right? Isn't that what that means"

"I guess it could mean a lot of things."

"I called Bobby to ask why they'd arrested Misty, but I got his voice mail."

"Call him back. Then tell me what he said."

I hung up and did as I was told. I couldn't very well get into any danger calling Bobby, surely. If he wanted to do something nefarious to me, he would have done it long ago when he had more justification than just me annoying him.

He answered this time. "Sloan."

"Bobby, I left you a message. Why didn't you call me back?" I knew why he didn't call me back. He didn't want to. But I liked to annoy him.

"Oh, Salem, good. I was just about to call you and fill you in on all the news about our latest arrest." Then he put the phone down with a clunk and laughed. Ridiculously loudly. Like a braying ass, in fact. Then he hung up.

I called Viv back. "I got nada," I said.

"We should go up to the police station and talk to him. We always get more information that way."

I considered that for a moment. We had gone to the police station a few times and tried to get information out of Bobby. One time Viv had even faked a heart attack, which is probably a crime, and I was definitely afraid we would be arrested then. Each time we went to the police station, in fact, I'd left feeling like I was lucky to get away. Calling Tony from jail was not something I wanted to do.

I do love you, but...

"Let's think of another way," I said.

"Back to Channel 11, then," Viv said. "Somebody there will know something."

"Now?" It was 10:30, and I was already up past my normal bed time. I did have work the next day. Besides, Trisha wouldn't be there, so the chances of us getting anything good were remote at best.

"Oh," Viv said. Not a big sleeper anyway, Viv sometimes had to be reminded that the rest of the human race needed more than two or three hours a night. "Well, as soon as you get off work tomorrow."

I tilted the phone away and looked at Frank. "Can you watch Stump tomorrow after work?"

He nodded toward the pile of plates on the coffee table. "Can you make more fajitas?"

I gave him a thumbs up and said to Viv, "Deal. As soon as I get off work tomorrow."

CHAPTER ELEVEN

Space Cops

Viv called me at work the next day to say she'd found out where Misty Monahan lived.

"How?"

"I was there when she posted bail and I followed her home," she said.

"Seriously?" That seemed so...simple.

"We'll go talk to her in person. She'll be caught on her back foot and we might be able to get something out of her."

I didn't care for the thought of facing Misty Mohanah again, but it did seem to be the next logical step.

I had to wait for my last dog to be dried before I could finish, so I checked my phone for the dozenth time that day to see if Tony had called. It was only one day. He'd said a few days.

I ordered myself not to be neurotic and needy. *Be a grown-up!* I said sternly to my reflection in the grooming shop bathroom mirror.

This did no good, of course. I decided that if I couldn't be a grown-up, I could at least be distracted. I mentally ran down the list of contacts and stories Peter Browning had done that could be connected to his death.

I couldn't bring myself to watch another video of David Baucum being vilified, but I realized that I had not re-watched the stories about the LPD Christmas toy scandal that had originally put Browning on the local map. I had seen the stories the first time, of course, but it might help to watch them again with the benefit of hindsight.

I found that link in the list Trisha had sent and played it.

"Patrice, we received an anonymous tip today on an allegation   that—while not felonious or violent—can be described as nothing but heinous." He punctuated that with a brief shake of his head, as if he couldn't quite believe what he was about to tell us. "Take a look."

The scene went to a shot of a giant red Santa bag overflowing with toys. Uniformed police officers stood smiling, shaking hands, and receiving gifts as people came up and handed them toy after toy.

"The generosity of the South Plains is well known. It's part of the culture. Part of who we are. And at Christmastime, we pull out all the stops. But this year, one generous gift garnered special attention."

Switch to the commercial for last Christmas' hottest toy, the Space Cop flying policeman. The Space Cop was impossible to get. The kind of thing that sold on eBay for ten times the retail price—which had been kind of high to begin with. Whether by chance or by design, the manufacturer had not anticipated such a response to Space Cop and hadn't supplied enough, creating the kind of consumer-driven frenzy that legends are made of. Toy stores were reporting fist fights over the few they occasionally got in stock, and there were online maps of Space Cop sightings. Before Black Friday, stores put out announcements that they had no Space Cops in stock, and there were real cops on hand to handle those who didn't believe them.

And for the police department toy drive, someone had donated a Space Cop.

The scene switched back to the giant Santa bag, but this time there were special effects lighting and hallelujah music, along with a pan shot of Space Cop on top of the rest of the pile. Misty Monahan had been the one to report on that story, and when she did, Patrice and her co-anchor, along with the weatherman and sports desk, had gone on for too long about how bad their kids wanted a Space Cop and the ridiculous lengths they were considering going to, to get one for them.

Then the donated Space Cop disappeared. It was just a rumor at first, and there were stories going around that it hadn't been lost, that it had already been given out, that it was just random and nobody knew what was in their gift bags until they left the police department. Browning did one story on it, a very friendly one in the chief of police's office, giving them the chance to explain how the toy distribution worked and to lay the public outrage to rest.

"Of course we keep everything anonymous and untrackable. Nobody wants to track down some eight-year-old and have them justify the gift they received from Santa. People just have to trust in the process and believe that they did a good thing for a lot of deserving kids and leave it at that. Gifts are gifts. No strings attached."

But then Peter Browning received an anonymous tip. One of the cops in charge of distributing the toys had a son who had received a Space Cop for Christmas.

The cop denied stealing the toy, of course. He said it was a gift from out-of-state grandparents.

The poor kid was the one I felt sorry for. A teacher from his school came into Flo's Bow Wow Barbers and talked about all the bullying he was getting. Kids were jealous, first of all, because he'd gotten a Space Cop for Christmas, and the rumors that his dad had stolen it were enough to turn the envy into righteous anger and then into full-on bullying. He'd taken so much crud over the next few days that his mom pulled him out of school.

One would think that would be enough to make people back off and consider that perhaps things were blown out of proportion, but, of course, it wasn't. Browning did a story on the bullying and the kid leaving school. Not a word about how his story had contributed to the furor, of course. Pandemonium erupted from all sides. People thought Browning should back off and quit stirring the pot. Others thought the cops were corrupt and used the charity as a front for furnishing their own Christmas mornings, and others declared they would never give to a police charity again. Rumors started circulating that the entire department was corrupt from floor to ceiling.

Within a few days it came out that the cop had, in fact, diverted the Space Cop to his own locker. His wife refuted the grandparent story. She was furious that her kid was being bullied, of course, and wasn't going to go down with her husband.

The cop posted an ill-advised diatribe on Facebook:

"You try working with these deadbeat parents day in and day out. See how they don't work, they don't take care of their kids, they don't even know where their kids are half the time. And think about them playing the hero on Christmas morning while their kid get the hottest toy around. Meanwhile, you, who's been putting your life on the line for those same deadbeats for the past year, wrap up a sad replica because you can't afford the real thing, despite working sixty hour weeks for months. See if you're not tempted."

The post was deleted soon after, but of course someone did a screen grab and it lived in infamy.

Poor guy. The theft hadn't risen to the level of felony, of course, but he was given the opportunity to quit before he was fired. This opportunity brought fresh outrage, and the police chief eventually decided he was fed up with the whole mess and retired. He'd been on the brink anyway. This was pretty much the last straw. On his way out the door, he made it very clear how he felt about having to lose a good cop over a stupid toy and how he thought the media was more interested in stirring pots than they were in anything the public had a right to know.

As I scissored my last dog, I thought about what Jessica and Bitsy had both said. People were angry at Browning for pursuing this story. People got a little crazy when they perceived the police or military weren't being fully appreciated. It was a matter of loyalty. That feeling of betrayal could stir up a lot of passion in some people. Could one of them honestly have been angry enough to kill him over it?

Stump and I drove home, and I thawed beef flank steaks for more fajitas. I checked the fridge and saw that I did not, in fact, have any of the other ingredients.

"I'll stop by the store after our interview," I promised Frank.

He grunted from the recliner, already wrapped up in his Telemundo soap opera.

Misty lived in a duplex—one of a row of duplexes—with a tiny front yard surrounded by a short brick wall. I didn't know what I expected from someone who'd been recently arrested for murder, but it wasn't to be greeted at the door by that person in bare feet, wearing gray sweats and a Red Raiders jersey. I hadn't even knocked.

Misty opened the door. "Did Patrice send you?"

"Ummm, no." I gave Viv a quick glance.

"Does she know you're here?"

Jeez-O-Peet , how did someone standing in bare feet and baggy sweats manage to be so intimidating?

"I—I don't know."

Misty frowned, then stepped back, holding the door open.

I looked again at Viv, who—for once—seemed as hesitant as I felt.

"Well? Come on." She motioned with her head for us to come inside.

I hurried in and sat on the edge of the sofa, making myself as small as I could so as not to give offense.

After another moment, Viv stepped into the room, shoulders back and nose high. She had recovered her inner snob, I was glad to see. One of us had to show some backbone, and apparently it wasn't my turn.

Misty sat in a recliner across from the sofa and crossed one leg over the other. "If Patrice didn't send you, why are you here?"

"I—uh—well..."

"We want to know why you were arrested," Viv said. Clearly, Viv wasn't going to be thrown by Misty's attitude a second time. "As I told you before, we're investigating the death, and this is obviously a development that is of interest to us."

Misty rocked a couple of times, her mouth set. She let out a breath audibly through her nose.

Then she uncrossed her legs and sat forward.

"Peter and I had—well, I guess you'd call it an affair." She rolled her eyes. "We had a relationship, and he told me he was going to leave his wife. When she became pregnant, I broke up with him. I'm not interested in wrecking anyone's family. Anyway..."

I did mental math. Misty was also pregnant—at least, she hadn't denied being pregnant when we confronted her in the parking lot, and she seemed like the kind of person who had no problem telling people they were wrong. But she also didn't look pregnant at all.

Bitsy was eight months pregnant. The fact had been well publicized since the third month. If Misty had broken up with Browning once news of his wife's pregnancy had become public, she would have to be at least five months along by now. But her stomach was flat. Darn her.

Misty waited, not bothering to disguise her contempt while she watched me process the information. Then she said, "We hooked up again about six weeks ago. We were drunk. It was—it was stupid. A mistake."

"And now you're pregnant."

Misty cut her eyes to Viv, but didn't respond with a yay or nay. "I tried to keep a decent working relationship going, but I think Peter was just freaked out by the whole thing. I told him I didn't expect anything from him. I'm a grown woman, and I know the way the world works. I made a stupid decision, and I was prepared to live with the consequences of it. But I wanted him to be aware, because it was, of course, his child, too. He refused to talk to me."

Misty blew out a breath and sat back in her chair. "He would communicate only be text or email, which I found to be ridiculous. We are adults and I, for one, wanted to act like it. I insisted Peter meet with me so we could have a face-to-face conversation. I—" She frowned and looked off, then turned back. "I threatened him. I told him if he insisted on treating me like a dirty secret, I would act like one. I would tell his wife, tell the station manager. I wasn't going to really do it, but I was so furious that he was acting like such a little...toad." She frowned and her lips thinned. "He said he would meet me after the 10:00 o'clock that night, so I drove to where we agreed to meet."

"And where was that?"

"Mackenzie Park, out past the amusement park."

I looked at Viv. That was pretty far from where Browning had been found.

"He never showed, of course. That was the night he..." She frowned again, but didn't break.

I studied her carefully. She was a few years younger than I was, but she seemed so...in control of herself. No nonsense. She was a person who had sight of what she wanted and poured her energy into getting it.

Even now, with this difficult conversation, she was remarkably calm.

She cleared her throat and went on. "He never showed. I waited for a while and then came home. The next day I found out that he hadn't gone home, and Bitsy was frantic. Didn't know where he was. He was supposed to come in to work at 2:00 that afternoon, but he never showed. That's when things really got crazy."

I nodded, stunned that she was revealing so much information, until it dawned on me that none of this really explained why she'd been arrested. "So, you were arrested because you and Browning had an affair? How is that obstruction?"

She shook her head and sighed. "It's not just that, of course. When his body was found, I just...I didn't want it coming out. About the affair. I didn't want Bitsy to have to deal with that, on top of losing her husband and the father of her child. So I logged into his email account and deleted all of our messages."

"You have his password?" Viv sounded shocked.

"Look, it's not that big a deal. I knew his password, he knew mine. We helped each other with assignments and things. It wasn't that big a deal," she said again.

"So you..." I tried to work it out in my mind. "Did you miss one or something?"

She shook her head. "No. At least, I don't think so. Patrice told them to look for other stories Peter could have been working on. Something about him working a new angle on something. So they did a deeper search and were able to see that I'd logged in remotely and deleted them." She gave a crooked smile and shook her head again. "I was afraid that the emails made me look guilty of something I didn't do. But deleting them made me look even more guilty."

"Wow," I said. This girl was in a lot of trouble. Now would not be the time to alert her to the fact that I might have set that particular ball rolling.

"Yeah," Misty said. "I'm pretty well screwed."

"Why are you telling us all this?" Viv asked.

"Because I need help, of course. My parents have hired a lawyer, but they can't afford a really good one—I can't either. The station pays crap, and I'm already up to my eyeballs in student loans. The police obviously think they've got me on something, and if it does turn out to be murder and not suicide, they're not going to look much further than me. Why would they? You know what's going to happen when the public finds out about the baby. Sweet petite Bitsy with the big blue eyes and little basketball belly. And then there's me, the hussy who tempted her man away and then killed him in a jealous rage, leaving her a young widow. I'm screwed," she said again. "I need help."

"You are in a spot of bother," Viv acknowledged.

"I know I didn't kill him, and I need help figuring out who did, or if anyone did."

"You still think it might be suicide?" Viv asked.

Misty frowned and leaned back in her chair, crossing her legs again. "I just don't know. I've been through it in my mind, over and over. He was acting weird those last few weeks. Almost desperate. He wouldn't talk to me. I think he was freaked out about the baby. Babies, I mean. My baby, and Bitsy's baby, too."

"Did he talk to you about David Baucum?"

"Oh yeah. We talked about that a lot."

"How did he feel about it?"

"He said to me that David Baucum was the very definition of hubris. Peter saw him as just another middle-aged white guy in the pocket of the oil companies. Someone who didn't care about anything except the bottom line. He truly believed Baucum was ultimately responsible for Meredith Logan's paralysis, and he deserved everything that happened to him."

I drew my head back. "Even death?"

"Of course not. That was Baucum's choice. That wasn't Peter's fault, and Peter didn't suffer any guilt over it. He thought Baucum was a spineless weasel who couldn't live with what he'd done. He said more than once that Meredith Logan was a hundred times braver than David Baucum would ever be. He thought Baucum was a whiny little baby. He had no respect for him and even less after the man died."

I made a mental note of that. I'd asked Trisha almost the same questions, and her take on Browning's philosophy had been much less harsh. Then again, maybe Browning didn't feel as free to reveal such harshness to Trisha—who would be his superior, even if she wasn't his direct supervisor—as he was with Misty, someone who was more his equal.

"So, if it was suicide, you're not buying that it was guilt over Baucum's death?"

Misty shook her head. "Not for a second."

"Did the police ask you anything about Peter being injured or being in a fight before he went missing?" Viv asked, and I remembered what Bitsy had said.

She nodded. "Yes, they did. I kept telling them, there was no fight. There was nothing. He was flat-out ignoring me. They asked if it got physical, but it didn't even get verbal. Aside from an occasional short text, he was completely shutting me out those last few weeks." She chewed her bottom lip. "So, did Patrice say anything about me? I'm meeting with her and the station manager tomorrow, but I really don't know what to expect."

"You saw the opinion segment he did?"

She nodded, and for the first time, her eyes filled with tears. She blinked them back. "I saw it."

"I think they want to stand by you," I said with a shrug. I might be blowing smoke, but it was smoke I felt okay about. "That's the impression I got. Their main priorities are honoring Peter's memory and cooperating with the investigation, but to me, he looked like someone who was anxious to find any reason to stand behind you and support you. My sense is that if you're as honest with him as you have been with us, you'll have an ally."

She closed her eyes for a second, and she suddenly looked very young. Poor kid.

"What's going to happen now?" I asked.

"They told me not to leave town without checking with them first. I was going to go to my parents' house for a while, but I can't, so they're coming here."

A car door slammed outside, and her eyes flew open. She turned in the chair and lifted the curtain.

"My parents are here," she said. Her voice was full of dread.

Viv and I stood to go.

"Let me know what you find out," Misty said as she held the door open for us.

"We're not working for you," Viv said.

"I don't care," Misty said. "I am an innocent woman facing a murder charge, and I need help. Letting me know what you find out is the decent thing to do."

Viv and I looked at each other, and I shrugged. Neither one of us could argue with that.

I climbed into Viv's Caddy as Misty's parents made it to her door.

We didn't know where else to go, so we did what we always did when we didn't know what else to do. We went to Sonic.

While Viv crunched on an order of chili-and-cheese-covered tator tots, I sipped my Vanilla Diet Coke and thought. "Is it just me, or does it make no sense that they would bring obstruction charges on something like this if they still think Peter killed himself?"

"Maybe they thought she did something to push him over the edge."

"But that wouldn't be obstruction, would it? Would that be...aiding and abetting?" That didn't sound right, either.

I finally gave up and pulled out my phone. "Windy, call Bobby Sloan."

"I'm gettin' him for ya now, Sweetie," Windy said.

A few seconds later, "Sloan."

"Bobby, it's Salem. I have Viv here with me."

"Hello, Mr. Hot Detective," Viv called in the direction of the phone.

Bobby groaned.

"We just finished interviewing Misty Monahan. Poor girl. She's terrified."

Silence.

"We did get some interesting information, though."

"Which you are legally required to pass on to the police. Unless you have a two-fer coupon for obstruction charges and want to share a cell with Ms. Monahan."

"Bobby," I sighed. "Bobby, Bobby, Bobby. Why do you think I called? Here is some information that could be useful to you." I was quite sure I didn't have anything he didn't already know, but I figured the more I talked to him, the greater the chances I could hit on something of value. "For one thing, it appears that Peter Browning was definitely murdered. It wasn't suicide."

"Yeah?" He sounded bored. "How do you figure that?"

"You don't file charges of obstruction in a suicide case."

"Oh my gosh." His voice was entirely flat. "You don't?"

"No. I mean, if she had encouraged him or drove him to suicide, that would be..." Here's where I lost my nerve a bit, and faltered. "Aiding and abetting?"

"Good try, Salem. No. That would probably fall more under the category of involuntary manslaughter."

"Oh."

Viv frowned at me. I wrinkled my nose and nodded in chagrin. I really was blowing this.

She took the phone out of my hand. "We also know for a fact that he was injured sometime before his death."

Silence.

"So, am I right?" Viv asked.

More silence.

"Also, we know that Peter Browning had a foot fetish."

"What?!" Bobby and I said at the same time.

"A fact," Viv said. She leaned back, a satisfied smile on her face.

"Eww," I said. "What makes you think that?"

"Neither Bitsy or Misty were wearing shoes when we interviewed them." Viv raised her eyebrows and said, smugly, "You see, but you do not observe."

Bobby laughed. Did I imagine it, or was there a hint of relief in his laugh?

"You got me there, Sherlock," he said. "Obviously a foot fetish."

Viv popped a tator tot in her mouth and smiled.

This was getting us nowhere. I decided to go for the gold. What did I have to lose?

"Bobby, Misty did tell us that she had deleted some emails that showed she and Peter were having an affair, and they planned to meet up. She said she did it because she didn't want his wife to find out about the relationship."

"Did she?"

I frowned, frustrated. "But you were checking his emails, so that means...something. That you haven't closed the book on this. You haven't definitely ruled it a suicide."

"Did I say we'd closed the book on it?"

"No, but..."

"How's the dog grooming business, Salem?"

"What? Fine. Why?"

"Because that's your job. You're a dog groomer. I'm a detective. How about we all just do our jobs?"

Viv winked at me, then said into the microphone. "Hey, Mr. Hot Detective. Can you remind me who caught the High Point Bandits?"

Silence.

"And Marky Patrelli?"

Silence.

"And Sylvia Ramirez?"

Silence.

I leaned over and looked at the screen. "He hung up."

She frowned. "Before or after I reminded him of our track record?"

I shrugged. "Probably before. But if it's any consolation, I think you're onto something about the feet. Not a fetish, I mean. But he seemed relieved when he said, 'Obviously a foot fetish.' Right?"

It was Viv's turn to shrug. "I guess."

"How do we find out?"

Viv finished off her tots. "We have to ask the right questions."

Sadly, Viv's "right questions" turned out to be really embarrassing.

We drove back over to Bitsy's house. When she answered the door, Viv got right to the point. "Listen, I hate to be intrusive and crude, but I'm sure you understand that, in order to get to the bottom of things, we need all applicable information. And, we don't really know what's applicable until all is said and done, so..."

Bitsy frowned, but she didn't say anything. She looked from Viv to me. Finally, she nodded.

"Did your husband have a foot fetish?"

Bitsy and I both gasped. I know Bitsy she did—she was shocked. I have no idea why I did. I mean, I should have known, right?

"A what? No."

"There's no shame in it, Mrs. Browning," Viv said. "Lots of people find pleasure in—"

"Stop!" I said. "Enough."

"Why on earth would you think...what?" Bitsy looked confused and a little panicked.

"You weren't wearing any shoes when we interviewed you the other day, and you're not wearing shoes now."

She looked at her feet. In fact, we all looked at her feet, with their neat, pink-painted nails.

"I'm pregnant. My feet swell."

Viv stared at her feet, silent. Then she said, "Oh."

Bitsy looked at me. I shrugged.

After a few more seconds of uncomfortable silence, Viv pulled out her little notepad and pretended to take notes, but it was plain to all of us that she was only doing it to save face. "Okay, then. That is helpful information, indeed."

"Is it okay if we call you if we have any more questions?" I asked. I backed up a half step in the universal it's-time-to-go motion.

"Please do," Bitsy said. Maybe she didn't mean for it to sound like, "Please call instead of coming to my door with this craziness." But I was pretty sure she did.

Viv and I drove in silence for a while. I wondered if she was telling herself that that had gone well.

I picked up the phone and dialed Misty's number. "I'll handle this one," I told Viv.

When Misty answered, I said, "Listen, I can't say much because I don't know what I'm looking for yet. But I have a hunch something in this case has to do with feet. Does that make you think of anything?"

"They took all my shoes except my heels, and one old pair of Tom's," she said. "When they came to take my computer, they took them all."

"Really?" My heart began to race a bit. I'd found an actual clue! I had no idea what it meant, but still...

"Really. They wouldn't tell me anything except that they would give them back when the investigation is resolved."

"Okay, that's good to know. That's helpful."

When I hung up, Viv asked, "What was that about?"

"She said the police took all of her shoes except her heels and one old pair of Tom's."

"Hmmm...so they have footprints."

"Right. That must be it. Right?" I wish I felt more confident that I knew what I was looking at. The high I'd felt off figuring out the one thing about the feet was sadly short lived.

At least I hadn't gone straight from feet to fetish, though.

I frowned and stared at my phone.

I do love you, Salem, but...

They took her shoes.

They wouldn't have taken her shoes unless they had something to check them against. You don't take shoes to investigate obstruction, do you?

"They took her shoes," I said to Viv.

"They jolly well did."

"All those shoe prints we saw out in the field—they must have been trying to match them up."

"They jolly well are."

I bit my tongue. I sighed. "They wouldn't have done that if they thought it was suicide."

"I thought we'd established that already."

"I guess. I mean, Bobby was in the 'neither confirm nor deny' camp. But up until now I was pretty sure he'd done himself in. Now..." A shiver went up the back of my neck.

I ran through a list of all the people we'd talked to over the last couple of days. Dorsett Oil. Bitsy. Jessica—although I found it doubtful that Jessica had anything to do with Peter's murder. Misty.

Something tugged at the edges of my conscience. Some kind of relationship between those three young Channel 11 employees.

Misty and Peter, having an affair.

Jessica and Misty, best friends.

Jessica and Peter. I supposed I would never know how Peter felt about Jessica, but Jessica didn't seem to have a lot of affection for Peter.

She did have a lot of admiration for Misty, though.

Misty and I are close, she'd said. Much more than she and Peter ever were.

But Misty was having Peter's baby, so they had been close on some level.

A thought occurred to me. Was it possible that Jessica was in love with Misty? Had she killed Peter out of jealousy?

I suggested this to Viv.

She shrugged. "Maybe. I doubt it, though. I'm not getting a killer vibe from her."

"Neither of us got a killer vibe from Mikey Patrelli, either. Or Sylvia Ramirez."

"Good point."

Maybe Misty really did murder Peter. Maybe everything she'd said to us was meant to lead us down a path so we, too, would create an obstruction for the police. Maybe she was using us to help muddy the waters, somehow.

I said a little prayer. *God, I need direction here. If I keep pulling on this string, I don't think Tony is going to like it. I assured him this was probably not murder, but now I'm pretty sure it is. But if I don't pursue it, an innocent woman might go to jail. It would be very helpful if you could just...point me in a direction. Is she guilty? Should I keep out of this?*

The thought occurred to me that it was, perhaps, too late for that option. I'd made a commitment to Trisha and Scott. Viv, my BFF, was counting on me.

I waited. Silence.

I sighed. "I need to get out of my head."

"Me, too," Viv agreed. "Give things time to percolate. Let's go out and see Serena again. Maybe she has some way we can increase our vibe detectors."

CHAPTER TWELVE

Vibe Detecting 101

I decided to just keep my mouth shut while we were at Serena's. Let Viv get all kinds of encouraged. I would keep my mouth shut and my aura to myself.

"Look at you!" Serena said as soon as we came through the door.

I checked behind me, then sighed when I saw that, yep, she was talking to me.

"You opened the floodgates."

This was too much. I jabbed a finger. "Yes, and it's your fault!"

She just kept up that annoying serene smile.

"Okay, it wasn't your fault, but it was a—a very bad idea!" I finally said. "I told you it was a bad idea, and it was."

"No." She shook her head. "Nothing is either good or bad. It simply is what it is."

Remember how you were going to keep your mouth shut? I asked myself. I held my hand up like a traffic cop. "Stop." I pointed to Viv. "Peddle it to her. Leave me out of it."

She and Viv went off on an oohhing and aaahhing spree over chunks of crystal and CDs of whale noises. I stood by the window until I saw G-Ma going into one of the new shops—the coffee shop. I could use some coffee. More than I could use Serena making me feel lousy about my aura.

This turned out to be a very wise choice indeed, because the barista was trying out a new Chilean hot chocolate recipe. I figured since I'd passed up on cheesy tator tots, I had some virtue points in the bank.

The barista poured a mug for each of us, then dropped a nice dollop of whipped cream on top.

I sipped. Then I gasped.

"It's fantastic, isn't it?" G-Ma said as she sipped.

"This must be what heaven tastes like." I took another sip. The chocolate was rich and creamy, and the chili powder gave it a kick.

"Your mother is driving me batty," G-Ma announced. "I'll be glad when this wedding is over."

I made a non-committal noise in my throat. I didn't want to think about my mother. Thinking about her made me think about Susan and her disgusting son and my fight with Tony. Serena could probably see the change in my aura from here.

"You're harshing my mellow," I said. "Let's talk about something else."

"Like what you two are doing at Serena's?" G-Ma asked, pointing toward the blue swirl on Serena's window. She had a whipped cream mustache.

I pulled a napkin from the dispenser on the counter and wiped her upper lip. "We're looking into this thing with Peter Browning."

"I heard it was suicide," G-Ma announced, as if that put an end to it. "He was wrestling with demons, you know."

"Yes, I have heard that," I said. "But nobody seems to know what kind of demons those were."

"Serena will know."

"Serena didn't know. All she would say is that he was wrestling with demons and that my aura is the wrong color."

"There's no such thing as right or wrong, Salem. It simply is what it is."

"Are you friggin' kidding me? You, too?"

She laughed. "No. That's hogwash. Take this hot chocolate, for instance. It's good. But still, Serena is very insightful. She told me the universe was telling me I had a gift for seeing the potential in every human and helping guide them into the fullness of their being."

I sipped my hot chocolate and thought about that. I didn't want to sound negative, what with G-Ma finally being happy and all, but I could honestly say that was not a quality I had noticed in her before.

But I nodded like I was not dismissing the concept out of hand. Then, on the off chance this was true, I turned to her and said, "That is excellent news because I have been wondering what my gift is. Tell me."

G-Ma frowned. "What do you mean, your gift?"

"Paul says everyone has gifts and they all work together. We're all part of the body, you know."

"Paul who? Is he that Hispanic guy that lives next to you?"

"No, G-Ma, the Apostle Paul. From the Bible."

"Oh. Him." She pulled a slight grimace and sipped her chocolate.

G-Ma wasn't heavily into the Bible, but I had a feeling that, even if she was, she still would have grimaced at the mention of Paul. I was heavily into the Bible, and he and I didn't always get along.

"So, what's my potential?"

She studied me. "Well, of course, you must be good at what you do. You know, with the dogs and stuff."

I nodded. Then I waited. "And?"

"Oh, you wanted more?"

"Well, yeah. I mean, you're a successful business owner here, and you always have been. But that's not the same as guiding someone into the fullness of their being, is it? That's more than just a job you're competent at. That's a gift."

She smiled smugly. "It is, isn't it?"

"So, guide me! I want to be in the fullness of my being."

She got a decidedly panicked look in her eye and took a gulp of her hot chocolate. "Ouch. Gosh. That is hot. Maybe I should warn her not to make it so hot, do you think?"

"You're stalling. Come on. It doesn't have to be anything huge. Just, you know, what have you noticed that I'm good at?" I tried to remember the different things I'd read about. "There's stuff like discernment, speaking wisdom, speaking in tongues and prophesying. I think encouragement is in there..."

"Oh, you can be very encouraging. And you're good at finding bad guys."

I nodded, but a sense of despair began to overtake me. G-Ma knew me probably better than anyone. She'd known me the longest, and even though she wasn't my mother, she had played a huge role in my upbringing and had certainly paid more attention while she was doing it than Mom had.

I tried to latch onto the "you can be very encouraging" bit. I mean, that was good, right? That was important. I could grow that.

I must have had a sour look on my face, though, because the panic on G-Ma's face turned somewhat desperate, and she stood. "Look, there's Serena. She'll know!"

Serena and Viv had walked out onto the sidewalk, chatting happily away like two people who were wallowing around in the fullness of their own being. "No, G-Ma, it's okay. You don't—"

But it was too late. G-Ma was out the door and headed for them.

I sighed and stood. God, I prayed. Now would be a really good time to hear from you.

"Salem wants to know what her gift is," G-Ma announced as she approached them.

"That is certainly important," Serena said.

"That's what I told her." G-Ma smiled and nodded at me.

I waited, looking back and forth between the two of them. Then, again, "Is that it?"

"It's important to know what your gifts are—what your identity is. Your identity informs every relationship you have, every decision you make."

"I know," I said, trying not to grit my teeth. "Jacob was called heel-grabber and look how he turned out."

"Exactly," Serena nodded. "He is one of the major patriarchs of the Old Testament."

I shook my head. "How is that—never mind. I just want to know what my gift is. Like, you told G-Ma that she helped people recognize their potential and all that."

Viv snorted. G-Ma glared at her.

Serena nodded and narrowed her eyes, staring at me. I held still, praying for her to say something good.

"What are you afraid of?" she finally asked.

I blinked. "What? Like...snakes?"

"No. I mean, what is your worst fear?"

"That I'll start drinking again."

She raised her eyebrows. "Very good. Very good."

"Is it?"

"She's afraid of Imogene Walker," Viv chimed in. "And she is very afraid of snakes, I agree."

"Who is Imogene Walker?" Serena asked.

I shook my head. "This is running off the rails. Imogene Walker has nothing to do with me."

"Not true. We're all connected, Salem."

"All connected," G-Ma piped up. "Like waves in the ocean."

I sighed.

"Why are you afraid of Imogene Walker?" Serena asked.

"Because she's scary," I said. "And this is telling me nothing about my gift. Why is it very good that I'm afraid I'll start drinking again?"

"Well, if drinking turns out badly for you, it's a good thing to be afraid of. Hopefully that fear will help you steer clear."

"Oh," I said. This was so sensible that it bordered on disappointing.

"Look, I don't know your gifts except that you seem to be a strikingly honest person. Honest with others, but most importantly, honest with yourself. That last one might not be what you're looking for, but believe me, it's a frightfully rare gift."

I blinked. I said again, "Oh." It wasn't what I was looking for, but somehow it still made me feel a slight twinge of...hope, was it? "Why did you ask what I'm afraid of?"

"Because our greatest rewards lie on the other side of our deepest fears. Not just for you—for all of us. And what greater reward could there be than knowing your true identity?" She leaned in and looked deep into my eyes. "Don't be afraid to fight for what you need, Salem. If you have to wrestle all night, do it. It'll be worth it."

I lay awake for a solid hour, back in my bed in Trailertopia.

Our greatest rewards lie on the other side of our deepest fears.

I sat up and punched my pillow in frustration, then flopped onto my other side.

Stump opened one eye, glared at me, then burrowed her nose back under the covers.

Basically, I decided, Serena was full of bull poop. She was nothing but a sham built on pretty rocks, weird moaning music, and Internet positivity slogans.

How could my greatest reward lie on the other side of my fear of drinking again? That didn't even make sense. If it did, that would mean I needed to start drinking again to find my reward. As much as part of me kind of wanted that to be true, I knew it wasn't.

I began to drift to sleep, satisfied that Serena was not something I needed to waste further mental energy on.

You did ask for a word.

I bolted awake. Was that God?

I listened intently but didn't hear anything else. Of course, I hadn't heard that. That had just been a thought that popped up in that in-between netherworld between wake and sleep.

I lay back down and took a deep breath. If that saying were truly from God, it would be in the Bible somewhere, and I was almost positive it wasn't. If it was, it would be printed on t-shirts and bumper stickers with the verse attributed. It was a positivity saying, basically devoid of any power, and that was it.

"Don't be afraid" is in the Bible more times than anything else. Gotta be some reason for that.

"Dadgummit!" I said out loud, sitting up and turning on the light.

I stared at my ceiling. "What? Are you talking to me or not?"

Silence. Of course.

Stump grumbled and burrowed deeper, getting away from the lamp light. I scooted down next to her and curled around her, getting comfortable once more. My eyes got heavy and I felt myself drifting off again.

Maybe drinking again isn't really your deepest fear.

"No!" I said. Kind of shouted, actually. "Right now my deepest fear is I'll never sleep again."

Silence.

But I was awake now—it's kind of hard to fall asleep when you're furious.

I sighed and picked up my phone, searching for the phrase Serena had told me that evening. Sure enough, it showed up in all kinds of beautiful Instagram-ready posts, in front of sunset beaches, in flourishing fonts imposed over snow-capped mountains, in stark black font on plain white backgrounds. Not a single one had a verse attached.

"Not from the Bible," I said to the ceiling. "And now I'm awake and can't go back to sleep."

With a sigh, I sat up and decided to go back through the videos Trisha had given us. Maybe I had missed something. I lay in bed and scrolled through my phone, but I didn't see anything I hadn't seen before.

I remembered that kid at the coffee shop who showed us how to reach the surveillance video history online. Maybe I could check some cameras around the TV station the night Browning disappeared. That could lead to something.

I typed in different addresses and dates, first on and around the days right before the disappearance, then further back.

I didn't see anyone I didn't recognize as working there, even if I didn't know all of them. But I supposed I could ask Trisha to take a look. Maybe she would notice something I didn't.

I checked the neighborhood around Browning's house, but I couldn't get much besides still photos, and there was no way of knowing how old those were.

For fun, I typed in the address for Trailertopia, but that only showed the entrance to the park, not down by my trailer.

I typed in Tony's address. The nearest camera was half a block down, but I could see his driveway and front porch.

I remembered the tortilla-making fiasco and thought about the date – two days after the Veterans Day service, so November 13. I typed in 13-11 and the year, but got an error message. I stared at the screen, annoyed, then realized I'd entered it backwards. There was no thirteenth month, of course. I'd entered it the way the British would with the date first. I'd have to let Viv know that her British invasion was working on me, too.

I corrected the dates and entered them, sliding the time line close to six o'clock. I watched as Tony's car pulled into the drive and he walked up the sidewalk.

My heart squeezed in my chest. I wanted to reach into the phone and latch onto him.

A second later, I watched him stand back out of the way as I came barreling through with a pan full of fire. Like a freak, I danced around on the sidewalk, looking for a place to set the pan.

Sitting in the safety of my bed, I actually felt my heart start to race and I worried for a second if I would actually do what I'd been afraid of last time—that I would set the entire neighborhood on fire.

Then, of course, it got through to my sleep-deprived brain that there was no this time and last time. It was all just one time.

I put the phone down, turned off the lamp, and slid down into bed beside Stump.

"No more mysterious revelations tonight, okay?" I told God. "Clearly, I need some sleep."

Around lunchtime the next day, Viv called me. "Well, you heard the woman. Our greatest rewards lie on the other side of our deepest fears."

"Yeah?" Oh no. What did this mean?

"So I went to Goodwill. Got me a Miss Marple outfit." She sounded thoroughly disgusted and resigned.

I, however, was relieved. I had thought for an insane moment that she was talking about my fears.

"How does it look?"

"I don't even want to talk about it. This had better work."

"What's the plan?"

"Just...be here by 3:00."

Stump and I did as we were told, but I thought I was going to have to drag Viv out of her room.

"I might change my mind," she called through the locked bedroom door.

I set Stump down to sniff around Viv's kitchen for crumbs. "Let's just look. It might not be that bad."

"Oh, it's that bad all right. It's worse."

"Let's just see."

After a second, I heard the lock turn. "If you laugh, I will shoot you," she promised. "I mean it."

"Of course, I won't laugh," I said.

I didn't laugh. It took everything I had not to gasp, though.

She wore a white blouse with a lace collar, buttoned to the throat, and a maroon cardigan over it. A blue skirt with tiny white flowers hung to just above her feet—clad in the most sensible shoes I'd ever seen—and what showed of her calves was covered by baggy tan stockings.

Her silver hair—her one normal concession to her age—was covered in a burgundy cloche hat, with a sprig of holly attached at the band.

Stump took one look at her and growled.

I waved a hand toward Stump to shush her. "Viv! You look amazing!"

"Amazingly awful?" She frowned and turned to study her reflection in the hall mirror.

"No, amazingly...sweet."

"Matronly."

"Comforting."

"Like an old sock." She sighed and checked her butt, which was hidden under the voluminous folds of skirt. "This shows absolutely none of my pizazz."

"That is not true. Look at the twinkle in your eye. The spring in your step."

She trudged a short pace before me. "There is no such thing as spring in these things. I swear I feel like my heels are dragging the ground in these."

Viv always wore, at minimum, a two-inch heel.

She took a few more steps, watching her feet glumly. "I don't know how you people walk in these things." She sighed and turned back to the mirror. "Nope. I can't do it. I can't let him see me like this." She reached to pull the pin from her hat.

"You know who you kind of look like? Anne."

At the sudden flare of her nostrils, I said, "I mean, like Anne's younger sister. Or daughter."

She cocked her head.

"I'm just saying, if Nigel is into the demure type—"

"Demure, but with hidden treasures only he can see."

"Right, hidden treasures only he can see—then you've nailed it. One hundred percent." I stood behind her in the mirror. "See, it's all about the hidden mystery, right? The enticing temptress under the angel facade."

She studied her reflection some more. "Enticing," she said. She tucked her chin and gave herself come hither eyes.

"Exactly."

She took a deep breath, then sighed and picked up a big tapestry bag with two knitting needles sticking out of it. "Okay, fine. It's worth a shot. Nigel and Anne play miniature golf out on the east side of the campus. Let's just take a walk out there and run this up the flagpole. See if he has anything left to salute."

We made for the door before she froze and said, "Wait!" She fished through the bag—which had no yarn for knitting, I noticed—and found a lipstick. "There's no sense in going completely mad." She applied the lipstick, made a duck face in the mirror, and then slipped the lipstick into her cardigan pocket. She checked her watch. "Crikey! Okay, let's move. I want to be in place before they come by."

I tagged along after her. "So, what are we doing now, anyway? Are we impressing him with your miniature golf skills?"

Viv looked at me like I was an idiot. "No. They have to pass the Baucum Local Hero memorial thingamajig, so we're going to be standing there, pensively studying the names when they walk by. Then I'm going to work in a little factoid I learned last night while I was doing research for this getup."

I raised an eyebrow as the elevator dinged. "What factoid?"

"One of the honorees after Baucum was a WASP pilot! Can you believe that?"

I shook my head. "I have no idea how shocked I'm supposed to be at this. What's a WASP pilot?"

"Women's Airforce Service Pilots. They flew the planes to the service men during World War II. One of them moved here after the war and became a Baucum Local Hero." Viv clapped her hands together. "What a stroke of luck for me! Now I can impress Nigel with my patriotic knowledge. England had their own branch called the WAAFs. Don't tell him I said this, but this is one time when the American word is better than the British word."

"My lips are sealed," I promised. "Is that what she got the award for, being a WASP?"

"No, it was..." She flapped a hand. "Teaching poor kids to read, or feeding homeless people. Cleaning up a park, maybe. One of those selfless things."

"Those are all kind of different selfless things," I pointed out.

The elevator stopped, and the door slid open. Viv strolled out. "Well, I read a bunch of profiles last night and they all kind of ran together after a while." She checked her lipstick and the sprig of holly on her hat as we walked by the big mirror near the back door. She hitched up her skirt and adjusted the lace collar.

I was glad to get the chance to see the Memorial up close. I had seen it from the parking lot—which is to say not very well— and it looked charming. A low stone wall surrounded a brick courtyard with a small fountain in the center. Benches sat along the edge of the circle, and baskets of flowers hung around the outside of the circle. "It's so cute. I thought it was just, you know, a place to sit."

We entered the circle, and I saw that some of the brick pavers had names on them. "These are the heroes?" I asked.

"Indeed, they are. Okay, help me look for...hang on." She dug in her cardigan pocket and drew out a slip of paper. "JoAnn Pepper." She held the paper up. "JoAnn Pepper. Sounds like someone who would be a WASP, doesn't she?"

I walked slowly around the circle, reading the names. "What year was it?"

Viv didn't answer. I looked up. Dang it. She was too busy looking for Nigel to pay attention to what we were doing.

Anne and Nigel came around the corner, her hand on his arm. He held their little miniature golf clubs in his other hand.

"Would you look at that!" Viv muttered. "She's dressed like a blasted teenager."

Anne wore jeans and tennis shoes with a blue and white striped zip-up hoodie. She looked adorable.

"You look great," I said under my breath. "Give him an enticing look."

Anne beamed when she saw us. "Viola! Don't you look lovely this afternoon."

"Viola?" Viv said. She scowled at Anne's hand on Nigel's arm, then forced a laugh. "You silly old nutter, you."

Anne laughed and shook her head. "I know, I'm terrible with names. What are you two up to?"

"We're actually out looking for one of the Local Heroes I read about last night. A fascinating individual named JoAnn Pepper. She was—"

Anne gave a little gasp and clapped her hands together. "Oh, I knew JoAnn! She was a WASP!"

The smile slid from Viv's face. "Yes. She was."

Anne put her hand back on Nigel's arm. "Did I tell you about JoAnn Pepper? We were in a Bible study together years ago. She was the most amazing woman I ever met." She tilted her head back as if remembering, a wide smile on her face. "She drove the most beautiful powder blue Thunderbird convertible. She called it Piston-Packin' Mama! Her nickname when she was a WASP was Pistol-Packin' Mama, so..." She laughed again, clearly transported back in time.

"Right." Viv said.

"I remember when she won the Baucum Local Hero award. No one more deserving, if you ask me."

Viv frowned and chewed her lip. "Right, it was...teaching kids to read?"

"Not just read! She started an entire Saturday morning program for kids, so they could come get a hot meal, play games, read books. She said she talked to a friend of her son's one Monday morning and realized he hadn't had a thing to eat all weekend. The only meals he got were at school. So she started a Saturday morning program where the kids could come to the community center, get a muffin and a banana for breakfast, a hot lunch, and a sandwich sack lunch to take home for the next day. I'll bet she had every person in this town volunteering for something in that program at one time or another. Making sandwiches or calling bingo or washing apples or something. Everybody was in on it."

"Yes, well..." Viv didn't appear to know what to say to that. "That does sound like an awful lot of carbs, but..."

I gave her a look.

"But, yes, a very impressive accomplishment." She tugged at the lace collar around her neck.

"Highly commendable," I said.

Viv gave me a look.

"But you should see Viv do yoga," I said. "Like nobody's business."

Nigel blinked. Anne's smile faltered a bit. No one seemed to know what to say to that.

"Nobody's," Viv confirmed.

I saw movement out of the corner of my eye and turned to smile at the couple walking toward us. I didn't recognize the old woman in the velour track suit, but—and I realized this with a gasp of dread—I certainly recognized the guy with her.

"Viv!" I hissed. "Look!"

It was the construction company guy, the one who had almost run over Viv after the Veterans Day ceremony. The one we'd made complete fools of ourselves in front of later that same day.

He recognized us, too—I could tell by the way he stopped dead in his tracks the moment he saw my face. The woman with him kept shuffling along toward the stone circle, though, and he had little choice but to continue toward us. He passed a wary look from me to Viv. He probably expected to get another bizarre third-degree interrogation right here.

I tried to give him a reassuring smile, but the truth was, I couldn't make any promises where Viv was concerned. I wanted to hightail it out of there, but Viv seemed locked into her plan to impress Nigel, come heck or high water.

"But unlike the rest of these people, JoAnn Pepper wasn't just a local hero," Viv said, stepping closer to Nigel. "She was a war hero, too. Like you." She batted her eyelashes.

Poor Nigel. He just gave a noncommittal smile and nodded.

"Indeed!" Anne said, not the least concerned that Viv was one step removed from a cat rubbing up against a man's leg with a soft purr. "JoAnn came all the way from Sioux Falls, South Dakota, when she was only twenty years old to train at the airfield in Sweetwater. That's a town south of here," she beamed at Nigel. "Over a thousand women trained to fly military planes so they could ferry them to the air bases for the men in combat. Such brave women! Of course, they weren't allowed to fly combat missions, but they freed up the servicemen so they could. In a lot of cases, they were the first ones to fly those planes, straight out of the factory. Can you imagine? How terrifying!"

"What are you, Wikipedia?" Viv groused.

"My father was a war hero," the woman in the track suit said.

The young guy drew his head back, scowling. He looked at the woman—his mother, presumably; he'd said his mother was here in the Alzheimer's unit—then to the rest of us.

"Is that right, dear?" Anne said. "Bless him."

The guy gave her a wry smile, then shook his head the slightest bit. Then he shrugged.

The woman didn't say anything else. She moved, slowly and silently, to the other edge of the circle and sat on the stone bench. She looked at the basket of flowers opposite her.

The young guy gave us another look, then moved closer to his mother without a word.

Fortunately—or unfortunately, depending on how you looked at it, Viv was too preoccupied with Nigel to give this guy any time. She looked around at the names on the circle. Her spine stiffened, and I saw the tell-tale signs of her thinking up another tactic.

"It's a shame they weren't able to give out the Baucum Local Hero award this year," Viv said. "My contact at Channel 11 said they just gave that story about the weather to hide the fact that they weren't prepared to give an award this year."

"Is that right, dear?" Anne said. "Well..."

"I have contacts at Channel 11," Viv repeated, leaning in a bit to gauge how impressed Nigel was.

He nodded and smiled.

Viv frowned. "With all the brouhaha over the Baucum Engineering thing, nobody thought to issue a call for nominations until it was too late."

Nigel nodded and made a noise in his throat.

Anne gave a sad smile and tilted her head. "Is that right, dear? Well..."

I liked Anne—I liked her a lot. She was a sweet lady. But I didn't care for the way it seemed she was being dismissive of Viv. Maybe she was more offended by Viv flirting with her boyfriend than I originally thought—and who could blame her if she was? Still, I felt the need to stand in Viv's corner somehow.

"That is what the reporter from Channel 11 said when Viv interviewed her," I said. "That Baucum Engineering always handled the nominations and awards, but when they went out of business, no one thought to take it up until it was too late." I twisted my lip. Hmmm...that didn't seem quite as strongly in Viv's corner as I wanted. So I flat-out lied. "I had heard rumors that someone was going to nominate Viv, for her...contributions to crime solving in the community."

Anne beamed once again. "Yes! Yes, she's certainly deserving. Well, perhaps someone will be more prepared to take up the mantle next year, and you'll have another shot."

Viv gave a beneficent nod. "Perhaps."

"Unless you plan to retire between now and then," Nigel said.

"Are you barmy?" Viv looked at him with mock outrage. "A woman in the prime of her life, retiring? Don't let these sensible shoes fool you. Believe me, I have scads of baddie take-downs in me yet."

"Scads," I echoed.

Beside the woman in the track suit, the construction guy shifted and frowned in our general direction. He said something to her, too low for me to overhear, and then bent and took her elbow.

She stood, slowly, and they made their way carefully back down the sidewalk. His Eagle Construction pickup waited in the parking lot, and he helped her into the passenger seat. As Viv went on in a monologue about our crime-solving exploits that made us sound much more capable than we actually were, I watched the pickup—full of boxes, I noticed once he'd turned it toward the exit – pull out and drive away.

I turned back to the group. Viv was prattling on, and it appeared that Nigel was doing his best to look attentive, but shifted from one foot to the other, looking down the path we blocked, to the door of Belle Court and his apparent safety.

Anne, though...Anne's gaze was focused in the direction the construction guy and his mother had just left. She looked suddenly unbearably sad.

Back at Viv's apartment, I tried to cheer her up. "Well, I think that went well," I said.

She scowled, but didn't say anything. She pulled the pin from her hat and tossed it on the sofa.

"Seriously. He's intrigued, I can tell. He probably just didn't want to hurt Anne's feelings."

Viv dropped to the sofa and put her feet up on the coffee table. "Anne! Anne would be just fine, I guarantee you. Anne is the type to always look on the sunny side, no matter what happens." She unlaced her shoes and toed them off. They fell to the floor with a clunk and Stump immediately went to sniff them.

I remembered the sad look on her face. "No reason to be cruel to her, though. Did she seem sad to you? Maybe she knew that woman who was with the construction guy."

Viv was too busy scowling at her feet to give it much thought. She shrugged.

"She's the one with Alzheimer's, I guess." I sat in the comfy chair across from Viv. "Remember, he told us his mother was in the Alzheimer's unit here." I cocked my head, realizing something. "Is it usual for them to leave like that?"

"Like what?"

"The guy put her in his pickup and drove off with her."

"This is not a prison, Salem. I leave all the time, don't I?"

"Yes, but you don't have Alzheimer's. And she was confused. She said her father was a war hero, when clearly he wasn't." *The guy's very slight head shake and shrug. Poor guy.* "There were a bunch of boxes in the back of his pickup. Do you think he was moving her?" That didn't seem right, though. Moving someone with Alzheimer's would be very traumatic to them, wouldn't it? Wouldn't they need structure and a familiar routine?

"I really don't know how all that works," Viv said. "I have other things to worry about."

I nodded. I'd learned long ago that Viv lived in a reality of her own making. In her mind, she and I were roughly the same age. The only reason she lived at Belle Court was because her fifth and last husband had set her up there before he died. I think her working hypothesis was that she lived in a very fancy full-service hotel, and it just happened to be filled with old people—aside from herself, of course.

I had no problem with going along with this at all. I wasn't above playing fast and loose with reality sometimes myself. Where was the harm?

I hated seeing her look so frustrated, though. Reality wasn't cooperating with her fantasy at the moment.

"Do you want to drive over and see if Serena has had any more visions, or whatever they are?"

But she shook her head. "No. I think I'll stay in and watch some BBC."

"More Miss Marple?"

"Ugh. No." She frowned and looked at the baggy toes of her brown tights. "I'm going to have to let that one do him for a while. Blimey." She groaned and leaned her head back on the sofa.

I nodded and stood, trying not to look too relieved. I didn't want to go to Serena's and have her say something like "Look, I see by your aura that your greatest fear is dying broke and alone!" with that serene smile.

Actually, I just wanted to get home and cuddle with Stump, maybe watch a sitcom on TV so I could forget everything sad for a while. I made my goodbyes to Viv and promised to be ready on a moment's notice when her next plan was ready to execute.

I drove the Monster Carlo out of Belle Court and pointed it for home. I wanted—wanted very badly—to swing by Tony's house, just to say hi.

He needed time. Just a few days.

I do love you, Salem, but...

I had run the words over and over in my head so many times, I honestly couldn't remember if he'd said the 'but' or not. On one hand, I knew he hadn't. On the other...it sounded so real in my head.

I sighed and pressed the pedal down toward Trailertopia.

CHAPTER THIRTEEN

Every British Man's Fantasy

Viv called me at work the next day. "What time do you think you'll be off?"

I checked my list for the day. I had three more dogs to finish up, and one was a bichon frise. Those took a while to scissor. But I also had two schnauzers, which were usually pretty quick. "Two hours," I said. "Two and a half, maybe. What's up today? More Marple stuff?"

"Are you kidding? I burned that outfit."

"You did not."

"Well, I did spend last night looking through every British show I could, and I think I have found the problem. Nigel is just not into detectives."

Which meant, of course, that she couldn't find a female detective she wanted to emulate. She sounded upbeat, though, and she obviously had some scheme in mind or she wouldn't have called me. "No?"

"No, but it's okay because in my research I hit upon the perfect persona to take on. Emma Peel from The Avengers."

I racked my brain. That spider thing that Scarlett Johansen played? I could definitely see Viv going for a full-body black leather look. But...

"But The Avengers aren't British," I said.

"Not those Marvel guys," Viv said. "The British spy series. From the sixties."

"Oh." Sixties British spies. This should be fun.

"Oh, Salem. The clothes that woman wore..." She was clearly in rapture. "And her hair. I don't have enough to pull off that hairstyle, but I've found a vintage clothing place in town, and I think I know where I can get a wig that would work."

"Awesome," I said. Good grief. The woman was around the bend. Up to this point, she had been a mild embarrassment to herself, but I'd let it go because where was the harm? But this... I mean, wigs? Period clothing? As her best friend, did I have an obligation to pull her back?

Viv was going on about how she should have put it together before. "Every guy in Britain had a crush on Emma Peel. The show would have been on during Nigel's thirties and early forties, so he definitely would have been the age to watch her.

And she was a spy! I mean, come on. What war hero isn't interested in spies?"

"Right. Listen, Viv..."

"So here's what's going down. I'm getting the costume, then you're going to come over and tell him we're rehearsing for a play."

I breathed a silent prayer of gratitude. A *play*. So she didn't plan to put on this getup and expect everyone to accept this as her new look. "That's a fantastic idea!"

"I know! Tonight is poetry night, and you can hear him read. Oh, Salem. It's like...bathing in warm chocolate ganache."

I pictured that and decided that it sounded gross. Do I want chocolate ganache in all my crevices? Do I want to *eat* ganache that has been in my crevices? No. No, I do not. Rather than say that out loud, I said, "Wow. Sounds great."

"Once he sees me in the outfit, it will trigger every Emma Peel fantasy he ever had."

"Do I get to be in this play, too?"

"And have you steal my thunder? No, you're going to be in set design."

Thank you, God, I said silently. "Fair enough. Stump and I will be there in a little while."

At Belle Court, I let Stump take care of her business in the dog walk area, cleaned up after her, and then dropped the bag in the metal box provided. I had just clanged the lid down and turned to go up to Viv's apartment when I almost bumped into Imogene Walker.

"Oh, jeez!" I said, jumping back.

She frowned at me. "What is wrong with you?"

I shook my head furiously. "Oh, nothing. Nothing. I was just...lost in thought, and you startled me." I gave an awkward giggle.

She continued to frown.

"Remember how you wanted that word?" a mocking voice in my head asked.

Oh, come on, I thought. *You cannot be serious. The clues to my identity and the fullness of my being do not lie on the other side of Imogene Friggin' Walker.*

Just to be sure, though, I leaned a bit and looked past her.

She turned her head to see what I was looking at.

We both saw nothing but empty sidewalk.

"I'm just...going up to see Viv," I said lamely. "She's been at play rehearsal."

She blinked and nodded once. She could not have looked more bored. She shifted to move past me.

"Chicken," the voice said.

I groaned. Then I moved to step into her way. "Actually, I jumped because I was just...thinking about you." Jeez-O-Peet , that sounded weird. "I mean, the other day Viv and I were at the Metro Tower building and I saw your picture."

Imogene's expression cleared. I mean, it wasn't as if she broke out in a welcoming smile or anything, but she looked markedly less annoyed. "Yes, my picture is there."

"You were one of the architects who helped make sure the building was safe for use again."

"I was. There was a whole team, of course. But I played a part."

"That is fascinating to me," I said. "Viv and I are looking into the thing with Peter Browning which has, you know, led to other things," I stammered. "We've been watching all the stories he did, and, you know, you probably remember, well, I mean of course you remember, it just happened a few months ago, and I'm sure there's nothing wrong with your rememberer." I laughed.

She went back to looking annoyed.

I cleared my throat and went on. "We've rewatched all the stories he did about Baucum Engineering and the earthquake and the school that collapsed and all that."

Her frowned deepened, but I was fairly sure it was about Browning and all those stories.

I shook my head, not entirely sure of what I wanted to say. "I guess I just never thought about it that much. How it's more than just building something—building a building, I mean. If something goes wrong, people could die."

"That's true."

"I mean, a lot of people could die, in the case of the Metro Tower. That must be...scary." Good grief, I was lame. "I mean, in my job, if I mess up, it'll probably just...grow back."

"Yes, well."

I racked my brain for something else to say. I wasn't seeing any fullness of being materializing in front of me, though. This was all just painfully awkward.

"Did you know him? David Baucum?"

"Of course. His mother lives—lived here. She and I were friends before she got sick."

I hid my shock that anyone could be friends with this formidable woman. "I'm asking this because you were in a related field, and you have experience with...I guess...umm...buildings and natural disaster type things—"

"What, exactly, are you asking me?"

"Did you, ummm, think he got a fair shake, with all that business with NorthStar?"

"No. I do not. There were, tragically, many factors that went into that event that were far beyond David's control. But people need a scapegoat, and unfortunately for David, he appeared to become just that."

At last, something we could agree on. "That's what's been bugging me. I can't understand why Browning focused on him so much. I mean, he brought every story back to Baucum, whether they were involved or not. My friend—who was his boss—said he just did that to keep it in perspective for the local viewers. Make it more personal, I think."

"Well, it certainly made it more personal for David."

"Do you think he meant to kill himself?" I said, reflexively lowering my voice to barely above a whisper.

But there was nothing wrong with her hearer, either. "I have no way of knowing, but I certainly wouldn't be surprised. He was quite devastated when the firm closed and all those people lost their jobs. He knew he wouldn't be able to afford his mother's care here anymore. I know that weighed heavily on him."

"You said his mother died. Was it after—"

"I did no such thing."

"Oh." I flinched like she'd hit me. "I'm sorry, I thought you said—"

"I said his mother lived here, and she did. She is being moved to another facility." She frowned and looked at her watch. "Now if you'll excuse me, I am due at the library desk."

My phone dinged. *"Come on up,"* Viv's text read. *"I need help."*

I lugged Stump inside Belle Court and up to Viv's apartment. I was kind of excited to see her costume, to be honest.

I tapped on the door and let myself in. "We're here," I called.

"Just in time to zip me up," she sang as she waltzed in from the bedroom.

She wore a one-piece fuschia body suit, with one black stripe down the outside of each leg and the length of each long sleeve, and a black patent leather belt low across the hips, fastened with a round silver ring low on her belly. Black heeled go-go boots completed the look.

She turned around, exposing her knobby spine to me. I tugged the zipper up past her black bra and patted her shoulder. "You're all set. Let's see."

She spun around, arms akimbo. The neckline of the outfit was a kind of mock turtleneck.

"Groovy," I said. Who cared if she had chicken legs, rounded shoulders, and a little pot belly? She was working what she did have for all it was worth.

"Wait until you see the wig," she said.

She moved to the side table, where a styrofoam head sat holding the wig in question. It was a nice shade of brown, and the style you think of when you think of sixties hair—all one length, brushed back at the top, bowing away from the cheeks and then curling up at the bottom in a big fat loop of hair.

With the fuschia outfit, it should have been perfect. Viv plopped it on her head and tucked stray white strands of her own hair under it, tugging here and adjusting there.

When she was satisfied, she whirled around again, her hands on her hips, a jaunty tilt to her chin.

She looked like an old man in drag.

"Wow, that wig..." I said.

"I know! It really ties the whole look together." She faced her reflection again and gave her curls a little bounce. She lowered her chin and gave herself a come hither look.

"Yeah, baby," I said, a la Austin Powers.

"That's right," Viv said. "Okay, let's do this."

Viv strode through the halls of Belle Court with even more vigor than usual, so I was forced to practically trot to keep up. Whereas, say, a normal person might feel somewhat abashed at drawing every available eye with three-inch heeled patent leather boots, fuschia from head to toe, and a bouncy wig, Viv met each gaze as if to say, "I know, right?! How freaking fabulous am I?"

When we got to the library, though, the little sitting area was empty.

Imogene was at the volunteer desk, sorting through books.

"What's going on with poetry night?" Viv asked. "I rushed here from dress rehearsal for a play we're doing, and now no one is here."

Imogene eyed Viv over her glasses. She took in the getup, starting at the boots and working her way up to the wig without a word.

"Well?" Viv

"Canceled," was all Imogene said.

"Canceled?!" Viv looked around, as if expecting someone to contradict this obvious impossibility. No one else was in the room, unfortunately. "But...I rushed back from dress rehearsal."

"You said that already. However, your rushing has no bearing on anything related to poetry night."

Viv frowned and put her hands on her hips. "Does this happen often with this—this poetry night thing? You get people all excited to hear—hear *poems* and then cancel it?"

Imogene went back to sorting her books silently. After a few seconds, she said, "Only when the founder is unexpectedly moved to the sixth floor."

Her voice was so low that it took a few moments for the meaning of those words to register.

Sixth floor. The Alzheimer's unit.

I looked at Viv. She was catching on at the same time I was.

Anne had Alzheimer's.

Viv and I walked slowly back toward her room. She looked like I felt—dazed. Anne? Sweet Apple Annie?

We had almost reached Viv's apartment when Viv spun on her booted heel. "I don't believe it."

"I know," I said. "It's heartbreaking."

"No, I mean, I really *don't believe* it."

I thought of Anne's difficulties in following her notes at the Veterans Day ceremony and the blank smiles she'd given Viv at the Memorial Circle when Viv talked about recent events. JoAnn Pepper from years ago, she remembered well. What was going on that week, she seemed very vague on.

I did believe it, I was afraid.

"I'm going to go up and check. I'm sure Imogene Walker is just mixed up."

I followed Viv back to the elevator and we rode silently to the sixth floor.

Inside the Alzheimer's unit, the woman at the desk raised an eyebrow at Viv and her getup, but didn't say anything.

"Anne Meyers," Viv said briskly. "She's not here, is she?"

"She is here. She just moved in today, in fact." She nodded toward the other end of the hallway. "I came from there a few minutes ago, though, and she seemed in good spirits if you want to go down and say hello." She nodded toward me. "You can't take the dog in there, though. Pets have to stay outside those doors."

"You can take her back to my apartment," Viv offered.

I imagined the screaming fit Stump would pitch if I left her alone for one second in Viv's apartment. Stump suffers from extreme separation anxiety. The whole of Belle Court would be thrown into Code Red status before I made it down the hallway.

"You go ahead and go visit her," I told Viv. "Stump and I will wait by the elevator."

We stepped outside the swinging door and I sat, cross-legged, on the floor beside a rolling cart.

The atmosphere was hushed. I fought the urge to run away. For a horrible, terrifying moment I thought about visiting Viv up here. It was easy to pretend that Viv was my age, because she acted like it. Her room at Belle Court was more like a high-end apartment than an assisted living place. But on this floor were real hospital beds. People walking around with trays of medicine and machines on poles.

I leaned against the wall, Stump curled in my lap, and looked at the cart. It held several closed boxes, with a couple on top that were too full to close. One was filled with framed pictures, the other with what looked to be knickknacks. A porcelain bust of a woman with a broad-brimmed hat, kind of like the one G-Ma had in her bedroom. What looked to be three or four folded scarves. A set of candlesticks.

Were these Anne's things, waiting to be moved into her room? Before thinking it through, I slid the box of pictures closer to me and flipped through them.

Anne wasn't in any of them, though. There were a few of what looked like old school pictures and some family photos—a blond boy holding a fish on a line, grinning proudly, a beautiful girl in a black graduation cap and gown, her family around her, an extended family gathered around a fireplace at Christmastime. The white-haired parents, the old man's arm around his wife's shoulder, and a grown man stood on the other side of her, his hands on her shoulders, leaning in and laughing. Someone had just said something funny, or the person taking the picture had done something funny, because his expression was more exuberant than just smiling for a family photo. A few more grown children and three or four grandchildren all smiling for the camera. In moments like that, no one thinks that one of those people will be dead soon. That the woman with the bright blue eyes and generous smile will no longer recognize them. I didn't see Annie in any of these pictures, though.

I realized with horror that this could be stuff gathered up from someone who had recently died, and it was waiting to be picked up by their family. I slid the box back onto the cart and scooted away from it.

Viv came out just a few seconds later.

"That didn't take long," I said as I rose, dusting myself off. "How is she?"

Viv shook her head. "I didn't see her after all. They had taken her for some tests. I waited a few minutes, but..."

She trailed off and turned to push the elevator button. She stared at the closed silver doors, waiting, looking lost in thought and forlorn. Without saying a word, she reached up and tugged the wig from her head. Her hair underneath was completely mussed, but she didn't even try to straighten it.

The elevator dinged softly and the doors slid open. Viv stepped in, almost colliding with a guy getting out. She didn't notice the irritated look he gave her. I put my arm out and gently steered her to the side.

I went back to Viv's apartment for a while, but neither of us had much to say.

"You ought to go talk to your husband," Viv said.

The thought of seeing Tony terrified me. At the same time, I felt an overwhelming need to do just that. Life seemed suddenly very tenuous, and I felt a need to hunker down on home base.

I stood and picked up Stump, who groaned when I did, then yawned and settled.

"Call me if you want to talk," I said. "We'll regroup tomorrow on this Browning thing."

I drove back toward Trailertopia, thinking that I might just text Tony from there. That would be the least intrusive way to contact him. See if he was ready to talk.

Then I thought, *You know what? You faced a conversation with Imogene Walker. You can face Tony.*

So I drove to his house. My heart pounded as I walked up the sidewalk, thinking about our last conversation.

I didn't realize what I was getting into.

I'd never failed before.

I do love you, but...

I rang the doorbell with my stomach clenched.

Tony opened the door and stood back to let me in.

I couldn't bring myself to step across the threshold, though. I hung back on the porch, unsure what to do or say.

"You don't want to come in?" he asked.

I shook my head. "I just..." I trailed off as Stump walked past us both and went to find her bed.

Tony smiled at her. "Stump came in. You should come in."

I followed him into the living room and we sat side by side on the sofa.

"I'm sorry I didn't wait for you to call first," I said.

"Are you? I'm not." He slid his hand up to cup the back of my neck, rubbing his thumb along my jaw line and under my ear.

This, as one might imagine, made me feel a bit more confident. But I didn't come here to ignore the elephant in the room.

I needed to ask him some hard questions. I reminded myself of Serena's advice—our greatest rewards lie on the other side of our deepest fears.

"I have to just—" I started. My throat closed, and I could only whisper. "The other day on the phone, you said you'd never failed at anything before. I just need to know..."

He leaned forward, his forehead touching mine. "What, Salem?" he whispered.

I had to know, but at the last second, I chickened out. I made a joke. "You should have asked me for advice," I whispered. "I've failed at pretty much everything at one time or another. It's not that hard once you get the hang of it."

He laughed, and the next thing I knew his arms were around me, he was pulling me into his lap, holding me so tight, kissing my hair, my face, my lips.

He took my face in his hands. Tears stood in the corners his eyes. "God, Salem. I do love you so much. I don't know how you do that."

"Do what?" I was crying, too, but hopeful, now. Surely we could be okay if he loved me so much, and I loved him so much.

"Make everything feel...okay. Like huge unsolvable problems are suddenly smoothed into..." He shrugged. "Not into nothing, of course, but into something manageable. Something we can handle together."

I ran my thumb along his lower lip. I didn't care for the sound of *unsolvable problems*. I swallowed. "I don't know. But there's a reason we talk about taking one day at a time so much in the program."

We held each other for a while, and finally he said, "Well, this is one day. And you're here. I'd like you to stay here, for this one day."

I felt something inside me unclench, and I smiled. "Me too."

CHAPTER FOURTEEN

What's in a Name?

Later that night, after I felt reconnected to Tony—somehow safer—I felt better able to ask him what I'd come to ask. I couldn't do it while looking at him, though. I lay in his arms, my face against his chest, and said, "I do have to ask you something, though, Tony."

He went very still. "Yes?"

I swallowed. "Do you still struggle with forgiving me? Or did it just—" I swept a flattened hand through the air. "Did it just go?"

He shifted, rolling toward me so that I lay on his arm, but I had to face him.

"Of course, I still struggle, Salem. Of course, I do. Sometimes I think about—about all that—and I want to just—just throttle you. Slam you against the wall. I want you to be broken and sobbing and—and I want you to feel how much you hurt me. And be sorry for it."

"I am sorry for it!" Tears sprang to my eyes and my chest caved.

"I know! And knowing that is what takes all the fire out of my anger. Seeing how broken you are..." He reached out and gently pushed my hair back from my face. "I think I want you to hurt, until I see how much you are hurt, and then I can't take it. It makes me see the whole thing for what it is. Just...pain that causes more pain. And the only thing I can think to do is hold you and try to make the pain go away, for both of us."

"You know if I could undo the past ten years, I would. In a heartbeat."

"I know that, Love." He kissed my forehead.

"Do you really think we can do this, Tony? Really? The fight the other day...it was so ugly."

He nodded. "Yes. It was."

Not the reassurance I had hoped for, but I couldn't fault him.

"I don't want that to happen again."

"Me either. But I'm not sure how we can learn to live together again without a few hard knocks." He slid his hand down my arm and gripped my hand.

I felt the blood thunder in my ears. "So...what does that mean?"

He gripped my hand tighter. "We're married, Salem. You and me. We're married. I don't intend for that to change. Not now, not ever. But...I wonder if maybe I was moving too fast." His mouth tilted crookedly. "I know you probably feel pressured to give up your place. I love having you here. I'd love to have you here all the time. But after the other day...I think maybe we just need to keep things at this level for a while longer. A couple of nights a week here, and you keep your place for a while."

The relief that flooded through me was almost palpable. He must have felt it, because he smiled.

"I do need to keep my trailer," I said. "For a while. Not to drink. Just to..."

"Just to relax. I know. I get that." He shrugged. "I relax when you're not here. I miss you. But I'm comfortable. You need to have space to feel comfortable, too."

I kissed him and snuggled back against his chest.

I must have dozed into the in-between land where I wasn't quite asleep, but my mind was already dreaming. I thought about Jacob becoming Israel.

"I want a new name," I said. I woke myself up saying it, actually.

"A new name?"

I came fully awake and started to pass it off as talking in my sleep. But I realized what half-asleep me had said was true.

"Yes. You know how, in the Bible, God gives people a new name when they go through big life changes. Saul became Paul. Abram became Abraham. Sarai became Sarah. I was reading about how Jacob—whichh means heel-grabber, by the way, did you know that?—became Israel. The devotional said that means "God contended." Because he fought with God. The others sound similar, but, from Jacob to Israel? That's like—a whole new thing. No more heel-grabber. Now you're a contender."

"Gotta admit, the guy had guts," Tony said. "Wrestling all night with an angel. That's pretty brave."

"Or brazen. At any rate, he knew what he wanted. I keep wondering what effect that would have on a person to be called 'heel-grabber' all your life."

Tony shrugged. "I guess everyone's name meant something back then."

"I guess. But it would have to have an effect, don't you think? Everyone knows you're a heel-grabber, so they treat you like a heel-grabber. 'Hey, here comes the heel-grabber, hide your stuff.' I mean, is it really surprising that he stole his brother's birthright? He thinks of himself as a thief."

Tony nodded and shifted his arm around me. "And how do you see yourself? What kind of name do you carry?"

I shrugged. "I don't dislike my name, but...remember Mom's friend Susan? She said that Mom named me after her first love—menthol cigarettes. I don't know if that's true or not, but I guess I always did kind of think of myself as...well, in the "bad stuff" category. I mean, not the really bad stuff, like bubonic plague or something like that."

"I hope not," he laughed.

"But I kind of always thought of myself in the category of the bad stuff that's still part of everyday life. You know, alcohol, smoking, foul language, maybe a little trash-talking other people. That kind of thing. And me."

I raised up and looked at him. He looked confused.

"I'm not sure I'm following you."

"I'm probably not making sense. It's not like anyone ever said anything like that to me – 'Salem, you remind me of all that is white trash.' It's just a sense of how I saw myself. Not one of the good people. One of the bad people."

"And how do you see yourself now? No longer one of the bad things of life, I hope."

I shook my head. "That's just it. I'm getting a sense that this—this labeling as essentially good or essentially bad—is basically groundless. I mean, it all comes down to choices, right? You can see yourself as a good person who continually makes bad choices, and the good is really just all in your own estimation. There's nothing behind it except maybe pedigree, or how others treat you, but it doesn't make your bad choices good. I'm starting to see everyone—myself included, which is nice—as more of a blank slate, and how our choices fill in the picture."

He nodded. "What would you like your new name to be?"

"No idea. I keep thinking about that. Where do I fit? What are my gifts? I wonder if there's a Hebrew word for 'at least she tried.'"

Tony laughed. "We can look that one up."

"I don't even know what my greatest fear is. Do you?"

"Why would I know what your greatest fear is?"

I poked him in the side. "Not mine. Yours. What's your greatest fear?"

He shrugged. "I don't know. I have a bunch of smaller fears, I guess. That something will happen and I won't know what to do. I won't be prepared for it."

"Something will happen to what?"

"Just...anything, basically. Something will go wrong with my business. Mom or Dad will get sick. Or one of the sisters or the nieces or nephews. And I won't be able to help them. So I'm always looking for what could go wrong so I can figure out how to take care of it if and when it happens. Whatever that is."

"You realize that all falls under the umbrella of loss of control, right?"

The corners of his mouth tipped up. "I have been called a control freak from time to time."

I snuggled back into the crook of his arm. My sleepy brain kept mulling over the problem. Finally, just before I dropped off, I said, "I have two greatest fears. One is that I will never figure out God's plan for me. That I live my entire life searching, starting and stopping all these different things, but that I never find my purpose. There's a specific plan for me, but that I never figure out what it is."

"And what's the other?"

"That there is no plan."

In the middle of the night, my bladder reminded me that it was fully functional, and I slipped out from under Tony's heavy arm. I went to the bathroom down the hall instead of the one in his bedroom, because I didn't want to wake him. Or take a chance on him hearing me pee.

I was in mid-stream, not even bothering to keep my sleepy eyes open, when my brain made one of those connections it can only make when it's not busy doing anything else.

The laughing man in that picture on the cart—the one surrounded by family at Christmas. I had seen that picture before, but I hadn't recognized it at first because the context changed the entire tone. With his family, laughing, a Christmas tree in the background, he'd looked joyful. With that laughing face cropped out and imposed over the rubble of devastation, that same smile had looked devious—evil, even.

It was David Baucum.

And the other guy, the younger one holding the fish. He was also in the Christmas picture, still with that same wide grin.

And now, maybe six or eight years on from that—he worked for Eagle construction and drove a white pickup.

I came wide awake, of course.

Was he the guy Viv had almost bumped into in the elevator that afternoon, leaving the Alzheimer's unit?

I was pretty sure it was.

It was him. I was positive. Almost.

What did this mean?

I washed my hands and thought.

Nothing. It meant nothing.

I stood in Tony's hallway but couldn't bring myself to go back to bed. Something was off.

The Eagle Construction guy was David Baucum's half brother. That stuff I'd read last week said David's mother remarried and had another son after Donald Jr. died. He must be the other son. What was his name? I didn't remember seeing a name, just that she'd had another son.

He hadn't said anything about being related to David Baucum. Why hadn't he said anything about it when we talked to him that day in the Eagle parking lot?

Why would he? We'd been talking about Peter Browning. We'd mentioned nothing about David Baucum or the school collapse.

Or had we?

I racked my brain, but my one and only eureka moment had been spent on making the connection of the people.

He was at the finding of Peter Browning's body. Killers always return to the scene of the crime.

I thought about what Imogene had said. I said his mother lived here, and she did. She is being moved to another facility.

Viv and I had seen him and the woman getting into his pickup, filled with boxes.

With the closing of Baucum Engineering, there weren't enough funds to keep her here, in the best Alzheimer's facility for hundreds of miles.

He'd moved his mother to a less expensive facility. He'd been coming back to get her remaining possessions.

It was definitely him. I was sure of it now. I felt a chill in the pit of my stomach.

I thought about Misty Monahan, unable to leave town and facing an obstruction charge. It was not difficult to imagine that morphing into a murder charge. A good prosecutor could turn the circumstances—her affair, Peter's rebuff of her, his chance for a better job while she's left to deal with her unplanned pregnancy alone—into a decent case against her. But this—this seemed to change the landscape. Didn't it?

Should I call Bobby? No, I would wake him and make him mad again.

Should I call Viv? I checked the clock. It was only 1:30 am. Viv didn't sleep much, and it was conceivable that she would be up.

I decided to text her instead, in case she was asleep.

"That guy who almost ran over you in the Belle Court parking lot is David Baucum's half brother. He was in the elevator today, too."

I hit send and chewed my lip, thinking. Why did this seem like such a big deal?

The phone rang almost immediately.

"Are you serious!?" It was Viv, of course. "It's him! He's the one who killed Peter Browning!"

"I think so, too, but why? Why do I think that? It wasn't publicized much, but after Donald Jr. died, his wife remarried and had another son. It's not a secret."

"He was secretive, though."

"Was he? I keep going through the different interactions we had with him, trying to find a time when he should obviously have spoken up."

"What about the other day at Memorial Garden? We were right there, talking about Donald Baucum."

"That's right, we were."

"His mother said her father-in-law was a war hero, and he denied it! He flat denied it!"

I remembered that tiniest of head shakes. Was that denial? Why would he deny his grandfather was a war hero when we were standing in the middle of the memorial built specifically for him? That was secretive. But why?

I sighed. "I don't know. I need to think some more. I'm looking at everything from a different angle, and I can't be sure it all adds up to treachery or just...weirdness."

"We have to talk to him."

"Yeah," I said. But in my head I was thinking, *no way is Tony going to be okay with me interviewing someone I suspect of murder.* That would not fall under the "Be Safe" umbrella.

"Let's go back out to Eagle tomorrow and lean on him a little," Viv said. "See what pops out."

"Gross," I said. "Listen, I don't think I can do that."

"Frank can watch Stump."

"No, it's not that. It's...it's Tony."

"Tony can watch Stump."

"No. Listen. Tony really doesn't like me doing this."

"So?"

"So, he's my husband. And I want to take his wishes into consideration when I do things."

"Well, you could..." She trailed off, though, coming to the same conclusion I did.

We could not interview the half brother, whatever his name was.

"I'll call Bobby tomorrow and tell him what I've found out. He's right, you know. He's the detective, not us. It's his job to take care of things like this. He's trained and everything."

"Yes. And if this turns out to be the guy, he will get all the glory. You know that, right?"

"I know that rubs you the wrong way."

"Yes, it does."

"But, that's just, you know, the way things will have to be."

She was silent for a long time. "What does this mean, Salem? Are we closing the agency?"

"We don't have an agency," I reminded her.

"We have cards. Plus, I was going to send in for a certificate."

"What kind of certificate?"

"Well, you just get it printed on this fancy paper. But I was going to frame it."

"Viv, the thing is, I just don't know if I'm going to be able to do these investigations anymore. Not and keep my marriage—which I want to do, by the way. I mean, in case that sounded like I was undecided. But that doesn't mean we can't still hang out. Do other stuff together."

"What other stuff could we possibly do?"

"I don't know." Suddenly tears welled in my eyes and my throat closed. This was so silly! What was I doing? Crying over giving up something that I wasn't even very good at. Something that was dangerous. "We have to find something, though." I didn't say it, but the thought of Viv finding another partner to solve crimes with made me feel bereft.

"I suppose we really could give gardening a shot. I look awful in overalls, though."

"We could be high society arts patrons, then," I said. "Although I am going to have a hard time pulling that one off. And we'll definitely have to use your money."

"The wardrobe will be better, but it still sounds boring. How does your husband feel about high-stakes illegal gambling?"

"Well, I could ask. But no. He will not feel good about that."

Viv sighed.

I sniffed back tears and reached for the box of tissues on the table. "We have to think of something. Because I can't lose Tony again. I have to respect what he's asked of me."

"Do you? I mean, has he respected what you asked of him?"

It was my turn to sigh. "He forgave me for leaving him and sleeping with other men."

"Oh."

See? There was really nothing that could be said to that. Nothing at all.

"Well, let's just go to bed and talk about it tomorrow. Things always look worse in the middle of the night than they really are."

"That's what Les says, too. I'll call Bobby tomorrow and give him the information, and then we'll be out of this case."

"Good night, Salem."

"Good night." I hung up and sat on the sofa, chiding myself for feeling like I'd lost something. I hadn't lost anything. Viv and I would still be friends. We would find something to do. And if she moved on, well, I had Tony. I had Stump. I had my actual job that I was paid to do. I had a lot to be grateful for.

I sniffed back more tears and blew my nose.

"Are you okay?"

I jumped and spun to see Tony standing in the doorway.

"You scared me!" I said with a shaky laugh, sniffing (softly, I hoped) and standing. "Yes, I'm fine. I just woke up to go to the bathroom." And now I was in the living room.

He looked at the phone in my hand.

I started to tell him I'd had a nightmare and that's why I was crying, but I couldn't bring myself to lie, not outright like that. He would be concerned and might even want to know what I'd dreamed about.

But I didn't want him to think I'd been talking to someone in the middle of the night, either. Even though I had. "I knew it was probably a mistake to get a smart phone," I said, tossing it onto the sofa. "Here it is the middle of the night and I've got it in my hand like a pacifier or something."

He smiled and put an arm around me. "Let's go back to bed."

Tony was already gone by the time I woke up the next morning. He had left half a pot of coffee, though, and a note that said, "Breakfast muffins in the freezer. Help yourself," with a little heart underneath.

I took a deep breath. My crying jag from the night before seemed silly now. Viv and I could find something to do. I was off work, I had time to think of something.

I showered and dressed, planning how I would tell Bobby what I'd discovered about David Baucum's half brother. I was fairly sure he would disregard it entirely, and I wasn't sure what I would do in that case. I had a gut feeling there was something off with the guy.

I remembered that night at the side of the road. "Vultures," he'd called the reporters, his voice dripping with hatred.

Or was I just remembering it that way because I'd decided he was a bad guy?

I dried my hair and decided I needed to lay everything out for Bobby. I would write down all the links, the stories we'd re-watched, and put everything together for him.

I shook my head, thinking about how mad Viv would be to have to turn all this over to Bobby so he could get the credit. I would have to remind her that we knew—and most importantly, Bobby would know—who was the real hero.

I found a pad of legal paper in Tony's office and sat at the bar in the kitchen to make my notes. I figured a timeline was probably the best way to start.

How long had the Baucum brother said he had been in Lubbock? A few months, if I remembered correctly. He hadn't given a number. But still, it kind of lined up with the collapse of Baucum Engineering.

I opened my phone and recorded the different URLs that Trisha had sent us. I wrote the one that was supposed to be for the security camera that captured the school collapse, but then decided I should include the one that the kid at the coffee shop had given us, too.

I started typing, and the memory filled in the rest, thank goodness. Just to make sure I had the right one, though, I filled in the date and waited for the image of an intact school to load.

The screen was so dark at first that it must have stalled. Then I saw brighter lights emerging and realized the screen was there, it was just dark.

Why was it dark?

I brought the phone closer to me and looked at the lights that moved slowly across the scene. It was raining.

I frowned. I'd typed in the wrong date again. This wasn't the bright March day of the earthquake. This was a dark rainy day in—yep, November. I'd typed in 11-3 instead of 3-11.

I started to hit the back button, then froze, watching the car that drove slowly, swerving slightly, past the school.

My phone rang and I jumped.

Viv's picture popped up in the top right corner of my screen. I tapped it and said, "Viv! What kind of car did Peter Browning drive?"

"A tan Honda," she said.

"A light-colored one?"

"Tan is pretty light, yes."

"I think I found a clue."

I dragged the blue dot on the video backwards, then let it play again.

The car slowed almost to a stop in front of the school. The video was grainy, but I was pretty sure I saw something. Something I had to share.

My heart began to thud heavily, and my mind spun. Viv rattled on, something about Nigel and Anne.

"Stop," I said. "Hush."

"Well," she said, but I think it was mostly for show. "I'll be by your place in fifteen minutes. Be ready to go to see Bobby."

CHAPTER FIFTEEN

Charade

It actually took me and Stump more like thirty minutes to get there, but Viv still wasn't ready to go. While she primped her hair and put on fresh lipstick, I pulled up the security camera footage again. I was glad to see her back in normal clothes today—chocolate brown slacks and a gold satin button-down shirt, with a brown jacket over it.

I found the right time in the video and rose to stand beside her. The picture was a bit grainy and dark from the rain, but it was still possible to tell what we were looking at. The front part of the school still stood, and if you only looked at that part, you'd never know anything was wrong.

"Okay, check the date," I said. I tilted the phone so Viv could see.

"November third?" she asked.

I nodded. "The day Peter Browning disappeared. Look at this."

The car entered the frame—a light-colored hatchback, the kind we knew Peter Browning drove. It entered the driveway to the school and then the parking lot, driving first straight down the middle of the drive, then hugging the right side of the road, then back to the middle. Even on this small screen, I could tell that the license plate would probably be easy to make out on a larger screen. The car drove slowly to the front of the parking lot, slowing even more as it reached the very front of the building where the sidewalks converged to provide one wide entryway into the building. It stopped there for a few seconds, then, with a quick burst, it sped out of the frame and presumably out of the lot.

"See that!" I said. "Did you see that?"

"What?"

"Did something move on the other side of the car? Look again."

I dragged the dot back a bit. Watched again as the car made its wobbly way up the driveway and to the drop-off loop.

"There!" I did see something. Something small and barely perceptible, but it was there. I was almost sure.

We rewound again. "Now look, there on the passenger side. Something moves right before he speeds up and drives off."

It was almost impossible to see, because the movement was on the other side of the car. And it could have been nothing— just a blip, some static or something, a glitch in the film. Except this was digital. Did digital recordings get blips? I had no idea. But it looked like just the merest hint of movement at the passenger door. A small triangle, darker than the rest of the area around it.

"Did the passenger door open?" Viv asked.

"That's what I am wondering."

We watched it again. And again.

It could be.

I tried to imagine Peter Browning's frame of mind as he drove up to the school that night. Driving by the school would certainly support the theory that he felt remorse for the death of David Baucum—this school was the scene of Baucum's own undoing, after all. It was the scene that Browning himself brought to the public's attention, again and again, relentlessly.

If he had swung by the scene of this devastation on the way to intentionally carrying out his own death, it could have meant that despite the self-assured face he put on, he was consumed by guilt over David Baucum's death, the shuttering of the firm.

But...was he alone? I tried to gauge the distance from the driver's side to the passenger door. Peter was a tall man, so he probably had long arms. The car was small. It was within the realm of possibility that he had leaned over and opened the door, before driving away.

But why? Had he thrown something out?

I took out the notebook I had been writing notes in. "We have to tell Bobby all of this."

Viv frowned. "We do?"

I chewed my lip. "Yes?"

She made a groaning noise. "This is rubbish. He'll probably get a promotion and a raise from this. You know that, don't you?"

"Yes, I know." I thought for a moment. "Of course, when it comes right down to it, I'm the one with the concerned husband. There's no reason you couldn't follow up on this lead."

She curled her lip. "That wouldn't be nearly as much fun."

Like the complete dork I am, I teared up.

She sighed and stood. "Oh, well. We might as well get this over—" She stopped when she looked at me. "Oh, good grief. Are you *crying*?"

"No," I said, through tears. "Don't be stupid." I sniffed and cleared my throat. "You're crying."

"You're not pregnant, are you?"

"No!" I hadn't meant for it to come out so loud. Even Stump flinched a little. "I mean, no. I don't think so. I'm just a little emotional. My aura's all out of whack."

"Well, get a grip. You're not a civilian yet." She locked up and we headed toward the elevator. "You need to keep a steely grip on your nerves for a bit longer."

"Okay, I have never had a steely grip on my nerves, as you well know." I pushed the elevator down button. "You should have seen me this morning when I realized that we had been talking to David Baucum's half brother and I hadn't even known it."

"Why should that scare you?" Viv fluffed her hair in the reflection of the elevator doors. She rolled her lips together and stepped back as the elevator dinged and the doors slid open.

"Because. What reason would he have for being so...secretive?"

"Well, he didn't do anything."

"Not that we know of. But...why is he lying about who he is? What reason could he have?"

"Has he actually lied?"

"Well, he hasn't been honest. I mean, we don't even know his name. We've had all these conversations with him. He's had every opportunity to tell us who he really is, and he hasn't. Doesn't that imply some ill intent?" I said as we headed for the front doors.

"It is odd."

"It's very odd. I think we should find out what it means."

I heard something around the corner as we approached it. I almost jumped out of my skin. I whirled and faced the perpendicular hallway in a crouch, fully expecting to see what's-his-name ready to bring something heavy down on my head.

Instead, we saw Nigel, frozen in the middle of the hall runner. He had a most definite "I'm caught!" look in his eye.

I stood with an apologetic smile for him. Poor guy. It must be wearing him out that Viv was after him so blatantly. He probably had all he could handle on his plate with poor Anne.

His eyes darted between the two of us. "I—uh, I forgot something in my room." He turned and hurried away.

Viv grabbed my shirt. "Come on!" Viv whispered. "I thought of another one this morning."

We quick-footed after Nigel, while Viv hissed, "You say, 'How long has it been since you've played cribbage.'" She gave me a raised-brow look, then nodded.

"What? What is that?"

She grimaced at Nigel's retreating back. "Just say it. Now!"

"How long has it been since you've played cribbage?" I shouted after Nigel.

"It's been at least a bloody fortnight!" Viv shouted back.

Nigel kept up the hasty retreat. I was getting out of breath, so I slowed.

After a few moments, Viv gave up, too. She watched Nigel around the next corner, then turned back, her shoulders slumped. "Come on. Let's go give Mr. Hot Detective the lead of his career."

There was a new receptionist at the police station and she got, frankly, quite rude when Viv and I walked through with Stump.

"Excuse me!" she shouted through her glass partition. She slid it back so she could direct the full force of her outrage at us. "Where do you think you're going?"

"We're going to see Detective Sloan about an important murder case."

"Do you have an appointment?"

Viv gave me the side-eye and waltzed up to the window. "Let me see. Do we have an appointment? Why don't you check your little book there?"

Her gaze never leaving Viv's, she said, "Nope. Nothing in my little book."

I joined Viv at the window and, just to be annoying, positioned Stump so that her front feet rested on the counter.

I checked the name plate. "Jeannie? Jeannie. Nice to meet you. I'm Salem, and this is Viv."

Viv gave her a flat smile. "Pleasure to meet you."

"I know who you are," Jeannie said.

I was guessing Jeannie was about ten years older than my mom. She had dyed long blond hair that swept back from her head in big waves. I had seen that style in pictures of the '70s. It was probably the style she'd had in high school, and she just never changed it. You had to admire that kind of commitment.

"So Bobby's told you about us?" I asked. "Good. We don't have an appointment, but we do need to see Bobby. It's important. We have a lead in the Peter Browning case."

"Have a seat."

"He won't mind if we go on back to his office," Viv said. "We've been there before. We know where we're going."

"Have a seat."

"Has he told you that we've worked together on other cases? Did he tell you we brought down the Hombres' cock-fighting ring?"

"Have a seat."

Viv's mouth thinned, but she said nothing for a moment.

"Maybe you could just call Bobby right quick and tell him we're here," I suggested.

"Have a se—"

"We're having a seat!" Viv barked. She stalked toward the plastic chairs at the other side of the room.

Jeannie picked up the phone and bent her head to look at the keypad.

The second she did, Viv raced for the door and jerked the handle.

The door rattled loudly. It was locked.

I looked at Jeannie, who stared stonily at Viv as she dropped the handle and stomped away grumbling. Jeannie talked into the phone. She hung up and slid the glass partition back without another word.

Stump and I had a seat. Viv stalked back and forth, her heels clicking on the tile floor. I pulled my phone out of my purse. "Windy, call Bobby."

"Gettin' him for ya now, Honey."

I got his voicemail. "Bobby, Viv and I are in the lobby. We have some information for you. The dragon lady at the front desk won't let us in. Come get us, please."

Ten minutes later, I called again. "Bobby, I'm quite sure I have at least two pieces of information you don't have. Come get us."

Fifteen minutes after that, I called again. "Bobby, come on. Tony doesn't want me to investigate any more, so I can't follow up on these myself."

Less than ten seconds later, he was at the door.

I picked up Stump and gave Jeannie a benevolent smile as we left. "Thank you so much."

In Bobby's office, I pulled up the surveillance video I had found. "See? That's Browning's car, right? And look at this." I jabbed my finger at the screen when the car stopped. "See?"

"What am I looking at?"

I dragged the blue dot backward. "Look at the passenger side."

We watched it again. "He stops, he goes again," Bobby said.

"Don't you see the door open? I think the door opened. The passenger door."

"The door definitely opened," Viv said.

Bobby groaned and watched the video one more time. Then he said, "What am I doing?" He hit the mouse on his computer, then studied my phone and typed in the URL. We all gathered around his computer and watched the whole thing play out again.

On the bigger screen, it was easier to see that something had happened on that side of the car, but it wasn't clear just what.

Viv and I waited while Bobby wordlessly watched the monitor. He dragged the car back and watched it three more times.

"Well?" Viv said. "Did you know Peter Browning had driven by that school the night he disappeared?" When Bobby didn't answer she said again, "Well, did you?"

Bobby sat with his hand on his chin, his finger over his mouth, staring at the screen.

Viv smiled at me. "He's stumped. We stumped him."

"Do you think he was throwing something out, Bobby?" I asked. "Like, a note or something?"

Bobby gave me a look, but said nothing.

I sighed. "Are you going to say anything? Anything at all? What do you think this is?"

He frowned, then leaned back in his chair, laced his fingers over his belly and said, "This is a good find, Salem."

I was so shocked I had to sit. "What?"

"Nope." He shook his head. "Not saying it twice."

Viv laughed and did a little victory dance, right there in Bobby's office. She mimed spiking a football.

Bobby let her indulge for a few seconds, then said, "We'll follow up on this. Now, go home and stay out of trouble."

"That's it?" I asked. "That's all you're going to say?"

"Your husband asked you to quit doing stuff like this, didn't he?"

I nodded.

"Smart man. Now, again—good job, go home."

Viv shook her head. "Sad. Your professional envy of us is just sad."

The corner of Bobby's mouth tipped up, but he didn't answer.

I wanted to argue, but there really wasn't much I could say, either. I told myself to be glad we had found something that could be helpful, and let it go. I mean, I should start getting used to that, right?

This was no longer my purview. I mean, it had never been my purview, but I could no longer play like it was.

I stood and hefted Stump on my hip. "Fine. We're going." As I reached the door, though, I turned back and said, "You could at least say thank you."

The look he gave me...I wasn't sure what to make of it. He sat with his elbow on the arm of his chair, his hand over his mouth. He was watching me walk out of the room, his eyes filled with something that might possibly have been...regret? Sadness?

Seriously?

He straightened, gave me a small smile, and said, "Thank you, Salem. This is a good find."

The ride away from the police station was a silent one. I kept seeing that look on Bobby's face. What had he been thinking? He couldn't possibly have been upset to know that Viv and I would no longer be bugging him for inside information or bringing largely useless information to him.

Could he?

To be honest, my feelings about Bobby were pretty mixed-up. I had had a crush on him for two solid years, from the beginning of the fourth grade through the end of the fifth grade. I had written Mrs. Bobby Sloan on every available surface. I had—to my undying mortification—written him love notes that I signed with my real name and left in his car.

It was kind of hard to get past all that, even now—even as a married woman who was in love with her husband. Bobby had kissed me, once, before Tony and I were reunited. It might have been an emotional impulse brought about by the fact that I had almost gotten myself killed.

But part of me couldn't help but entertain the notion that Bobby was a little, teeny-tiny bit attracted to me. And that part couldn't help but be flattered by the idea.

However, that was a thought I had to put out of my mind. Tony didn't deserve a wife who was playing imaginary flirting games with another man. Even if I was sure nothing would ever come from it—and I was quite sure of that—Tony didn't deserve for me to even contemplate it for a minute. I knew how I would feel if I found out Tony had the slightest attraction for another woman—violence and destruction on a massive scale came immediately to mind. So, no. Bobby Sloan needed to be evicted from my head space before he could put down roots.

"You forgot to tell him your theory about David Baucum's half brother," Viv reminded me as we pulled into the Belle Court parking lot.

"Shoot." I frowned at my phone. I dialed Bobby's number and put him immediately on speaker.

"Bobby, I forgot the other bit of information we had for you," I said as soon as he answered.

"Let me get a pen," he said.

I looked at Viv, who gave me an 'I'm impressed' eyebrow raise. We had definitely earned some props from Bobby by finding that surveillance video. He'd never bothered to write down anything we said before.

"Okay, you know David Baucum?"

"Yeah?"

"Well, he has a half brother who is here in town, but he hasn't told anyone that's who he is."

"What do you mean?"

"I mean, he's David Baucum's half brother. But he hasn't said that."

"Is he going under a different name or something?"

"Well, I don't know that." He hadn't introduced himself, so I couldn't say for certain he was using an assumed name.

"What name is he going by?"

"I don't know that, either. That's the thing. We've talked to him on four separate occasions now—" I held up four fingers and gave Viv a questioning look. She nodded. "Four different occasions, and he never once mentioned who he was."

Silence on the other end.

"Okay, I understand that it doesn't seem like much. But why is he being so secretive? We saw him out at the scene when Peter's body was found. Not a word. We talked to him in the parking lot where he works—"

"Where does he work?"

"Eagle Construction."

"And he's using an assumed name there?"

"Well, I don't actually know that. I just think it's noteworthy that he had several opportunities to mention who—I mean, we were talking openly about Peter Browning's death, so you would think—but he never revealed that information."

More silence. Then, "Did you ask him his name?"

I looked at Viv, and we both shrugged at the same time. We didn't remember if we had or not.

I felt my lead crumbling pitifully around me.

"Tell him about the other day at the Baucum Memorial," Viv said.

"Yeah! We saw him and his mother—his mother has Alzheimer's, he did tell us that much—at the Baucum Local Hero memorial thingy, and she said that her father was a war hero, but he—he kind of shook his head like he was denying it."

"Did he come right out and say she was wrong?"

"Well, no, it was more of just a tiny shake of his head—"

"So it could have been anything."

"But it wasn't anything. He was denying that his grandfather was a war hero, because we were standing right there in the tribute built for his grandfather the war hero, and he didn't want us to know who he was. That's noteworthy, don't you think?"

Bobby sighed, and even though I couldn't see him, I knew he was rubbing his forehead in exasperation.

"Salem," he finally said. "Maybe—and hear me out, I'm just spitballing here—but maybe he was just a guy who has been through a lot of upheaval over the past few months and didn't want to get chatty with a couple of nosy women asking intrusive questions."

I drew my head back. I looked at Viv. She looked as offended as I felt.

"His brother faced professional disgrace and ruin and is now dead, his mother is very sick and will never get better, and the family business is in the can. And here come two—"

"If you say nosy women again, I swear I will make you regret it," Viv warned.

"Two people asking a bunch of questions," Bobby said. Now, though, I could hear the smile in his voice. "And he doesn't feel like getting involved. I see nothing really noteworthy about that."

I stared at the phone for a while. Viv killed the motor.

Finally, I said, "Thanks, Bobby," and hung up. I slipped the phone back into my purse, feeling better.

"You look happy. Why do you look happy when he insults us?"

"His condescending attitude means I don't have to worry that my childhood crush gets revived."

Viv shrugged and opened her car door. "Whatever gets you through the day, I suppose."

As we walked back through the halls of Belle Court, I said, "Let's go see Anne."

"We can't. You've got your kid." She nodded toward Stump.

"Shoot. That's right."

"I can watch your dog."

I turned and froze in shock. Imogene Walker stood behind us.

When I just stood there, mouth slightly agape, she said again, "I can watch your dog. You should go see Anne. She's having a good day today."

I looked down at Stump. "She has...issues. Sometimes she freaks out when I'm gone and starts..." I searched for the right word.

"Screaming bloody murder," Viv said.

I gave a grudging nod.

"She'll be fine." Imogene reached for her.

Reflexively, I tightened my grip. Stump groaned.

Imogene fixed me with her steely gaze, and I dropped my hands.

I'm sorry, Stump, I said silently as she was lifted away from me. I was the worst mother ever.

But Imogene cradled her close, the way Stump liked to be held, and looked down at her. The closest thing I'd ever seen to a smile played at the edges of her mouth. "You look a bit like my Mookie," she said.

Stump stared up at her, then gave a loud belch.

When Imogene did no more than raise an eyebrow and say, "Is that so?" I felt like things were probably going to be okay.

"We'll be in my cottage," Imogene said as she walked away.

Viv grabbed my elbow and dragged me down the hallway. I watched them go, thinking this was what mothers must feel like when they drop their kids off at kindergarten the first time.

We were two or three hallways down Belle Court's labyrinthine structure when Viv said, "I'm proud of you. You've gone probably a good 75 or 80 yards without turning back."

"Only because I'm too afraid of Imogene not to do what she tells me to."

"Still."

I had noticeably slowed, though. I was falling behind Viv and looking back over my shoulder, listening for the telltale tortured howl that meant I needed to go running, when Viv suddenly stopped in mid step.

I crashed into her back.

Facing her in the otherwise empty hallway was Nigel, holding the handle of a rolling suitcase. He carried a box under his other arm, and a smaller bag hung from that hand. His eyes were wide, his mouth open.

"I haven't done anything!" he shouted. Then he pulled himself back at the shoulders and nodded once, his mouth firm. "I have done nothing illegal, and there's not a thing you can do to me."

Viv and I looked at each other. She looked as confused as I felt.

"Is that right?" I asked, not knowing what else to say.

Then it dawned on me. What he'd just said was not in a British accent. What was going on here?

The best defense is a good offense, I remembered from the poster hanging in my middle school gym. "How can you even say that?" I stepped around Viv and crossed my arms over my chest, tossing my nose in the air. "*Done nothing wrong,*" I echoed with a sneer.

"I said I've done nothing illegal." He continued to eye Viv with distrust. "For that matter, though, I have done nothing wrong. I gave Anne what she needed and what she wanted. She wanted a charming gentleman to keep her company as her brain cells slowly dribbled away, and that's what I gave her. I have made her happy for a few weeks, and I would have gone on making her happy if you would have kept your clever little nose out of things—" He jabbed a finger furiously at Viv. "You with your—your taunts and questions at every turn, trying to trip me up."

Viv sneered back at him, tossed me a look that clearly said she had no idea what was going on, then turned back to him and crossed her own arms. "Yes, well..." She nodded decisively as if to say, "Heck yeah."

"You're not even British!" I shouted.

"I never said I was."

"Seriously?! You said you were an RAF pilot, you told people you were a war hero. You talked with a fake accent!"

"Which is not illegal, I again point out."

"It's illegal to pose as an RAF war hero," I said. I had no idea if it was or not, but I seemed to remember from some TV show that it was illegal to pose as someone from the US military, so probably...

"No, it's not!" The vehemence in his voice told me that he was someone who had studied the statutes very well. "Not unless you take some kind of benefit from it—a free meal or a free bus ride or something."

"What about free *nookie*?" Viv shouted. "It's probably illegal to pose as a war hero so you can get free nookie!"

"That was mutually given," Nigel said. "An even exchange, thank you very much."

Since we were smack-dab in the middle of territory I didn't want to explore further, I said, "What's your real name? I know it's not Nigel."

"Exactly," Viv said, fighting to catch up now that she'd caught on. "That's the most ridiculous name I've ever heard, by the way."

"It's very British," not-Nigel said.

"It's too British. It's the Britishest British that ever Britished! And I can't wait to tell Anne what a charade you are."

She stalked past Nigel toward the elevator to the fifth floor.

Viv worked her mouth in anger all the way up to the Alzheimer's unit. "That—that fool! What in the world was he playing at?" She shook her head, her mouth a thin line. "He must have loved how he had all those poor women fooled."

I checked her reflection in the elevator door. I did not say anything.

"Poor Anne. She was so—so taken in by him. Bless her heart."

"Well, if she'd had all her faculties, like you do, maybe she could have spotted it—"

"I know what you're thinking," Viv said, glaring at me. "And I'm not having it. Yes, I was attracted to him. He's an attractive man. But I knew, on a certain level, that he wasn't legit."

"Did you?" I raised my eyebrows innocently.

"Of course, I did! Why do you think I kept trying to trip him up like I did?" She tapped her temple. "A sharp mind is always working, Salem. Always working. My subconscious obviously knew the score, even if my conscious mind hadn't caught up to it yet."

I nodded as the doors slid open. "Whatever gets you through the day, I suppose."

Viv marched up to the desk. "We're here to see Anne," she said to the nurse. "We have some shocking news that she needs to hear."

"Well then, you better just march yourself right back out that door," the nurse said, pointing back the way we'd come. "Because we do not do shocking news on this floor."

Viv frowned. "Look. Anne has a very close friend who, it turns out, is not who he said he was. She will be expecting him to come see her, and she needs to know that he's a louse who is hightailing his chicken butt out of town as we speak."

"Were they close?"

Viv's frown deepened. "Yes."

The nurse frowned, too. "Well, then. We will give this information to her family, and we will let them and her doctors decide if and how to tell her."

Viv appeared to be thinking about it.

"I mean it, Ms. Kennedy. A shock like that could really set her back. Alzheimer's and dementia are greatly exacerbated by trauma."

"She will need to know that something has happened, though. She'll wonder why he isn't coming to see her."

"And we will send his regrets until such time as she is ready to hear it. Or else we won't. But that won't be for you to decide." She put her hand on her hip and studied Viv. "Now. Do you still want to see Anne? Because if you go in there spouting off, I'm gonna tell the nurses on your floor to slip some powerful laxatives into your morning coffee."

Viv raised an eyebrow, but said nothing.

"I ain't playin', Viv."

"Fair enough," Viv said. "Please arrange to have her family get in touch with me."

The nurse looked at me. "I'm counting on you to remind her of her responsibilities."

A chill went through me. I wasn't sure I was up to the task.

I followed Viv to Anne's room, looking back over my shoulder at the nurse. She watched me with a lifted eyebrow.

Viv took a fortifying breath outside Anne's door, then knocked lightly.

Anne stood beside the table in her new room, going through a stack of folders and loose papers.

"Viv! Salem! This is a nice surprise!"

"We came to see your new digs!" Viv planted her hands on her hips and surveyed the place. "Very nice. I like the colors."

Anne gave her a patient smile. "You don't have to put a positive spin on it, Viv. I know where I am and I know what's going on. I do pretty well, still, as long as the sun is up. For some reason the night time gets me confused. But right now I am lucid enough to know why I'm here and the situation I'm in."

"I"m sorry," Viv said, and she seemed as close to tears as I'd ever seen her. Which made my own throat close up and my eyes burn.

"Oh, I know. You're sorry, I'm sorry, everyone is sorry. Not a thing any of us can do about it, though." She dropped into a chair and shrugged, a stack of papers in her hands. "But, it's not really that bad. I mean, I would have liked more. But it's not as if I didn't have a fantastic life. I was just sorting through these papers and reliving my teaching days. It's silly to keep them all this time, I know." She leaned forward and gave me a conspiratorial smile. "But I only kept the best. My teacher's pets." She laughed and shuffled through the papers. "I know we're not supposed to have them, but we do. Favorite students. I had so many, too! Precious kids who became precious adults and are friends still. Do you know, I have students who still come to visit me? They graduated forty years ago and still come to see me. Because I taught them about Dickens or Poe, or helped them learn how to appreciate a poem. Now, someone who has lived that kind of life can hardly complain, can they?"

Viv and I agreed, but it still seemed too sad.

Anne took a deep breath and slapped her hands onto her knees. "And just where is Nigel, anyway?" she asked. "That scoundrel. He promised he'd come see me this afternoon and it's almost—" She looked around for the clock. "Why, it's almost dinner time."

Viv and I exchanged a look, which was a mistake.

"What?" Anne asked. "Why are you looking at each other like that?"

My heart thudded. I looked at Viv.

"Look," she said with a sigh. "We didn't want to have to tell you this."

"Viv," I said.

"Salem, she needs to know. She's going to find out sooner or later."

I stood. "Viv, don't—"

Viv put her hand out to stop me. "Nigel's kids came and got him. This afternoon."

"What? Why?"

"Apparently they wanted him to live with them all along, but he didn't want to be a burden to them. You know how...selfless and considerate he was." She had to spit the last words out, but she got it done. "Also, I remember him saying something about what a control freak his daughter is."

Anne frowned, putting her hand to her mouth. She looked unsure. "Yes..."

"They showed up with no warning. His daughter made a big fuss and he couldn't very well say he'd prefer to live here than with her and her family. They have an entire suite for him in their house. They brought all these brochures for programs around there that he can be involved in. Even a World War II veterans group that he can be a part of. They had it all worked out."

"That sounds wonderful," Anne said. "How nice for him." She looked genuinely pleased.

"Doesn't it?" Viv looked out the window then back at Anne. "Anyway, he said he would be fine, of course, and expects to be treated very well even if he is constantly fussed over. He was quite upset that they wouldn't give him time to say goodbye. But hopefully he can come back for visits from time to time."

"Oh, that would be nice."

"And, he said that he would write to you as soon as he can."

Anne smiled. "Of course. Of course he will write." She frowned again. "I can't remember, Viv. Where does his daughter live?"

"Florida," Viv said. She stood and smoothed at her blouse. "She lives in Port St. Lucie. Right on the coast."

"He'll be by the ocean again, then. That will make him happy."

"Exactly. Well, we need to be going. But we'll be back for visits, and maybe you can still hang out with us. Poetry night and all that"

"I will, if they let me out," Anne said with a laugh.

"Why Florida?" I asked, just to have something to break the heavy silence on our elevator ride back to Viv's floor.

"I have a friend there. She can postmark the envelopes for me."

"Envelopes?" Then it dawned on me. "You're going to write her letters? As Nigel?"

"Of course I am. I can't let her sit here and pine away for something from that loser, can I?"

I shook my head. "Definitely not." I put my arm around her skinny shoulders and gave her a slight squeeze.

"Get off me." She batted at my arm.

I grinned but withdrew and said no more.

CHAPTER SIXTEEN

You Still Have Your Health

We walked in silence to Imogene's cottage, down a winding sidewalk from the main Belle Court building. Imogene answered the door. I felt a moment of panic when Stump wasn't at her feet to greet me, but then saw her in the recliner, where apparently she'd been sitting beside Imogene the same way she always sat with Frank.

"There's my girl," I said. *Any recliner in a storm, huh, Stump?*

"How was Anne?"

"She was remarkably well," Viv said. "You may as well know—Nigel is not who he pretended to be. We caught him sneaking out with his suitcase and all his belongings in a cardboard box."

"I figured as much." Imogene shook her head in disgust.

"You did?"

"Of course. You were very smart to keep calling him out the way you did with all that British trivia. He knew you were on to him and he panicked. I just didn't have the heart to tell Anne."

"No," Viv nodded, as if she'd been of the same mind. "What, exactly, made you realize he was such a faker?"

"Well, I started wondering about him at that poetry reading. He's clearly a trained actor."

"Clearly," Viv said.

"And I just don't trust actors."

"Exactly."

"And then when you kept so subtly questioning his story, and he couldn't really provide any answers..." She held up her hands. And the Veterans Day ceremony, with his laryngitis or whatever." She shook her head and snorted. "Too afraid to even attempt to answer questions. Such a phony. If Anne had had all her faculties around her, she would have seen through such a charlatan in an instant."

"She asked about him just now, and I made up a story about his daughter taking him to Florida."

Imogene nodded her approval. "Good idea. She'll miss him, but I think it would crush her to know she was fooled by such an obvious con man."

Viv's shoulders, already slumped, drooped even more. "Yes. Well..."

"We need to be going," I said. "Thank you so much for watching Stump. There aren't that many people she feels comfortable with."

"Anytime," Imogene said, because apparently this was the day for shocking revelations.

We walked back toward the main building, but Viv stopped in the middle of the sidewalk.

"What's the matter?"

Viv looked up at the building. "I can't go back in there. Not yet."

"Let's go get some coffee then."

She didn't respond.

"Or tea? I'll bet that new coffee house on 19th knows what Earl Grey hot is."

She frowned. "No. Coffee's fine. But you have to drive."

We drove to a small coffee shop where I could park close to the windows. I rolled the window down for Stump and told her to sit and be quiet. I closed the door and hoped for the best. Before I'd reached the front door, though, she was already howling.

"We can sit outside," Viv said.

The November air was chilly but not freezing. I ordered two black coffees while Viv let Stump out, and they claimed a table on the deserted patio. Viv buttoned her coat and sat, hunched, staring at the wrought iron tabletop. Stump lay at her feet, her nose between her paws.

We sat and drank our coffee in silence for a while. I had no idea what to say, but I was growing more worried by Viv's demeanor by the minute.

Viv stared straight ahead, then made a frustrated, groaning noise. She frowned at her coffee.

"Nigel?" I asked.

She just frowned deeper. "Yes. No. Not him, exactly. Me. You might find this hard to believe, but I really hadn't caught on to the fact that he was faking. Not really. I mean, I would have. Like I said, it was all there in my subconscious. But on a conscious level..."

"Me either," I said. "It seems obvious now, after Imogene pointed everything out."

"I hate that I made such a fool of myself for no reason."

I reached across and took her hand. "If it's any consolation, I almost got a little crush when you played that recording of him reading that poem. The only reason I didn't was I didn't want to move in on your territory."

She drew her hand back and stirred her coffee. "You're a good friend. And you're right—we do not need to be competing over men. I've lost too many friends that way. They never forgive you for being the one chosen."

I nodded, judiciously deciding not to challenge her assumption that Nigel would have chosen her over me, because it was entirely too weird.

She sighed. "He was a hottie."

I nodded. "He was. And you were only human."

"I know. It's just that now...he wasn't really British. He wasn't really a war hero. Does that mean he wasn't really even hot? I mean...I feel very confused now."

"Well, it's a confusing situation. You'll work it out, though."

She sighed and rested her chin in her hand. She stared down at the cup. "This is not what I want."

"Do you want me to get the tea after all?"

She shook her head, still in her hand. "No. I want a bottle."

"Oh." Oh. I felt a moment of panic. I was used to being the one who needed support. I didn't have a lot of experience being the one who provided it. Viv very rarely talked about wanting to drink, and when she did, it was more in passing. Never had she said it while she was looking so dejected.

What would Les do, if this were me?

Les would sit back, let me rant and rail against the unfairness of life and how hard things were, and then say something infuriating like, "You're doing great, Salem."

Since I didn't know what to say, I sat back and said nothing, waiting for her to go on.

"I think my whole life I've wanted to be someone else."

I blinked. "Seriously?"

She nodded, still staring at her cup.

"But...you're so cool."

She shrugged. "That was just me, trying to be someone else. Anyone else."

Poor Viv! I chewed my lip, thinking about all the things that had been running through my own mind over the last few weeks—all the labels I'd had during my life. Most of them were labels I hadn't wanted but that had given me some sense of perspective. Even if I didn't like where I was, I could at least look around me and see where I fit, how I fit. In school, I was with the kids who hid behind the gym and smoked, who poured

Jack Daniels into their Sonic cokes, who laughed at the failing grades on their report cards. Then I became a teen pregnancy statistic. After I left Tony, I was with the gang who hung out at the bar, who turned every occasion into a reason to drink.

When I met Viv, I became part of the duo who went nosing around in other people's business and sometimes solving crimes.

I studied Viv, who stared glumly at her cup. It was impossible to imagine her feeling those same things, though. Viv was someone who always seemed fully, joyously herself. It broke my heart to think that she ever felt as miserable in her own skin as I did in mine.

I reached out again and took her hand. I prayed that God would give me the right words to say.

"Listen, Viv. I know how you feel. That, deep inside you, the person the world can't see is just not good enough. That the very essence of you is damaged, somehow. But I know you, and I know you have a lot left to offer."

She drew her head back and gave me the are-you-crazy look. "What?"

"I just mean that I can empathize with that, wanting to be someone else. Because it's so hard to be who you are. You feel like you're all wrong, somehow, that you're destined to fail at whatever you do."

"But I succeed at everything I do."

"I know, but—"

"You know, don't take this the wrong way, but you suck at this."

I drew back and blinked. "I...what?"

"Seriously, you're horrible. What a load of hog spit. Deep down, the very essence of you is damaged. What a load of baloney."

"I—but—you're the one who said—I wasn't saying you were actually damaged!"

"There is no deep down essence, sister. We are what we do, period. We're all trees and we're known by our fruit, right? That's what the man said."

"Um, I guess so."

She stood and pulled the belt of her coat tighter. "Listen, you started out okay, there. *'But you're so cool.'* That's what you said. That was a good start. But then you went off into all this existential psycho-babble and it went completely off the rails." She glared at me. "And what the heck was that, 'You have a lot left to offer' bit? A lot left? That's like saying, 'You still have your health'! Come on! That's what you say to *old* people!"

I nodded, but I felt quite off kilter, and a bit annoyed, too. "What should I have said, oh great and wise one?"

"Clearly, what was needed were Exhibits A through Z in the 'but you're so cool' defense." She held up her hand as if it should have been obvious. "Good lord. Deep down essence. Sheesh." She shook her head in exasperation.

"I see."

"Let's go." She headed for the car. Without asking, she got behind the wheel.

I stood and picked up Stump and sat us in the passenger seat. As I handed Viv the keys, I asked, "Where are we going?"

"Anywhere. I've had my cry in my drink. Now it's time to get moving again."

"Moving again to what?" I asked as she swung the car out of the parking lot.

"This is our last case. We could have ended on a high note—the lead from Browning's car at the school. But no. We had to foul it up by throwing out that dead-end bit about Baucum's half-brother and then get our butts handed to us by Imogene Walker, of all people. I can't quit on this sad note, Salem. One more win, that's all I need."

"I can't go chasing after bad guys, Viv. I kind of almost made a promise to my husband."

"Kind of almost is not a promise, Salem."

"I should also mention that I don't want a marriage that's based on splitting hairs."

She sighed. "Gag. Okay. What if we don't get out of the car?"

I considered this. It would be kind of hard to get into trouble if we didn't get out of the car. "If we see a bad guy, we have to run the other way."

"If we see a bad guy, I intend to mow him down with the car."

Of course, neither of us said the obvious—that our history of *identifying* the actual bad guy always came the moment after it was too late to extricate ourselves safely.

But I supposed even the best of plans had their flaws.

"Did I tell you I started watching that show, Vera?"

"Another British detective."

"Yep. Looks like a human-size Paddington Bear. And you know what Vera would do if she was at a dead end?" Viv said. "First, she would stare at the tri-fold white board for a while. Then she would holler for her hot young detective sergeant and they would jump in the beat-up Jeep to make the circuit of all the places she'd already been. See if it stirred up any new ideas."

"I can play the hot young detective sergeant," I said. "Just as long as we stay in the car."

"Done. First, we'll go by Eagle Construction and, if we see someone, I'll just roll down the window and ask all the questions we should have asked in the first place."

I thought this through. The place was well-lit, in a high-traffic area. If, by chance, the mysterious half brother was there, and if he really did have nefarious tendencies—something that, admittedly, seemed far-fetched considering the holes Bobby had poked all in my theory—he probably wouldn't do anything.

I thought how I would explain this to Tony, if I needed to.

Viv was depressed and she wanted a drink. It was a choice between a bottle and driving around chasing dead ends.

This would, very likely, lead to nothing, and I would have no need to explain anything to Tony. Just in case, though, I said, "You have your gun, right?"

"Naturally. Get it out of my purse, though, so I can have it handy."

I dug through her purse and gingerly handed her the gun.

She leaned forward, tugging at her coat. "Help me," she ordered.

I tugged at the back of her coat, then her jacket, then her blouse. By the time I got the gun tucked into the waistband of her pants, I was sweating and secretly glad this was our last case. I hoped I didn't shoot her in the butt. That would not end our PI careers on a high note.

I breathed a sigh of relief when Eagle Construction was closed. I figured it probably would be—it was after 7:00—but not being entirely familiar with the construction business, I hadn't known what to expect. I felt pretty virtuous for having stuck to my guns with Viv, though. So to speak.

I was less relieved when she circled the building for the third time. "Viv, there's no one here," I said, fearful that some late-working executive, who was secretly a bad guy, would emerge from the building, and then we'd have to roll down the window and talk to him and possibly get shot for who knows what reason.

"I'm just making sure we've covered everything thoroughly," Viv answered, her mouth set in determination. "Finish strong."

"Well, consider this angle covered. What's next? The Metro Tower building?"

"Nope."

"The place where Browning's body was found?"

"Rabid possums? No, thank you. Let's go back to the best lead we did have—the school."

I thought for a moment. This one did seem, also, safe. A residential neighborhood. The school was empty, and the last I'd heard the rubble still hadn't been cleared away, even though the earthquake had happened months ago. The rumor was that there were pending lawsuits that had held up the clearing away of the debris. All kinds of things still being investigated.

"What are we looking for there, though? Browning's drive-by there was almost two weeks ago."

"Yes, but nobody's been up there looking for clues, have they? If he dropped something, like you said, it could conceivably still be there."

I shrugged. "I guess. But I'm not getting out of the car."

She gave me a look. "I hope your husband appreciates the sacrifices I'm making for him."

"I'll try to communicate the enormity to him," I promised. To be perfectly honest, I wanted to follow up on this one. Bobby had said it was a good find. He hadn't dismissed out of hand my theory that Browning had tossed something out of the car on his way through.

We drove to NorthStar Elementary, and, as promised, Viv slowed the car to a crawl in the driveway, but didn't stop.

"Hang on," I said, opening the flashlight app on my phone. I opened the door and leaned out, shining the light against the curb.

We crawled along with me leaning out the door as far out as I dared, braced against the seatbelt. Nothing. A few clumps of leaves that I poked at, but nothing that could be considered a clue. Plus, the blood was rushing to my head from leaning over so far.

I groaned and rose, dropping my phone onto the seat. The car door swung out of my grip.

Stump pushed off from my lap and jumped out the door.

"Crud!" I shouted. "Stump, get back here."

She was already gone into the dark, though.

The car kept rolling.

"Viv! Stop the car."

"You said not to - "

"Stop the dadgummed car!" I punched the button on my seatbelt and leapt from the car, stumbling as I hit the pavement.

Viv finally stopped, and I reached back in and grabbed my phone, fumbling for the flashlight app. "Stump! Come here, baby." I tried to keep the panic from my voice.

I scanned the front of the building. It stretched far on either side, but since the landscaping hadn't been completed when the earthquake happened, the front of the building was fairly flat and unobstructed. Not knowing which way she'd run, though, made my heart thud painfully.

I stepped backwards to get a broader perspective and saw a flash of movement at the corner of the building. I took off running in that direction.

The back of the building was fenced in, to keep people out of the rubble, I supposed. From the street lamp on the next corner, I could see heavy equipment. Apparently work had begun on clearing the area, but it was still a mess.

I swept the beam along the ground, picturing Stump rooting under the fence, getting crushed by falling concrete rubble. "Come here, Sweetie. Come to me."

I could hear her sniffing and snorting around at the fence. I couldn't imagine what she'd found that would keep her so focused, but she was not paying a bit of attention to me.

Another flash of movement caught my eye around the tires of that equipment—a small bulldozer or something.

I heard something behind me and turned to see Viv picking her way across the dirt toward us. "I want to go on record as being the one who tried to stay in the car," she said.

"Fine, I'll be sure Tony is aware. Help me find Stump."

"I'm helping," she said. She pulled her own phone out of her purse and tapped the flashlight app. Nothing. She tapped it again. Nothing.

"What the—" She turned the phone over to look at the light and it flashed in her face. "Oh, crap!" She stumbled back, blinking furiously.

I giggled.

Then I heard paper rattling. I whipped my flashlight back to the ground and spotted Stump behind one wheel of the dozer, tearing into a Taco Juan's bag. "No! Stump, no!"

"What?" Viv shouted, panic in her voice.

"She's found a leftover bean burrito!"

Viv snorted. "Good grief. Is that all? I thought she'd found a bomb or something."

"She did." I got down on my knees and lunged for the bag. "It's a delayed explosive device, believe me. It'll go off in my bedroom floor about three o'clock tomorrow morning."

Stump growled and tugged at the bag, backing further under the equipment. I lunged after it, touching paper with the tips of my fingers, but couldn't reach. I got down on my belly and stretched. Stump gripped the bag in her teeth fiercely and continued to back away. I slithered after her.

I finally managed to get enough of the bag in my grip that I could pull on it. Stump growled and tugged back, but she couldn't get it out of my grip. I tugged hard, the bag tore, and I wadded it up in my hands. Yep, I could feel the remains of a cold bean burrito in there. Stump ran to me and sniffed furiously, pawing at my hands.

"I got it!" I called to Viv. "Crisis averted." Stump clawed so furiously that she scratched my lip. "Ouch, Stump! Quit it."

I slid back toward the edge of the dozer, now completely covered in dirt but relieved that I wouldn't have to stay up all night waiting for Stump to exhibit signs of gastrointestinal distress. I rolled over and was about to push myself up when something struck me.

Viv was completely silent.

I aimed my flashlight in her direction. She stood stock still, her arms raised. Beside and slightly behind her stood David Baucum's half brother. He held a gun to Viv's temple.

CHAPTER SEVENTEEN

Truth Defender

"It's him!" Viv hissed.

I stood on wobbly legs, my phone dropping from my suddenly numb hand. "I see that."

"What the freak are you two doing?" he said through gritted teeth. "You two clueless idiots!"

"Hey," Viv said in protest, turning to glare at him. "That's not nice."

"You're so stupid! I didn't want to have to kill anyone else. I did not want to do this. I just came to get justice for my brother, and then I was going to leave again and everything would be fine."

A few things clicked into place for me, and despite the situation, I felt kind of proud for having spotted a motive, although I didn't know that's what I was looking at. I pictured every movie I'd ever seen where a sympathetic ear turned a bad guy into a good one. "What Peter Browning did to your brother was wrong," I said. "Unfair."

"What he did to my brother was *criminal!*" he shouted. "He should have been tried for manslaughter, at least. But instead he was turned into a hero, and he was about to ride that train all the way to stardom." He looked at the rubble. "David was not to blame for this. He should never have taken the fall."

"You're right," I said. I took a small step closer.

Behind me, Stump had taken advantage of the distraction and was ripping into the paper bag. She growled again, but this time it had more of a triumphant overtone.

I looked at Viv and the guy. They were both looking at Stump. I decided maybe I could take advantage of this.

"Can I just—if she eats that she's going to be—" I turned and bent, edging carefully toward Stump. If I could somehow whisper into my phone for Windy to get Bobby...

He cocked the gun. "Don't move."

I straightened and raised my hands, just like Viv did, and froze.

"You two have only yourselves to blame for this. Following me around, asking stupid questions. You know this would have eventually died out. It looked like a suicide. I was very careful about that. I gave him the exact same things David took. I made him write a note. People would have realized what a jerk thing he'd done, and they would have seen him for the opportunist he was. It would have blown over." He gave Viv a disgusted look. "You deserve this. Cocky. Driving circles around my office like you're taunting me. You asked for it, old lady."

I felt my own eyes go wide at that. One did not simply call Viv an old lady.

She narrowed her own eyes, and then, with a banshee scream, she whirled around, her coat in her hands. "Grab my gun!" she screamed. "Grab it! Hurry!"

For a second, the guy was too startled to do much besides stand there looking confused. I scrambled with Viv's wildly flapping coat, struggling to get through the layers of fabric.

The guy reached for her. She slid to the side. I went after her, fighting to get hold of anything.

"Get it, Salem! Get it and shoot him!"

"Be still! I can't get hold of—"

Stump decided then to get involved. She danced around us, barking furiously.

The guy drew back his arm and backhanded Viv across the side of the head. She dropped like a rock.

I froze again, breathing hard. I raised my hands. His eyes on me, the gun pointed at me, he squatted and patted Viv's back. He ripped aside her coat, then her jacket, then her blouse. He tugged the gun from the back of her pants.

He stood, his gun still trained on me, his eyes on me, and slid Viv's gun into the pocket of his jeans.

"Look," I said. "You can't get away with killing us. My friend is a detective with the Lubbock PD, and I've already told him about you. If we're killed, he'll know who did it."

He didn't look nearly as concerned about this as I would have liked.

"But it's not too late for you to get, I don't know, leniency, maybe? What Peter did to you—he ruined the family business. He practically killed your brother with his own hands." I remembered the poor woman he'd ushered through the Baucum

Memorial and what the nurse had said about shock exacerbating Alzheimer's. "The shock of his death drove your poor mother's failing health right over the edge. Peter Browning made you a desperate man. I think a jury would take all that into consideration."

"I wasn't desperate," he sneered. "I did what had to be done to avenge my family's honor. I made sure he knew it, too. The little weasel. He sat there, holding his broken hand and promised me all kinds of things. He would set the record straight. But I could see what a lying weasel he was. Trying to manipulate me just like you're trying to do now."

My heart thudded, and I fought to stay clear headed. "His broken hand? How did he break his hand?"

Then a thought occurred to me and I blurted it. "You drove him through here before you took him out of town. You were driving the car."

"Sure. He had to know what was going on. He was pretty out of it by then, but he knew enough to put two and two together when we came through here."

"When the passenger door opened—Peter was trying to get out. Trying to escape."

He didn't answer, but it made sense. The injury Bitsy had said the police asked her about, the fight they asked Misty about—if he'd tried to escape and this guy had slammed his hand in the car door to keep him in—that added up.

It also scared me.

"*Trying* is the operative word here," he said. "I don't let people escape."

"You will not get away with this," I reminded him. "I don't know your name, but I told Bobby all about you, where you worked, that you're David's half brother. He will easily be able to track you down."

He shook his head. "Do you honestly think that really matters to me at this point? I came into this knowing that I could go to prison for it. I've got my eyes wide open." He shrugged. "From what you say, I'm probably going now anyway. Might as well go for three murders as for one."

My heart stopped beating. I opened my mouth to speak, but couldn't. What did you say to someone who has nothing left to lose?

"What *is* your name?" I finally croaked, because I literally couldn't think of anything else to say.

He stared stonily at me for a long time. Then finally, he said, "Jacob."

Everything inside me went suddenly very still. It was as if I'd come to a pinnacle moment. A mountaintop moment, when everything in my life and my consciousness coalesced to one pinpoint moment of clarity.

Jacob, the heel-grabber.

Jacob, who wrestled all night with an angel.

Don't be afraid to fight for what you need, Salem. If you have to wrestle all night...

I took a deep breath, then took a step toward him.

I couldn't believe how calm I felt. I suddenly wasn't afraid at all. God was on my side.

"Freeze," Jacob said. He leveled the gun at me.

I kept coming, crossing the space between us quickly.

"I mean it," he said. "Don't try me, girl."

I stepped closer. I could touch him now. "You aren't going to shoot me," I said.

He shoved the barrel of the gun hard into my chest.

I fell back. "Ow!" That had, unfortunately, brought me out of the numb reverie that had made me cross to him. Reflexively, I grabbed his wrists. "That hurt!"

He jerked his hands back, but I tightened my grip and held on. We were locked together—I could feel the length of his body against mine, feel the muscles in his forearms that were stronger than mine, feel the power of his thighs against my own. He was clearly so much stronger than I was, but I couldn't let go.

We stumbled around in the dirt, with me gripping his wrists for all I was worth. The gun was cold and hard between us, and I knew it could go off at any moment, killing him or me.

Wrestle all night if you have to.

Already, though, I could feel his strength winning over my own. I gripped my hands tighter, but it felt feeble against the muscle and sinew of his arms.

"Windy!" I screamed in the direction of where I'd dropped my phone. "Call Bobby!"

"I'm getting him now, Sweetie," she said.

Jacob looked, startled, in the direction of the phone. That bought me half a second, and I shifted a bit and re-tightened my grip.

"Sloan." Bobby's voice came through the dark night and I almost sobbed in desperation. I had all my strength focused on hanging on to Jacob's wrists, so focused that I couldn't force words out of my mouth. It took all my strength to grunt, "Bobby, help!"

"Salem?" he sounded frantic. "Salem! Hang on! I'm on my way."

Jacob frowned at the phone, then at me. Then, a decision came into his eyes. He shifted his feet apart and bent his knees.

Behind Jacob, Viv stirred.

Seeing her triggered another memory, and I knew suddenly what I had to do.

I tightened my grip hard. Then, as quick as I could, I released my grip.

He stumbled, just a bit. I dropped my hands to his front pocket. I felt Viv's gun there. I pulled the trigger.

The gun went off with a boom.

"Salem!" Bobby screamed through the phone.

Jacob dropped to the ground, moaning. I kept my hand gripped on the gun, and it slipped from his pocket as he fell. I pointed it at him. The thigh of his jeans was already growing darker with the blood seeping out through the hole the bullet had made.

He pointed his gun at me, his teeth clenched with fury and pain. "You stupid—"

Behind him, Viv stretched out and kicked his elbow. The gun flew from his hand and landed on the ground near me. I moved toward it, then put my foot on top of it.

Through the roar in my head, I heard sirens. The furious sound screamed closer, then headlights bounced over the ground, a car racing across the dirt toward us.

I narrowed my eyes against the bright light, but I couldn't move. Jacob was on his knees on the ground, slumping more by the second. Viv lay behind him, breathing hard. Stump sniffed around my feet at the gun but I was afraid to move. I felt such a tenuous hold on safety that I couldn't unclench.

Two more cars tore across the grass, red and blue lights flashing. I heard car doors opening, saw Bobby running toward me in the glare of the headlights.

"Salem! Put the gun down! Put it down!"

I heard him, but I couldn't think. The boom of the gun had been so loud, the shock of it so powerful, it was as if everything in me had shut down in response.

Bobby was running toward me, and I could hear him screaming at me to drop the gun. I looked beyond him at the other officers, standing behind their open doors.

They all had guns pointed at me.

"Hold!" Bobby shouted, turning back to them. "Hold fire!"

He turned back to me and ran closer. He had his own weapon out, I saw. He looked desperate. "Salem. Honey. Drop the gun. Put it down."

They were going to shoot me, I realized, but only through layers and layers of numbness. I was standing with a gun in my hand, pointed at someone on the ground.

But I was frozen. I couldn't move.

I heard Stump snuffling at my feet and I thought, *A stray bullet could hit her.*

"Salem, baby, *please.* Please put the gun on the ground."

Something about the desperation in his voice finally got through to me, and I jerked myself back into the moment.

I raised my hands, dangling the gun by the butt. I held it far from me and slowly bent my knees, showing with exaggerated motions that I was putting it down. Once I'd dropped it into the dirt, I stood straight and held my hands wide.

Bobby took over then, shouting for an ambulance, putting handcuffs on Jacob, ordering me and Viv to not move a muscle or, he swore on his mother's life, he would arrest us both. I watched everything as if from a distance.

Viv sat in the dirt, criss-cross apple sauce, her hands held up near her ears, and watched everything going on around her. She, too, looked dazed.

An ambulance appeared quickly, and they immediately went to work on Jacob's bullet wound.

I remained frozen, but I said to one of the ambulance people, "You need to check Viv. He hit her in the head."

"Are you injured?" he asked me.

"No, no, I don't think so." To be honest, I had no idea if I was injured or not. But I had seen Viv get hit, seen her go down, and I knew she needed help. "Viv got hit. Take care of Viv."

Bobby was getting the scene wrapped up quickly, but he kept turning back to look at me. "Salem, are you hurt? Did he hurt you?" He looked at my mouth, then reached out and ran his thumb over my lip where Stump had scratched me.

I couldn't answer. I couldn't think. All I could do was stand there, holding my arms up. Suddenly, I felt very strongly that I was probably going to cry. "Bobby, can I hold my dog?" My voice cracked on the last word.

"Can you..." He scanned the ground, saw Stump. He scooped her up and shoved her at me. My arms dropped, folding around Stump. He took half a step back, then closed in again, holding onto me fiercely, taking me and Stump both into one tight hug. He kissed the top of my head, then my forehead, gripped my shoulders and searched my face. He kissed my forehead again before he let me go.

Bobby took me and Viv to a small emergency clinic a couple of blocks from the school. He told us the ambulance would take Jacob to the county hospital where he would be treated under guard.

The little ER decided Viv needed to be observed overnight, so that meant she'd be taking an ambulance ride to the other big hospital in town.

They were loading her in the ambulance, with me and Stump waving from the sidewalk, when Tony pulled up.

He didn't even close the door on his truck. He saw me and was by my side in an instant.

"I did not go chasing after him, Tony," I said as he barreled toward me. "We were just—"

I had to stop talking then, because Tony held me too tight for words.

His heart thudded against mine, and somehow, this made all my emotions—which had been locked up somewhere—come flooding back. All of them at once.

I could have been shot.

I almost *was* shot. The hard shove of that gun barrel into my chest felt suddenly as big as the world.

I shot someone.

I could have been shot by the police.

Suddenly, I was crying. Ridiculous, hard, hiccuping sobs in Tony's safe arms. Stump grumbled and shoved her feet against me, and I bent and put her on the ground with strict but unintelligible orders to stay, and then I launched myself back into Tony's arms.

I heard footsteps behind me and turned to see Bobby coming toward us.

"Your wife is a hero, man," he said, and held out his hand to shake Tony's.

"I know," Tony said.

The obvious ridiculousness of this struck me as funny, so then I was crying and laughing at the same time.

"How did you get there so fast?" I asked Bobby, wiping my eyes and sniffling. "It was like you were around the corner."

"I was around the corner. I was watching that video you showed me, and then I heard a call come through that somebody in the neighborhood of the school had reported two women screaming something about bombs, and I figured..." He held out his hands. "Two women. It had to be you, right? So, I checked the live feed and saw your car, then saw the Eagle truck pull up."

"Can I make some kind of arrangements for you to just keep her under surveillance 24/7?" Tony asked. "It would be a good use of my tax dollars."

Bobby shook his head. "You need a whole security detail for this girl," Bobby said. He gave a crooked smile and left.

I watched him go, trying not to notice that he looked sad and lonely. He was a grown man. A *handsome* grown man. If he was sad and lonely, he would probably have no problem finding someone to help him take care of that.

I turned back to Tony. "I really didn't go chasing after him. He came after us."

Tony put his forehead against mine. "I believe you, Salem."

"I really was trying to honor my word to you."

"I know."

"I'm sorry I almost got myself killed again."

"Shhh." He kissed me. "Let's go home."

So we went home, and he didn't let go of me all night.

The next week was blessedly back to normal. I went to work. I watched Misty Monahan report the news about Jacob Starr's release from the hospital and arrest into the county jail with charges of murder and attempted murder. When I got tempted to freak completely out about that attempted murder thing, I visited Viv back in Belle Court, and together we went to see Anne.

The nurse who had warned her about the laxatives gave Viv the stink eye as we walked by. "I told you we were going to let her family decide what to tell her. Then you went and gave her some bull hockey about him moving in with his daughter in Florida."

"Which gave her a great deal of comfort," Viv said, leaning over the counter to give her own stink eye right back.

"Which is why I'm letting you off with a warning this time. But you just remember." She leaned forward and met Viv's gaze. "I have the power to make you all sorts of uncomfortable."

Viv straightened. "I am not afraid of you." She strolled away.

I followed after her, looking back over my shoulder to make sure the nurse wasn't about to chunk anything at us. I was afraid of her.

Anne seemed tireder than she'd been the last time we visited, and I felt guilty when I realized she was working very hard to make us feel better about her situation, which seemed like an unreasonable thing for anyone to expect. So I entertained her with some stories of my own school days, and we both agreed that she was lucky she hadn't had me for a student.

When we left her room and headed for the elevator, I noticed something that made me stop dead in my tracks.

"Mrs. Starr is back?" I turned to the nurse and pointed to the room where the woman we'd seen at the Baucum Memorial had just been wheeled in.

The nurse nodded. "Yeah, she just got moved back in yesterday. And you know, I think she's better already. She's comfortable here."

"But..." I leaned close, my surprise outweighing my fear of her. "I heard that she couldn't afford to stay here any longer. I mean, that's gossip, but..."

"She couldn't." The nurse flattened her lips. "What with the one son dead, the other one in jail, and all the business assets tied up in litigation, she's flat broke, I think. But then all of a sudden, she got a benefactor. Which is a good thing, because she needs to be here."

"Salem, would you quit gossiping and come on?" Viv stood holding the door for me.

In the elevator, I let this sink in. I opened my mouth to say something to Viv, but stopped. She stared straight ahead, ignoring me as hard as she could.

I smiled. I shifted toward her and lifted my arm.

"If you try to hug me again, I will slap you."

I stopped, put my arm down, and grinned.

That night, Tony and I went shopping for clothes to wear to my mother's wedding. I have to admit, it was fun going into a nice department store and picking out something new, instead of Walmart or the resale store. I found a chocolate brown sweater dress that would look nice with my riding boots, and Tony got a new shirt and tie of almost the same color. We would look perfect for a "rustic" backyard wedding.

The next day, I stood in front of the mirror, turning to look at the back view, then the side view. I placed my hands on my stomach. It was hard to say if it would ever be flat again, now. I tried not to worry about it, though.

Tony came up behind me and wrapped his arms around me, his gaze meeting mine in the mirror. "You are beautiful," he said.

I reached back to put my hand on his head. "I love you."

He leaned over, opened a drawer on the dresser, and pulled out a wrapped gift box.

"I have something for you."

"It's a little early for presents, isn't it?" I couldn't help but smile, though. And take it.

"There will be more for Christmas, don't worry."

I untied the ribbon and slipped it off. My heart thudded when I realized this could be a key. To his house. And he was asking me to move in permanently. It only made sense, but...my heart still thudded painfully at the thought.

But it wasn't a key. It was a small stack of business cards.

Discreet Investigations, it read. Salem Solis and Vivian Kennedy. Our phone numbers. All in tasteful black type on a plain white card.

"Tony?" I looked at him.

"Look." He framed my face with his hands. "I can't ask you not to do this. You love doing this. I heard you the other night, talking to Viv. And maybe you're right—this could be God's plan for you. Who am I to get in the way of that?"

I threw my arms around him and held him so tight. "Do you mean it?"

"I must. I had cards made."

"Oh my gosh, these are so much better than Viv's cards."

"Tell me about it. Those things were horrifying."

I studied them through tears. "But—and I'm just checking here—is this your way of trying to get rid of me? Give me free rein to go chase after bad guys in the hopes that one of them will actually shoot me?"

He laughed. "Not a chance." He lifted the stack of cards and I saw something beneath it. A folded piece of paper. I unfolded it.

"An application for a concealed handgun license?" I looked at him. "Are you serious?"

"Deadly. Salem, if you're going to be out there dealing with people who kill people, you have to protect yourself."

"But...I don't want a gun."

He cocked his head and gave me an unyielding look.

"Viv has a gun."

"Viv is also bad with that gun."

"That's true, but..." I remembered the feel of the gun going off in my hand and shuddered.

"There's also this." He pulled another piece of paper out of the box.

"A self-defense course. Well, okay!" I said. I could get on board with this.

He kissed the top of my head. "Good. If you're going to be fighting bad guys, you might as well be prepared. Okay, one more thing." He pulled back and drew something from his pocket. It was a silver bracelet with oval discs linked together. He held it out to me.

"What is this?" I peered closely at the word inscribed on one of the discs. "A...*minta*? Aminta? What's that?"

"I think that's how it's pronounced, yes." He fastened the bracelet around my wrist. "You wanted a new name, so I looked up the Hebrew word for truth – because when I think of you, that's always the first word that comes to mind. Truth. Aminta. It also means defender." He gave a slight shake of his head. "Truth defender. Sounds like you all over."

"Aminta," I whispered, studying the bracelet through fresh tears. "Truth."

Epilogue

Perhaps it was the combination of narrowly escaping death and being in the company of my own amazing husband, but I went to Mom's wedding feeling magnanimous toward everyone.

When Mom introduced me simply as "Salem" instead of "my daughter, Salem," I smiled, shook hands, made small talk – all the things expected of me.

When I spotted Susan across the expanse of Neely Bates' charmingly rustic back yard, I slid my arm through Tony's and turned the other cheek. At least she met me halfway by avoiding me, too.

When someone bumped into one of the tables and spilled three round trays of champagne flutes onto the ground, I tamped down the flicker of schadenfreude that reared its ugly head and offered Mom consolation that was almost one hundred percent authentic. I did, in fact, feel genuine compassion for her, but I kind of hated that champagne for being there and looking so pretty, so I was glad to see it go.

A large part of why I felt so good, though, was the discussion Tony and I had before we left Lubbock.

As we stood watching the bride and groom dance awkwardly on the rented dance floor under the gigantic tent, I leaned in to tell him, "I'm going inside to call Viv."

The huge house had, I kid you not, *two* guest bathrooms off the mud room leading in from the garage. I pretended I was waiting for the women's to be empty, but really, I just wanted a chance to talk to Viv in private.

"I have news!" she said as soon as she picked up.

"No, me first," I protested.

"I'm older. I go first."

"Tony said I could keep doing investigations with you," I blurted. "He even had business cards made for me, and pre-paid for self-defense classes." I decided to leave out the part about the gun. "There. I was first."

She made an impatient sound, then said, "Well, okay, you're forgiven, but only because that's really good news. And just in time, because of *my* news."

"What's your news?"

"Nope. You took my turn, you're going to have to drag it out of me."

"Seriously? Come on, I – "

"That weasel Nigel stole Anne's brooch. That old turtle thing she wore sometimes? With the emeralds and pearls? Turns out it was worth about twenty-five grand! And now her daughter's up here pitching a conniption fit!"

"Viv," I hissed. "You really need to tone down your glee a bit. This is *bad* news."

"Of course, it is. Horrible. Tragic." She laughed, and in the background I heard her clap her hands together. "We're gettin' the band back together, man!"

Want more of Salem and the gang? Sign up for my newsletter and get free short stories, excerpts from upcoming books, and publishing news. Go to www.KimHuntHarris.com to sign up!

If you enjoyed Knickers in a Twist, I would love it if you could take a few minutes to leave a review on Amazon, iBooks, Kobo, Barnes and Noble, or GoodReads.

Titles in the Trailer Park Princess Series
Titles in the Trailer Park Princess Series
The Middle Finger of Fate (Book One)
Unsightly Bulges (Book Two)
Caught in the Crotchfire (Book Three)
Knickers in a Twist (Book Four)
'Tis the Friggin' Season (Short Story)
The Power of Bacon (Short Story)
Mud, Sweat, and Tears (Short Story)
Frankincense, Gold, and Murder
(short story coming December 2017)

ABOUT THE AUTHOR

*This is me. I bought this outfit
and got my roots done for this picture. You can't tell, but I also got
a pedicure. It was a big day for me, let me tell you.*

The award-winning author of the Trailer Park Princess comic mystery series. Kim Hunt Harris knew she wanted to be a writer before she even knew how to write. When her parents read bedtime stories to her, she knew she wanted to be a part of the story world. She started out writing children's stories, and her stories grew as she did. She discovered a gift for humor and a love for making people laugh with her tales, and the Trailer Park Princess series was born.

Kim loves to not only make her readers laugh and entertain them with a good mystery, but also to examine the issues the everyday people face...well, every day. Issues like faith and forgiveness, perseverance, and tolerance. Set in Lubbock, Texas, the fun books feature a cast of quirky characters, outrageous situations, a drama queen of a dog, and from time to time, a tear or two.

Kim lives with her husband of more than thirty years and two kids in West Texas.

www.ingramcontent.com/pod-product-compliance
Lightning Source LLC
Chambersburg PA
CBHW070349260626
47161CB00001B/77